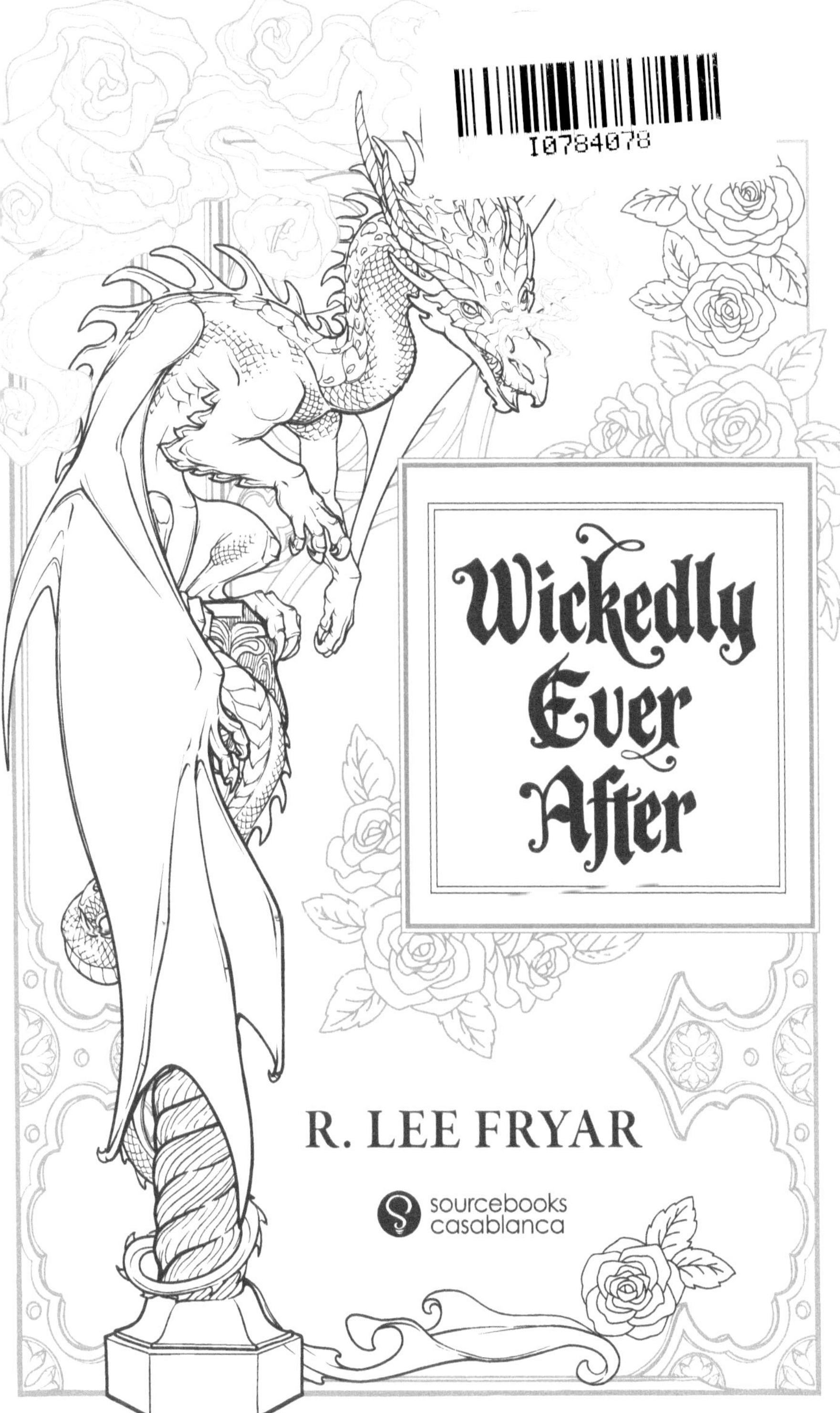

I0784078
Wickedly Ever After
R. LEE FRYAR
sourcebooks
casablanca

Published by Sourcebooks Casablanca, an imprint of Sourcebooks
1935 Brookdale RD, Naperville, IL 60563-2773
(630) 961-3900
sourcebooks.com

Cataloging-in-Publication Data is on file with the Library of Congress.

Printed and bound in the United States of America.
POD

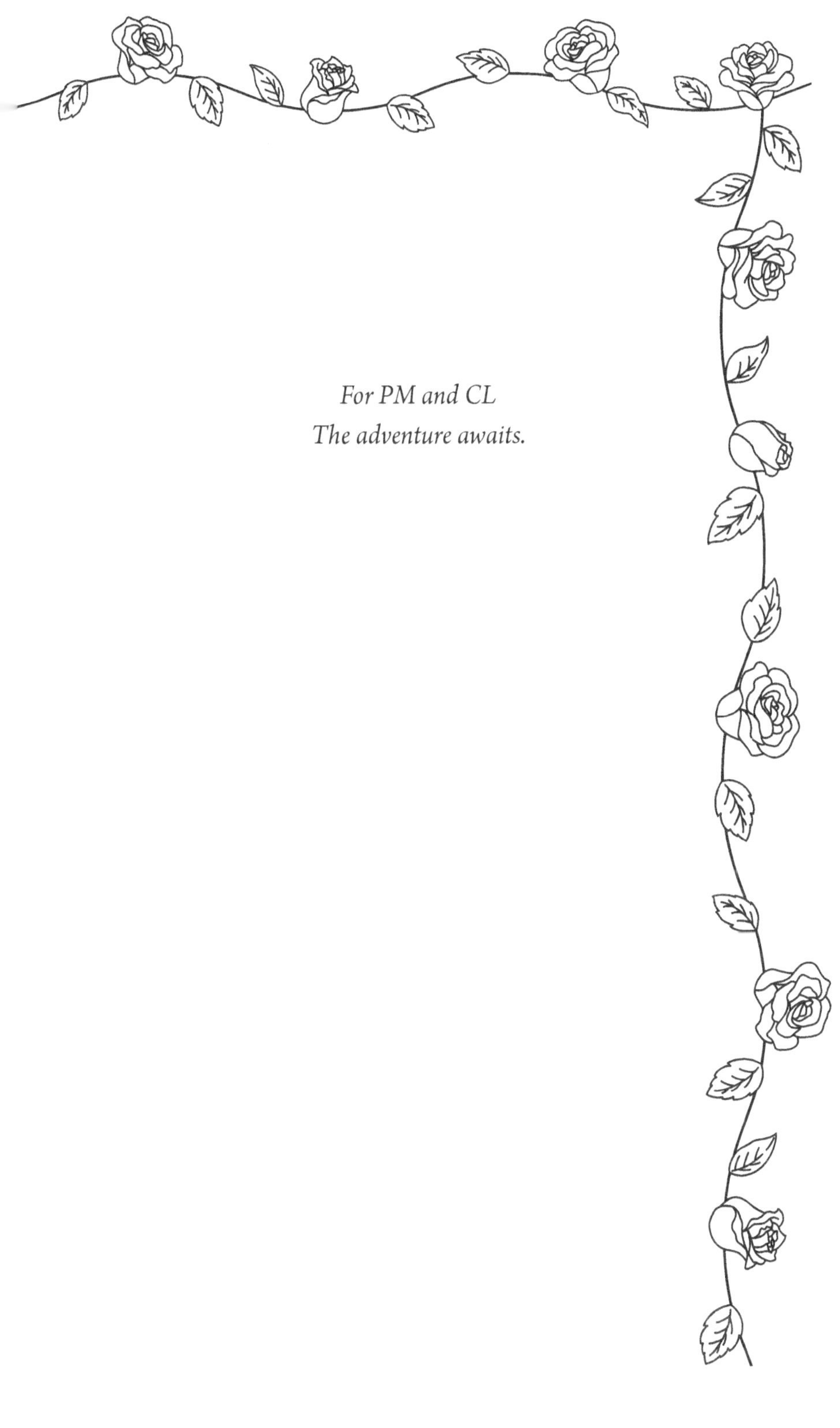

For PM and CL
The adventure awaits.

PROLOGUE

Hector

ON A DESERTED BATTLEFIELD, THE SCENT OF SMOKE and death steams in the mist trailing from the nearby fens. Ravens are hard at work on the corpses. Mire imps pick over what the ravens don't dare to touch, but much remains uneaten. Necomantic constructs aren't meant to be ingested. Not voluntarily anyway.

Not far from the corpses, a fire has been kindled under a cauldron. The flames are blue, gold, red, and green, all the colors of magic. A boy stirs that cauldron, the sleeves of his black tunic rolled up to his shoulders, which are knotted in equally complicated folds. His long black hair sticks in strands over his forehead, but he doesn't touch his face. Like the ravens, he knows better.

With an ominous rattle, a construct approaches, an ancient skeleton held together by sinews and magic. It gazes at the apprentice through hollow eye sockets. A question shines in the red light glowing in the darkness there as it holds up a twisted root.

"Put it in—but carefully."

With a soft plop, hemlock slides into the black soup.

"Thank you," the boy says. It's never felt awkward saying thanks to the dead. He's never had a problem with them. It's the living who irritate him the most—the people who have gone to war over this particular patch of ground so many times that the compacted soil has long since turned to bone dust and blood meal. The boy has been tending this cauldron for hours— seven stirs counterclockwise, seven clockwise, seven counter- clockwise, all day long. But it won't be long now. He has a clear view of the great snowcapped range of the Dread Mountains, and the sun is kissing the peaks of Mount Dragon right now. In the chilly mists stealing across the plain, he sees the newcomers approaching. Three of them stride across the field, two in white robes, one in black. They are all old women, and they walk with purpose.

"Gretel?" His voice cracks. "They're here."

His mentor puts a hand on his back. "You can stop stirring now, Hector. It's as done as we can make it."

He steps back, arms aching, more alert now than he's been all day. He's been working with Gretel on this piece of magic for his entire apprenticeship, but for her and the other Cardinal Witches, it's been the study of their long lives.

The oldest of them, a sharp-eyed crone with faded hair and a deeply wrinkled face, gives the boy an appraising glance. "What is *he* doing here, Gretel?"

His mentor smiles all over her grandmotherly face. "That cauldron is heavy. I needed a young back and strong arms. You should consider getting an apprentice yourself, Hilde. You're not getting any younger either."

The old witch snorts. "When I do get one, it will be a fine, upstanding young lady, not some stray farm boy I picked up out of the woods."

"Farm boys have a way of turning into heroes if you don't catch them soon enough," Gretel says. "There's plenty of precedent. Besides, he's good with the plants. Did you bring the wine?"

From the folds of her white robes, Hilde pulls out a flask filled with a liquid so bright that it puts the rays of the setting sun to shame. "Golden wine from the frost grapes of the north— the last of it, I believe. No one grows them anymore, not since the famine."

"And the other items? Rosalind? Judith?" The other witches come forward, holding out two objects. One of them, the boy has only heard of in legends that his uncle used to tell, before the long war took him like it took so many members of his family. It's an ancient crown that once belonged to the high king, back when there was such a thing, and not this splintered kingdom where every family with a drop of royal blood has decreed themselves king. The other item is something he's quite familiar with. It's a simple workman's hammer, probably taken from some camp forge.

Gretel nods in approval. "Now all we need are the elementals. Hilde, will you call them please? My hands are full."

The apprentice is so enthralled by the elementals, he forgets to ask his mentor if there's something he should do to help. He's never seen one before, except in Gretel's books. The books didn't do them justice. The earth elemental starts out as a toad, and then becomes a tall, thin green person with hard onyx eyes; the sylph materializes from the mist as a moth before becoming blue from the hair to the feet; the green undine swims through the nearest dewdrop as a tiny fish before taking their shape; and the salamander! They are a lithe blue, gold, red, and purple entity, sliding out from between the coals beneath the cauldron. When they take their form, they turn their bright blue eyes on him, and he feels like he's been looked through from head to heart in a glance.

"Hector?" Gretel's voice recalls him. "I need the stone knife."

"Coming." He turns around to the bag to fetch it. Witches don't react well to iron, something he's been coming to terms with since he found out he was destined to be one. It was highly disconcerting to find out he could prick his finger on a nail and wind up in bed for three days. But he's so interested in the spell being chanted and items being added to the cauldron by the elementals, he can barely concentrate.

"What are they doing?" he whispers to Gretel.

She explains patiently, as she always has. "Elementals are the guardians of magic, Hector, and this is a very complicated spell. We needed their help to build it. A thousand years of peace is a long time to ask of magic."

"A thousand years of war would be longer," he says.

"That's true." Gretel pats his arm as if hearing his bitterness. "The earth elemental has brought a grain of sand from the far reaches of the south seas, the sylph has a breath of the north wind in their wings, the undine has brought a drop of water from the driest desert in the east, and the salamander has come all the way from Mount Dragon itself with a tongue of dragon flame."

"And the crown and the hammer?"

"Watch and see. The knife please."

The boy hands it over. What he sees next will haunt him for the rest of his life. Gretel takes the knife and plunges it into her own chest. "Gretel!" He reaches out to stop her, but it's too late.

The blood slides over her hands and she smiles at him. "Don't worry, child," she says. "It doesn't hurt much as long as it doesn't belong to anyone else." In front of his unbelieving eyes, she removes her heart from her chest.

"Hilde?"

The great northern witch sighs. "Not something I've been looking forward to," she says, taking the knife from Gretel.

"Then get it over with." Gretel smirks. "We both knew it would need this."

"That doesn't mean I have to like it," Hilde says. But she cuts her own heart out with a wince, and the boy wonders who might have part of Hilde's heart for her to react that way.

All four witches approach the cauldron, two with dripping hearts, one with the crown, one with the hammer. Chanting fills his ears.

> No longer will war take its toll,
> Nor famine make the round
> Two hearts combined do make a whole
> When hammer weds the crown
> Preserve this peace with truelove's kiss
> In a rose conceal
> Red rose will bring eternal bliss
> Black rose will make it real.

There's a blinding flash, brighter than the sun at noon, a noise like ten thousand thunders shakes the hills, and the scent of roses fills the air—wild, intoxicating, magical. The blast throws the boy ten feet through the air, and he lands unceremoniously on his rear end in a puddle, but the witches and the elementals are unmoved. The potion he labored on all day bleeds out into the fire through the shards of the cauldron.

He gets to his feet warily. Over the past four years, he's learned several things about magical potion making: First, always wash your hands before and after; secondly, never, for any reason, stick your burned finger in your mouth when you're stirring the pot; and thirdly, spells that explode often have a second stage. But nothing else happens, and gradually he approaches.

"Did it…did it work?" he breathes.

Gretel bends over the wreckage and takes something from the bottom of the shattered cauldron—two seeds. One red. One black.

She hands the red one to Hilde. "Well?"

"I thought it might be something like this," Hilde says thoughtfully. "A thousand years is a long time after all. You're right, Gretel. I need an apprentice."

Gretel turns to her apprentice. "This is yours, Hector, dear." She drops the black seed into his hand. It weighs next to nothing, but it feels like he's holding the whole world.

"I…I'm not ready," he says. "Maybe you'd better take it."

Gretel smiles, but he thinks she looks sad. "Believe me, child, I wish I could. But Happily-Ever-After is your burden now. You might as well take care of it from the beginning."

She was right, of course. Gretel usually was. But whenever I cut a bloom from the black rose that grew from what I planted, it feels just as heavy as the seed did so long ago.

A THOUSAND YEARS OF WICKEDNESS: A MEMOIR

HECTOR WEST

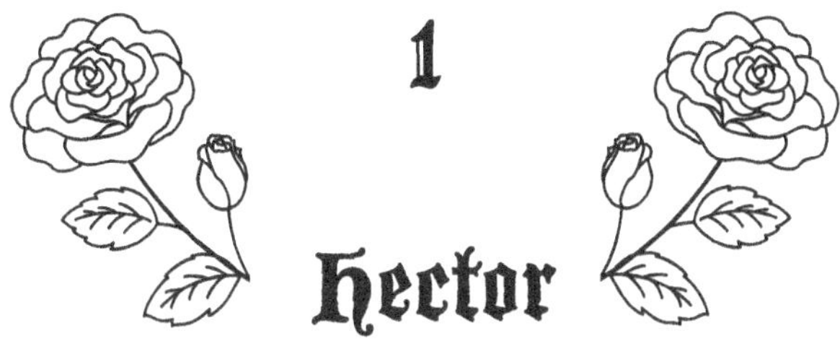

1

Hector

My Dear Detested Ida,

I hope this letter finds you poxed, feverish, and confined to your bed. Alas, I'm sure you are well and as hateful as ever.

Regarding the plague you're complaining about, you didn't need to flatter me, but I appreciate it. As to the illegality, I suggest you take it up with this year's Witches' Council after the Happily-Ever-After. Pestilence and natural disasters are an acceptable, if messy, means of balancing the good and evil in our world. I'm perfectly within my limits to send a plague when I feel like it, and if it happens to blight roses as well as people, I can only applaud my ability to wreak a two-for-the-price-of-one kind of havoc.

I took exception to the dandelion seeds you sent on the wind to spoil my lawn. But next time, you'll want to give more attention to their vulnerability to goat-urine herbicide. I'm pleased to say I've eradicated them, and your attempt to sabotage my entry into the Witches' Weeds Annual Gardening Contest has failed, yet again. By the way, how are your Cinderella pumpkins? Thriving? You might want to check.

Wickedly yours,
HECTOR WEST

HECTOR SIGNED THE LETTER WITH HIS TRADEMARK flourish and folded it exactly five times before inserting it into the envelope along with a curse for blistered fingers. Ida would probably defuse it before she even touched it, but he could hope. Sometimes he could still get one past her. Satisfied, he sealed it with his personal ring in the hot wax dripped from the human fat candle that Adorphus handed him.

"Will that be all, Hector?" Adorphus asked, putting the letter in the outgoing mail.

"No, my dear fellow." Hector sighed. "I need more goat-urine herbicide." Ida's stupid dandelions. But he would get rid of them all, even if he had to dig them out by the light of the crescent moon and recite a cease-and-desist over each benighted hole in his lawn. Irritating old witch.

"I don't know if they made enough for a bottle. You bought me out the last time you were in." The little goblin disappeared entirely when he stepped off the ladder. His sharp ears moved like disembodied puppets behind the long black counter before he emerged through the swinging door at the end. With a sudden, stinking smell of billy goat, he disappeared down a trapdoor.

Hector helped himself to a pickled eyeball from the counter jar. He still had six weeks until that infernal competition, and he intended to win this time. He wanted to rub it in Ida's face after the Happily-Ever-After. But he wouldn't put it past her to curse his sawbriers to puny brambles or send thrips to attack his death lilies. She certainly knew how to get him where it hurt the most. Curses! And for a good witch too. Her great-great-great-grandmother must have had a touch of fae in her. She'd inherited both their fabulously good looks and eviscerating wit. The first time he'd seen Ida North, he'd completely underestimated the power of both.

He'd been twenty-six at the time. It was his first formal function as the Wicked Witch of the West, and although he would never have admitted it to anyone—a sure way to get himself hexed to infinity—he was nervous. He'd never been good at speeches, and with the newly minted Witches' College first-year class staring at him like a parliament of wide-eyed owls, and the remaining two witches from Happily-Ever-After basking like ancient dragons on the stage behind him, he tripped over half his words and almost over his own robes on the way down the stairs.

When the young woman came up to the punch bowl where he was eating his anxiety in the form of dead man's peanut butter fingers, he was relieved to find he could crack a smile. She was lovely, like some fairy at her christening had dispensed gifts with the randomness of a drunk uncle—breathtaking beauty, sparkling presence, a dazzling smile, and the longest eyelashes he'd ever seen. Red hair fell in waves to the middle of her back, and both it and her eyes seemed to change color in the light. They shifted from evening blue to morning lilac when she looked up at him.

"Nice save," she said, dipping a glass of blood-colored punch into a crystal cup. "I thought you were going to go heels over broomstick there for a minute."

"I thought the same myself." He laughed.

"Not the sort of thing I'd have expected from the youngest-ever Wicked Witch of the West." She sipped her drink. "Did you mean what you said about a blight in the north being good for the economy of the southern regions, or was that just a bad joke like all the others?"

He almost choked on his cookie. "I beg your pardon?"

"Because if you're going to make a habit of turning us into your perennial target with your dastardly magic, I'm going to fight you. I didn't spend the last three years working on a new breed of grain for you to wipe it out in a week, is that clear?"

"I…well…" He had a million things to say, most of them quotes from his reams of notes he'd taken in case of questions about the balance of good and evil, but somehow, under that serpent stare of evident dislike, he couldn't find anything to say, at least nothing diplomatic. "It's my job to be wicked," he finally managed. "You don't have to like it, but you do have to live with it."

"We'll see." She turned her back on him and sailed off, trailing pixie dust from her long blue cloak, which had been bewitched to resemble the night sky shedding stars.

Flabbergasted, he turned toward a sprite popping a fresh batch of frosted strawberries into a silver bowl below the rose-chocolate fountain. "*Who* was that?"

The sprite looked up. "Ida Moonshadow—apprentice to the Good Witch of the North."

He'd hated her on the spot.

Two years later, when she took her place across the table from him as a Cardinal Witch, he'd made an enemy for life.

A thud behind the counter told him Adorphus had raised the trapdoor. He folded his hands in front of himself, as if he'd not been pilfering eyeballs.

"Here you are, Hector," Adorphus said, placing a gallon of yellow and green goat-urine herbicide on the counter. "Anything else?"

"Perhaps a small jar of these eyeballs—"

Adorphus glanced suspiciously at the counter jar. "You know what Tinbit says. Those things make your gout worse."

"Tinbit has been saying that forever," Hector argued. "And I'm not laid up in bed yet."

"It's your funeral." Adorphus wrapped a small jar of the pickled eyeballs in crisp brown paper before adding it to the basket holding Hector's weekly groceries: a pound of liverwurst, a half-pound of boletes, pasta shells, a portion of gorgonzola, and two pounds of lamb, along with his usual magical purchases of nightshade berries, henbane leaves, and hemlock roots.

"Oh, and one of those flats of skunk cabbages outside," Hector added, unable to resist the charms of the small plants reeking their fetid odor into the shop when the door opened. They'd be beautiful in a drift next to his bat orchids.

"Oh, congrats on the Unicorn Jubilee. One thousand years of Happily-Ever-After is a credit to you, Your Wickedness," Adorphus yelled after him as he left the shop.

Hector carried the flat of skunk cabbages home himself, refusing Adorphus's offer to bring it by the next day. Once he'd set his heart on a plant, he didn't like to leave it behind. Adorphus was a businessman and his head was filled with shopkeeping, receipts and tallies—turning a profit, not turning the soil. Specialty plants came from one of his fae suppliers. This particular species was carnivorous, requiring a bog culture. A grin curled Hector's mustache as he considered diverting a suitable spring beneath their bed to provide them with the optimal habitat at Castle Grim. Within a month he'd have them big enough to take out an army of knights even if they came in with their noses pinned shut. *Beat that, Ida North.*

It wasn't entirely a dark witch's province, this fascination with gardening, but he couldn't help himself. He'd loved plants from an early age, and his parents—long dead now—indulged his rambles through the forest and neighboring bogs. At least, that's how he liked to remember it. Once upon a time, his parents didn't actually care if he got lost and died. He was the third child of seven, not a number anyone gave significance to, and he could hardly wait to go on his own quest to see what the world held for him.

No one was more surprised than he when he dutifully journeyed to the Dread Mountains in the West, twisted his ankle outside a charming gingerbread house, and was rescued by the person who lived there. The Wicked Witch of the West turned out to be a gentle and intelligent old woman who seemed to know that, at sixteen, he wasn't as brave or bold as he'd hoped to be. She gave him a plate of gingerbread and offered to tell his fortune by the knucklebones. Knowing this to be a good way for a young man to find out everything, from the location of a sword in a stone to who his future enchanted bride might be, he happily acquiesced. Thankfully, he was sitting in bed with his ankle wrapped in a block of never-melting ice when she told him he would be her apprentice.

"But I'm a boy," he'd protested.

She shook her head and gathered up the bones. "It doesn't matter. The bones never lie. If they say you're a witch, you're a witch."

"Do I have to wear the hat?"

"Why wouldn't you? They're quite comfortable, and the brim is excellent sun protection for your ears. You'll never get skin cancer."

"What about the broom? I don't think boys can ride a broom like that."

"If you don't want to ride astride, you can always try sidesaddle."

He took a bite of the gingerbread. "Maybe I can manage. This is delicious, by the way."

She patted his shoulder. "It's world-class bait for children who need to be fattened up for their first quest. My own special recipe."

He laughed. "Why, you're not wicked at all."

She shook her head. "Oh, my dear boy. You have so much to learn about being a witch. Now, pass me the eye of newt and I'll teach you how to brew poison apples."

Hector smiled at the memories as he set the baby plants on the skullery table.

"Not there, you horrible old man!" A giant voice boomed up at him from beneath the table. "I just cleaned that!"

He snatched the cabbages up quickly. "Tinbit. I didn't know you were back already. How is Crowbone? Better, I hope?"

A shock of black hair and a flash of red eyes and Tinbit, his gnome, popped up from beneath the table. "Dragon-flu is a bitch," he said. "I took him some carrot and ginger soup."

"Good, good." Hector tried to hide the plants behind his back. "Ginger is excellent for colds."

"What in the name of all that's evil did you want those for?" Tinbit eyed the plants. "I hope you don't expect me to take care of them. I've got more than enough to do, supervising your skeletons. Did you know one of them dyed your boxers blue this morning? You left indigo in your robe pockets again."

He winced. It could've been worse. It might've been madder root. "I'll try to be less careless next time."

"See that you are." Tinbit slapped a folder down on the table. "Three questors are waiting for you in the dungeons, here's a request for a pair of red-hot dancing slippers, oh, and the Flamelord asked you to visit tomorrow. Something about the Happily-Ever-After."

"I'm supposed to visit at the end of the week. What's so important that it can't wait?"

Tinbit shrugged and took the tray of skunk cabbages. "It just said visit him tomorrow. You know how dragons are."

"But what did he want?"

"No idea," Tinbit said, walking out of the room. "The message burned up the minute I read it, but if you want to dig through the ashes, that's your prerogative. It's in the fireplace. Do you want watercress sandwiches or cucumber with your tea?"

"Watercress, I suppose." Hector sat at the table, fingering the correspondence: bills, a letter from the king, a few fan letters—even wicked witches had admirers—and a notice for the annual greenhouse sale at the fae university. What on earth did the Flamelord want with him that couldn't wait? And he'd intended to spend the next day puttering around in his garden too.

But he was the Wicked Witch of the West.

Pulling his robes straight, he headed to his evil lair, which doubled as his library, to deal with his afternoon appointments before tea.

2

Ida

Dear Horrible Hector,

Sorry to disappoint you, but I'm healthy as a horse and so are my roses—your plagues never amount to much in the great scheme of things.

My Cinderella pumpkins are thriving and will be ready in time for the contest, not to mention the Unicorn Jubilee parade for the Common Princess. I must say that infestation of vine borers was beneath you—such a small-scale attack on your part—are you feeling well?

By the way, have you prepared the chosen dragon for his role in the upcoming Happily-Ever-After? I expect you to uphold your end of the magic and provide a suitable reptile for the occasion, not like the miserable excuse for a dragon we had last time. Hopefully this one will breathe a little more fire and less poetry.

Sincerely wishing you the worst,
IDA NORTH

HECTOR'S LETTER LAY OPEN NEXT TO IDA'S MOTHER-of-pearl penknife, stained the most appalling shade of green-black. She'd learned to be careful opening his letters. Hector liked to send hexes by mail and she couldn't always remove them by first counter-cursing the envelope. He'd always been clever, she'd give him that, even if sometimes he acted nine years old and not nine hundred ninety. She rubbed the blister on the tip of her index finger with a smidge of calendula cream.

She rose, folded a letter precisely into thirds, and set it aside to ripen. Potent charms like the one she'd added needed time to embed properly in the paper.

"Nearly noon—oh, goodness." She pulled her dressing gown over her shoulders and slipped out onto the balcony where she always took breakfast, a very late breakfast. At her age, she'd long since resigned herself to the flipping of her days and nights, a chronic insomnia that, over the last four hundred years, had become her normal. She rose around eleven, ate breakfast, then saw her appointments from noon to four. After lunch, she took a nap, and worked in her garden or greenhouses until nine, at which point she'd eat dinner and retire to her spellroom for the remainder of the evening and go to bed around three in the morning. No one minded this unusual schedule. She was the Good Witch of the North—her castle, her rules.

Northern spring days were chilly, but the noon sun warmed her face. The twinges of pain in her hands and wrists began to fade with the calendula cream she'd worked into her skin. Getting old didn't bother Ida greatly, except for the damned arthritis. She sat in her chair and gazed proudly at her garden. The Happily-Ever-After rose was in full bloom. The enchanting fragrance wafted on the cool breeze, some musky, others sweet. The red roses sprawled wildly through the trees and over the garden walls, tenacious as any weed. It always made her happy to think how well they'd naturalized since she'd planted that seed in the ground—the first magic her mentor had entrusted her with. Now everyone could have one of these roses in their own garden. Granted, they weren't magical like hers, but still, they smelled and looked good, a constant reminder of how beautiful Happily-Ever-After was.

"Aren't they lovely, Hari?" she asked the gnome when his light footfall pattered up the stairs.

"Yes, my lady," came the glum reply. He was definitely unhappy about something. Hari was one of the few servants who heeded her when it came to not calling her that.

She half rose from her chair. "Hari, what on earth are you wearing?"

He stood before her in a brown hunter's jacket, a tight white shirt, brown breeches, and shiny black boots, a huge change from his usual flowing tunic and smart red-and-blue trousers. With his long brown curls and deep brown eyes in his pale face, he resembled a pert mushroom. She would've laughed if he didn't look so miserable.

He set the breakfast tray on the table. "Will that be all, my lady?"

"Don't you 'my lady' me, young man," she scolded. "Why are you wearing that ridiculous outfit?"

"With the princesses coming this week, I was told to wear a uniform."

Ida shook her head. "You know I don't insist on uniforms for anyone, least of all you."

A small smile appeared on his face. She smiled too. Hari looked so much like his great-great-great-great grandfather. She could admit she missed old friends. That too was one thing she didn't like about the immortality that came with being a Cardinal

Witch. After the first eighty years or so, everyone she'd ever loved had died. The only people left were her colleagues. And Hector. He hardly counted. But she always made new friends. Like young Hari.

"Go change, immediately. You look like a starched fungus."

The smile broadened to a grin. "I feel like one. I won't bother to tell you where this outfit rides up, but it's not pleasant."

"I need to have a talk with the housekeeper about you."

He winced, pouring her cup. "I wish you wouldn't. She already calls me your favorite, and I don't think you talking to her would make it any better. I'll change and tell her you asked me to water the roses."

"Well, go and do it soon," she said. "You're a cloud on a sunny day when you frown, Hari."

He chuckled. "I'll try to frown less, my lady."

"I ought to make you wear a tie for that."

"Don't tell her. She'll take it as a command. How are your hands?" He reached out and took them in his tiny ones, massaging the bones gently.

"Better," she said. "Your calendula cream worked wonders."

"It's a friend's recipe. He claimed it would even soothe a dragon burn," he said. "Got to keep your fingers nimble if you're going to keep writing letters to his Wicked Witchness."

"Speaking of Hector West, did you get the last of the moth larvae out of the vines? I can't lose anymore coaches to that pestilence of a man."

"Done," he said. "But the chickens are refusing to eat them now. I think they're sick of worms."

She sighed. "At least we saved a few of them. Of course, I told him his plan failed utterly."

"Somehow, I don't think it will deter him. Perhaps, for a change of pace, you could tell him what a great job he's doing as Wicked Witch and how much you admire his nasty necomancy. See if that works."

She drained her teacup and rose. "That will be the day. I'll take my breakfast in the reception room. I want to see the preparations for the princesses for myself. I'm not too hungry—there is no need to bring me more than a cup of fruit and buttered toast."

"I'll bring it myself," Hari said, collecting the cup.

"No. I want you go to the garden and bring me a dozen roses. Have the housekeeper bring breakfast."

Hari glanced at her sharply. "You won't—"

"I won't." She watched him go, smiling. Good witches weren't supposed to lie, but that didn't mean they had to tell the whole truth either. She wouldn't consult *the housekeeper*. But she absolutely would talk to Hari's mother.

The reception room was Ida's favorite place in the castle. She'd designed it herself, along with the rest of the Castle Peerless. Immortality guaranteed a woman one great privilege—the delight of designing and building one's own house. She knew every stone of this place intimately.

By day, massive skylights admitted all the glorious sunlight ceiling to floor, giving the pure white marble hall a dazzling radiance. Whenever she entered it, she thought of snow—snow and home. But home had not been a tenth of the size of this room, let alone a castle.

She'd been born in a tiny cottage with a thatched roof,

coming into the world as her mother left it. Her father remarried when she was twelve. Her stepmother was a witch.

According to the new rule of Happily-Ever-After, an evil stepmother was just the thing for a girl growing up in poverty in the cold mountains of the north. Ida jumped around, clapping her hands in joy. Then she ran upstairs and put on her most ragged dress and grabbed a broom, ready to enter a life of servanthood until she would be chosen as the Common Princess, go to her first ball in uncomfortable glass slippers, and meet a prince. But as soon as her new stepmother came in, she spotted the broom, grabbed her own, and took Ida out for a ride in the moonlight. By the time they came home, windblown and laughing, Ida's new mother was her best friend.

She taught Ida potion making, the growing of herbs, how to speak to the trees, how not to ever laugh at a dragon if you met one in the mountains, and complex mathematics, along with the reading and writing of the languages of magic. By the time she turned eighteen, Ida was a witch herself, and apprenticed to the ancient Good Witch of the North, well on her way to becoming a preeminent sorceress.

She toured the snow-white room, breathing in the scent of roses. Every vase in the room overflowed with them—white roses, pink roses, yellow roses, red roses, even a purple kind that flirted with being blue. Dense fragrance surrounded her as she sat on the White Throne, a grand name for the most uncomfortable chair in the world. Even the seats in the Witches' Council Chamber weren't so bad. She might've padded it with a velvet cushion, but as she often told Hari, the chair served as a constant reminder that governing the balance of good and evil in the kingdom was her job, one she took seriously enough to endure the ache in her tailbone as she lowered herself onto the stone seat. Almost a thousand years she'd been doing this, and it never got any easier.

Wicked magic didn't take the effort good magic did, or at least Hector never seemed to exert any effort thinking up the plagues and pestilences that fueled his magic. He wasn't fooling her when he said he was just doing his job—the man loved it, even stuffing the more minor of his magics in an envelope simply to annoy her, and all at the expenses of someone else's life. Ida's spells brought life into the world, which required more responsibility than killing for every spell you made, like Hector's necomancy did.

With a long sigh, she sat down on her throne. A thousand years of Happily-Ever-After, a thousand years of peace and prosperity, a fairy tale come true, and it was largely up to her to maintain it. She was the one with the red rose. She had to arrange the happy marriage of the crown prince to a commoner, joining the two hearts required to maintain the spell. And on top of all that, as a good witch, she had to think of something nice for the world at least once a week, not to mention thinking up new and wonderful happy endings for every farm girl with a wicked stepmother who actually was wicked, and not a witch. And yes, she was proud to be helping to preserve the world, but there were certainly times when the weight of it felt heavy.

Meanwhile, Hector lounged around his castle for decades, waiting for the next time he got to stick his long and pointed nose into the affairs of the kingdom every time a crown prince turned twenty.

She fingered the red rose sitting by itself in the vase beside her.

One of these days, she thought, feeling rather vicious, I'd like to trade places with that second-rate witch, and make him see it's far harder to be good than bad. And then I'd pop a blister-butt hex in an envelope and see how he likes it. She hoped her laughing charm made him miserable for a full twenty-four hours. Would serve the bastard right.

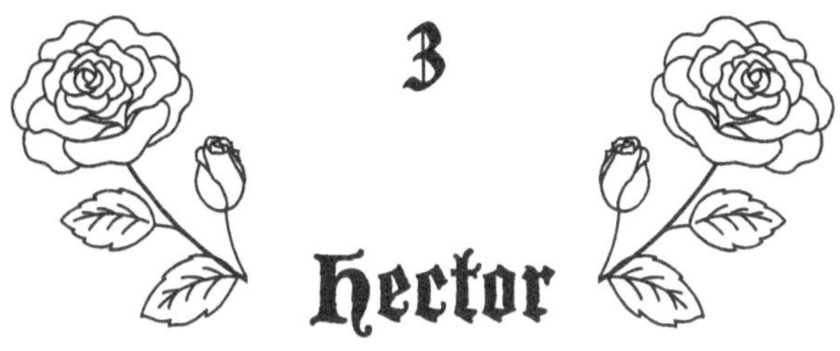

3

Hector

My Dear Detested Ida,

There's friendly rivalry, and then there's war.

HECTOR WEST

HECTOR LAY ON HIS BACK, SOAKING IN A GRAY-GREEN bath of marshmallow root and slippery elm bark. He'd smudged the letter disgracefully, but his fingers were singed and raw, along with the rest of him. He groaned and set the page back on his bath table, an invention he'd designed and given to himself for his five-hundredth birthday, and sank down into the water. He found his best creative moments came when relaxing in the warm water with all his long salt-and-pepper hair floating around him like drifts of silver seaweed.

Tonight, it looked like smoke on the water as he stewed in his rage. Irresponsible, foolish, reprehensible, old…

"Witch," he muttered.

He had so much more he wanted to say but couldn't bring himself to say what he wanted, not even in his own thoughts and certainly not in a letter. Even unintentional curses had a nasty way of coming true. He had a sudden vision of Ida North, dressed in her most becoming white robes, greeting the candidates for Common Princess, transforming into a replica of his hellhound and eating half the eligible girls in six big snaps. It would serve her right, though.

He settled down lower in the bath. He'd come up with something—something really nasty this time, something that would make her smart as much as he was smarting now. The nerve of that woman! Now everything was ruined.

It had started out as such a nice day too.

Tinbit began it on a good note by bringing him breakfast in bed.

"What did I do to deserve this?" Hector set his memoirs aside. This was an ongoing project, begun in his seven-hundredth year when he became worried that his memory might fail him on the more obscure details if he waited much longer. "Thank you, Tinbit."

"Mmmph," Tinbit grunted, opening the curtains.

Hector spooned chokeberry jelly into a bowl where he could break up the hot buttered scone and eat it submerged in his favorite jam. Sweet, but still retaining an acidic, poisonous tang, it came from his own garden. The espaliered trees were the pride and joy of his orchard.

Tinbit squatted beside the fireplace, scraping at the coals from the night before. He added a few fresh juniper sticks, grumbling under his breath.

"What is it, Tinbit? You're frowning."

"I always frown; you know that."

Hector set his spoon down. "But not down to your shoes. What's wrong?"

"It's just you show more appreciation for the little things I do around here than Crowbone does, and it makes me want to thump him. You know what he said yesterday when I scolded him for not eating his soup? He said I was a meddlesome old hen and to go cluck somewhere else."

Hector repressed a sigh. He'd once lectured Tinbit's grandmother on the feasibility of maintaining a relationship with no mutual respect and admiration. He struggled to recall the exact words. Something like "tell that man to go choke on his own selfishness; you can do better," and she'd listened. Perhaps that might work here.

He glanced at Tinbit.

Perhaps not. They'd been through this before and not only with Crowbone. "Don't worry, Tinbit. One day, he will see how amazing you are, and carry you off on his best bullfrog to his home in the swamp and you'll live happily ever after."

A ghost of a smile appeared, and the laugh was harsh and dark, which sounded right for Tinbit. "What would you do without me? Get your own breakfast? Clean your own clothes? Sweep this castle on your own?"

"Nonsense," he said, spraying crumbs. "The skeletons do that."

"Next you'll be telling me you like bone broth in your coffee every morning."

Hector eyed his coffee suspiciously. "You didn't!"

"No, but I ought to, you old relic," Tinbit said, jerking Hector's second-best robe out of the closet and tossing it unceremoniously at him before heading back to the fireplace, this time with his broom. "You'll have to wear this today. I'm still trying to magic the indigo out of your better one. It may be ruined."

Hector tasted his coffee dubiously, rolling the first sip

around, checking for the foul concoction Tinbit always tried to slip into his meals one way or another. "You know I wouldn't keep you here if it negated your happiness."

Tinbit's shoulders stiffened. "I am happy. Anyway, if he loved me, he'd have come to work at the castle. And aren't you a little wicked to be matchmaking? That's Ida North's job."

"Since I get the distinction of choosing the villains in the story, I can say I'm an excellent judge of character."

Tinbit stopped sweeping ashes. "You don't like him, do you?"

"I don't know him like you do, Tinbit." Hector blew on his flaxseed meal to cool it.

With a sigh, the harsh veneer vanished, and the surly, grumpy gnome Hector had known since he was a gnomelet slumped all over his little body. "I think I love him, Hector, but when I do something nice, like applique his jacket so he can go on the big frog hunt, he doesn't even thank me. He grabbed it and left—bye, Tinbit, see you this weekend—like I'd just be there when he got back. And now when I try to be nice and forget the whole thing, he calls me a meddlesome mother hen. I don't know what to do. I just want someone…someone to love me."

Hector stirred the gruel, thinking. Roughly six months had passed since he'd found Tinbit crying in the skullery, declaring he and Crowbone were done. He'd thrown a plate across the room and said he didn't ever want to see the arrogant, toadstool-barf of a man again. A month later, Crowbone came to the castle with a bouquet of swamp saxifrage, asking for forgiveness. Tinbit took him back without even asking for an explanation. Now it looked like they were separating again, and Hector was fairly sure it wasn't really about the jacket or the soup. Regardless of his opinion of Crowbone, it hurt him to see his favorite so depressed. Tinbit deserved a nice gnome who would love him in all his grouchy, overbearing, completely devoted mother hen obnoxiousness. It would be a happy ending for once. But as Tinbit had reminded him, Hector wasn't in charge of those.

"Do you want me to go with you to see the Flamelord today?" Tinbit asked.

"No, I'll have Pocket with me."

"You're sure?"

"Absolutely," Hector said. When it came to dragons, a taciturn temperament was useful. Dragons could be touchy, and Tinbit lacked tact, especially when he was grumpy. The giant, at least, would be quiet.

Hector left Castle Grim immediately after breakfast. A trip into the mountains, even in a basket perched high on a giant's shoulders, took most of a day. He'd packed a good book to read as well as his personal correspondence. He spotted Ida's thin script on one of the envelopes and smiled grimly. She never wrote back so quickly unless she was furious. He imagined ravenous moths descending on her pumpkin patch and swelled with professional pride.

"Are we there yet?" he asked, taking her letter from the pile on his lap desk and settling back in the comfortable nest of blankets to enjoy it.

Pocket's voice rumbled up to him. "I can see the Flamelord's lair now, master."

"Pocket, I'm nobody's master."

"As you say, master."

Hector growled under his breath. In the past thousand years, significant social changes had happened. With his reforms, all giants were paid appropriately, and given pensions and paid time off from pillaging, carrying off fair maidens, and building castles in the sky. Your Wickedness or plain Wickedness was the appropriate address for him, but he'd found it impossible to get them to drop an honorific carryover from the time when giants were pawns, used in war to cause as much destruction as possible and then discarded like the rubbish they left behind. Giants could be set in their ways. It had taken him six centuries to convince them they could eat something other than magic beans, at what point the air quality in the Dread Mountains became much better. Now one only needed a mask on the cloudiest days when the dragon smoke mixed with the fetid mist that settled in the mountain valleys.

He slit the envelope open with his obsidian penknife. Ida's charms were potent, and he'd found them unpleasant on every occasion when he didn't neutralize them, but obsidian usually did the trick. He pulled the letter—ivory stationery strongly smelling of roses—and read the contents.

He burst out laughing.

The giggles shook him to tears. "Pock…Pocke…Pocket…" but he couldn't stop chortling. He gasped, he cried, he snorted until he hiccupped. Nothing was funny. He stared at the letter, eyes wet, furious. And burst out laughing again. A mirth charm, laughing gas, the shits and giggles, and he couldn't stop. Quickly, he zipped his mouth shut, all but the very center, and spoke through the hole, "Poookett, hume." He couldn't possibly be diplomatic with dragons while laughing his fool head off.

"We're here, master."

"Cwap."

A sudden drop told him that Pocket had set his basket on the ground. Hector rummaged in his satchel for a mirror. Below his angry green eyes and beetling brows, his mouth turned up at the corners in the worst kind of smirk. Frothy giggles trickled out of his lips. Crap indeed! He couldn't even go in to make an apology looking like this. The worst thing a person could do was laugh at a dragon.

His gaze fell on his mask.

Thoughtful, thoughtful Tinbit! Hastily, he tied it on, pulling it well up over his nose, mouth and beard, and tightened it around his ears. He'd go in, find out why the Flamelord had asked for him, and leave before his muffled snorts and chuffs would be taken for anything other than a bad case of dragon-flu.

He feigned a particularly loud sneeze followed by several collapsed giggles and approached the Flamelord waiting at the entrance to the cave.

Hector

The only thing more offensive than laughing at a dragon is refusing to have tea with one.

A THOUSAND YEARS OF WICKEDNESS: A MEMOIR

HECTOR WEST

THE FLAMELORD ADAIR WAS A BEAUTIFUL DRAGON, more than ten feet tall, with blue eyes the shade of a summer sky and shiny red hair trailing well past his shoulders. When he smiled, rows of fabulously sharp, serrated teeth sparkled like rubies in the sunlight. He used this human form for visitors, but Hector had seen him in his true shape, soaring over the mountains as a twenty-foot dragon-king, all smoke, fire, and roar. He was red then too, with massive, webbed wings and a heavy, armored tail complete with razor-sharp spikes.

"Hector!" The dragon grabbed Hector's hand in both of his. "What's with your mask? We specifically had a no-smoking order for the last week in anticipation of your visit."

"Dwagon foo," he spluttered through the tiny hole he'd left between his lips, turning another giggle into a cough.

Adair grinned. "Got my vaccination earlier this year. Hector,

Hector, Hector. When will you ever learn you're not completely indestructible?" He clapped Hector on the back.

"Can't shay long. What's wong?"

Adair still smiled, but it looked forced now. "I need you to talk to Alistair. Come in and I'll explain. Morga has made your favorite, toffee cakes and chamomile tea."

A laugh shuddered through him so suddenly, he almost didn't suppress it in time. He patted his throat. "No fanks."

"Just the tea, then." The Flamelord put his arm around Hector and propelled him into the cave.

Once upon a time, Hector believed dragon caves were just caves—uncomfortably large spaces underground, featuring ridiculous faux dwarf interior design, straight out of the overactive imaginations of second-rate writers. He also believed they should be filled with treasure, mostly of the shiny variety, equating dragons to oversized magpies with an unfortunate craving for fresh princesses with a side of butter and a hot roll. He was sixteen. By seventeen, he'd met his first Flamelord and been reeducated.

The room Adair led Hector into was indeed a cave but spacious, airy, and beautifully decorated. The walls were polished black granite, with sensible furniture carved of the same. No gold lay about—the dragon kept that in a safe deposit box. But the room was filled with treasure, although the average person might be hard-pressed to see its value. The Flamelord collected obscure folk art—the more inscrutable the design and obscure the artist, the better.

He'd acquired a new piece since Hector had been here last.

Adair paused a pregnant moment to let Hector admire the animal in the corner, an odd combination of a horned animal and a fish, covered in black and white spots, made of driftwood and shells. "Beautiful, isn't it?" he said, looking gratified by Hector's stunned silence. "It's called Sea Cow. It was made from natural materials, locally sourced, by an old mermaid who lives by the coastal city of Myst."

"Mmm." He'd call it more striking than beautiful, but he wasn't artistic, unless he counted picking the right color of orange prickly poppy to contrast with black pussywillow. All the works of art in his castle came from friends, including the young dragon who slouched through the hallway at the back of the gallery clearly trying to be invisible.

"Alistair!"

The boy paused. He turned slowly. "Yes?"

"Don't you go flying off," the Flamelord said. "Hector has come to see you, and after I talk to him, I want you to hear what he has to say." He sounded unnecessarily loud. Alistair must have been listening to that heavy metal dwarf group again—Smashing Mountains? Crushing Gravel? Hector couldn't keep track of them anymore. That might have been the Flamelord thirty-odd years ago. Funny how parents could never remember how rebellious they'd once been when their teenagers turned against them. He smiled. A small bubble of giggles trickled from the hole between his mostly sealed lips. He turned it into a coughing fit.

The Flamelord patted him on the back. "Dear me—you really do need a cup of hot tea. Morga! Hector's here."

Morga swept into the room in her human form, long black hair swinging down to her ankles. "Hector!" She took his hands in her own and held them up to her mouth to kiss them. "Oh, I'm so glad you're here. Addy and I need your advice on how to deal with Alistair. You see, Hector, he doesn't want to kidnap the princess!"

"Fwat?" An explosion of furious laughter almost burst out of him.

Morga looked at Adair in confusion.

"He's got dragon-flu."

Morga rolled her eyes. "Didn't you get a shot? Hector!"

"That's what I told him. A big grown-up witch shouldn't be afraid of a little needle." Adair sat in one of the huge granite chairs. "Now, how about a cup of your lemon-chamomile blend and a slice of cake for him?"

"No cake." Hector sat and removed his mask. His nose was practically bumping the edge of the table, but he didn't like to ask for a booster seat. In the middle of the table sat the magical centerpiece: the everblooming black rose shedding petals on the stone table. Of all the foolishness. Alistair had been groomed for this position since he was a twelve-year-old wyvern-sized drag-onet. Now at eighteen he was getting new ideas?

"S'why?" he asked as Morga plunked a flagon full of tea at his elbow. At least it was large enough to hide his grin when he drank it, and he'd have to. It would be rude not to.

"It's all those weird books he reads," Addy said. "At first, we thought it was a phase—him reading outside of the traditional fairy tales. And frankly, Morga and I were just glad he *was* reading. You remember how hard it was for us to get him to give up comic books."

"Graphic novels, dear," Morga said.

"He thinks girls shouldn't be forced to go with a dragon against their will. It's like he doesn't believe it's the way the whole world works. I've tried to tell him how good it is for the

Common Princess, how it greatly improves her life, how it lifts her out of her usual station and lets her become a queen. But all he keeps saying is he won't support a practice that has its roots in medieval…abduction fantasies."

"Talk to him, Hector," Morga said. "Alistair respects you so much, and you are, of course, human and can explain it so much better than we can. Addy has gone over the dragon's role in the Happily-Ever-After with him—how he doesn't even have to touch the girl's hand if he doesn't want to, and how he's to be a perfect gentleman and furnish her a cave as befits a princess. I even suggested he decorate it with his art for her—he wasn't having any of it. Please, Hector. We're at our wit's end."

Cwap indeed. The date for kidnap was barely a week away. Ida would be interviewing the candidates today or the next. He'd have to find some way to talk to Alistair without laughing. A teenage dragon was about ten times as volatile as a grown one. He lifted his empty cup and set it down beside the slab of cake Morga now pushed hopefully in his direction. "I'll twy," he said.

Alistair's studio used to be his bedroom. Hector had been there countless times in the past, when Alistair was a young, wiggly, excitable dragonet who couldn't keep his form from one second to the next. Sometimes he was a wild-haired, brown-skinned, blue-eyed little boy with grabby hands, rushing from one treasure to the next, eager to show off his latest toys. The next minute, he was a hard-scaled, lithe little snake with undeveloped wings, fawning against Hector's ankles, climbing up his robe with razorlike claws, panting in his eagerness, a typical dragon child. His room used to be the typical room of a dragon child too—brightly colored stone furniture, windows open to the sky, a balcony from which to take the air, and a large, open bathing pool for shedding skins—in short, everything to make a dragon prince feel like a king.

Not anymore.

Hector coughed. Smoke billowed out the moment he opened the door, although the crystal windows stood open, admitting a stiff, cold breeze and plenty of sunlight into what had essentially become a volcanic vent.

Everything was black—the curtains, the walls, the asbestos bedding. Even the ceiling was black. The bright furniture had been removed, leaving a long, sterile-looking sleeping couch completely covered in ashes. The swimming pool-sized bath was empty and soot colored. The reason for all the cinders was evident immediately. Alistair had completely filled his room with fire sculptures.

The closest one roared all the way up to the ceiling, flying up as a man, crawling down itself as a dragon. It stood far taller than the dragon himself, breathing out enormous jets of fire onto a granite base, shaping them boldly with his hands.

Alistair wasn't as tall as his father yet—he had years of growing left to do—but he wasn't the vampire-thin, scrawny boy he'd been a year ago. Working with fire had given him an upper body a dwarf would've been proud of. His muscles rippled as he worked; his skin glistened in the heat. Hector was somewhat surprised to see Alistair caught between dragon and man—his human legs were covered in his dark scales and he sported crimson wings from his shoulder blades. Only when Hector saw the mirror did he understand.

Alistair was carving a self-portrait. Every now and then, he'd check the mirror and blow another long, flaming breath into the sculpture. He glanced at Hector, smoke leaking from both nostrils.

With the greatest of care, Hector fully unzipped his lips. A smile still curled the corners of his mouth but no giggles emerged. The worst might be over, and this wasn't the sort of conversation one could conduct through a blowhole.

"Very nice. What do you call this one?" he asked, gesturing to the sculpture.

"*The Quintessence of Being*," Alistair said. With a broad slap of his large hand, he carved off a substantial chunk of semi-soft lava. It shuddered in the air and fell from the pedestal as a pyroclastic cloud. "I know why you're here, and you're wasting your time. I won't do it. Find another dragon. There must be any number of hotshots who want the notoriety."

"Notoriety is not the point," Hector said. "Alistair, you are the prince. Every Flamelord for the last thousand years starts his reign by kidnapping a princess. Your father did. Your grandfather did. Your great-grandfather—"

"And my great-great-great-grandfather did, yes, I know. You sound like Dad. But it's not for me. I don't want to be the Flamelord. I'm an artist. And I don't want to take an innocent girl, trap her in a cave, and fight some stupid prince when I wanted nothing to do with it in the first place."

"It's not like that at all, not now," Hector said, seriously disturbed. "It's not a real fight—no magical weapons allowed. And your scales will turn any blade that isn't enchanted."

"Dad got wounded."

"That was a…misunderstanding." It wouldn't be happening again. A stint in his dungeon had taught that royal fool a lesson.

"Well, if dragons aren't supposed to be wounded and it happened anyway, what makes you think the princess actually wants to be shut up in a cave and kept as a prisoner until she's rescued? What if she wanted to rescue herself? What if she didn't want to be a princess at all? Have you ever thought about that?"

"Frankly, no," he said. "That's not my department. But I can assure you that the princess does *not* want to rescue herself and she *does* want to be a princess. It's all included in the spell."

Alistair snorted sparks. "Yeah, right. Because you say so, it has to be true."

"Fine. Don't fight the prince. Leave the princess in the cave and come right home. I'll find some way of making it work—an illusion of some kind, perhaps. But you can't overturn centuries' worth of tradition because of human feelings."

"Maybe they are dragon feelings. Did you ever consider that?"

Hector's lips trembled, curled. *Oh no. No, no, no, no.* He laughed.

Alistair caught him full in the face with a blast of ultra-hot dragon fire and roasted him like a marshmallow.

Adair was incensed. He stormed off to Alistair's room, promising to ground him for the rest of his life.

Morga bandaged Hector tenderly, apologizing until she literally turned blue in the face.

Pocket, bless his kind heart, wrapped Hector carefully in blankets, tucked him in the basket, and ran all the way home with him.

Tinbit, all concern and very little sarcasm, made Pocket tell him what happened about ten times while he undressed Hector and hissed with sympathy over the crispy bits while Hector tried to assure him he'd gotten worse in his lifetime, which he had, but a very long time ago, back when the dragons were wild, ungoverned, and particularly suspicious of wicked witches, who compelled them to fight in the wars. What was wrong with kids these days? No respect and irresponsible to boot. But he would have handled it better if he hadn't been laughing.

Hector glanced again at the unfinished letter lying on his bathtub writing table.

He crumpled it up and grabbed a fresh sheet of paper.

If Ida wanted war with him, he'd give her one.

5

Ida

Hector,

That was uncalled for. I meant no harm with my laughing charm, and if you found a way to get yourself barbecued as a result, it's not my fault. If you want to stop our correspondence, I can assure you, it won't bother me to take you off my mailing list.

I hope you got second-degree burns.

IDA NORTH

A TEARDROP SPLASHED ONTO THE CREAMY WHITE paper Ida was writing on and blurred the ink. A tiny little laughing charm, that's all it was. His retaliation was unconscionable, and if she hadn't been so angry, she would've summoned him up and yelled at him face to face in the crystal ball. But her face was puffy from crying all night, and she'd never let him see he'd made her cry. Never. That ass of a man! Now she was crying again.

A timid knock on the door made her wipe her eyes hastily. "Come in, Hari."

The gnome poked his head around the door. His eyebrows

crinkled in deep concern. "You didn't send for breakfast. I thought you might be ill."

"No," she said, voice cracking. "I'm not ill. But I'm not hungry."

"Can I come in? I brought oatmeal."

She waved her hand at him.

He slipped in, back first, and shut the door gently with his foot before carrying the tray to her writing table.

She glanced at the bowl and the wineglass. "That's not oatmeal, Hari."

"So I lied," he said, shrugging. "Raspberry sorbet goes well with white wine. And I put mint chocolate syrup in it."

She rubbed her forehead with both hands. "Do I really seem so upset?"

He pulled up a footstool, clambered onto it, and dug his tiny hands into her shoulders. "It'll be all right. You tell the Council the truth. No one should ever get in trouble for telling the truth."

Oh, sweet, wonderful Hari, but so, so naïve.

The truth? She'd sooner let Hector see her cry than let the Council know what had happened. The truth would get her fired.

Hector's letter arrived on the afternoon Ida met with the contestants vying for the role of Common Princess. She hated this day with all of her heart and soul, but it hadn't always been that way.

Once upon a time, the position of princess was hereditary. The rival factions of royalty fought each other for the kingship, marrying their sons and daughters by betrothal, all in the name of power. The world was awash in magical chaos from the witches fighting for the various sides. Plague, pestilence, famine, and unimaginable poverty blanketed the land.

Ida had been a child during those dark days, but she certainly remembered them. It would have taken an army of witches centuries to clean up the mess that centuries of war had caused—everything from salted earth to battlefields so piled with corpses there weren't graves to bury them all.

Until Happily-Ever-After.

The first Happily-Ever-After was a beautiful one. The crown prince married a common girl, the first of many such marriages. Ida remembered the story well—the downtrodden servant with her wicked stepmother and two horrid sisters, the glass slipper, the elegant ball where her luck changed. It was the day everything changed. From that time forward, magic worked for the good of the people, for the good of the land, for the good of all. It was her job to maintain that, and one she took very seriously.

Ida had a great deal of sympathy for the girls who came from farms, smithies, salt mines, orphanages, and taverns. This used to be a difficult but rewarding part of her job, choosing girls for a royal Happily-Ever-After. They all deserved Happily-Ever-Afters in her opinion. Everyone did. She wished she could give a fairy-tale princess crown to every last one of them. But she couldn't. Therefore, she devised quests for the girls, challenging them to various tests and trials to prove their worthiness. At the end, the victorious princess claimed the red rose imbued with Happily-Ever-After magic, ensuring them a wonderful life with their prince.

That's how it used to be.

But five hundred years ago, the commoners decided no

witch deserved so much power in choosing the royal family. If the common folk became royalty, they wanted a say in the process. Ida had been all for it. It seemed fair. Only it didn't quite work out that way. It got political, then literary, and when things get literary, there's not much even a very great witch can do to make things better. Now the position of Common Princess was decided by a committee composed entirely of various upper-class citizens, mostly belonging to the Storyteller's Guild. They decided every elected princess needed a story worthy of the fairy-tale rags-to-riches legends of the past.

This year, they'd chosen The Little Match Girl Gets a Happy Ending. The lucky recipient was Mildred Cheapstreet, an orphan with an upbringing to make even someone as hard-hearted as Hector cry. Mother died when she was three. Father was a drunk. At five, he sent her out to sell matches, which she dutifully did, and with very poor sales, since no one in the kingdom had used matches since the dwarf Nikel Tessler made electricity free for everyone. This enabled her to spend her days doing good for anyone who passed her street corner, where she dispensed everything from advice to little dolls for babies that she made out of matches tied together with strands of her long blond hair. They were a choking hazard, but it was the thought that counted. From her bald head to her chilblains, this was certainly a girl who deserved a happy ending to her story.

Ida would have agreed, if she hadn't known it was completely fabricated.

The girl in question did come from a common background, but her father was no drunk, and he didn't make her sell matches.

He was a popular tavern owner, and she was a spoiled only child. Her indulgent father called in a bar tab with three of the committee members. But that was how the cookie crumbled these days. It could be worse. There was the current queen—now that had been a fiasco.

Still, as Ida sat in her receiving room, in the uncomfortable, ass-biting chair, fiddling with the red rose, she wished she could give it to any other girl but Mildred Cheapstreet—like the little seamstress who had just left the room weeping.

Hari passed the girl on her way out, carrying the tea tray. Ida was never so glad to see it. She set the rose down in her vacant seat and joined him at the table.

"Tea, quiche tartlets, and prosciutto and honeydew," he said. "Don't worry. Mother will see to the rejected princesses. She's laying out a high tea for them right now. She saved you some petit fours if you want one."

Ida shuddered. "I couldn't possibly." She helped herself to the melon. "How many more are there?" She downed the tea, wishing it were wine.

"Only two. This came for you." Hari set a letter on the table with the sugar tongs. Hector's thin, intricate script was on the envelope. A proper precaution—it wouldn't be beyond Hector to give her a sudden and acute case of diarrhea. She'd never ripped open a letter so fast.

Hari spooned the required sugar into Ida's second cup of tea. "Is that wise?"

"At this point, Hari, I'd welcome one of Hector's curses if it would postpone the rest of this day until I'm ready to deal with it."

She pulled out the soft gray linen stationery and read.

Ida,

What you did was completely reprehensible. You put me in serious danger. I might have been killed. I only escaped incineration by using a sculpture as a shield when a dragon took exception to being laughed at. I'm tired of your little jokes.

Consider this my final letter.

HECTOR

She crumpled the letter in both hands. In all the years they'd corresponded, he'd never sounded so…angry. From the straightforward address to the furious tenor of the last line, this was a Hector she didn't recognize.

Hari held out the teacup. "Are you all right?"

"Hector's hurt. A dragon attacked him."

Hari's eyes widened. "But he's okay? I mean, he's a witch. He could protect himself, right?"

"Oh, he's fine," she said, throwing the letter on the tray. "Well enough to write. Well enough to tell me he won't write again. Well enough to tell me he doesn't like my 'little jokes'!"

"Ida?"

She waved her hand distractedly. "I don't care. I don't care if he's alive or dead, hurt or well. Send the next princess in. I'm tired. I want to finish my work and go out to my garden and forget this. Forget everything."

She blinked fiercely. They'd been writing each other almost as long as they'd been practicing, as long as they'd been in charge of tending the delicate balance of good and evil in the kingdom. And they respected each other—a grudging respect but respect all the same. At times, she'd even detected a teasing, needling amusement in his letters when he spoke of how he'd thwarted her latest spell, and it had made her happy to think he probably struggled to contain her magic as much as she fought to deal with his.

She took her seat and tossed the rose angrily on the armrest. Two girls entered the room together, one of them a wreck of rags and pitiable countenance with a balding head, the other dressed in her finest work dress, clean and starched for the occasion.

Gods. All she wanted to do was get this over with and go upstairs to cry or break something, possibly both. What was it about that man? A thousand years of rivalry, of working against each other, and here she was crying because she wanted him to respect her?

She stared them both down fiercely. "Which one of you is Mildred the Match Girl?"

The ragbag started sobbing. "I'm Mildred, your ladyship. This thug attacked me in the hallway!"

"I did no such thing. I'd only attack a person if they could defend themselves. You couldn't even flatten a gnat." The girl in the new dress gazed up at Ida with the kind of steady confidence that she'd expect from a witch, not a princess. She had a striking face, pretty, even with the clear light of anger in her soft brown eyes. Her reddish-brown hair was pulled into a thick braid that fell halfway down her back, and her lips were so tight they looked pale against her tan. A farmer or a blacksmith, perhaps. Her arms were muscular, and she looked strong. "Your Goodness, my name is Amber. I know you've been told Mildred is a match girl, and that she tore all her hair out to make dolls out of matches, but that's a lie, and a wig. I've known her for years. Her family owns the biggest tavern conglomerate in the capital. My father works for them—he's makes the iron rings for the barrels. She's not an orphan. She's not poor. She's not been through any real hardship. It's not fair they didn't tell you, and it's not fair to the other girls either."

"She's lying, Your Goodness!" Mildred wept. "I *am* a match girl. Amber is just jealous of me. She always has been. She knew she could never be a princess because she's from a good family! She wants to smear me so *she* can be the princess!"

Amber's face twisted into a disdainful sneer. "I don't want any part of that nonsense. I'm a smith and a damn good one. I'm not giving that up."

Mildred's tears turned to angry sobs. "This is your way of getting even because Timothy Greene liked me instead of you in the eighth grade!"

"Oh, for Gods' sake. You can choose who you want to marry or if you want to marry at all! Those other girls don't have half our privilege—"

Mildred slapped Amber. "You think any one of those other girls has any idea how to be consort to a prince? They wouldn't know how to embroider a pillow! Some of them probably don't know how to read, let alone compile a guest list for a party!"

Amber's bright eyes sparkled, but she didn't retaliate. "If they get a chance, they'll learn all they need and more, and you're denying them—"

Suddenly, it all seemed so revolting, so worthless, so inane. One thousand years, and this was the best magic could come up with? Of course, it wasn't magic that had come up with this travesty; she hadn't even been consulted in centuries for the choosing. She was supposed to be. She'd have never gotten the committee's proposal past Hector if that wasn't in there, but the reality was somewhat different. They'd turned the whole thing into a massive politically motivated beauty pageant. The nerve of Hector, calling her irresponsible but…maybe he had a point. Here she was, about to rubber stamp another princess, one that even other commoners knew wasn't deserving. This wasn't like Queen Annabeth—at least the committee had been duped on that one as much as she had.

Her temper, already at the breaking point, snapped.

"Stop." Ida cut both girls off with a swipe of her hand. Mildred went on shouting in complete silence. Amber whirled around to face Ida, face red, eyes glittering with fury, but she stopped talking. Smart girl.

Ida rubbed her temples. "A thousand years ago, my mentor, the Good Witch of the North, placed a single red rose in the hand of a struggling servant girl and changed the fate of the world. This is supposed to be a solemn, reverent moment, not some tit-for-tat on a daytime crystal ball talk show. You should both be ashamed of yourselves. But so should I." She picked up the red rose and held it carefully while the water dripped from the stem onto the folds of her robes. "Once upon a time, magic chose the girl who would become the Common Princess. Maybe it's time to return to tradition."

She descended the stairs, holding the rose. "My duty for the last thousand years has been to place this rose in the hand of the worthy princess, who will be taken captive by the evil dragon and rescued by the good prince, to ensure that this magic—the magic that saved us from ourselves—will continue to protect us and preserve us. Hold out your hands."

Mildred stuck her hand out at once. But Amber folded her arms over her chest.

"You would really refuse this test as a person who has been

the recipient of Happily-Ever-After your whole life?" Ida stared directly into Amber's deep brown eyes. "The magic will choose. Not you. Not I. Not some committee who gives out favors to those who can buy them. Isn't that what you wanted? Why you came?"

Amber's face turned red and her frown deepened into a gulch, but she slowly held out her hand.

Ida held the rose out like a wand. She touched Mildred's left hand. The rose shivered between her fingers, but nothing happened. Then she touched Amber's.

For a moment, Ida thought perhaps nothing would happen at all. She was on the verge of stepping back, calling Hari and telling him to send all the other girls back into the room. That would probably be the right thing to do, the fair thing. Then the rose warmed in her hand, first the stem as it filled with magic, and then the sepals, the petals, the stamens. With a sudden burst of dark smoke and the smell of a rose garden, the rose flared with crimson light.

Amber's mouth fell open. Next to her, Mildred Cheapstreet broke into silent sobs, stamping her feet and yelling soundlessly at Ida and Amber in turns. Well, that would never do. She'd not be able to make herself heard over that once she lifted the spell.

A flick of the rose and Mildred was a match. Ida picked her up and tucked her gently in her pocket. It would do the girl good to spend some time reflecting on her life and what she might want to do with it now. Perhaps a room full of matches in which she needed to find herself would be just the thing—Ida used to do that with grains of wheat sometimes. Very meditative, sorting wheat. But right now, she had a princess to deal with, and a very angry one to judge by the color in Amber's cheeks.

"Congratulations," Ida said. "The magic chose well. I wish you the best Happily-Ever-After, my dear."

Amber's red face turned purple. She opened her mouth, as if uncertain whether or not she could speak, but the words poured out in a torrent. "I told you, I don't want it! I have a life. I don't want to marry some prince. That's not my idea of a Happily-Ever-After! You can't force me to do this!"

"I'm not forcing you to do anything," Ida said. "The magic—"

"The magic can go get—"

"Listen to me," Ida said, holding up her hand. "You've been chosen, Amber Smith. You can either embrace your destiny or you can run away from it. That's the real choice you have to make now. Is it really so bad to be saving the world?"

If Amber's glare were turned into a sword, it couldn't be sharper. "You're going to regret this."

She threw the rose down on the floor and stomped out.

6

Ida

My advice to any young witch—always maintain a polite, friendly demeanor when corresponding with rival witches. Unless, of course, they are complete assholes.

MAGIC AND MISCHIEF—A THOUSAND
YEARS OF HAPPILY-EVER-AFTER

IDA NORTH

FOR THE REMAINDER OF THAT DAY, IDA HAD NOT known exactly what was wrong with her. She left the room, feeling vaguely that she'd made a mistake. Still, it was oddly satisfying to have picked, regardless of the circumstances, the most suitable girl for the position. Amber, clearly from the most middle of the middle class, a blacksmith with a stable career—and here she laughed at her own bad pun—was as common as common got. And yet, the girl had an uncommon temper, a fine sense of morality, and clearly cared about the downtrodden. She would make an excellent queen.

But she began to suspect something wasn't quite right that evening, far too late to save the day.

As usual, Hari was involved.

Ida had a frank discussion with her chef about the petit fours in the kitchen. "I really feel serving so many sweets at these functions sets a bad example."

"But—but you've always liked my Angel's Dream Cake!" the tearful man protested, twisting his chef's hat into knots, and glancing around the kitchen nervously. The cooks kept their attention on the stoves, but the housekeeper left her station where she was consulting with Hari over the folding of the napkins—delicate white swans on a blue bifold—and came over, looking concerned.

"Actually, I've never liked your Angel's Dream Cake. It's more like a sugar-spun nightmare, in all honesty—how much butter can you cram into a cake before it's a frosted heart attack? From now on, I want a simple fruit tray and crudités. Is that clear?"

"Yes, my lady." He sniffed.

"Good," she said. "Now, if you'll pardon me, I believe I will skip the princesses' dinner and ball. Make sure the soup and salad are served first, not with the meal."

The housekeeper protested. "But, my lady—it is traditional for the Good Witch to congratulate all the girls for their participation! You must attend."

Ida waved her off. "Gods, can't a woman buck tradition once in a thousand years? She touched the rose, the spell is set, and nothing in my job description stipulates I must be present for a dinner I don't want to eat, and a ball at which I won't dance; and I simply can't deal with all the fragrances girls wear nowadays."

"But, my lady—"

"Ida. It's always been Ida. Now excuse me, I have a witch to burn." Hector's letter galled her. How dare he write and accuse her of deliberately trying to get him killed? If she'd wanted him dead, she wouldn't send something like a laughing charm. It was a joke!

Hari brought her a bowl of watercress soup and a beef sandwich for dinner at ten. But he wasn't his usual self—he tiptoed around the room, hanging up the dress and putting away the gloves that had been set out in the hopes she'd change her mind.

"Are you sure you won't go down?" he asked, picking up her shoes. "You wouldn't need to stay long—just make a showing?"

"No! I'm tired, and it's almost over anyway. I hope they are all leaving right away. I've no desire to watch people weep into their tea at breakfast."

Hari snorted. "Oh, yeah? After this afternoon, I rather thought you enjoyed watching people weep."

Ida set her sandwich down. "All right. Out with it, Hari."

He squared up to her, shoulders back. "Out with what? Do you need anything else, my lady?"

She rolled her eyes. "If you don't say it now, I'll have to hear it later, won't I? You might as well speak—I'm not going to bite your head off."

"I don't know that you wouldn't," he said. "It's not like you to snap at the cook, and my mother is downstairs crying. You did it in front of the whole kitchen too."

Unwelcome remorse bubbled up. "I suppose…I suppose I was a bit sharp."

"I'm not saying you weren't right—at least about the frosted heart attack—but you've never told the man you didn't like his cake. Instead, you tell me to feed it to the pigs so you won't hurt his feelings. And my mother was only trying to make sure things went right—the girl you chose, Amber? She wouldn't wear the dress they brought for her. Told the hairdresser to 'get lost' and given how dutiful our sprite is, she might be wandering around the castle crying because she can't find her room. Just what was in that letter?"

She huffed. "Mostly Hector's raw ass crack. He's mad about the laughing charm."

"That's not what I meant. When you opened it, your whole face changed, like a spell had come over you. You looked…devastated." He sat on the footstool next to her and took her hand in both of his tiny ones. "What's wrong, Ida?"

She burst into tears. "I don't…I don't know! When you've known a man for so many years, even someone as awful as Hector, you expect to keep on knowing them. When he said he didn't want to even hear from me anymore, I felt like someone died. I know that sounds stupid."

"It doesn't sound stupid at all," Hari said, stroking her hand.

"I don't like the man. I've never liked the man. But I respected the witch, and it was nice to know he'd always be there, at least until he retired, and maybe I'd hex his cabbages to glow pink so he'd remember me. I guess I thought he…"

She stopped. Hari was right. Something was wrong. She shouldn't be this open with anyone, even Hari, even after two glasses of wine. She always concealed her emotions from her staff, the way a witch should.

Hector. Her lips tightened. "Did the trolls take out the trash yet?"

Hari pulled the letter out of his pocket, still wadded up like a snowball, carefully wrapped in a protective layer of wax paper.

"You didn't touch it?"

"Picked it up with a fork," he said.

She dumped it out on her dressing table with care. The paper had been plain and gray. Now it had turned dark and smoky, inked with blood.

Ida donned a white kid glove and flattened out the paper.

One ill turn deserves another.

"Hari," she asked hesitantly, "did I tell you exactly how I felt about you too?"

He smiled. "Nothing I don't already know. You think I'm artistic, funny, and very gay. You consider me a friend as much as a manservant. You're thinking about promoting me to steward, but you haven't done it yet because you worry you wouldn't get to be friends with me anymore. You think I have a green thumb with the roses, but it's the chicken shit, not me. And you wish I'd settle down with a nice man and have a family, but I only know that because my mother said you told her."

Ida palmed her face. A candor curse! That irresponsible, foolish, deplorable, ancient, old…witch! He knew the princesses were coming today. He knew how much she detested the event. He'd heard her go on about it during Council meetings . Oh, Gods. She'd elected the wrong girl! Mildred was probably halfway home by now, she'd sob to her daddy, he'd go to the board, and they'd go to the Witches' Council…

Of course, she could possibly get around that by telling Hector what had happened, how she'd simply gotten tired of the whole thing and decided to throw caution to the wind and let the magic choose, but that would involve telling him and the other witches that for years the committee had made the choice. Then they'd want to know why she'd done something so reckless as asking the magic itself to choose without telling the Council first, her letter to Hector would come up, and then…

She bit her lip.

"What are you going to do?" Hari asked.

What indeed?

The fact she and Hector didn't like one another was well-known. The fact they both wanted to see the other's expertly crafted and maintained castle and grounds decimated by cutworms and weevils was legend. But very few people knew they'd been corresponding and hexing each other by mail for centuries. That sort of thing, if it got out, would bring endless speculation in the kingdom. She could see the headlines.

The *Sorcerer's Star*, that horrible tabloid, would probably publish something like:

ELDERLY WITCHES SECRET LOVE AFFAIR—COUPLE
HAS HOT PHONE SEX ON CRYSTAL BALL

The *Kingdom Wall Journal* would read:

WITCHES, WIZARDS, AND GRAFT—CORRUPTION
AT HIGHEST LEVELS OF MAGIC

Witches' Weeds would say:

WITCH RIVALRY LEADS TO GOOD/EVIL IMBALANCE
IN KINGDOM: CROP FUTURES DECLINE

SALE ON JACK-IN-THE-BEANSTALK'S
MAGIC ROOT POWDER!

SHOP CINDERELLA'S EMPORIUM FOR
ALL YOUR GIANT PUMPKIN NEEDS!

She crumpled the paper up and tossed it in the trash. "I'm not going to do anything," she said. "Hari, I know it's late, but would you go find our sprite and make sure she isn't lost in the north tower again?"

Amber would make an amazing Common Princess. She certainly had the drive, ambition, and good sense to make an excellent queen. Far better than that horrible Mildred.

No one needed to know. Everything would be okay.

7

Hector

THERE WAS NO MAIL. THIS SURPRISED HECTOR.

Tinbit had lingered at the store a full thirty minutes waiting for it before buying liverwurst, mountain goat butter, and a pack of moss compresses for Hector to apply to the burns on his lower legs. This he did as soon as Tinbit got home. The others required a more personal treatment.

The gnome worked his legendary calendula salve into Hector's buttocks thoroughly, clucking under his breath. "Why in the name of the Gods did you go bare?"

Hector half-turned his head. "Because you had my favorite silk boxers soaking to get the indigo out." He yelped when Tinbit's careful fingers worked the lotion into places he didn't ordinarily let anyone touch. All the concern of yesterday was gone, and Tinbit was back to his usually scheduled acerbity.

"Wear briefs. Cotton won't kill you. Quit squirming or I'll never get this finished."

Hector growled under his breath and held still. Ida's silence worried him. She wasn't one to let him have the last word. He'd expected a thunderclap of a missive, something involving doing anatomically impossible things with his private parts. She wasn't delicate when she was angry.

A loud shriek of warning from the klaxon on the roof made him grab for his robe. Tinbit pressed a hand firmly on his back. "I'll answer it. If it's our reluctant dragon, I've got a few choice words for him." The gnome stomped off, leaving Hector to dress slowly, careful not to undo all the good Tinbit had done with the salve.

It was the dragon. He could hear Tinbit yelling those "choice words." With a sigh, he went out to his balcony to keep his gnome from needing calendula cream too.

"What is it, Alistair?" he said, leaning against the iron railing.

The young man was in dragon form today, probably because no dragon likes to grovel, and groveling is impossible to do as a fire-breathing monster.

"First of all," Alistair said with a soft puff of white smoke, "I'm sorry for burning your bottom."

Hector waved it off. "I'm not upset." He wasn't—not now. Even his most scalded parts felt better when he saw the black rose tucked under one of Alistair's chest scales. "I'm glad to see you've chosen to uphold tradition."

Alistair shrugged his wings. "Dad told me he'd destroy my sculptures if I didn't. But this is all I'm doing. I'm taking the princess captive, and once she's comfortably settled in the cave, I'm leaving. I refuse to wage a mock battle with the prince. That's just stupid."

It wasn't stupid. It was tradition. Hector thought about arguing, but the burns were fresh.

Once upon a time, dragons ate people. They were particularly fond of nobility, who seemed to taste better, no doubt because they ate a more varied diet. But now only the very elderly dragons sat around their caves, playing backgammon and talking about the good old days when their great-grandparents could buy Knight-on-a-Stick at roadside stands after Princess Day. Perhaps this too should change with the times.

"That's fair," he said. "And thank you again."

He watched Alistair flap away, so relieved he risked a smile for the first time since he'd been roasted. He'd not been looking forward to telling the Council an adolescent dragon got the better of him and his backside. It would lead to questions, like why he'd been foolish enough to laugh at a dragon. Then he'd need to tell them about Ida and her letters, and he didn't want to even think about how that would go over. The press would have a field day.

"Tinbit," he said when he walked back inside, "would you be so kind as to get my stationery and bring it to the bedroom? I think I'll start on the quest map, the various pitfalls, traps, and so forth. Don't let me forget I need to talk to the chief ogre on Wednesday about setting up an ambush for the knight attendants, and I still need to send a raven to the swamp to borrow a fire-toad from Crowbone. Or would you rather go?"

Tinbit grimaced. "No…no, I think I'll stay here. We're not talking now, you see. And besides all that, I've met someone else. It would be awkward."

"Met someone else?" Already? He'd expected Tinbit to be out of sorts for months. But he didn't say that aloud. Tinbit had always been touchy about his love life as long as Hector had known him. "Do I know him?"

"No." Tinbit squirmed. "I haven't exactly met him. We're… we've been…corresponding."

Hector blinked. "When did this start?"

More squirming. "After I broke up with Crowbone." His

eyes grew hard and bright. "And don't you dare say anything. He dumped me—not the other way around!"

"I wouldn't dream of it," Hector said, smiling. "What's his name?"

Any more twisting and writhing, and Tinbit would corkscrew into the floor. "Uh…Hari. I don't know his surname—at least not his real one."

Hector sighed. "Tinbit—are you using The Web?"

The gnome's cheeks turned crimson. "So what if I am?"

"I hope to goodness you didn't give them any personal information! Those dating websites are nothing but spider scams. And don't you dare set up a meeting with this man unless it's in a public place where everyone can see you. Anybody can put up a profile."

"It's not like that at all," Tinbit said. "It's the paid service. Verified users—he's absolutely a flesh-and-blood person."

Worse and worse. The way the spiders ran their threads through the warp and weft of the magical communication net, it was all too easy for "verified flesh and blood" to end up in an eat-cute. Hari was probably a hairy tarantula looking for a good meal of fresh gnome.

"I saw his profile and sent him a letter. He likes gardening, silk shirts, long romantic walks in the enchanted forest, and he can make spinach strawberry salad."

"Who puts spinach strawberry salad in their dating profile?"

"Somebody interesting." Tinbit turned almost purple. "Anyway, I said I'd meet him when I go with you to the capital city for the Council meeting next week. He works for a witch too, so he'll be there for the Unicorn Jubilee. I'm meeting him for dinner at The Golden Dragon Hotel—he's got a reservation."

"Do I need to get another room?"

"Really, Hector? On a first date? A lot would need to happen between the appetizer and dessert."

Hector's face burned. He wouldn't call himself prudish, but he'd always been shy where matters of the heart—and matters concentrated rather lower than the heart—were concerned. He'd been interested in girls, then boys, and finally, around the age of twenty-two, he'd concluded he liked dragons, giants, gnomes, ogres, vampires, shapeshifters, ghouls, demons, and even sea serpents, but he couldn't go further than that if he didn't become friends with any of them. Which shouldn't have been a problem—Cardinal Witches weren't supposed to fall in love. But he'd been a little too lonely at times…

He forced a smile. "Well, that's fine. Do I get to meet him?" he asked.

"Of course. He was excited to find out I work for a witch too. I told him you liked gardening, and he said the witch he works for is an amazing gardener herself. She has this lovely herb bed. So I sent him my recipe for calendula cream, and he sent me the recipe for the carrot and ginger soup you liked so much."

Hector considered. It had been first rate soup. Maybe this one—this one might not be all bad? "He sounds nice."

"He is. He's sweet, he's funny, and…and I like him." Tinbit sounded slightly astonished. "This guy—I feel like I know him and I don't even know what he looks like—he didn't include a picture. But he could have warts all over his nose and a hump on his back, and I wouldn't care. I like getting his letters, opening them, and knowing he's thinking about me, wanting to share everything that's happened in his life with me. I was surprised he wanted to meet so soon, but it's only dinner."

"I'm happy for you," Hector said, but a horrible, miserable feeling congealed in the pit of his stomach. Tinbit might fall in love—he was prone to it. Lonely people were. And if there was one thing Hector understood about love, it was this: Love meant losing people.

For the remainder of the day, he buried himself in work, his sure remedy for anything that touched him too deeply or lingered like the taint of something rotten in his soul.

He would never stand in the way of Tinbit's happily-ever-after. He'd been preparing himself for this eventuality when Tinbit met Crowbone and dissolved into a puddle of romantic goo. But Crowbone was a local. Gnomes could be so inflexible when it came to moving from their ancestral homes to other parts of the world. What if this new man wanted Tinbit to go with him? He'd be dealing with despondent, defeated, and depressed Tinbit again. With a sigh, Hector pulled out his stationery. He had so many letters to write this afternoon, to swamp gnomes, ogres, and yet...

He took up his pen.

> Dear Ida,
>
> I'm sorry. Please forgive me. It was thoughtless of me to write the way I did, even if I was angry. The truth is, so few people that I care about remain in my life. Immortality—as magical as it is—weighs rather heavily on me these days. I keep remembering people I knew who are no longer with me, and their memories are now so faded that I sometimes wake up in the middle of the night, terrified I'm forgetting them.

I strain to see their faces, like looking back into the grainy tintypes they used to make so we could have photographs of our loved ones—do you remember those? You used to be able to go down to goblin market and step in one of those little booths and they were five for a copper penny.

I'm rambling now. But all I wanted to say is that no matter how I detest you, and no matter how you despise me, I treasured our relationship. Sometimes enemies do make the best friends.

Wickedly yours,
HECTOR

He burned the letter in the fireplace.

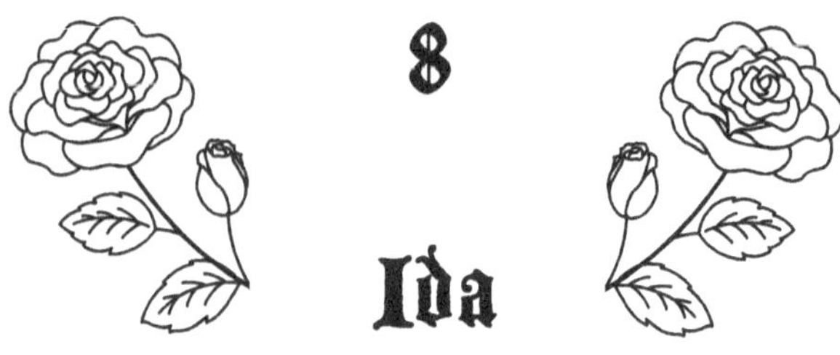

THERE WAS MAIL. NOTHING FROM HECTOR, THOUGH.

Ida thumbed through the morning stack at three in the afternoon. She shouldn't expect to hear from him. After composing six different ways to tell Hector she wasn't speaking to him anymore, she'd decided not to speak at all. Coming about twelve hours after the effects of the spell wore off, this epiphany seemed more a stray bubble of the enchantment than a return to her usual diplomatic self.

She apologized to the pastry cook and told him she loved his cakes, cookies, and pies. She'd simply not been herself when she called his claim-to-fame cake a heart attack. He was so happy, he made cream cheese Danish pastries for breakfast. She made a mental note to tell Hari not to feed them to the pigs because now she was worried about the state of *their* arteries.

She sent a note of profuse apology to the Princess Ball Committee, excusing her absence from the festivities due to a sudden and serious attack of diarrhea. Diarrhea of the mouth was a serious illness.

Hari had found the hairdresser sprite confused and sad in the north tower. Ida heard the poor creature out over what the Common Princess said about putting her fairy powders and pixie dust into the anal orifice, and assured the sprite nothing like that would ever happen again. She suggested the sprite retire and open her own hairdressing shop at Ida's expense. She had the money and who didn't love a tax deduction?

She stared glumly at the remaining correspondence on her desk to be personally answered: Invitation to the Witch of the South's soiree (regretfully decline, alternate engagement); the Gardening Club's tea party (attend, grateful for the opportunity to speak on magical rose breeding); the Council itself, needing to know if she would speak to the Young Witches Society as part of the Unicorn Jubilee festivities (yes, but dinner invitation declined); and an invitation from the palace for the Prince's Dinner (delighted to accept, can't wait to see you again, dear Annabeth!). She'd have liked to get out of that last one. She couldn't stand Queen Annabeth.

Beside her, Hari answered fan mail and the graceless requests for money, magic, and time. He put most of the petitions in the wastebasket, which happily devoured them along with the small stack of Angel's Dream petit fours left over from the reception.

"Lady Jane, asking you to come visit," Hari said, holding up a letter.

She rubbed her temples. "Throw it away. If I open it, I'll say yes, and I can't say yes again. I've said yes to everything except Tara South's soiree."

Hari chuckled. "Still remembering the last time you said yes to that?"

She gave him the fish eye. "Three hundred years isn't enough time to recover from that gallbladder attack. I don't know how the woman isn't translucent. Every one of her recipes calls for a stick of butter. Besides, my schedule is packed."

"You could turn down the garden meeting. Or the Young Witches."

"I can't turn the Young Witches down! And the Garden Club has been asking me to speak about my rose breeding program all year." She sighed. "If I turned down anything, it would be the dinner with Annabeth, but I can't. That's the toast to the prince. I have to be there for that."

"You're going to wear yourself out."

She leaned back in her chair. "When this week is over, I'm spending a month in the gardens and greenhouses. I need to get my hands dirty, plant some seeds, talk to the chickens. I'm nine hundred eighty-four years old. I'm allowed to be an eccentric old Baba Yaga."

"And you don't look a day over nine hundred." Hari held a letter in his hand as if it might bite him, but he didn't throw it in the trash. Instead, he set it aside. It was a small square envelope, addressed in a firm, bold hand.

"Who is that one from? A fan?"

Hari blushed. "It's…uh…it's for me. I hope you don't mind. I used your box—I didn't want my mother asking questions."

"A secret admirer?" she asked.

"Sort of." He turned crimson.

"Well, I'm going to ask questions too," she said, leaning forward. "What does he look like? Is he handsome?"

"I…I don't know. Uh…we didn't exchange pictures."

Ida tensed. "Hari—this isn't one of those Norn services, is it?"

He sighed. "What if it is?"

"Those fates are notorious for jinxing happy endings! Have you told your mother about any of this?"

Hari's face flamed. "No. She'd read me the riot act about how I can't commit, how every time I date a guy, it all falls apart. She's already disappointed in me."

"She is not really disappointed. She only wishes you'd settle down, marry a nice gnome, build an addition onto her house, and have children."

"Grow up, in other words." He pocketed the letter. "I don't need to hear it from you too."

"You know I didn't mean it that way," she said.

"She doesn't mean it that way, either. But it hurts anyway."

"I'm sorry. But for my part, it doesn't matter what anyone thinks, including me, Hari. I want to see you with a good man, and if you have to leave to find him, you should. I'll bawl my eyes out and send you care packages five times a month, but Gods bless you, sweetheart, you deserve all the happiness in the world."

Hari laughed. "I'm not leaving for any man. If he's the right one, he'll come here to live with me."

"You're not going to find the right one by asking the Norns," she said.

"I've tried everything else," he said. "You've been so helpful, setting me up and all, but it just hasn't felt right until now. This guy—he's different. He's kind, and thoughtful, and he's got this sarcastic sense of humor I love. And he works for a witch too. He won't say who, but I haven't told him I work for you either. Got to be careful, after all. I mean, like you say, I don't know him. Yet."

"Yet?"

"I told him I'd be in the capital next week and if he was there, you know, with all the witch conferences going on, we might, well, meet up."

Ida's stomach squirmed unpleasantly, probably as a result of the cheese Danish she'd forced herself to eat as penance, but it bothered her far more than lactose intolerance usually did. Was Hari actually serious about this gnome? He was romantic, like most of her staff, but he was usually sensible about most matters, especially ones of the heart. This gnome, whoever he was, had clearly sidestepped Hari's usual caution.

"Are you sure that's wise?"

"I'm going to be careful." Hari gave her a curious look. "We're going to meet at the hotel for dinner. Lots of people there. It's not like I'm going to have my own room. I'm staying with you."

"Oh, nonsense, I'll update our arrangements—"

Hari set his hand on hers. "You don't understand. I want to stay with you. I don't want to take a chance something might happen to make me want something I don't already have. I love it here with you. I don't want to go anywhere else. And if I like this guy, there's one person he has to impress more than me, and that's you, Fairy Godmother."

She refused to cry. Happily-Ever-After was her business, and if a person found one without the help of a witch, it was even better. Those were genuine. They weren't tangled up in any more magic than people wanting to be together for the rest of their lives because they loved each other. She let out a sharp, happy laugh and hugged him. "Go read your letter." She kissed the top of his head. "Your young man is going to be very lucky if he impresses you, and if he's done that, he won't have any trouble impressing me."

"Are you sure?" The gnome's face creased into folds of concern. "I can get through the rest of the fan mail first."

"It will wait. And anyway, Hector isn't writing, so I don't have to be afraid of getting a vomiting spell or something worse."

"Yeah," Hari said, still looking worried. "Yeah, that's true. Okay, then. But you let me handle it. You've got enough to do with the personal mail today."

"I'm going for a walk in the garden as soon as I finish answering the invitations," she promised.

When the door closed behind Hari, Ida listlessly set the remainder of the letters aside. Normally, she felt stressed before the week of a Happily-Ever-After, but also excited. She loved the festivities associated with the kidnapping of the princess at the end of the week: the dinners, the garden parties, the Bards' Festival—she certainly appreciated a good lute duet—not to mention seeing friends she only saw once a year. And this was the Unicorn Jubilee. She should be celebrating a thousand years of love and happiness. But this year, it didn't feel that way.

Blast Hector, blast him. She couldn't even be properly happy for Hari.

Her eye fell on the crumpled letter she'd drafted.

> Dear Hector,
>
> Your refusal to write to me is your choice. If that is how you feel, then that's how it should be. But I can't say it causes me happiness to know you think I sent the laughing charm in order to hurt you. That was never my intention.
>
> At my age, it's easy to dispense advice to young men and women who come to me for help when one or the other has torn a rift in their relationship. It is somehow harder to give the same advice to myself. But if I had it to do over again, I would never have caused you pain.

Please forgive me.

Love,
IDA

She tossed it into the hungry wastebasket, which devoured it with great papery crunchings and gave a contented, inky burp.

9

Hector

Dear Hector,

I know you aren't one for visits, and I wouldn't ask, but I must talk to you about Archie. No need for a formal visit—I'm attending the Rogues and Thieves game on Moonsday. I would be happy if you honored me by accepting these tickets.

Thanks,

KING RUPERT I

HECTOR HATED TRAVELLING. THIS WASN'T LIKE HOP-ping on a broom for a quick ride to Goblin Town. A trip to the capital city meant harnessing the undead horses, making sure the coach was properly enchanted with antitheft hexes, asking his banshee neighbor to water the greenhouse while he was gone, arming a few skeletons to ride post, and then sitting in the most uncomfortable seat outside of the Council chamber for two whole miserable days. The coach rocked hard as it hit the millionth pothole, and his teeth slammed against each other. King Rupert's letter almost flew out of his hand.

Tinbit bounced halfway across his seat, cursing. "Dammit, Hector, you said you were going to fix this."

Hector folded the letter, tucking it away in the pocket of his second-best robe for safekeeping, and adjusted the cushion under his backside. "I didn't see the sense in pulling ogres off duty for road work. Besides, heroes can use a few more hemorrhoids in their lives."

Grumbling, Tinbit shoved his pillow into a comfortable position. The poor gnome had been up until midnight making arrangements for their week away from the castle, and as most places on Hector's side of the kingdom weren't equipped with crystal balls, that meant summoning carrier bats for reservations. At least there'd been no need to do that for the hotel in the capital city, although he remained uneasy about that. The Golden Dragon was Ida's favorite hotel. Well, maybe he wouldn't see her there.

"It's almost time for afternoon tea. Would you like to stop and stretch?"

Tinbit's eyes widened. "Oh, shit. I forgot to pack your favorite tea."

"Don't worry about it." His stomach would rot on the swill they made in the village. But the gnome had been so stressed.

"It slipped my mind," Tinbit said. "I was trying to decide what flowers to send to Hari. A rose? But what if he thinks that means I'm in love with him? What if I'm not? Maybe a poppy. But poppies make people sleep, and he might think I want to go to bed with him. Argh!"

Hector chuckled. "I'm sure you'll find the flower that says what you want it to say."

"Yeah, aconite. I can poison myself and make a quick getaway in a healer's wagon."

"Are you truly that nervous about meeting this man?"

Tinbit folded his arms over his chest moodily. "Haven't you ever wanted to make a good first impression on someone?"

"Can't say that I have." Maybe Ida. But he'd been younger and considerably more foolish back then.

"Daisies. Yeah. Not too formal. Friendly," Tinbit muttered to himself.

Hector almost suggested gardenias. If he remembered his language of flowers correctly, gardenias meant 'go away.' Or was that sweet peas? He couldn't remember anymore. Centuries had passed since he'd read a book on the language of flowers for his examination as a Cardinal Witch. He'd not had cause to use it since.

"What are you going to do when you aren't at the Happily-Ever-After?" Tinbit asked. "You made me turn down every invitation, even the one to the Gardening Club."

"I'm a Wicked Witch. I'm supposed to be unsociable." It hurt him to turn down the Gardening Club. They'd wanted him to speak on "Sentient Plants and Their Special Requirements." He'd planned to bring his sensitive fern. But Ida would definitely go to the Gardening Club. If he could get out of the Prince's Dinner, perhaps he could avoid her altogether except for the Happily-Ever-After. He fingered the king's letter. "The Rouge Rogues are playing the Marketown Thieves on Moonsday. I'll go to that."

"That's one night out of three. You can't just lie around in the hotel and do nothing."

That was exactly what he planned to do. It was all he ever did on these trips to the capital city. Entertainment could be found there, but none that entertained him. "You know how boring I've gotten in my old age. Turn in every evening at eight, and seven if it's dark out."

Tinbit eyed him distrustfully.

"You packed my swim trunks. I can go to the spa." He wouldn't be caught dead in those things. He was a good-looking man for his age, but his knees were knobby and he was somewhat bowlegged, a sequela from riding a broom for most of his younger years. He'd hate to see anyone turned to stone for staring at his legs.

"I wish you'd get out more," Tinbit said. "I'd hate knowing you're lonely."

"I'm never lonely." It wasn't the truth, not exactly, but after nine hundred ninety years, he'd learned not to bother his butler with trivial things like how he sometimes paced his bedroom at night, about the doses of belladonna he was taking for his insomnia now, or bigger things like the pit of despair inside at the thought of losing someone so dear to him as Tinbit to that monster called love.

He grabbed another cushion, shoved it under his head, and closed his eyes.

Darkness had fallen when the coach stopped in the largest town on the border of his evil realm. As he stepped down, he took a long breath of the fog drifting in from the marshes, a pleasant stench—herbal, rotten, with a hint of blood. People who lived here grew up strong and tough on such an aroma.

A thug was busy gutting a man in the shadows beside the inn door. He looked up with an eye for a new victim, but Hector's bodyguards, both tall skeletons with heavy jaws and heavier punches, flexed their clavicles and pounded their bony phalanges against their equally bony metacarpals. The man slid back into the dark.

The lawlessness was part of the place too, like the smell. But it bothered Hector that the townsfolk didn't stop at terrorizing visitors. He'd always hoped they would band together instead of murdering each other. Over the years he'd gotten goblins to unionize and set up pensions for their elderly, the dragons to quit cooking knights à la carte, and the giants, bless them, were well on their way to outlawing the murder of anyone named Jack. But ordinary humans didn't seem to understand it wasn't nice to knife each other for no good reason.

Tinbit stuck close to Hector as they walked the distance from the stable to the inn.

Once inside, Tinbit took Hector's coat while he waited a respectful distance from the fire. His burns were still somewhat sensitive. The décor appeared in good order for an evil tavern— bright fire, greasy tables, a few tired men by the bar, and a maid who looked quite capable of moonlighting as an assassin. The smoky air irritated his throat, and he coughed into his elbow. He didn't want the innkeeper to think he disapproved.

Tinbit came back from the desk with their room key. "I've asked them to bring the food upstairs and confirmed we'll be putting our own hexes on the doors and windows, and I asked for a dehumidifier for the damp. Sorry about this—they didn't have a non-smoking room."

"It's quite all right," he said, noting with approval the man with a long pipe in the darkest corner. "Give that man a tip," he said. "He's the best dark and brooding stranger I've seen in a while."

The upstairs room was only slightly less smoky than down-stairs, but a quick spell applied to the large, ornate four-poster immediately stunned the bedbugs.

"I hope you don't mind sharing," Tinbit said apologetically

as the assassin laid out their evening repast on the table. "I didn't feel comfortable taking a separate room."

"I don't kick too hard," Hector said, adding a few more gold coins to the oak tray for the maid's trouble. Over the centuries, he'd learned a healthy tip was key to staying healthy in a place like this. He noted how she removed the wine carafe immediately and promised to bring a fresh one—there was a fly. Yes, and a lovely quantity of poison hemlock. He'd make sure he mentioned that in his review.

"I've been thinking about our reservations in the capital," he said. "I wish you would let me upgrade them to two rooms. I feel I might be a distraction."

"No—don't," Tinbit said, blushing. "It's not that I don't appreciate it, but I'm counting on you to keep me honest. You know what I'm like. I don't want to get into a situation where he asks me if I have a room and I'd need to lie. I don't know how this is going to go." He hopped up on the bed and sat, legs dangling. "Maybe I shouldn't have said yes to this meeting, but if there's a chance…well." He sighed. "You're lucky, Hector. You don't have a heart to lose anymore."

"That is one of the perks of being a witch," he said, smiling.

He didn't tell Tinbit the rest of it, the part about how much it hurt, cutting his own heart out, locking it in a stone box, and hiding it away from the world. He'd buried it under a magnificent apple tree in his garden long ago, the first time he lost someone dear to him. He ought to have destroyed it then. It was clearly a liability, but something about stabbing it, burning it, or simply blasting it out of existence seemed so…final. And if it had hurt so much to take it out, how much worse would it be to destroy it?

He pushed the memories away. "Now, how about dinner?"

After the dinner, which Tinbit refused to eat—too many mushrooms, any one of them might be an amanita—Hector lay down next to Tinbit, listening to the gnome's squeaky little snores. He watched the fire burn on the hearth, sending out a strong, smoky aroma of pine, and thought about the ashes of the letter he'd written to Ida, still sitting in the grate at home.

A moment's weakness, that's all it had been. A moment's weakness, not a feeling that for the second time he'd cut something out of his life that hurt as bad as his heart.

10

Ida

My Dearest, Sweetest, Bestest of Good Witches, Ida,

I'm so delighted you can attend the banquet! I can't wait to see you again! So exciting! I invited the Common Princess to tea, but she wouldn't come! Can you believe it? I don't know how they got her past the committee, do you? I can't wait to pick your brain. I mean, if the little bitch is going to marry my son, I think I should know all the dirt.

Oh, Ida, it will be just like old times. Do you remember when I came to your castle as the Common Princess? I was so scared, even though I knew I'd be selected. I thought maybe you'd give me a test, like picking up grains of rice in a room, and I've always been petrified of enchanted mice. But you were so sweet. One look at your pink, godmotherly face and I knew we would always be the best of friends.

Oh, by the way, Rupert says to invite you to the Rogues and Thieves game Moonsday night. Won't that be lovely? Those fae hurling players are oh so much eye candy. You can drool with me. Let Rupert keep the other guests busy. You and I will have such a good girly time together! Squeee! Can hardly wait!

Your best princess, Queen of the Four Kingdoms,

Sweetheart of the Commoners,

Annabeth

IDA BRUSHED HER SHORT HAIR AND SURVEYED HER-self in the mirror. "What do you think?"

The mirror image compressed her shell-pink lips back at her. In a sultry, provocative tone very different from Ida's own, it said, "Delicious, my dear, but may I suggest the white hat with the lilacs would go better with your purple blouse and—"

"No, you may not," she said, adjusting the brown hat with the violets. Hari had said it made her look like a wee mouse. Very well. She felt like a mouse, a mouse who wished more than anything to crawl into a hole in the wall in her castle and stay there. Hari was right. She should've refused the Young Witches. After her packed schedule, she wouldn't have time to do much more than unpack at the hotel, get a bath, and change from her sensible slacks, shoes, and blouse into witch's robes, then climb back in the pumpkin to drive to the palace for a dinner she didn't want to eat.

Hari poked his head around the door. "The white horse is lame. The coachman wanted to know if the gray would be all right with you—he's almost completely white except for his nose."

"I don't think anyone is going to be checking horse noses at the palace." She sighed. "Tell him it's fine. I'm ready as soon as he is." Her coachman had a prickly disposition, and he tended to get his beard in a knot if she appeared on the steps of the castle two minutes before or after he pulled the coach up. Sometimes she wondered why she kept all these temperamental staff, but nearly all of them came to her with a hard-luck story she couldn't ignore. This man was the youngest of seven dwarves, all living in the same house, mining diamonds for a living, but diamonds weren't as easy to come by as they used to be, and his share was so small that when he finally retired, he couldn't even pay the rent. It didn't help that he and his brothers almost went bust supporting a sleeping maiden they'd found in the woods. Gold digger if Ida ever met one!

She rose and followed Hari out the door. It was only a few days. And she had the game between the Thieves and Rogues to go to on Moonsday. She'd packed her Rogues jersey. Nothing like a game of good fae hurling to take the edge off her worry over the princess selection fiasco.

Hari's mother had told her that Princess Amber had left in a huff without even making an appearance at the ball, and when the enchanted clock himself offered to turn into a footman to escort her home, she clocked him. The poor old grandfather was still getting his gears repaired. What had been in the Happily-Ever-After magic to select that spitfire, she'd never know. Hector might—he'd been there at the beginning after all—but she wasn't talking to him. She picked up her valise and left the room.

She found Hari waiting for her in the coach, sitting back comfortably in his soft leather breeches and flowing white smock, a letter dangling in his hand and a dreamy expression on his face. It had been ages since she'd seen him so happy.

"From your friend?" she asked, taking her seat opposite him.

"Yes. He—well, Tinbit says he's looking forward to meeting me." He sucked in a great gulp of air, let it out, pulled it in again. "I know I shouldn't be this nervous. I mean, it's only dinner. But Gods! I want him to like me. And I want to like him as much as I do when I read his letters. And I'm scared I won't. Then I'm scared I will. Oh, Ida! It can't be love if you're scared, can it?"

"Well, now, that's something I can answer," she said, smiling although she ached inside. "All happily-ever-afters are scary in the beginning, even the natural ones."

"Really? You make it look so easy."

She picked at a frayed red thread in the cushion. "It's actually quite complicated. The variables are difficult to control. For instance, it's hard to get two people who truly hate each other to fall in love. And it's just as difficult to get two people to fall in love if they are already close in some way."

"Close?"

"Friends," she said. "Some friends can't be swayed in a romantic fashion at all. Others must be friends before they can be in love. I do a full analysis on every princess and prince before casting—or I used to." Once upon a time, she spent about six months in matchmaking for every Common Princess applicant and made her selections based on science and her good intuition, not committee—a committee that would probably want her wand for not sticking to the established protocol. She'd have to do something nice for Mildred's family. Fifty years of perfect ale ought to be a sufficient bribe, and after all, she had to trust that the magic really had chosen well. The prince was handsome, and soon enough, Amber would see what a good thing it was to be given this opportunity. She seemed to be a smart, ambitious girl—rather like herself when she'd been that age…

Hari's voice recalled her from her musings. "If I asked you, would you cast a love spell for me?"

She laughed. "Oh, no, honey, you don't need me to do that. Magic is a tricky thing to get right. It's better to let your heart do the magic for you. They're powerful things, hearts. That's why we witches take ours out. They aren't safe to be carrying around inside—we are too easily moved to make magic where there shouldn't be any."

If only she'd remembered that a day ago! While she didn't have her heart inside her, she kept it at home, locked in a golden chest. Most witches destroyed them—she bet Hector had taken his to the highest peak in the Dread Mountains and fed it to an eagle who'd probably died of indigestion a few hours later. She should have done away with hers more humanely, but she didn't feel right about not having a heart. Surely Good Witches should keep them, albeit in a safe place. So it stayed in that chest under her bed, covered in dust, keeping safe all the memories of the people she'd loved over the years.

Hari set his little hand on hers. "But how will I know if this love is real? I've met so many people I thought I would love, and then it just didn't happen. They were nice guys, good guys. But when it came down to it, I never really felt like I was in love. Does that make sense?"

"If love made sense, my job would be simpler. But it doesn't. And like most magic, it won't take if it happens at the wrong time. Or with the wrong person. Why do you think love potions are outlawed?"

"Maybe love should be outlawed too," Hari said, folding his letter up. But he tucked it in his breast pocket, which was a good place for it to be. Love letters carried a magic all their own, and if the man Hari was interested in did indeed work for a witch, residual magic probably was in the ink.

Many witches employed gnomes. They were highly devoted, friendly, and best of all, not afraid to speak their minds, qualities witches respected—at least good witches. Wicked ones like Hector probably barbecued a gnome once a week to feed his cockatrice or something. He still kept a cockatrice, didn't he? He used to talk about it, a bantam, with black wings and a yellow head-crest that liked to scream at one in the morning. He'd compared it to her going on about brownie rights in the Council session. Horrible, horrible man.

Hector might be staying at the Golden Dragon. He preferred out-of-the-way places, but his usual inn, Mage Suites, was being renovated. If it hadn't been for Hari meeting his young man, she'd have changed her reservation, even stayed at the palace perhaps, regardless of how she despised Annabeth. But if this man was Hari's match, it couldn't be helped. One thing Ida knew—never interfere with a happily-ever-after in progress.

Hari would meet his man. He'd see if it was right for him or not. And they would go home at the end of the week with a resolution either way.

She sighed.

It was a big hotel. Maybe she wouldn't see Hector at all.

11
Hector

It's that time again! Happily-Ever-After, the most magical time of the year, when wedding bells ring for the king- and queen-to-be. But don't be too sure! This just in, Prince Archie in love with the Captain of the Guard! Exclusive to The Star, Prince plans to jilt the Common Princess and propose marriage to his lover over the dragon's corpse! Full article on page eleven!

Rumors continue to circulate of a snafu in the selection process. Heartbroken "real" princess Mildred Cheapstreet reveals all to The Star! Good Witch Ida North, formerly Ida Moonshadow, implicated in the mix-up! This paper wonders if a thousand years of magic has led to senility. Should witches over the age of five hundred be compelled to retire?

—THE SORCERER'S STAR

THE GOLDEN DRAGON WAS THE NICEST HOTEL IN Kingsmanor. Towers crowned with silver shimmered in the afternoon sunlight, bright as stars. A thousand crystal windows glittered like a goblin's fever dream. The doors were gold-plated. Hector had seen it too many times to be awed.

But Tinbit shrank in his seat. "It's like a mountain—a shiny, bright mountain."

"It wasn't always this high-rise," Hector said. "This used to be farmland once upon a time."

"Sometimes I forget how old you really are," Tinbit said.

Sometimes Hector forgot too. Remembering made him feel old in a way his bones and joints didn't quite feel, not yet, even on the coldest of winter mornings.

Once upon a time, farms came right up to the bailey. Back then, the castle itself was a wooden building with fine buttressed ceilings made of rough-hewn fir with a thatched roof. The Hall of Witches was the only stone building in Kingsmanor. He'd been appointed Wicked Witch of the West there, an honor he still felt he didn't deserve. All he'd done was enchant dragons to make them harder for knights to kill. He'd long felt that the knights had too much of an advantage over people who could only breathe fire to protect themselves. He'd turned their scales into proper armor to give them a fighting chance.

Of course, that didn't last long. Ida Moonshadow became the Good Witch of the North on the strength of her magic that gave an ordinary sword magical powers against dragon armor, a feat of metallurgy he could have appreciated if it hadn't left him gnashing his teeth and scrambling for a new solution.

A hundred years later, they'd knocked down the old hall and paved the lot with cobblestones so a new, improved building could be raised. A hundred years after that, they tore it down and built the new hall adjacent to the castle—largely because the king at the time wanted to make sure the enchanted sword went to his son, the crown prince. No more sticking it in a stone to see which of the noblest knights were the worthiest of a Happily-Ever-After. Despite Hector's best efforts, he'd never managed to beat Ida's enchantment on that damned sword. He agreed; the sword stayed in the royal treasury in exchange for the promise that no more dragons would die. The Hall of Witches had remained next to the castle ever since. So much for the separation of magic and state.

He shrugged off the irritating memories like an old coat. "Are you meeting your young man tonight?"

Tinbit, still goggling at the building, shook his head. "No, tomorrow. He said his witch needed him tonight—something about a dinner she had to go to."

Hector winced. "That will be Tara's shindig. I hope she likes butter."

Tinbit grunted. "Hector, do you think he'll make me choose the wine? Shit, I don't know anything about that."

"A good pinot noir is never a bad choice," Hector said. "Unless he orders fish."

"He won't. He's allergic to fish."

"Well then."

"I didn't realize it would be so grand," Tinbit said in an awed whisper as the skeletal horses pulled up under the golden fabric canopy with a loud clatter of coffin bones.

"Wait until you see the inside."

The skeleton coachman opened the door, and Hector stepped out onto the slick cobblestones. He eyed the liveried doormen with the kind of scorn he usually reserved for over-dressed royalty.

"Is that unicorn horn?" Tinbit asked as they walked through the doors inlaid with a shimmering material giving off the faint glow of moonlight.

"No, it's narwhal," he said. The last of the unicorns had been rounded up centuries ago and put in a magical preserve to prevent their extinction. The last mare still lived there. Her horn had been removed to save her life. All the wild ones had been killed by the royal family on their magical game hunts. The ones in captivity committed suicide. It kept him awake some nights, thinking dragons might have gone the same way had he not protected them. Unicorn Jubilee indeed. A thousand years and nothing had ever really changed when it came to the upper class. Maybe princes no longer killed dragons, but the royal family was still the royal family—grabbing swords, power, and constantly making sure they kept witches and monsters in their places.

A footman with rough hands, dressed as splendidly as a duke that belied a farm boy come to town to make his fortune, carried their bags into the glass elevator.

"Where's the dining room?" Tinbit asked, voice quavering.

The farm boy gave him a dismissive look. "Which one?"

"There's more than one?"

"Yes. Where are you from, Westfale or something?"

Hector stepped in. "I'm Hector, the Wicked Witch of the West. My butler was inquiring about the Golden Dragon's Claw. I have a hankering for frog legs tonight," he added with a menacing glare.

The farm boy turned the color of buttermilk. "Third floor, down the hall, first door on your left. Would you like me to reserve you a table by the balcony or the fish tank?"

"Neither," Hector said. "I'll send for *you* when I'm ready to eat."

The footman unlocked their door and bolted.

Tinbit chuckled. "Could you really turn him into a frog?"

Hector smiled. "I don't do much transformation anymore, but I suspect I could still manage a bullfrog. The trouble with frogs, though, they whine about wanting to be human right until they see water, and plop, off they go, and they never look back. The ponds in this valley used to be swimming with half-human tadpoles."

He opened the room door.

"Wow." Tinbit stood paralyzed.

Personally, Hector thought the place had come down a notch since the last time he'd stayed there. The golden carpets looked cat-picked, and they rolled themselves up at the edges protectively. Customers hunting for cheap souvenirs liked to take threads. Do that often enough to sentient rugs and they started thinking about smothering you in bed. He reached down and patted each one respectfully while Tinbit unpacked his own trunk and put his clothes in Hector's wardrobe. He was still clearly overwhelmed.

"Who pays for all this?" Tinbit asked, eyeing the stained-glass wash basin and the silk sheets.

"The king," Hector said. "Which means we pay for it. Taxes."

"But they pay for our castle in the mountains too. Why isn't it this nice?"

"Two reasons," he said, unpacking his trunk and setting aside his best robe to air out for the Happily-Ever-After. "First, I'm a man of simple tastes. Secondly, when one gets the plea-sure of presenting one's expenditures to a new king every half-century or so, a man soon finds that a king's grandson doesn't care quite so much about updating the plumbing his great-great-great-grandfather installed. Ah, the mail." A pile of it appeared on a fine cherrywood table that trotted over like an obedient dog when he beckoned.

"That reminds me, I need to leave a letter at the front desk for Hari, let him know I've arrived."

"You do that. Then what about a late lunch? I'll let you order for me."

"Frog legs?" Tinbit grinned.

"I believe so."

With a chuckle, Tinbit left Hector to finish sorting out his clothes and the mail.

Hector glanced at the headline on the complimentary paper, but it was the *Sorcerer's Star*. He tossed it in the trash where it belonged.

The first letter came from Queen Annabeth—a command invitation for the Unicorn Jubilee dinner and reminding him about the Thieves/Rogues match on Moonsday and insisting that he wear his best robe. Hector read it glumly. King Rupert he could usually handle, but Annabeth was a whole level of irritating he'd hoped to avoid. He'd had the distinct displeasure of her company the entire time he'd had her dear husband in his dungeons educating him on what happens to heroes who break the rules. On the whole, he thought she might have him beat when it came to torture—so much whining about everything from the bugs to the blood on the walls.

The rest of the letters contained requests for curses on ex-husbands, neighbor's farms, wives, and ten concerning meddlesome mothers-in-law. He burned these rather than feed them to the wastebasket. He didn't want to deal with a nauseated trashcan burping up paper scraps on the floor all night. He'd eat his frog legs, turn in early, and tomorrow he would go to the game, Annabeth or not. He didn't want to mess up Tinbit's date.

And he was wearing his Thieves jersey, damn it.

12

Ida

Dearest, bestest Witchy-Woman Ida,

Confirming you're coming to the game on Moonsday. Ticket for you. It's the King's Box, of course. I hope you don't mind, but I've invited some of the ladies and lords to come party with us! And I've ordered that delicious rich cake you served for me at my Common Princess election— Angel's Dream Cake. Yummy!

Confidentially, I don't believe a word those awful tabloids say, but is it true Amber shouldn't be the Common Princess?

Love,
ANNABETH

IDA'S HEADACHE, ALREADY AT A LEVEL FOUR FROM the carriage ride and a busy day, escalated to an eight. She lay back on the garish pink comforter and pulled the heart-shaped pillow from the mountain of surplus over her head.

Of all the princesses in her life Ida regretted, none bothered her more than Annabeth. The dossier called her a dairy girl with a buxom physique, blond hair, and blue eyes, possessed of a sweet, kind nature. Birds flew down from the trees to sing on her shoulder. Butterflies followed her wherever she walked. Sometimes she sang for no apparent reason while she worked. Classic princess behavior. Ida didn't think she could do any better, really—the crop wasn't great that year.

Only afterward did the dirty secrets come out. Annabeth was no common dairy maid. She was the daughter of a popular duke's herdswoman, but it turned out she was actually half-royalty, her farmer "father" being somewhat notable for having no other children with his wife. She'd bought a glamour off a hedge witch to entice birds and butterflies. She "borrowed" the voice of an operatic mermaid and never gave it back. Her hair was her own, but that was about it.

It was quite the scandal when the story broke. Damned investigative trolls. Ida wanted to tell them the truth—that for the past few hundred years, the contest to become Common Princess had become a farce, with every girl hiring personal coaches and trainers in order to get their grabby hands on the tiara. But that would have meant a grilling by Hector, and so she held her tongue and appeared as the good witch to Hector's bad at both the wedding and the christening of the prince the following year. Annabeth never publicly treated Ida as anyone but her agent of good fortune. But she was a notorious gossip. No wonder the *Sorcerer's Star* got the exclusive.

Ida tossed the letter on top of the complimentary copy of the paper.

"Coffee?" Hari poured a cup for himself and took a raspberry tart.

"I suppose," Ida said, rubbing her temples. She'd love to nurture this headache into an excuse to get out of dinner, but that sounded more like something Hector would do. She, at least, wouldn't shirk her responsibility.

Hari paused pouring, then resumed. "A nice cuppa always helps a headache. After that, do you mind if we visit the gardens before I do your hair? I got a letter from Tinbit saying he's arrived. His witch is all settled in, and he invited me to take an evening walk."

She smiled. "Well, I didn't think you'd want me along for that."

"But I do. I'm…I'm scared." He glanced down at his feet in a shamefaced way.

"Oh, Hari, it's in the open, there're lots of people—"

"No, you don't understand," Hari said, shaking his brown curls. "I'm scared I'm not going to like him. I'm terrified it's going to be like all the others. No spark. No nothing. No feelings at all. Oh, Ida, what if I'm one of those people who never falls in love? What if I'm alone for the rest of my life?" His face blanched. "Worse, what if he sees me and hates me? What if he thinks—" he swallowed hard. "What if he finds out I'm…I'm ugly?"

Ida sighed. "Sweetheart, you *aren't* ugly. How many times do I need to tell you that?"

"I know—but he'll have to know about it someday, and—"

"And if he's the man for you, he will love you, even then. Give it a chance. For all that love at first sight is wonderful, real love happens when the magic wears off and you see the person you married across the table, shriveled and gray, eating prunes for breakfast, and you realize that if you were eighteen, you'd do it all over again because you're still in love with them. The spark will happen for you if it's right, but it won't ever happen if you don't let it kindle."

Hari didn't look convinced.

"I'll go with you," she said with a sigh.

He grinned and squeezed her hand. "Thanks."

The gardens attached to the hotel were some of the finest in the kingdom. Her own surpassed them, and truthfully, she'd been far more interested touring the Garden Club grounds to view their rare and magical plants, but she always took pleasure in walking through a well-tended rose trellis. She leaned forward, brought one of the fragrant sprays toward her nose, and inhaled appreciatively.

"We should plant musk roses around the chicken house next year," she told Hari. "It would help with the smell in high summer."

"I don't think any kind of rose would help the smell of chickens." Hari glanced around again, anxiously looking through the thorn-covered canes, peeping past leaves and heavy, red blossoms.

"Hari…"

"I don't want him to see me first," he hissed.

"We've been walking the gardens for the past half hour and we've seen no one. Do you think he might be doing the same thing, hiding from you? You are a rather secretive people, after all. It's instinctive."

Hari rolled his eyes. "It is not." A robin breezed through the arbor, and Hari ducked.

"It was a bird."

"Shit," he muttered, clutching his heart. "Let's just go back to the hotel. My hands are sweaty, my heart is pounding, and I feel like I'm about to puke. He's not here anyway."

"You don't know that. Tell you what, Hari, let's split up," she suggested. "I want to see the goldfish pond. You take the forest trail where you can hide behind ferns if you'd like, and I'll find you at the end and tell you if I've seen any gnomes, yes?"

"Yeah—yeah. That would be better." Before she could ask him how long he wanted to take, he was gone, running down the arbor path. He hopped headfirst into some azaleas.

"Not instinctive, my ass." She set both hands in the middle of her back and pushed as she stood. Crouching in the bushes was a pastime for kids, not grumpy old witches.

She left the arbor and moseyed across the open ground, stopping to admire a drift of cosmos that changed color based on the mood of the person passing. She got a lovely pastel shade of robin's-egg blue with saffron streaks. Which color was lingering irritation about Annabeth's invite and which was amusement over Hari's romantic anxiety? The goldfish pond wasn't far away, but given how Hari had hidden in every bush on the way, it might not be a stretch to assume his suitor might be disguised in the pachysandra. She found no lurking gnome, however, and made her way to the pond. She'd give Hari another half hour in the woods before going to find him.

Voices drifted over the green, coming toward her.

"Hector, I can't do this. My heart's doing dragon flights, and I keep forgetting to breathe. Let's call it and go in, okay? He's not here. I scared the hell out of him and now he's gone for good."

"Calm down. He may be at the pond."

Ida dove into the nearest rhododendron bush. She crouched, trying not to breathe herself.

Hector came into view. His hair and beard were more silver than black now, but his green eyes were as vivid as she remembered. Even in ratty old trousers and a weathered and ridiculously outdated red tunic, he still impressed her as he had so many years ago, back when his hair was the color of midnight and the startling green eyes stared out of a younger man's face. He leaned on his blackthorn staff, gazing at the vivid red and yellow goldfish and their fabulous tails with interest. "These are lovely. I'd like a fish pond in our court-yard, but with razor-toothed redfish. I always wanted a pool of redfish."

"We'd have to put in a heater. They'd freeze in winter," said a disembodied voice somewhere on Hector's right.

"Maybe I'll buy *The Quintessence of Being* from Alistair. It would go some way to getting him to forgive me for insisting he do his dragonly duty."

Great. First a poet and now he sends a sculptor. What is it about dragons and fine arts? Ida leaned into the bushes, trying to see the other speaker.

Hector sighed. "Tinbit, come out of the daisies. He's not here."

"What if he's in that rhododendron, watching me? That thing's so huge you could put a whole family of gnomes in there." A wild, disheveled little gnome with black hair and flame-colored eyes appeared, brushing a forest of leaves from his gray overalls.

Hector shook his head. "You told me you couldn't wait to meet him."

"I did, but I didn't know I'd be sick to my stomach about it! I can't take any more of this. Let's go back. He doesn't want to see me. If he did, he'd have come out to meet me."

"Oh, for mermaid's tears, Tinbit! Something must have come up, that's all. I'm sure he'd be here if he could."

"Maybe you're right." Tinbit relaxed a fraction. "Can we go back anyway? If I saw him now, I'd have to explain this." He gestured to his clothes.

"I could say I pushed you into the leaf pile," Hector said. "I am a wicked witch after all. I'm supposed to mistreat my servants."

"Yeah right," Tinbit said. "He'd take one look at you and know you never did. You couldn't keep a straight face."

Hector chuckled. "You're probably right."

"You really think he couldn't come? He didn't stand me up? Because I don't think I can take it if he doesn't come to dinner on Moonsday. Oh, Gods, Hector, what if he doesn't? Maybe I should just say I can't make it, send him a letter—"

"You'll do no such thing," Hector said. "I'm going to the game, you are going to dinner, he will show, you're going to have a great time, and I'm not coming back early, in case something happens."

"Nothing is going to happen," Tinbit said, blushing furiously.

"Well, if it does, I'll be out of your way." Hector strolled around the pond and set off across the lawn.

Tinbit kicked a hazelnut that rolled almost to Ida's feet. "I swear, Hector, you're enough to make me want to thump you." He trotted off after his witch.

So that was Tinbit. Hari had said the name, but it hadn't meant anything to her. Hector had never mentioned him before. Of course, he hadn't. He'd set this up. More payback for his scalded behind.

"Of all the reprehensible, vindictive, petty…" She crawled out of the shrubbery on all fours, shaking with rage.

Well, she'd just have to put a stop to it. Hari was *not* going to fall in love with Hector's gnome.

For the rest of the evening, it was all she thought about—how best to thwart Hector's diabolical plan. Hari styled her hair for the dinner, valiantly prattling on about how it was okay, he hadn't promised Tinbit he'd come to the garden and maybe they had just missed each other. She fumed, hearing the heartbreak in his voice. It made her want to stomp out of her room, go find Hector, and scream in his face about just how much he couldn't take a joke. But that would mean admitting he'd gotten her with his spell, and she would never give him that kind of satisfaction. No, she'd have to get Hari out of this carefully, or more things than Hari's heart could be hurt.

"I may be back late," she said. "Annabeth hinted at something like a palaver afterwards and you know she can go on and on when she's in the mood. Are you sure you won't come? The castle library is one of the finest in the world, and it might take your mind off…things."

"No, I'll be okay," he said. "Now you, I worry about…"

"I can control my temper," she promised. *With Annabeth.* But if Hector so much as showed his long nose tonight, she wasn't sure she could do the same with him. Then again, he never went to these things if he could help it. He hadn't cared about her end of the magic almost since the inception of it, so why would he change now?

Glumly, she opened her valise and pulled out a slender glass vial adorned only with a golden stopper made in the shape of a rose to identify it. This was the second half of her part of the Happily-Ever-After, a love potion brewed from rose petals, the same rose that the Common Princess had crushed under her heel when she left. She gave it an experimental shake, and all the gold and red within swirled inside like a romantic dream, or a freshly opened wound.

There were times when she was sure that love magic should never have been the province of a good witch. It looked too much like poison.

13
Hector

Dear Rupert,

I regret missing the Prince's Dinner last night. Unfortunately, the journey left me with a severe case of indigestion. I remained at the hotel in hopes that my health would be better for the game on Moonsday.

Sincerely,
HECTOR

"YOUR PREOCCUPATION WITH TELLING THE TRUTH IS beginning to sound like I need to get you a tonic," Tinbit yelled.

Hector groaned. A self-induced gastrointestinal earthquake had been a small price to pay for skipping out on last night's royal dinner. It was traditional for the crown prince to take the potion that would make him fall head-over-heels in love with the Common Princess at this event, which meant one thing. Seeing Ida. An overdose of Hex-Lax certainly hadn't been pleasant, but it beat the alternative.

"Hector?"

"I'm fine." Shakily, he rose, feeling like he'd lost ten pounds. "I need to take it gently for the next hour or so."

"So no grilled sausage with chili at the game tonight?" Tinbit asked.

"I absolutely intend to eat a sausage with chili! What's a hurling game without that, I'd like to know?" A huge belch escaped him. He wiped his mouth and, straightening his shirt, left the garderobe. Indoor plumbing had been installed about five hundred years ago, but he still called it the garderobe. "I intend to enjoy myself this evening."

"You'll be the only one," Tinbit said. "Mark my words, I'll find a letter in the mail tomorrow morning from Hari saying, 'regret missing dinner; I got hit by a dung cart and died.'"

Hector almost quipped that lying beat hexing your own bowels to get out of a dinner date, but Tinbit didn't appear in the mood for levity. "Stop catastrophizing. He'll be there."

The gnome didn't look up from his ironing.

Hector glanced furtively at Tinbit. "Did…did he send you a letter about missing you in the garden last night?"

"No. But this is better. If he saw me in the garden and decided I was hideous, I'd rather not know. I'll go to dinner tonight, he won't be there, and that will be the end of it."

"Tinbit—"

"Hector, I'm okay. You warned me. These pen-pal things never work out, not without some happily-ever-after magic involved. Love isn't for people…like…me. I'm fine. I'm—" His shoulders started to shake.

Hector managed to rescue his jersey from the ironing board before Tinbit covered his face with it, and steered the gnome to his bed. He sat him down on the edge. "Tinbit, Tinbit, honey, don't cry. You know what that does to your face."

"I know, I know, but, Hector, I wanted him to be the one. I've waited so long."

Hector hugged the gnome, letting Tinbit bury his face in his shoulder. "Don't give up hope. He might have been delayed. The coaches were rolling up almost until midnight—I know, I was in the garderobe. And if your poor fellow was unlucky enough to try even a bite of Ida North's Angel's Dream Cake at that soiree, he probably was, too."

Tinbit's muffled sob became half-laugh, half-cry of misery. "Oh, Hector."

Hector continued to hold him, feeling utterly helpless. This was completely out of his realm of experience. Yes, he did his part with Happily-Ever-After, but his job involved putting obstacles in the way of the magic to make it stick—that was what the black rose was for. To make it real, there must be suffering along the way. It was an immutable law of love. If people became friends, fell in love, never fought a day in their lives, lived a long, happy life together, and died peacefully within months of each other, what kind of a romance was that? But he'd never wanted so much to take away every obstacle for Tinbit. Sometimes suffering for love is just suffering.

For the rest of the day, he handled Tinbit like a bomb that might explode. Tinbit went back and forth. He would go to dinner. He didn't mind eating alone. He'd get a table for one. He was fine.

The next minute he wouldn't go. He couldn't get through it without breaking down in public, and he wouldn't embarrass Hector by doing that. He'd order room service. Eat in bed. Watch the game on the crystal ball.

Each time, Hector supported him. It took his mind off the

unhappy consequences of the Hex-Lax. His stomach still wasn't right. Or maybe it was Tinbit. The last time he'd seen the gnome so upset, Tinbit had completely fallen apart. The thought of that made him even queasier.

At precisely six, he dressed for the game, regarding himself in a full-length mirror. A gray, tired man in faded black trousers and a vintage game jersey stared back at him. When had he bought it? The Thieves hadn't worn this particular design in centuries. He was old, and tonight, he felt it. He sighed.

"I've decided I'm going to dinner," Tinbit announced, handing Hector his blackthorn staff, freshly polished.

"I think that's a good decision," he said, wiping the extra beeswax off on his sleeve.

"I'm not staying long. He won't be coming."

"Would you like me to come back early? I can leave the game in the last quarter if it's not close."

"No, don't do that. I'll be fine. Enjoy yourself."

As if he could. This Hari, whoever he was, deserved a boil hex on his behind if he was just stringing Tinbit along. Of course, given the way Tinbit acted, Hari might have been hiding in a bush somewhere.

Hector left the hotel in a hired coach. He'd have rather taken his own, but it was bad luck to bring bones to a Thieves game. Once upon a time, in the year when Hector got real plumbing in his castle, the Thieves had been up on the Rogues by thirteen points, in itself a bad omen. A fan let loose a skeleton cat, which ran across the field, stopping play. After that, the Rogues scored. They won the game, sixteen to thirteen, and the

Thieves, favored to win the coveted Golden Cauldron, lost it that year after having won it the past five. They hadn't won it since. The saying "when pigs fly" had been replaced by "when the Thieves win the Cauldron." An ardent Thieves supporter, Hector wouldn't even wear his favorite bone cufflinks to a match.

He arrived about thirty minutes before the coin toss. The moment the coachman let him out, he found himself immediately surrounded by guards.

"What is the meaning of this?"

"Your Wickedness?" A mustachioed knight came forward.

"Yes?"

"Security detail," the guard said. "King's orders."

"I'm more than capable of defending myself," Hector said, irritated. "I've never needed a security detail before. May I ask—"

He didn't get any further. A blinding flash of light, a puff of pixie dust, and he threw up his hand in a ward.

"No flash photography!" the guard yelled. Two knights jumped forward to deal with a rather irate photographer and his partner, a tiny green pixie with dragonfly wings doing his best to bite the knights' fingers off.

"What in the enchanted kingdom was that?" Hector asked.

"Pixarati. We've had a real problem with them in the last five years."

The remaining knights clustered around Hector like a swarm of bees, but the flashes of pixie dust continued unabated until they entered the stadium.

Hector scowled and straightened his jersey. "Pixarati?"

"For the *Star*," the mustachioed knight said. "Tabloids— worst kind of trash. They'll lie about anyone for a story, and their photographers are the worst. You'll be safe now." He aimed Hector in the direction of the royal box and gave him a push.

Hector went, not without a final glare. Rupert didn't care about tabloids. He rather liked the publicity. It was more likely he'd sent the guards to make sure Hector didn't slip into the stadium and promptly vanish.

"Hector!" The king boomed from the first landing. He came downstairs, arms out, dragon scale coat flashing in occasional bursts of light from above. Hector shuddered. The garment was ancient, made in the centuries before he'd protected the dragons, but he could never look at it without wondering which poor dragon grieved themselves to death for their deceased mate or child. But Rupert didn't care. As long as Hector had known him, he'd never had an ounce of compassion for anyone or anything.

The first time Hector dealt with him personally was at Rupert's Happily-Ever-After. Rupert had been a fine, fit prince when Hector devised the traps and impediments designed to make his Happily-Ever-After stick with the Common Princess, Annabeth. Hector had his reservations about her too—scuttlebutt said she'd bribed the committee—but after Rupert completely destroyed Hector's troll and wounded Adair, a flagrant violation of the established rules, and then bragged about it, Hector wouldn't have helped Rupert out of his Happily-Ever-After if it had been as easy as waving a wand. His reservations about Annabeth slipped by the wayside as he patched up Adair and then arranged a nice retirement in the mountains for the troll, wishing he'd never tasked that gentle soul to fight a prince. He still felt horrible about it.

"Rupert." He made no attempt to rid his voice of the stiffness.

"Come right up!" Rupert said. "Archie's here. He wants you

to give him all your pointers on fighting dragons. You haven't seen him since he turned eight—you won't believe how much he's grown."

Hector dragged himself up the stairs. Unless someone had put a shrink spell on the child, he'd have grown quite a lot. Whether he'd grown in intelligence or morality was less certain. Hector remembered a surly blond boy, with a pale complexion and freckles, who showed him a collection of dead beetles stuck on pins under a glass case. Hector had asked him what kind of beetles they were. The boy had looked at him dully. "I don't know," he'd said. "I just like sticking bugs on pins."

Hector despised that kind of base cruelty. If a man must be cruel, he ought to at least be intentional about it. Evil should be an art, not a hobby.

No, he didn't look forward to meeting Crown Prince Archibald Quentin Rupert II again.

A sudden commotion came from the stairs on the left, and he came face-to-face with the one person he wanted to see less than dear old Archie.

Ida North.

14
Ida

The one awful thing about being a good witch? You aren't allowed to throw a decent hex to save your life.

MAGIC AND MISCHIEF—A THOUSAND YEARS OF HAPPILY-EVER-AFTER: A MEMOIR

IDA NORTH

IDA WANTED TO TAKE OUT HER TRAVEL WAND AND HEX Hector with a terrific case of butt boils. But she was a good witch.

There he stood on the landing, glowering down at her from his considerable height advantage. How unfair. She was shrinking as she aged, but he stood straight and tall as a dragon-lance, the asshole. A frosty smile turned the left corner of his mouth upward, but the rest of his face could have been made from marble and the expression fixed somewhere between annoyance and outright dislike.

Big old butt boils, the kind that would mean he couldn't sit for a solid week. She gripped the handle of her wand and forced a pointed smile. "Why, Hector, I didn't expect you to be at the game. I thought you couldn't stand seeing the Thieves lose in person."

"Oh, I would never miss an opportunity to watch the Rogues go up in flames."

King Rupert laughed, a large, hearty guffaw, as he clapped his meaty hands on her shoulder and Hector's, pulling them together. "Now, you two! Save the trash talk for the big day tomorrow."

Boils for him too, right on his forehead, in a pattern that read, "Royal Prick." Nobody ever taught that man to respect his witches.

"Shall we?" she said, shrugging out from under Rupert's arm and waving Hector ahead. "Wickedness before goodness?"

"In that case." Hector stepped aside.

So they proceeded up the stairs ahead of the king, stride for stride.

"I didn't expect to see you here, Hector," she said. "You usually shun company."

"I thought it would be nice to get out of the hotel tonight."

"Oh, did you?" Ida's words slipped between her teeth. That ass. She was right. He had planned it after all. His gnome was probably just as bad as him. Neither one of them would have any reservations about destroying literally the sweetest soul in the world to hurt her. She'd spent the better part of the day begging Hari to go to the game with her and not to dinner with Tinbit.

"But I can't," Hari had said miserably as he'd styled her hair for the game. "I won't stand him up."

"But he stood you up, didn't he?" Lying hurt a little, but she was responsible for his happily-ever-after. If Hari ever found out that he'd been used as Hector's pawn to punish Ida, he'd never forgive himself. Worse, he might never trust anyone ever again. She couldn't live with herself if that happened. Damn Hector. She'd never wanted to permanently curse him into stone so much in her life.

"Maybe he came before us. Or after us. It's not his fault. It's mine."

She reached back and touched his hand. "It's absolutely not your fault! Did you tell him you'd meet him in the garden? No. He did. And he's the one who didn't show up. He's not worth your time. And I don't want you to be hurt, sweetheart. You mean too much to me."

He squeezed her hand back. "I know, but you're right. I need to give this a chance. I've never talked to anyone who I connected with so well."

Oh, she could kick herself for that "let love kindle" talk. "You haven't talked to him at all! You can't get to know someone through letters, Hari." She turned back to face the mirror with a huff.

"I don't know about that. You seem to know Hector pretty well," Hari said. The clipped tone in his voice let her know she might be overstepping the bounds of their friendship.

"That isn't the same thing! Those letters are—They were—"

Hari pulled a curler out of her hair. "Were what, exactly?"

She pursed her lips. "Jokes," she said. "It started as a joke." Up until five hundred years ago, she and Hector only really interacted at the Happily-Ever-After and at the Witches' Council afterward, secure and comfortable in their mutual loathing for one another. Any letters that passed between them were short and to the point. But one year she needed to ask him a question regarding his dragon. What was it? Something about the arrangements for the cave lair and the princess being allergic to something. Oh, yes, nettles. The poor child had been knitting shirts made out of the nasty things since she was twelve and now they broke her out in hives. On a whim, she'd slipped a tickle charm in the letter to annoy him. He'd written back taunting her about how he planned to hex the princess's lips with a fever blister curse that would make hives seem like a spa treatment and sent a sample. She'd turned his hair green in retaliation. He said baldness would be the next fad in hairstyles, and then she'd needed to buy a wig…

"I suppose I simply like sparring with him," she said, knotting her scarf in her lap. "And anyway, he's not writing to me now."

Hari stabbed her gently with the blunt end of a hairpin. "You were lonely, Ida. That's why you wrote to him. And I bet he's lonely too. So don't tell me you can't get attached to somebody because of letters."

"Hector is not my friend."

"I didn't say he was."

"Don't go to dinner with that gnome."

"Is that an order?"

She turned toward him, frowning. "Call it a premonition. I feel it's wrong for you and possibly wrong for him."

He raised his eyebrows. "I'm a big boy. I can take care of myself."

She sighed. "Well, I'm coming home at halftime. I don't want you here all alone when things don't work out."

Hari smiled. "You won't. The Rogues are going to win and you'll want to celebrate."

"You are more important to me than a game."

"Are you sure you're not sick or something?" Hari scoffed. "You're going to be late."

Way too late. If she'd been on time, she could've stopped Hari from ever sending his first letter to Hector's gnome: Tinbit. What a ridiculous name. Probably Hector gave it to him when he was a gnomelet, a moniker to make him feel subservient. That would be properly wicked.

But as she walked beside Hector now, almost the same way Tinbit had walked with him last night, she wondered. He hadn't quite sounded like an evil overlord conversing with his henchman. He sounded more like her when she talked with Hari. Yes, Hari was her manservant, but she never called him that, never thought of him that way, never wanted him to feel anything less than her equal. And he'd more than equally told her to mind her own business when it came to his love life. Had Tinbit done the same to Hector?

Maybe she was wrong. Hector might not have set this up. He might be as much in the dark as she had been. Things like that could happen, particularly when the blasted Fates got involved. Perhaps she should pull him aside, and just ask…

"Where were you last night?" she asked. "You weren't at the Prince's Dinner."

"I didn't feel well."

"That makes what? Zero dinners you've attended in forever? You might at least try to show some enthusiasm."

"That's your part of the magic, not mine. Love potions— ugh. Never touched the things, even when they weren't illegal."

"Clearly," she jabbed. Time to test her suspicion. "Where exactly are you staying?" she asked, innocently. "Mage Suites was closed, or so I heard."

"The Golden Dragon."

"I didn't see you arrive."

"I came a little early to settle in."

"Travelled alone, did you?"

"Not this time," he said. "My butler came with me. He had something he wanted to do in town."

So Tinbit was his butler. Not a henchman at all then. That explained the deference. Hector probably didn't want to be prematurely poisoned.

She forced a smile. "What a coincidence. I brought my man-servant, Hari, with me. But you know I usually do. I enjoy company, unlike you."

"I don't dislike company," he said. "Only present company. Excuse me." He sailed off with Rupert as Annabeth pounced.

"Ida! Idaidaidaidaida—my dear, Ida! Isn't this the most delish?" She wrapped her arm around Ida's waist and pulled her forward into the crush of evening gowns. *Evening gowns at a sporting event? What on earth?* Ida straightened her jersey, glad Hari had insisted on silk pants and sequined flats. She'd have preferred khaki shorts and a low-slung sandal, as spring was so warm in the capital city. Meanwhile, Hector strutted around in that ancient jersey and equally ancient pants, carrying an ancient staff, and somehow he managed to look more put together than anyone there. It was the way he carried himself, wearing that aura of dangerous magic like robes—perfectly poised. He hadn't even flinched when she mentioned Hari's name.

"Let me take you away from that horrid Hector," Annabeth said, sticking out her tongue in Rupert's direction. "You come with me. I'm just dying to hear about this Common Princess and how you came to pick her for my son. The *Star* says you went against committee to do it, you naughty thing, but then you were never one for rules, always said you'd do exactly the right thing no matter what, you're such a rebel, and—"

Amazing. Annabeth didn't seem to need to breathe. Ida let herself be swept into the well-dressed crowd of socialites.

"So tell me, darling, what is the deal with this girl?" Annabeth popped a pastry in her mouth, but she didn't stop talking. "Won't come to tea, won't come to the gown fitting for Happily-Ever-After, you should see the dress I've picked out, it's absolutely dreadful, I'm not going to just take rudeness from my future daughter-in-law, I plan to spit in her eye, I mean Happily-Ever-After doesn't apply to mothers-in-law, does it? Oh, wait until the wedding reception, Ida, I ordered red-hot dancing slippers for her, I plan to take her shopping before the big day, I can't wait to see her howling all over her smug little face when she puts them on, don't worry, I'm blaming an evil fairy…"

Ida pasted a pleasant smile on her face and tried to focus on Annabeth's endless prattle. She might be worried for nothing. Tinbit was likely to be like Hector—acerbic to the point of absolute acidity, evil to the bone, and far more likely to break a person's heart than carry it off with him on a white horse. Tinbit would stand Hari up. Hari would be inconsolable. Surely Hector wouldn't let it go further than that. Afterward, she'd sympathize with Hari, soothe him. She'd tell him that he was lucky he'd not lost his heart to someone so wicked and it would all be fine.

Speaking of wicked, she'd better send a message to Amber in the morning advising her to never go shoe shopping with the queen. Ten hours and blisters were even worse than red-hot dancing shoes.

15

Hector

Once upon a time, the royalty insisted on having their sons and daughters cursed for their sixteenth birthdays. I always refused. I saw no good reason to give a perfectly healthy prince an obsession with golden apples or a princess an unreasonable shoe size that would mean she'd always need custom orthotics. Plenty of hedge witches deal in that kind of chicanery. A Wicked Witch charged with maintaining the magic of Happily-Ever-After has far more important matters to think about.

A THOUSAND YEARS OF WICKEDNESS: A MEMOIR

HECTOR WEST

IDA DIDN'T LOOK A DAY OVER FIVE HUNDRED. HER hair floated ethereally around her shoulders, still colored the strange shade of mutable red Hector called rose-gold, red in some light, almost golden in others. The faint silver traces didn't make her look like the mangy old badger he'd become. They made her look wise, sophisticated—every inch *the* Good Witch. Some people had all the luck when it came to aging.

"Archie! Come over here, son," Rupert boomed.

He had grown. Hector wasn't a small man, but the crown prince moved out of the crowd of the swooning ladies-in-waiting like some graceful stag emerging from the mists of swirling evening gowns. He had Annabeth's blond hair and blue eyes, but he'd inherited his father's muscular upper body and thighs—extra apparent since he was wearing the most confining set of trousers Hector had ever seen outside of a torture chamber. But above them he wore the matching vest to go with his father's dragon coat. Not "that" changed then. Hector fixed a false smile on his face.

"Father. Wickedness." Archie's voice was melodic, clearly trained—or borrowed. Hector thought he remembered something about his mother bamboozling a mermaid.

"I was just telling Hector how much you were looking forward to tomorrow," Rupert said. "Got your armor all picked out for the big day?"

"Caedan picked it out for me," Archie said in a bored tone. "But I'd rather it had come a month later. I'm missing the golden bird hunt for this."

"There will be other seasons to hunt birds," Rupert said with a hint of irritation. "This is your destiny, son. Tell him, Hector." He turned to Hector with a bright grin on his face.

"Tell him what?" Hector asked, equally irritated. What was Rupert playing at?

"What you told me, of course! When I was in the dungeon!" Rupert grabbed Hector around the shoulders and shook him. "About how this was destiny, me and Annabeth, how the whole country depended on our Happily-Ever-After, how I couldn't flinch from my duty because it was destiny. It. Was. Destiny."

Oh, yes. That little talk. Well, spiders in one's armor tended to make a man regret all his life choices, including marriage. Rupert had been rather a mess by that point in his punishment. But in Hector's opinion, Rupert had deserved every last bite.

"I know that," Archie said in that bland, emotionless tone. "You've told me that story a thousand times, Dad. What I want to know is why I have go through this charade—a quest, killing a dragon, rescuing a princess—when you just plan to marry me off to this girl anyway. It's stupid."

"Marry you off—son, this is Happily-Ever-After! Look at me and your mother, and how happy we are!" Rupert smiled at Annabeth, chattering away at a rate to make an auctioneer jealous. "You're a very lucky young man."

Archie stared at his own father with something akin to flabbergasted annoyance. Hector smiled grimly. Rupert and Annabeth, wed until death did them part, would never see the other as anything but their perfect match. Wonderful stuff, Happily-Ever-After, he supposed. For himself personally, he preferred to see people as basically flawed but worth his affection, like Tinbit. And Tinbit certainly felt the same way about him— never wasted an opportunity to let Hector know when he was being unreasonable. Hector reached into his pocket and touched the glass marble he'd brought with him. Still cold. Tinbit, wherever he was right now, didn't need to talk to him.

He'd insisted on taking the pocket glass before he left. "What if—and this is simply hypothetical—this gnome doesn't show? What will you do?"

"I told you," Tinbit said, in a morose tone. "I'll watch the game on the crystal."

"All the same, I'd feel better if you had a way to contact me." He reached into the folds of his best robe and found the magical travelling pocket connected to his desk drawer at home. Groping around, he pricked himself on the nib of his writing pen and upset a bottle of ink before he found them, a silken bag filled with two marbles of astonishing moonlit brilliance. He took one and put it in his pants' pocket. The other, he gave to Tinbit. "You call me if anything—and I mean anything—comes up. Let me know what's going on so I can come back if I need to."

Tinbit took the marble grumpily.

"And, of course, if I need to take my time coming back, well...uh..."

Tinbit turned crimson. "That won't be happening."

"Of course not," Hector said, trying to smile. But he knew Tinbit. If things went well, *that* might happen, and he didn't want to walk in on his gnome having sex again. Once was enough.

Hector stuffed the cold marble back in his pocket and tried to concentrate on what Archie was saying.

"Look, I don't mean to buck a thousand years of tradition, but I don't see why we're still doing this. I mean, why does it have to be a commoner? There are a lot prettier people in this world." The prince glanced back at the serving table where Ida stood, the only normally dressed person in the disturbingly elaborate swirl of ladies in long gowns and noblemen dressed in their very best. The tall guard who had saved Hector from the Pixarati was there too, nibbling politely at a slice of cake whiter than the plate it was sitting on. Hector resisted the urge to call out a warning. The stuff should come with a skull and crossbones label.

Rupert's voice became stern. "It's for the good of the king-dom! Marrying a commoner is an excellent antidote to magical birth defects and whatnot—no lingering curses by fairies, wicked witches, and so forth. Plus, you don't have to watch them around sharp objects like spinning wheels because of Hector's narco-lepsy spells. It's a good deal, son. Plus, it makes the people happy."

"I've never cursed a princess like that," Hector protested.

"Come off it, Dad. We both know my enchanted marriage isn't going to make anyone happy—it's tax breaks, it's keeping the miners in the Mystic Mountains from unionizing, it's making sure nobody knows the hurling games are rigged—not Happily-Ever-After! It's an archaic custom that's had its day like the witches who came up with the damned magic in the first place."

Rupert gasped and glanced furtively at Hector. "Archie—"

"Excuse me." Archie turned his back on them and glided back to the table. The ladies swarmed him like moths to a candle.

Rupert sighed. "I don't know what I'm going to do with him, Hector. I really don't."

Hector's face was burning. Had its day like the witches who came up with the damned magic...what were royal princes learning these days? Clearly, not history. At least Alistair knew why he had to participate. Archie didn't seem to have a clue. He cleared his throat. "It's normal for a man to have—"

"Cold feet, yes. I had them. I had no idea what Annabeth would be like or if that nasty stuff I had to drink would make me love her as much as I do. But this is different." Rupert flopped into a chair and patted the seat next to him. "Game's starting."

Hector sank into the plush seat. The hurling game was now not remotely interesting.

Rupert's eyes never left his son, eating cake with the tall

guard. "Tell me you've got a pep talk for this, Hector. I'm at my wit's end. I kept hoping he'd come around, but he says he isn't going to go through with it."

"Not go through with it?" Hector gaped. "But…but it's his duty!"

"I know, right? It started last year—this foolishness of his. I blame his friends, filling his head with all this progressive non-sense, especially that one." Rupert jerked his head irritably in the direction of the tall guard, now hovering behind the prince like a buff bodyguard. "Ever since he arrived, Archie's been moody. He spends hours hanging out with the guards, or in the library reading." He shuddered. "Not normal at all. At least he's still into hunting and hawking, or I'd think he'd been enchanted or something. I tried to get him interested in the dragon fight—I told him to go for the wings, that's where I cut the one that had Annabeth. Even made a big deal out of giving him Excalibur 350 for the battle. Maybe that will put the fervor for being king in his veins—something had better."

Gods. Hector's face had to be on fire, it burned so much. "I hope you also told him that it's illegal to wound the dragon."

Rupert waved his hand carelessly. "Rules are only rules if people catch you breaking them. Frankly, between you and me, I wish he could kill the monster like in the good old days. Boy needs to grow up—get off his horse and back in the castle where a king belongs. He spends all his time with that Caedan. *He* put this foolish notion of what the people want in Archie's head— taxing the rich, free education for the masses, even a parliament. A parliament of commoners! Can you imagine that?"

A niggling doubt crept into Hector's mind like an unwel-come spider. "I thought I saw something in the paper—"

Rupert snorted. "Don't get me started on the *Star*. That tabloid will say anything to sell their rag. Caedan and Archie are friends, that's it. Between you and me, I'm sending Caedan on that quest for the Holey Pail with Pin-Dragon and the others tomorrow. That will get him away from Archie. If I'm really lucky, he'll get himself eaten by a griffin and we'll have no more of this 'what the people want' nonsense. What they need is Happily-Ever-After—at least that's all *we* need to keep them quiet." Rupert rose as the referee called offsides. "What I want you to do is take him aside and tell him it will be okay, that once it's done, once the potion sinks in, he won't care about anything but what's right for the kingdom. He'll believe it coming from someone other than me. I hope."

"He hasn't had the potion yet? But…the dinner—"

"Annabeth decided to do it here. More festive this way—you know how she feels about all that pomp with no party." He sauntered over to the table to where his wife and child waited and poured himself a huge flagon of dwarf-brewed beer.

Hector sank deeper into his seat, wishing he had a drink too. First a reluctant dragon, now a rebellious prince. Could this Happily-Ever-After get any worse? Granted, it sounded like Archie had acquired some common sense, at least in regard to what made a kingdom happy, and it almost made Hector feel a bit sorry about the zombie flies he'd come up with to torment Archie in the marshes.

"Gather around, people, gather around!" Rupert boomed, raising his glass. The room didn't quiet—if anything, it got louder and the tittering of the ladies-in-waiting sounded as shrill as the buzzing of hornets.

"I have a surprise for everyone. In light of the importance of this occasion for all the people"—Rupert stared rather pointedly at Archie—"we've decided that everyone should get a seat at the Prince's Dinner. Gentlemen, ladies—I give you the future king of our country, Prince Archibald Quentin Rupert the Second!"

The clapping in the room suddenly became a roar. Hector, baffled, glanced out at the field, where the game had stopped and a giant picture of the prince, looking startled and more than a little embarrassed, appeared in the crystal ball hovering over the field.

Ida sat down beside Hector, pointedly staring at anything but him.

"Your idea?" he said, making no attempt to hide his scorn.

"Hardly," she said through clenched teeth.

"This was supposed to be done last night."

"If you'd been there, you'd know why it wasn't," she interrupted. "He wasn't there."

"What?"

"The crown prince. He wasn't there. Not feeling well, Annabeth said."

"You could have—" He stopped in the middle of his sentence as his own face and Ida's appeared on the crystal to more cheers. Ida smiled and raised her hand as if casting a good luck charm over all the spectators. The crystal panned back to the royal family. Now Rupert was shaking Caedan's hand and saying something about "exemplary kindness" and "noble values" and how after his quest, he'd be knighted so he could always have a seat beside the prince. The young man didn't look very happy about it. Probably knew the king was hoping he'd end up in a griffin's stomach.

"This is utterly inane," Hector snarled. "You should have gone to the boy's room and given him the potion."

She sneered at him. "Oh, that's the way we do it, is it? We ram potions down people's throats like medicine?"

"You know perfectly well that's not what I meant—"

"Now, I know it's not tradition," Rupert said, smiling indulgently at Annabeth, "but we just couldn't have a special event like this without inviting all of Archie's friends and our loyal subjects to share this happy occasion with us." He raised a glass to the screen. "Please join our royal family in a toast to the happy prince and his future bride!"

Caedan, frowning almost as much as Hector, came forward, bearing a golden goblet filled with a wine that shivered red and gold, reflecting in the mirror finish. "My prince," he said, dropping to one knee.

Hector glanced at Ida. "If this was your idea of forcing me to attend one of these, I don't approve."

"Hector, believe me, the only event I ever want to attend with you is your funeral."

More cheers. The prince had just raised his glass to the crowd.

Hector rose. "You stay and see this through—I'm done with it."

"Go on, palm the whole thing off on me! That's what you always do, isn't it?"

Ramrod straight, he stalked away. He wouldn't be baited into arguing further. This wasn't the venue, but tomorrow at the Council meeting, he'd have plenty to say. He was all for progress, but when royals turned the single most important piece of magic that kept their world afloat into a spectacle, like some political propaganda, lines had to be drawn.

He grabbed the marble out of his pocket. "Tinbit, I'm headed back to the hotel. Could you order me a bottle of wine? On second thought, something stronger."

The gnome's face appeared, very flushed. "Oh, uh, Hector, I—" Tinbit gasped.

"Tinbit? Are you sick?"

"No, I just…didn't expect….oh, wow—"

"Tinbit? Are you all right?"

"Perfect—just kind of busy…"

Hector's face burned. "Oh. No need to explain. How…uh, long do you think you'll be?"

"I don't know—oh, wow, Hari, oh—please—don't stop."

Wait a minute. Hari? "Tinbit?" he yelled at the marble, now showing him a room rolling away.

"Tinbit!" No answer. Hector brought the marble up to his eye, staring furiously at two small figures more or less attached from the hips down.

A raucous cheer from the crowd let him know Rupert was talking again. Probably announced something like ale for the whole crowd. Rage filled him. It could not be coincidence, Ida North mentioning "Hari" just before he heard Tinbit moaning that name in complete ecstasy. She'd done it on purpose. She'd put her gnome in touch with his to get back at him for that candor curse. How dare she! He hadn't loved Tinbit all his life to see him break his heart over Ida North's manservant. He charged back up the stairs.

Ida North ran smack into him, headbutted him in the chest, and sent him tumbling sideways.

"Watch where you're going!"

"You watch where you're going," Ida retaliated, face flushed.

"Trouble?" Hector asked, ice dripping from his voice.

"No," Ida said with equal frost. "I have a headache and wish to return to my hotel room."

"Is that so? No plans for your manservant Hari to fix you a hot toddy?"

She glared at him. "No. Get out of my way."

He moved back into her path. "Did you know your gnome and my gnome would be together tonight? Did you send your gnome to seduce mine?"

Ida's pink cheeks turned maroon. "How dare you! You know damned well your gnome has been sending mine letters!"

"I didn't know who Tinbit was writing to or I would've forbidden it!"

"Bullshit! Hari is like a son to me, and you allowed your butler to seduce him—" She drew her wand.

He didn't even think. He waved his staff. A thousand spiders poured out of the sleeves of his jersey and galloped over Ida. They immediately set to work, throwing threads, spinning, pulling everything together they could—her shirtsleeves, her pants, the curls in her hair, her eyelids—

She screamed and blasted him.

Bright yellow butterflies descended on his head in a golden horde. They beat his face with their wings, hard as tiny hailstones. They stabbed him with tongues as sharp as needles.

He struck at her wand, catching it between his staff and the railing. It broke. Spiders and butterflies exploded, multiplying from hundreds into thousands, and from thousands into millions.

16
Ida

Exponentially, dear readers, this was a disaster. The spiders sewed up the players' jerseys, starting with the Rogues', no doubt a ploy the Wicked Witch of the West, Hector West, formerly Hector Prim, devised in order to give his favorites, the Thieves, the victory. They were thwarted by the myriad of attack butterflies, created by the Good Witch of the North, Ida North, formerly Ida Moonshadow, which descended on players and fans alike. The insects then infiltrated the royal box and caused much excitement when the spiders sewed up the queen and her ladies inside their dresses, while the butterflies, armed with curiously pointed proboscises, amputated the king's nose. See related story on page eight: Rupert's Magical Nose Job: Queen Says New Nose Matches King's Member in Length and Shape!

–THE SORCERERS' STAR

"How do I look?" Ida asked, turning around once in front of the glass.

The mirror said nothing. It wasn't enchanted. But Hari,

walking through with the blue robe she'd foregone in favor of the ecru one, spoke for it, and with much more candor. "White's not for you. Makes you look like a ghost."

She frowned. "I know, but it's traditional, and after last night, I need to do everything I can to appear like I generally uphold law and order."

"Instead of starting a riot?"

"I didn't start the riot. Hector threw the first punch, metaphorically." Hari was right about the ghost business. Gingers going silver probably shouldn't wear white even to their own funeral. Maybe a band of ivy and pink roses on her hat would help.

"Heels or flats?" Hari asked.

"Heels," Ida said firmly. She'd done enough looking up at Hector yesterday. Even an inch would be an improvement.

Hari returned from the wardrobe with her white pumps. His eyes were bloodshot this morning, and he squinted as if they stung. He'd been crying ever since she'd told him who Tinbit actually worked for and how everything must have been a trap to trick him. He stood listening while she confessed that she'd discovered it when Tinbit and Hector came to the garden, color draining from his face like she was a vampire sucking every bit of the happiness out of his body. And when she apologized brokenly for not telling him sooner, for not speaking up after the garden, he only said, "Thanks for telling me. I guess he didn't stand me up after all."

It wasn't as bad as she'd feared—it was worse.

She'd already cancelled all of her engagements after the Happily-Ever-After except the annual Witches' Council meeting this afternoon. Taking Hari home would help. Time cured all wounds—or at least she hoped it would. But she was worried. Two people couldn't exchange letters and then fall in love the moment they met—that only happened with magic. Probably, Hector had put a love potion in the ink. He'd have found that incredibly funny—Gods, she wanted to smack him so hard.

"I'm ready. You may call the coachman."

She rose, tucking her second-best wand in her robes. Hari would be all right. So would she. Everything would work out in the end.

The castle grounds were a splendor of gold and purple banners. Enchanted flowers sang in perfect tune from every flowerbed, and the lawn had been manicured into diamonds of spring green and emerald. Even in the carriage, she could catch a hint of fragrance coming from the ever-scented roses blooming on every trellis. A dance of dryads performed on the lawn, singing down charmed birds and bees for the little children of all the lords and ladies to play with, and even the common people, who had to be content with lottery seats on the west side, looked happy about the many kegs of dwarf-brewed beer on tap. Some of them had brought picnic baskets, and the meadow sprouted a tapestry of various checkered cloths.

It didn't please her the way it would have a day ago.

She glanced at Hari sitting across from her, tiny hands folded in his lap, eyes downcast. "I wish you'd stayed at the hotel. A letter would do to break it off with him, surely. You don't need to confront him. Hector put him up to it anyway."

"I have to tell him why it's all over," he said. "Because Hector might tell him you did it on purpose, sent me to distract him, and I don't want him to think that for a minute. He deserves the truth—even if he won't give that to me."

Oh, bless him, still wanting to see the good in everyone. She didn't have the heart to tell him that this Tinbit was probably as much of an asshole as his witch. Instead, she reached for his hand. "Dear, promise me, whatever he says, you won't take it to heart. I couldn't forgive myself if this hurts you further."

"This can't hurt me further," Hari said in a dead voice. He gazed blankly through the windows.

The carriage jolted to a halt. Hari rose, opened the door, and stepped down to hold it for her. She glanced around, startled by the cheers of the many common folk without lottery tickets who had turned out to watch the dragon carry off the princess from any vantage point they could find. A few knights extricated a family of gnomes from a grumpy old tree, reminding her forcefully of Hari.

"Stay with the coachman," she told him. "This won't take long—it's just the dragon coming to take the princess and then the prince's declaration speech."

"But I need to find Tinbit—"

She took hold of his shoulder. "I know. But I want to be with you when you do."

"Ida—"

"Please. Count it against what I owe for not being there when you needed me the most."

"You've always been there when I needed you," he said. He patted her hand.

"No hunting for Tinbit."

"No hunting for Tinbit," he sighed and climbed back in the coach.

Oh, when she saw Hector today, she would give him a proper piece of her mind.

"Your Goodness?" The Captain of the Guard stood just beyond a bower of white and red clematis, looking dashing in a chain mail waistcoat and light helmet. He extended his hand to take her arm when she approached the bower. "I'm here to escort you to the Witches' Box." His teeth shone amazingly white beneath his dark mustache.

She took his arm. "You're Caedan Cay, aren't you? I didn't get a chance to congratulate you on your first quest last night. I hope it's a very fruitful and fulfilling experience."

His jaw tightened, but his smile never wavered. "I'd rather hoped I'd be joining the prince's retinue on the rescue, but a quest is a great honor, of course. Good weather we are having for the day, isn't it?"

Of course it was. It always was. She made it that way. Bright sunshine, warm as summer, shone over everything like a benevolent God of Love, glazing every tower gold and making the white marble walls glitter like diamonds. Every banner hung still or stirred only briefly in the light breeze. Flights by dragon were never comfortable things for any princess, and anything to make the journey more pleasant was a good thing.

Ida glanced at the tall man by her side, noting the way he threw his shoulders back, the way his hair waved when he lifted his chin. He looked every inch the knight she was sure he would be. No wonder the *Star* seized on this man as a candidate for the prince's affection. The tabloids loved a sensational story on the brink of Happily-Ever-After. What had it been for Annabeth and Rupert's big day? Oh, yes. Annabeth had been carrying on with a baker's boy, and Rupert paid off a tavern wench who threatened to expose him in a sex scandal with a threesome of randy elves.

"Can I get you anything? Refreshments? A cushion for your seat?"

"No thank you. I don't expect I'll need either. You should return to the prince. I'm sure he wants you by his side when the dragon arrives." Caedan stared over his shoulder at the large pavilion where the prince would be waiting for his cue to rush to the rescue of the princess. A large white charger, arrayed in festive red and gold blankets, was being led toward the tent. "Yes, I'm sure he does. Don't hesitate to ask if you need anything, Your Goodness."

She smiled. What a nice young man. She had her doubts about Prince Archie—he'd never seemed all that kind as a child, and at the game he'd looked downright surly—but with a good wife in Amber, and thoughtful people like Caedan surrounding him, he'd do fine. But then, almost anything would be an improvement on Rupert.

"Ida, dear, come up and visit with me!" Tara, her Good Witch counterpart from the South, waved her toward the stand. "The princess just arrived. The attendants have their work cut out for them—she arrived in a leather apron and breeches, can you believe it?" Tara looked scandalized.

"She's a working blacksmith," Ida said. *That girl.* But at least she had shown up. After the fiasco last night, Ida had begun to wonder what would go wrong next. That whole "the prince is sick" lie Annabeth had orchestrated rankled almost as much as Hector's letters. For once, she was on the same page as he was— this event was getting entirely too political. *Ugh.* She couldn't believe she was actually agreeing with him!

"Interesting." The chill voice of Agatha cut in. "You always did pick the most…unusual…princesses." All in black, Hector's counterpart, Agatha of the East, fanned herself with a copy of the *Star*. "The papers are saying the most outrageous things about the girl, and about you." She smirked. "They say you deliberately yanked the rose out of the Common Princess's hand and gave it to this one, a girl chosen by some committee?" Her lip curled.

"The *Star* is hardly noted for telling the truth." Ida took her seat beside Tara, pointedly ignoring the front-page photo of her and Hector wrestling in a most undignified way on the stairs.

The smirk on Agatha's face got wider. Evil old witch. She was almost as old as Ida, but not quite, and she'd always wanted to be in charge of the Witches' Council. No doubt she completely approved of the riot. It irked Ida deeply that she'd wind up paying for Hector's part in that mess if Agatha decided to blame it on her. He'd probably lean back in his chair and gloat. Where was that man? It wasn't like him to be late, not even fashionably late. She craned around, searching for the dreadful coach and his skeleton horses.

Speaking of the bastard, here he came, jogging across the field, wearing ratty dark robes that looked like they'd been hand-dipped in indigo. He climbed the stairs, distinctly out of breath. "Sorry I'm late," he said, tipping his hat. "One of my carriage horses broke a leg this morning."

"Oh, what a shame. I hope you buried the poor creature decently." Agatha sniffed.

Hector's green eyes lit up. "A silver bone plate and it will be as good as new. I'm not about to bury a good horse simply because he's old." He gazed around the field, at the knights on parade, the military band warming up next to the stands, and at the brightly colored pavilions set up on either side of the field where the drama would play out. "Pardon me if this is a foolish question, but where is the princess? Should she not be presenting herself by now?"

Ida rose. The princess's tent stood on the left-hand side of the field, a flamboyant affair with decorative turrets and flags of blue and gold covered in fanciful stars and crowns. The princess should have been visible through the open doorway, but the tent flap remained stubbornly closed.

Agatha glared at Hector. "For that matter, Your Wickedness, where is the dragon?"

Hector's mouth became a concerned, tight line.

Good. He needed to squirm.

"You go see about your dragon. I'm going to go down to the tent to give the girl a last bit of advice," she announced. She hurried down the stairs and breezed across the field to see a princess about her destiny.

17

Hector

The role of the four Cardinal Witches encompasses these aspects of magic deemed too dangerous or delicate for average licensed witches:

Item 1) The maintenance and care of sensitive and/or sentient magical species, including, but not limited to giants, trolls, dragons, unicorns, manticores, gnomes, dwarves, dryads and drus, naiads, undines, merfolk, and sea serpents;

Item 2) The construction and breaking of various enchantments from animal to human and human to animal;

Item 3) To oversee the breeding and regulation of dangerous magical plant species;

Item 4) To regulate the use of potions, balms, essences, and various liquid enchantments; and

Item 5) All enchantments related to Happily-Ever-After.

*RULES AND REGULATIONS, COUNCIL OF
WITCHES, ROLE OF CARDINAL WITCHES*

HECTOR LEFT THE STAGE IN A HURRY. HIS SCRYING mirror was in the coach along with all his luggage—he didn't intend on staying in the capital city one hour more than necessary, not after last night. He'd had Tinbit check out of the hotel and see to the loading of the coach first thing that morning. Whenever the gnome was deeply upset, the best way to keep him from brooding was to give him something to do.

The nerve of Ida North, having her servant seduce his! It would be like her to brush a love potion on the letters, a patently illegal thing to do. He wished Tinbit hadn't burned all of Hari's letters last night in the hotel fireplace. If he could prove she'd done it, he'd haul her up in front of the Council and censure her for the next century over it. She deserved it. Tinbit was utterly undone.

At first Tinbit refused to believe him. "Wait a minute," he'd said, waving his hand, grin fading from his face. "Hari is Ida North's manservant?"

"I'm afraid so."

"You do realize Hari is a common name for gnomes. Granted, he's a lot less hairy than most Hari's I've met, but—"

"Tinbit—"

The gnome began to pace, wringing his hands. "No! It's not true. I don't believe you." He turned to Hector, his face a mask of fury. "I'm telling you, you've got the wrong guy. Nobody who gives a blowjob like that works for a good witch!"

His cheeks burned, but Tinbit was truly upset. Best keep it matter-of-fact. He didn't want Tinbit weeping. "I'm sorry, but there's no mistake. She said she saw you with me in the garden."

Tinbit froze. "He came?"

"It seems so."

Tinbit began to shake. "Oh, Gods, Hector. Tell me it's not

true. I haven't been like that with a man in forever. Everything was right, it was—" Tinbit stopped, staring at him. "Well, I guess you couldn't understand that, being a nine-hundred-ninety-year-old virgin."

Hector flinched. "No, I guess I couldn't. But it's true."

Tinbit wilted. He dropped on the bed and covered his face.

Hector's professionalism dropped like the façade it was. This was Tinbit—his Tinbit. He sat down beside him, and wrapped the little gnome in an embrace. "Tinbit, Tinbit, honey, please don't cry…I'm so sorry. If I'd known Ida would do something like this…she's supposed to be a good witch, but I suppose when it comes to getting back at me, she doesn't care who she hurts. This is all my fault."

"It's not your fault," Tinbit said, dry heaving to avoid tears. "You warned me."

"I didn't want to be right."

"And I totally fell for it." Tinbit slumped. "I really liked him, Hector. We talked together so easily—it was like I'd known him for years. I told him I'd meet him at the Happily-Ever-After tomorrow. I wanted him to meet you."

Love potion for sure. Oh, he was going to roast that woman!

Tinbit drew himself up, face twitching as he tried not to cry. "Hector, I want to go home. I can't stay here, not in this hotel, not knowing he probably set this up, used me to disgrace you."

"We'll go as soon as I'm done with the Council meeting. Why don't you stay with the coach today? That way you don't have to see him again." He wiped the tears accumulating in the corners of Tinbit's eyes with his handkerchief before they did any harm. He had limited experience with broken hearts, but one thing he knew for certain—time and distance helped.

In the stables, Hector found Tinbit working on the horse. He bent over, drilling holes in the horse's left front cannon bone while the skeleton coachman stood nearby, helpfully torquing a silver plate to fit. The patient, happily removed many years from the pain of such proceedings, stood three-legged, munching on a feedbag. It held chaff, which dropped to the floor through the open jawbone, but the horse didn't care, and Hector preferred them to remain as horse-like as possible after death.

"Almost done with Napoleon Bone-Apart," Tinbit said with a snort. "Maybe next time you resurrect a horse, give them a little more sense about not jumping at shadows that can't hurt them anymore."

"I'll consider it." Hector gave the horse's long frontal sinus a pat. "I need my scrying mirror. Where is it?"

"In the bag with your dirty jersey, I think. Those butterflies shat all over it." Tinbit wrinkled his brow. "Why do you need a mirror? And why don't I hear Alistair roaring?"

"That's why I need it. Our dragon prince hasn't arrived yet."

"Oh, shit," Tinbit said, straightening. "I only brought the medium distance one."

"If he's not in range of that one, I couldn't bring him here in time, anyway." The dragon had better be in range. His hands shook as he fumbled with the mirror. "Alistair," he breathed, fogging the glass. It remained passively gray.

The one day he needed a dragon to actually act like a stereotype—one day—and the chosen dragon had chosen to act like himself. It was one thing for him to know the fire-breathing reptiles were actually sensitive, deeply intellectual men and women, but the people of the kingdom shouldn't know that about their traditional creatures of fight and fear. That was part of the magic—there had to be something to test the magical love in order to make it stick. The black rose had to meet the red. If Alistair didn't come…

He didn't want to think about that, but his thoughts strayed back to an abandoned battlefield, the bodies lying there, a cauldron full of magic and hope, and the desperate understanding that if Happily-Ever-After ever fell apart, all he'd given up his life for would fall apart too. The kingdom would split into factions again with each nobleman trying to seize power. Within a decade, war, plague, famine, death, and destruction would follow, and none of it meted out carefully by witches who actually cared, and he'd go down in history as the wicked witch whose incompetence destroyed the world.

He slapped the glass angrily. "Alistair! Answer me right now or I'm calling your father!"

A few wisps of darker gray swirled in the atmosphere. He caught a glint of white and blue, clouds and sky, and finally the burning sapphire of a dragon's eye.

"What do you want?" A low, grumpy growl came from the mirror.

"Where are you? You should be here by now."

"What if I've decided I'm not coming?" Alistair's sharp teeth snapped in the glass. "What will you do then?"

"Your father—"

The dragon's voice climbed in pitch. "My father can burn his behind. Let him destroy my sculptures. Let him kick me out. I don't care!"

Hector shook his finger in the mirror. "You listen to me, young reptile! You're the prince, and this is bigger than both of us. You don't have to believe Happily-Ever-After is the right thing, or want anything to do with ruling the dragons, but I'm asking you on behalf of your people and as a friend, think of somebody other than yourself for once!"

"You are a friend of my father's," Alistair hissed. "Not mine."

"I *am* your friend. I've known you since you were a hatchling, and I've watched you grow from a thin, scrawny dragonet to a fine young dragon. You will be Flamelord one day, and I know you remember our lessons on your duty. Your privilege."

"I remember," Alistair growled. "You tweaked my tail when I didn't answer your questions right."

"Answer me now," Hector said. "What is the first duty of the Flamelord?"

"I'm not coming!"

"First duty of the Flamelord!"

"We dragons have been used long enough!"

"Alistair!"

Hector seldom raised his voice, and he'd never done it with Alistair, not even when the young dragon blew insolent smoke rings at him during his school sessions. He didn't like to do it now. If Alistair wanted, he could lift up and fly the other direction, and probably take himself out of range. If Hector wanted, he could put a spell on Alistair to make that impossible. Probably. There was the question of range. From what Hector could see of the sky behind Alistair, it looked like he might still be in the mountains.

"The first duty of the Flamelord is to his people," Alistair recited with a huff of smoke, "to protect their interests, to safeguard their families, to uphold their traditions."

"That's correct. This is the oldest and grandest tradition

of your people. For millennia, dragons kidnapped princesses. Once, they did it for food. Now, it is the key to peace. You are young—you may know the history of dragons, but I was there for it all. I was there when Happily-Ever-After was created. I was there when princes killed dragons to preserve that magic. I held some of their hands while they died. And as one voice, they judged it a death worth dying, and do you know why?"

"Those times are past, Hector—"

"Why?" Hector demanded.

Alistair growled low in his throat. "For their participation, the king and his court promised to kill no dragons except those elected to embody evil during the Happily-Ever-After. Without this protection, we would soon have faced extinction—I know all that Hector, but that's not going to happen now!"

"No. It won't, because I won't let it happen, Alistair, and neither will you. You know as well as I do that the monsters aren't us—the monsters are *in* all of us. Only Happily-Ever-After keeps them in check. We have to do this—we must be the evil that holds the kingdom together. That's what it takes to preserve the peace, including the peace of dragons."

"When the peace of dragons depends on the abduction of a woman who is no more a willing participant in this charade than I am, it isn't worth the word, let alone the meaning of it!"

"The princess knows what is expected of her as much as you do—she is a willing participant. It's the law of the land."

"No person restrained by magic just because it's been the law for a thousand years is truly willing. I don't care if she grabbed the rose out of Ida's hand like I took mine out of the vase—I didn't want it, and I'm sure she didn't either! We were forced into it."

"Alistair, don't make me *really* force you."

The large blue eyes narrowed to angry slits. "You wouldn't."

Hector raised his staff, set the head of it against the mirror.

"Piss off." Alistair's voice sounded rough, raspy, angry.

"You promised. And if you don't keep your word, the weight of it will be with you for the rest of your life, and that will be far worse than if I compelled you to come."

"Then why don't you?" Alistair flapped his wings, disturbing the clouds, but his eye didn't move. He was stationary, wherever he was.

"I don't want you to hate me for the next hundred years," Hector said with a sigh. "But I'd rather you hate me than hate yourself. Don't endanger your people, Alistair."

"I am not endangering—oh, balls!" Alistair gave an angry, futile hiss, and the blue eye vanished, to be replaced by shining obsidian scales as he launched himself skyward.

Finally. Hector tucked the mirror in his robes.

"Did you get him?" Tinbit asked.

"He's coming," Hector said. "He'll be late, but fashionably so. Not a bad thing. It will allow the princess and prince more initial bonding time."

"How do you know he'll be late?" Tinbit asked.

"I saw clouds—he's in the mountains, most likely, probably a little west of here—"

Tinbit raised one eyebrow. "Are you sure it wasn't smoke?"

"No. Why?"

Tinbit pointed out the door of the stable. "Because the palace is on fire."

18

Ida

As the single most important magic of our history and critical to the well-being of our kingdom, only the oldest and most experienced witches on this Council will be trusted to manage the Happily-Ever-After: the arranged and magically binding marriage of a royal to a commoner, thus ensuring that the magic made so many centuries ago to save our world continues to function and preserve the peace.

Any failure to carry out these duties shall be deemed reason for immediate expulsion from the Council and the revoking of the immortality granted only to Cardinal Witches.

RULES AND REGULATIONS, COUNCIL OF
WITCHES, ROLE OF CARDINAL WITCHES

THE FUTURE QUEEN WAS IN HER PARLOR, BUT SHE wasn't eating bread and honey to judge by the noise. Ida slipped into the tent, admiring the way the enchantments had held up over the years. Meant to be a foretaste of the splendors awaiting a queen, the cloth walls shimmered and took on the appearance of a polished marble façade as Ida walked through. Curtains of blue and silver silk framed a fainting couch absolutely awash with dresses. A lady-in-waiting moved around the room, muttering angrily and picking up discarded garments and hairpieces.

"Where is Princess Amber?" Ida asked.

"Oh, Your Goodness!" the lady exclaimed. "I'm so glad you're here. Please, talk some sense into her ladyship. She simply will not wear the dress the queen chose and sent as a gift this morning!"

Ida's gaze fell on a revolting thing of pink flounces with purple petals. Annabeth hadn't exaggerated—it was hideous and probably infested with an itching hex. "I'll do what I can." She paced through pillars and into the parlor.

On a solid chair of oak and gold sat the princess, still wearing her blacksmith apron and leather trousers. However, it wasn't fair to say she hadn't dressed for the occasion. She'd donned a mail coat and was polishing a poleax with a whetstone.

"What in the name of magic are you doing?" Ida asked.

"Preparing to rescue myself," Amber said with a low grunt.

"Put the weapon down. You'll cut someone with it."

Amber squinted at Ida. "Well, you're the first person who hasn't said I'd cut *myself* with it. You may have selected me for this stupid stunt but if I kill the dragon, I've saved myself, and that's what I'm going to do. I don't care if it's against the rules. I'll destroy this blasted tradition before I marry any prince."

A chill ran down Ida's spine. Hector would kill her. No dragons had died in Happily-Ever-After in centuries. There had been some maiming, but nothing a dragon couldn't heal from.

"You're behaving like a child," she said, primly arranging herself on a chair out of Amber's swing range. "Try to act like a queen."

"I'm acting like a woman who is going to save herself," Amber retorted.

"At what price?" Ida asked.

"What do you mean?"

"This magic isn't a game, Amber. It's not some foolishness you can discard on a whim. You know that, deep down. Long ago, four witches in their wisdom realized that only by coming together could people find love and peace in their lives. And so they arranged for a royal prince to marry a common princess, so that never again would the leaders of the world be able to exploit the people the way they did, turning the world into a ruin. This 'tradition' saved the people—it gave us this world we live in now. It gave the commoners a voice."

"Some voice, when someone like Mildred can buy a crown," Amber said with a snort.

Or Annabeth, but Ida didn't budge. It was too important. "I'm not saying there aren't still problems. Magic can't fix everything. But when it can't, it's our own choices that fill in the gaps. You say you want to save yourself, and you're willing to kill for it. Now, is that bravery, or is it plain, old selfishness?"

"I am not being selfish." Amber rose, gripping her weapon. "I'm my father's only child. I plan to take over his blacksmith shop when he retires so I can provide for him. What happens to that if I become queen? What happens to him? It's been in our family for generations."

"You'll be the queen. You can build a house as big as a palace for your father, or he can live in the palace with you. Move the whole shop if you want and open it on the grounds. You can have anything."

"Do you honestly think the prince will let me take out my

feelings in a smithy? Carry a hammer instead of a handbag? Shoe my own horse?"

Ida hesitated. She couldn't see Archie understanding why anyone would want to do those things. But Happily-Ever-After would make him invested in his queen's happiness. And Amber would care about him and his happiness as well. She'd forget her dream of owning the smithy the moment Archie saved her from the dragon and gave her truelove's kiss. Happily-Ever-After made everyone happy. Look at Annabeth.

Well, perhaps not. Annabeth hadn't changed much. She'd been a conniving, irresponsible, mean girl, and now she was a conniving, irresponsible, mean queen. In many respects, King Rupert deserved her.

But Archie wasn't Rupert. He listened to people like Caedan. And if he listened to people like Amber, he might be the greatest king their world ever had.

"Have you considered how much influence you would have as queen? How much good you could do for your people? A queen is more than a figurehead. She is more than a consort to the king. Annabeth has influenced everything from the accessibility women have to magical enhancements to court fashion— not always wisely," she added, thinking of the pink monstrosity of a dress. "But she did it because she embraced her role and used it. When she and the king step down and you and Archie take the throne, all the power to do good for the world will be in your hands. *Your* world, Amber. Think about that."

"I don't want that power," Amber said. "I want to choose my own destiny."

"In this world we very seldom get that chance," Ida said. "But you can change the destiny of many people—including your father. I think he'd like you to make the most of your opportunity. After all, he's not here with you."

Amber's tough façade cracked slightly. "He had to work."

"He told you not to waste this chance, didn't he?"

Amber blinked, and the brown of her eyes became harder and sharper with a thin sheen of tears. "How…"

"Because the same thing happened to me." Ida crossed her legs and smoothed her robes out. "I was about your age when I had the opportunity to apprentice with the Good Witch of the North. I felt much like you do now. My stepmother was a common hedge witch, and that was my world. I didn't want any other. I saw myself living in my village for the rest of my life, mixing medicines, performing charms for the farmers, mending relationships with magic—all small things my stepmother taught me how to do. To take the position as the Good Witch's apprentice would close all those doors to me. If all went well, I'd be a Cardinal Witch. I would outlive everyone I knew—all my family, all my friends. I'd never fall in love, I'd never marry, I'd never have children. And I'll admit, I had second thoughts."

She shook her head slightly to disrupt the regrets before they settled in like an unexpected guest. "My father saw my indecision. So he took me aside and told me something that has stayed with me to this day. He said every person on this earth is like a stone thrown to make waves. Most of the time, people are little stones. The ripples they make only affect the pond around them. But some of us are big stones, meant to affect a whole ocean. What I did with my life would affect the world. He made that very clear to me in a way I'd not thought of before."

"But you had a choice in your destiny!" Amber said. "I didn't get one."

Ida raised her eyebrows. "Didn't you?"

Amber fell silent.

"You chose your destiny when you came to my castle to right a wrong. You didn't have to. You had no desire to be princess yourself. You came because you saw wrongdoing in the world and you wanted to correct it. I call that fine and honorable, and it's the truest measure of your worthiness for this role." Ida rose. "The magic chose you. Now it's time to find out if it was right—if you are the person who could make the biggest difference for the common people in an age of queens. Amber, will you be a little stone or a big one?"

Amber gazed unhappily at Ida, then at the tiara waiting for her on a blue velvet cushion. With a sigh, she jammed it on her head. "Fine. But I'm not wearing that dress."

Ida smiled. "I quite agree—that thing is awful. Go as you are, but perhaps you could leave the poleax behind—"

A blast of searing air tore through the tent with a roar. The crowd shrieked in terror; a sudden *whish* suggested that about half the stands had just gone up in flames.

A rumbling voice like the earth opened up, belching frothy hot rage. "Well? I'm here. Let's get this stupid farce over with so I can show you what a dragon really is!"

19

Hector

I consider it one of my most abject failures as a witch—I've utterly failed to impress upon the dragons the importance of a less combustible temper. On the whole, I find them an eminently reasonable folk, no more prone to impatience than any other people. In fact, they seem to excel at defusing arguments among themselves. But when a dragon loses their temper, the results are always explosive. Therefore, they can never be members of proper society.

I envy them. Proper society often enrages me.

A THOUSAND YEARS OF WICKEDNESS: A MEMOIR

HECTOR WEST

ALISTAIR HAD ALWAYS BEEN IMPRESSIVE, EVEN AS A skinny dragonet with immature wings and a mouthful of deciduous teeth. Today, he looked every inch the future Flamelord. Wreathed in fire, eyes flashing, scales shining, he stood in the middle of the field, rampant, claws extended, while the stands burned and people ran for their lives.

All but one. A knight in shining armor raced across the field, long hair streaming. It took Hector all of three seconds to realize the knight wasn't a knight. Nor was it the crown prince, who joined his own knights, hastily evacuating over the fence.

It was the princess.

She was tall for a woman and exceptionally built in the upper body. She wore a mail shirt over what appeared to be a farrier's apron and wielded a long poleax. "You can take yourself right off. I'm not going anywhere with you," she said, voice magically amplified as it would have been for the event. Everyone enjoyed a love confession after all. But this…this was so far from what should have happened, Hector felt paralyzed. He should put out the bleachers. Or at least summon a raven brigade to evacuate the injured. People might have been hurt when Alistair set them ablaze. But he could do nothing but watch in dazed embarrassment and horror at the melee unfolding in front of his eyes.

Alistair bit the poleax, yanking it out of her hand. He tossed it aside. "I'm not taking you anywhere. I came to make a statement. Now get out of my way."

Hector gripped his staff until his knuckles blanched. Once the magic had been set in motion, trying to exert control in the middle of it could be disastrous. But he'd never seen a Happily-Ever-After go this wrong. Not only had Alistair behaved far worse than expected, something was dreadfully wrong with this princess. She should've run like all the rest. Instead, there she was, staring down an angry dragon with all the poise of an ancient knight, and she looked like one too as she yanked twin daggers from beneath her leather apron.

"If you think you can scare me by blowing smoke, you're wrong. So you'd just better keep your forked tongue behind your teeth, and get ready. I *didn't* come here to make a statement. I came to fight!"

Hector caught a glimpse of white as Ida stormed out of the tent, wand raised.

"Who are you?" Alistair said.

"Amber Smith, and you're a dead worm."

Alistair hissed and backed up. Hector raised his staff, ready to throw a shield between Alistair and the princess if worse came to worst, but Alistair's form had already begun to shift.

No, no, no, no—Alistair! But there wasn't a thing Hector could do about it. Alistair's scales retracted inward, his wings folded against his back, the long snout changed, flattened, and he stood, a man—a completely naked man, wearing only the last vestige of flames about his penis, smoke trailing over his shoulders along with a river of black hair. He opened his arms, exposing his chest to the princess, along with everything else. "Well?" he said. "Get on with it. Weren't you going to kill me? Go on. Show everyone here who the monsters really are."

The princess gaped.

Thankfully, the stands were empty now. The only people left to see were the witches and two startled gnomes hiding beneath the bunting. Tinbit and Hari peeped out from between the folds of fabric, bright eyes glowing.

"You—you—are—you're not a…you're a—" Amber stepped back, dropping her knives and spluttering.

"A dragon," Alistair said. "This is what I am. What we are."

"Alistair!" Hector raised his staff. He had to stop this now, whatever the consequences.

Across the field, Ida raised her wand.

At the last second Alistair turned, lunging toward Hector. His spell hit the princess right in the chest.

"Oh!" She tumbled backward.

Ida's spell caught Alistair in the shoulder.

"Shit!" His voice sounded high-pitched, frighteningly human. He doubled over in pain.

Ten knights charged onto the field from the corner where they'd gone over the fence. But they weren't wearing the ceremonial togs normally donned for the festivities. Led by Caedan, they wore traditional armor. A few sweaty and panicked pages backed away from the fence, carrying everything from feathered helmets to decorative lances. In the middle of the group charged Prince Archie, similarly attired, except for the visor and helmet. He carried a large, less-than-ceremonial sword, the enchanted sword his father had used when he'd gone on his quest to save Annabeth. Hector prepared for the worst—a stab to Alistair's gut and then a decapitation. He'd never be able to face the Flamelord again.

The princess jumped in front of Alistair and took up a fighting stance. "Run! Or fly! Or whatever it is you do!"

Alistair shook his wings out, desperately trying to regain his form, but it took dragons longer to change from human to reptile than it did the other way around.

"Will you get going?"

"What about you?" Alistair bared his dragon fangs at the oncoming knights and cast about for the amputated poleax.

"Don't worry about me. It's you they want to kill. Get out of here!"

"Wrong!" Alistair shook the last of his form free and rose into the air. "They'll kill you too. It'll just take longer." With a blast of flame in the direction of the knights, he grabbed the princess in his claws and took off. In a short time, her screams faded into the distance, and Alistair became a black spot against a wall of clouds, darkening the blue sky as they rolled in.

The prince panted up. "That was something else! I have to hand it to you witches, you really outdid yourself this year."

Caedan stared after the disappearing spot on the horizon. "I've never seen anything like it. Was he—was that really a dragon?"

"Illusion," Hector muttered. Amber's screams echoed in his ears, but not as loudly as Alistair's words. *They'll kill you too. It'll just take longer.* What on earth had Ida hit him with? It sounded almost like an empathy spell—something intended to give a person deep, abiding insight into someone's soul.

Thunder rolled. Lightning flickered in the distance.

Ida, red hair falling into her eyes, glared at him, but she looked as worried as she was angry. She was probably thinking the same thing he was. What happens when a Good Witch's spell hits a dragon? And what happens when a Wicked Witch's spell hits a princess? Nothing good, that was certain.

"What did you do?" she hissed when the prince moved off to congratulate his knights, clapping them all on the backs. "Why did your dragon take human form? They're not supposed to do that."

"Who gave the princess a weapon? She wasn't supposed to fight! What game are you playing here?"

"I didn't give her a weapon. Anyway, your dragon set the whole place on fire. They're not supposed to do that either, and she was only trying to defend herself—"

"There's no reason for her to even want to do that! Dragons never harm the princesses!"

Lightning cracked the sky, and the roar of the thunder shook the ground. Rain began to pelt Hector in the face, great, heavy drops, plunking down like hailstones. A blast of wind as freezing as snowfall enveloped him in an icy embrace, whipping his robes around like smoke. Ida's too.

She wrapped her arms around herself. "Oh, for Gods' sakes, what are you trying to prove, Hector? Turn it off."

"You think I did—" He glanced at the clouds roiling overhead, suddenly horrified. It was his province—storms and other natural disasters, to be distributed fairly and equitably over the kingdom—but this was nothing he'd done. Something was very wrong here. He glanced at Ida, into her violet eyes, shimmering with fury. She couldn't know. She'd roast him if she knew he was responsible for Alistair's interference with her magic. It was his job to keep his monsters in line after all.

He drew himself up, as tall and regal as he could make himself given that sleet was freckling his clothes and the wind had turned his hair into a badly disheveled eagle's nest. "I had to do something," he said in lofty tones. "You've turned this whole thing into some kind of publicity stunt for yourself after all."

"What?"

"First the Prince's Dinner and now the Happily-Ever-After itself—if this is another one of your 'let's let the people participate' schemes, I can assure you, I won't be supporting it!"

Ida gaped. "Of all the—your dragon burned down the stadium and you say I'm the one who made this into a publicity stunt?"

"He didn't burn down the stadium!" He glanced at the ruin. "Only…part of it."

"Now the whole kingdom is going to think dragons are out there walking around like ordinary people, setting things on fire whenever they feel like it. Good job, Hector. How do you plan to hush that up?"

He drew himself up even further, cloaking his fear in indifference. "An illusion. My work to create confusion by which the dragon takes the princess captive, meant to terrify her."

"That was not the look of a woman terrified."

"What was it the look of?" Hector snapped back. "Love? I can't believe that even *you* could mess up that badly."

"Fuck you." Ida thrust her middle finger up in his face and stomped off.

Hector slammed his staff down on the ground and stomped off in the opposite direction. Curses tumbled through his mind unadjusted. Damn Ida. Damn himself. Damn dragons and damsels, witches and princes, and damn Happily-Ever-After. He had to get this straightened out before anyone discovered he'd mismanaged his end of things.

Alistair might be in great danger. So might the princess. The kingdom certainly was. Something had gone dreadfully wrong with Happily-Ever-After.

The clouds opened up, and torrents poured down.

 **20** 

Ida

DRAGON KIDNAPS PRINCESS: PRINCE TO ATTEND ROYAL BALL WITH CAPTAIN OF THE GUARD

The long-awaited Happily-Ever-After for Prince Archie and the Common Princess got off to a flaming start when the dragon arrived late to the ceremony and set the palace on fire. Damage is estimated at several hundred thousand gold pieces, including damage to an enchanted spinning wheel and three hundred bales of straw waiting to be spun into gold. No word yet on whether the royal treasurer escaped. Is the straw standard doomed? Details on page eight!

Witnesses say the dragon assumed a human shape and the princess herself seemed captivated by the tall, incredibly sexy man who appeared naked in the field to the astonishment of all. Could we be looking at the first lover's triangle in Happily-Ever-After history? Or is this more evidence of a snafu caused by the missteps of Witches Hector West and Ida North, who may be going senile in their great age? Are heads about to roll? This paper says yes!

—*THE SORCERER'S STAR*

IDA COLLECTED HERSELF ALONE IN THE TENT WHILE buckets of water sluiced down from what had been crystal clear skies. She shouldn't have interfered. Only the complete desperation of knowing the princess might hurt the dragon—*really, Hector, could you at least pick a dragon without a sensitive side as long as his tail*—had made her step in. What had Hector used on the girl? It looked like a compulsion of some kind, no doubt designed to make the dragon carry out his side of the magic without hesitation. It must have been a powerful one to make the princess decide to take on a whole group of charging knights to save a dragon.

She rubbed her temples in agitation. Hector's words jangled in her ears. Just how badly *had* she messed this up? Could it be related to how she'd picked the princess? Her head was spinning with questions, and none of them had answers. At least no answers she wanted to believe.

"Ida?"

She flinched, then relaxed as Hari slid in through the tent flap, wringing out his sleeves. "Yes?"

"The coach is waiting. Hector and Tinbit have left. So have the other witches. The stadium looks like a complete loss, but the fire's out at the castle, thanks to the rain—no serious damage there, the steward says. The dragon lit the north tower on fire, the one with all the spinning wheels, but they say the royal treasurer got out in time."

She rose, trying to pull herself together. "Good. Where is Prince Archibald? Has he left in pursuit of the dragon yet?"

Hari hesitated. "Uh…no."

"He hasn't?" Ida yelped.

"He said he'd start out tomorrow," Hari said. "He had an

issue with his armor he wanted to get hammered out. He went off with the captain of the guard to fix it."

Not good. A prince under the influence of Happily-Ever-After should be horsed and on his way before the dragon was a distant dot in the sky. He might not go far, horseback riding being out of favor with many modern men of leisure, and he'd find himself a comfortable inn where he'd spend the night instead of camping under the stars in this rain, but he would go. The potion would ensure he did.

Amber might be in great danger. So might the dragon. The kingdom certainly was. Something had gone dreadfully wrong with Happily-Ever-After.

"Very well. I'm ready to go." She conjured an umbrella and walked out into the rain. She had to get this fixed before more than the weather went wrong.

The Hall of Witches had changed a great deal over the centuries, but entering always made Ida think back to the first time she'd seen it, when she'd been apprenticed to the old, and very good, Good Witch of the North. Filling those shoes had been the hardest task of her life. She felt like she was tripping over them now as she walked through the ancient wooden pillars, relics of the oldest days, and into the inner sanctum. Hari waited in the coach. No non-witches were allowed inside, with the exception of the elementals, the guardians of magic.

They had no gender, and indeed seldom took physical form of any kind, only wearing a shape when necessary to service the Hall and attend to the Cardinal Witches. Ida passed an undine dripping water on the floor, mopping as they went. They bowed deeply to her, and went on cleaning the dark slate floor and silver grout. The undine's skin shifted colors as they mopped—blue, green, and yellow—mirroring the ocean perhaps, or a clear pool in a mountain grotto.

When Ida entered the Council's chamber, the room was still largely dark and rain drummed heavily on the roof. The royal blue curtains were tightly drawn, and the lamps had not been lit, but a salamander, bright orange eyes aglow, was lighting a fire to burn until the meeting concluded, and no longer.

"Your Goodness." This elemental also bowed and went on with their work.

Ida took her seat at the table, the northern end, and watched the salamander feeding the flames with a few flakes of birch and cedar, coaxing the fire like a nervous animal from the hearth.

"Can I get you anything, Your Goodness?" the salamander asked, flame flickering around their mouth and nose. "A hot drink? A pastry?"

Ida's stomach rolled. "Tea," she decided. "Hot herb tea with a lavender tea cake, and this morning's copy of the *Kingdom Wall*. No, the *Sorcerer's Star*."

The salamander, to their credit, didn't ask why she'd asked for the city's most infamous rag. In a quick puff of brimstone and smoke, they vanished.

For all their heat, salamanders were the calmest of the elementals, the least emotional. Perhaps that was why the Wicked Witch of the West was represented by them. If so, what did a sylph say about her? Was she flighty, prone to temper, to changing her mind, to adapting to each situation as mutably as the wind? She wouldn't have said so a day ago, but thinking over things now...

A sudden guttering announced the salamander's return. They set the tea and cake at her elbow and the paper in front of her.

Ida split the ribbon with her finger and unrolled the paper on the table. She skimmed the article. The only good news: the true nature of the dragons remained a secret. The tabloid made mention of a snafu. At least they hadn't gone further. The paper had a reputation of jumping to conclusions faster than a pair of seven-league boots. She'd half expected to see the headline:

TOP CARDINAL WITCHES BOTCH PRINCESS ABDUCTION! HAPPILY-EVER-AFTER IS DEAD! WORLD ENDING SOON! SEE YOUR DOOMSDAY HOROSCOPE ON PAGE SEVEN!

The terrifying thing was that for once in its long history of wildly inaccurate reporting, the Star actually might have stumbled on the truth. If Happily-Ever-After had gone wrong, the world really might end.

It would be like shattering a magic mirror, although this would bring far more than seven years of bad luck. More like seven centuries. Happily-Ever-After was potent stuff. If it escaped from the confines of the spell, her vivomancy would spread through the land unregulated. Crops would ripen at the wrong time. Children would be born, but there would be nothing to feed them. Whole families might go to war over love matches that should never have happened. And what about Hector's side of things? She shuddered. That didn't bear thinking about.

A sudden gust of wind, and a slender sylph in blue opened the door and held it open. "Your Wickedness."

Hector stepped into the room. He looked even more tired than he had that morning and also soaked. She noted the deep, black circles under his eyes, the stringy, greasy cast to his long salt-and-pepper hair, and the way his mouth tightened when he saw her. If he weren't such a complete asshole, she'd almost have thought he looked as scared as she felt.

"Anything I can get for Your Wickedness? A drink? Something to eat?" the sylph asked.

"Just tea," Hector said in a heavy, gravelly voice. "Nothing to eat. Later, perhaps." He carried his staff, the first time she'd seen him take it into a meeting, like he expected trouble. He sat in the chair nearest the fire, lowering himself like every muscle hurt.

"We need to talk," Ida said in frosty tones.

"We do," he replied. "But not here."

"No. We're going to do this right now, before you blame this whole thing on me. If you so much as insinuate that I picked the wrong princess, I'm going to tell the Council that you sent me a candor curse. What's more, I'm going to the *Star* with it. Is that clear?"

He folded his hands on the table in front of him. "That's supposed to scare me?"

"It should. Agatha would love to take your place."

"And curse you so she can take leadership of the Council. I suggest you remember that. The last person who crossed her ended up a rather hairy creature confined to a drafty castle with only a bunch of furniture to take care of him."

"That's supposed to scare me?"

His stare would have turned a Medusa to stone. "It should. Forever is a long time to have fleas. And while we're on the subject of threats, if you even mention that candor curse, I'll have something to say about laughing charms and just how little regard you have for the magic you've been entrusted to protect."

"You think I haven't spent every waking minute of my eternity protecting and preserving Happily-Ever-After? You've no idea of how hard I work. All you ever have to do is manage the monsters." She huffed. "You've got all this time on your hands to come up with diabolical plots—like picking a dragon to act the fool and burn up the stadium."

"I did not—"

"And setting your gnome to seduce mine because you knew it would humiliate him and hurt me."

Hector's face flamed. "I never—"

"You did it to get back at me for my laughing spell. Burned your balls, did it?"

He sat back in his chair, arms over his chest. "Oh, for the love of magic! I wouldn't be so petty. That's more your thing— putting love potions in the ink so poor Tinbit would fall in love with someone he'd never met! Don't think I don't know one of your schemes when I see it—"

Her cheeks grew hot. "I did nothing of the sort! I'm a good witch—I don't go around trying to break people's hearts!"

He leaned forward, fist balled as he set his elbow on the table. "That's rich, you talking of hearts when you've never had one."

"Nor did you," she snapped back. "You've never cared about anything or anyone in your entire life."

"I care about Tinbit." His teeth were bared, his eyes sparked with fury. "I would never, ever, in any way, do anything that would hurt him. I set a rather high value on hearts, particularly the hearts of people under my protection. Like Tinbit. Like Alistair."

"I care about the hearts of the people I love as much as you do. Hari is like my son, and the very idea that I would do anything that might cause him pain is unthinkable."

Hector's eyes glinted. "I don't believe you."

"I don't believe you either." But she almost could. There was a sincerity in his hard, angry face, almost as if he really did care about his gnome and the dragon. Alistair. So that *was* the dragon's name. She never bothered to learn them. They weren't part of her side of the magic.

A sudden smell of earth and moss accompanied a small earth elemental, beetle-black eyes glinting, who entered the room with a soft brown velvet cushion, which they placed in the chair to the left of Hector.

Tara came in, smiling in her butter yellow robes. She smiled as she seated herself across from Ida. "Are you well, my dear? Such a fright today with the dragon. I wonder that you had the courage to face it!"

Oh, that was a slight if ever she'd heard one. "One does what one must. I am not afraid of dragons or any serpent." Ida sat back in her chair. Tara hated snakes. Let her chew on the insult instead of the strawberry Danish with rose water cream the earth elemental set in front of her.

A blast of humidity signaled Agatha's entrance. She waved the undine, the one with the mop, away with an impatient hand, and sat, digging her sharp nails like talons in the end of the table. "Sorry to be late. I was delayed. Reporters for the *Star*, you know."

Hector grimaced. "I really think, given the delicacy of the situation, none of us should be talking to reporters right now."

Agatha smiled, showing all her teeth. "Oh, I don't know about that Hector. People will want answers. Something seems to have gone wrong with Happily-Ever-After, and just between us, if what I'm hearing is accurate, if it isn't fixed, a couple of witches might as well turn over the keys to their castles and start looking for huts in the woods in which they can spend their retirement."

21

Hector

When one has been a Wicked Witch for most of one's life, one acquires many important skills. One also learns to refer to one's self in an oddly unnatural way, to monologue when necessary, to never seal one's power in things like magical rings, or if one must, never live close to an active volcano where heroes are itching to throw your magical doodad in the lava, and a million other things to keep one's self alive and largely intact. These are all excellent things to know.

Unfortunately, handling a whole council of squabbling witches isn't taught as part of any curriculum, and has turned out to be about as rewarding as asking the mermaids to stop eating sailors.

A THOUSAND YEARS OF WICKEDNESS: A MEMOIR

HECTOR WEST

PERSONALLY, HE'D LIKE SOME ANSWERS TOO. THE immediate problem—his protection spell had struck a princess right in the heart—he could explain, even if he was reluctant to do so. Not that the thing was exactly illegal, but the fact that he'd had to use it at all was certainly suspect, and it would lead to more questions he didn't want to discuss. Like why the dragon had needed convincing in the first place.

What he'd wanted to do was give Alistair a strong desire to take the princess in his claws and carry her off to his lair where he would guard her until the prince arrived to rescue her. When it hit the girl, it gave her a frantic desire to protect Alistair, the effect of Hector's dark magic on a good and valiant heart. Which meant—and this was a particularly irritating admission—Ida had picked one gem of a woman to be the Common Princess. And if nothing was wrong with the princess, he couldn't blame Ida at all, which was even more irritating, and deeply concerning because he couldn't, for the life of him, confess that *he'd* made a mistake. He'd been in charge of Happily-Ever-After forever—he couldn't make mistakes.

He faced Agatha, deliberately disguising his weariness as boredom and said what he'd been rehearsing during the coach ride to the Council Hall. "You're quick to demand solutions for a problem you don't understand, Agatha."

"Then you admit something is wrong with this Happily-Ever-After." Agatha crowed like she'd scored a point.

"That's patently obvious to anyone with magical sensibility," he said, reaching for the dark cup of smoke-flavored tea the salamander set before him.

"Then what went wrong?" Tara asked with genuine curiosity, like she'd never once considered that magic *could* go wrong. In Hector's opinion, she was by far the weakest of all of them— far too many of her spells involved cooking and nothing else. She didn't take real risks.

"I'm not sure," he said. "Yet."

"Well, whatever happened, we will fix it," Ida said, leaning forward. "Repairing Happily-Ever-After is not a matter of saving our reputations. This is about saving the world."

Agatha struck faster than an injured griffin. "And I suppose you aren't claiming any of the blame? Your princess charged the field like a knight, not a maiden. Just who is this girl?"

Ida flushed an angry shade of mauve. "A *princess*. And I absolutely take full responsibility for her behavior, which I personally found quite understandable under the circumstances. But this is not the time to be deciding who is to blame. Hector is right. No one needs to be encouraging the *Star* in their speculation—they'll do that on their own without our help."

Ida was actually agreeing with him? Had she struck him, he couldn't have been more surprised. But almost as soon as he felt gratitude, he squashed it flat. Of course, she was. She was reminding him of exactly what she'd do if he so much as mentioned the laughing charm.

"Ida is right," he said, gazing at her pointedly. "When the magic is corrected and the princess wed to her prince, we'll see who assumes full responsibility. First, we need to seek out the princess and the dragon and bring them here to untangle the magic. I will go in search of them both. The Dread Mountains are my domain."

"Not by yourself, you're not. I'm going too," Ida broke in. "I don't trust a Wicked Witch to be versed in how to alter my magic."

"I can handle your good magic," Hector said, nettled.

"You couldn't even handle your own dragon today," she retorted.

Hector's reserve, always so easy for him to maintain in public, felt as loose as his stomach right now. "But he is *my* dragon. I see no reason for you to come," he said.

"She's *my* princess. I'm coming."

Was she insinuating she would take responsibility with him? He felt like he'd stepped out of reality and into a whole new fantasy world. "Very well," he said, now completely wrong-footed. "Can you be ready to leave this afternoon?"

"We can leave now. My carriage is waiting outside. I'll transfer my belongings and send the coachman and my…manservant, home."

"This is all very responsible of you; almost chummy," Agatha said with a sneer. "One would think that both of you have something to hide. One might think you've joined forces to cover up your mistakes rather than fix them. One does find this very interesting, and others might also find it…interesting."

"You do know that talking about yourself like that went out of style about five hundred years ago," Ida scoffed.

"Agatha's right, though," Tara said. "I, for one, want another observer along. But someone…more unbiased." She shot a suspicious glance at Agatha. "Perhaps, I should go."

"Out of the question." Hector shook his head. "I can't guarantee anyone's safety, especially that of a good witch. We're talking dragons here."

"I can take care of myself," Ida said icily.

Agatha glanced at the salamander, standing respectfully near the fireplace. "What is your name?"

Fire-bright eyes contracted down to narrow black coals. "I'm Cear, Your Wickedness."

"Can you travel, Cear?"

"Yes, Your Wickedness. If I must leave the hearth, I travel in a flame."

"You'll accompany them. A salamander can't be burned by

a dragon. They don't need protecting. And they always tell the truth. Hector will prepare a flame jar for you to travel in," Agatha said.

Hector eyed the salamander. It had been a very long time since he'd spent any length of time with an elemental guardian of magic. In Council, they kept largely to themselves, only attending their respective Witch and maintaining the hall before disappearing back into their meditative existence. But he knew they were as long-lived as any Cardinal Witch. This one might even have been the entity staring him down at the dawn of Happily-Ever-After. Carrying them around in a can seemed demeaning. He could practically see the blue flames of anger lighting in the salamander's orange-and-red body. "Only if they wish to go. I wouldn't presume to order an elemental to do anything," he added, shooting a warning look at Agatha.

"I will prepare the jar," Ida said. "I can make it as large as a fireplace on the inside. I've done things like this before."

"Not for elementals surely," Hector said.

Ida's jaw tightened. "For dryads. Before the forests were protected, I helped them transplant saplings from areas being developed for farmland. I used magical pots. They needed to be transported with their soil linked from one place to another to keep them from reverting into screaming babies. Cear, I would be honored if you would help me prepare the firepot. I'd like to make sure it is exactly what you need." She bowed to the salamander.

Cear's fathomless eyes softened. "I will, but only if his Wickedness assists. Your magic feels odd," they said, reaching out a hand to touch Ida's collarbone. "Almost as if something, or someone, has broken it."

"I'm sure I don't know what you mean," Ida said, flushing purple.

"I have felt such things before," they said, withdrawing their hand, "when the land was broken and magic with it." They glanced at Hector. "It was long ago, but his Wickedness remembers. He was there."

"I'll fix it," Hector said firmly.

Agatha's face became a glow of happy accusation, and Tara smirked. Hector had never wanted to curse so much in his life.

 **22**

 **Ida**

My dear Malia,

I'm not coming home as anticipated. Matters have arisen that I need to attend to. I expect to be delayed for at least a week, possibly longer. I'll say no more here. I'm sure you've seen the news.

I'm sending Hari home. I'll be giving him additional responsibilities at the castle that should keep him busy, but please, please, please be gentle with him.

IDA

P.S. I know your maternal instinct will be to ask him all about his trip, but I'm begging you, don't. He'll tell you when he's ready.

HARI YELLED AT HER WHEN SHE TOLD HIM TO GO BACK to her castle. She'd never seen him so incensed, not even when the chickens got out and tore up every last one of the newly planted pumpkin seedlings.

"What do you mean I'm not coming with you? Of course, I'm coming. I'm not leaving you to deal with Hector on your own."

"I can handle him. I've always been able to handle him. I want you to manage things at home for me, particularly the garden—"

"That's all I am to you? Your servant?" His face flamed.

"Sweetheart, you misunderstand me," she said. "I'm promoting you. I want you to be my steward."

But Hari looked angrier than before. "Fine," he snapped. "As your steward, I say someone from your estate needs to come with you to take care of things like hotel expenses, and to see that you actually eat a decent meal. Left to your own devices, you'll forget to sleep, work all the time, and not eat, and you know it."

"Hari."

His jaw jutted out stubbornly. "You'll have to order me to go home."

"Hari, go home."

He gaped. His eyes widened. He'd not expected her to do it.

Ida turned away from him, empty chest aching. "I'm ready," she said and walked around to the far side of the coach where she couldn't see Hari's stricken face.

The rain had slackened to a drizzle by the time Ida carried Cear's firepot to Hector's coach. The skeletal horses glanced curiously at her through burning eye sockets. The red glow followed her as she passed.

Hector waited beside his coach, leaning heavily on his staff. He'd not spoken to her after the meeting, only helped her with the firepot, then walked out to alert his coachman to the change of baggage.

Cear looked impassively at the bone horses. "I won't ride among the luggage," they said.

"Of course not, you're riding in the coach with us," Hector said. "And we will feed you fuel as you need it."

"I prefer to sit with Ida."

"As you wish," Hector said.

Tinbit glanced down at Ida from his seat by the coachman, a mushroom-like hat pulled down almost to his shoulders against the weather. Like Hari, he stood about two feet tall and had sharply pointed ears and a nose to match, but his expression tended toward the sour rather than sweet, like Hari's. She watched her carriage pull away slowly, with Hari slouched next to the driver. It rounded the curve in the street and vanished out of sight.

She turned to face Hector sitting across from her. "I sincerely hope you don't expect me to make polite conversation."

"I didn't think you could be polite if you tried."

"Glad we have an understanding."

"In fact, I'd like it better if we didn't talk at all." Hector closed his eyes and leaned against the wall of the coach. In seconds, he was snoring.

The salamander…well, did whatever salamanders did when they rested. Burned. Smoldered. Glowed like a deep blue gem in the depths of the firepot. Ida watched them at first, and then decided it was like watching another person sleep, and while Hector had practically invited her to watch him saw logs, the salamander had not. Ida placed the urn slightly off to one side where she would not be tempted to look into the flame and wonder if the bright changes of color and intensity were dreams and gazed out the foggy window.

She'd not been this way in recent history. She'd traveled it once about six hundred years ago, when consulting with a dryad queen in one of Hector's forests as part of a National Forest Protection Act. It saddened her to see so much of the countryside tamed. Well-ordered farms dotted the landscape between greenbelts, and here and there, a baron's castle jutted up from a knoll. After miles and miles of the same scenery, she wished she'd thought to pack a few more books.

Hours later, Hector finally jerked awake when the coach hit a pothole. He'd drooled on himself, Ida noted with disgust. He wiped his beard in a self-conscious way, smacked his lips together, and stared out the window at the gray rain falling over the fields, green with early grain. How long they would stay that way was anyone's guess. Rain today—it might be snow and hail tomorrow.

"How far is it to the mountains?" Ida asked.

He stretched and his joints popped audibly. "Two days' journey to my castle if the roads are good and the horses fresh, and a day by giant to the dragons."

"Good. The sooner this is done, the happier I will be."

"I assure you, the feeling is completely mutual—but we may not get as far today as I'd like. It's not wise to push a magical repair on the first day. We'll have to camp somewhere tonight for the sake of the horse."

"Camp?"

"You can sleep in the coach." Hector's eyes glinted. "I will sleep outside."

"Then we'd best stop in a forest—there aren't enough trees here for you to hang from, you old bat."

"I think we'll stop in the Mire-Imp Swamp. I'm pretty sure you have relatives there."

Motion outside caught Ida's attention. She moved closer to Hector to get a better look. "What is that?" she asked first, then gasped. "What are they?"

Gruesome apparitions danced through the fog. They looked something like giant dolls, with bodies made of fabric stuffed with straw that poked out around collars and cuffs. Stick arms and legs protruded at awkward angles, and last autumn's rotting pumpkins served as heads. They galumphed happily in a ditch below a blackberry hedge where a farmer and his wife appeared to be herding them out of the damp.

Hector leaned back against the seat. "Scarecrows. The crows here are frightened more of magic than monsters, so I animated them to make them more effective."

"Are they—are they alive?"

"Not in the strictest sense of the word," Hector said. "Why do you ask?"

Ida's mouth twisted. There was something about the creatures that seemed different from a typical golem: Maybe it was the light in their carved eyes, the way their mouths moved, or the way one of them cavorted closely with its companion, linking arms before crashing with it into the blackberry hedge, ripping off its plaid shirt. The farmer's wife yelled and beat the scarecrows angrily with her broom while the farmer tried to pry them apart with a pitchfork.

"Uh—Hector?" Ida's face burned, but she couldn't turn away from the spectacle.

Hector's jaw dropped.

"If they aren't alive—then why are they—"

Hector coughed, blinking as he turned away from her, face as red as a ripe plum. "They are capable of reproducing; it saves time and magic."

The coach slowed and after a minute, two other scarecrows appeared, naked, trailing hay, bouncing off into the mist.

Hector's mouth firmed. "This definitely shouldn't be happening. The pumpkins are just now flowering. They'll have no proper heads for their children and have to settle for turnips."

Ida sat back in her seat, a profound sense of doom settling in her midsection. "They don't usually breed at this time of the year?"

"No, and not so…publicly. They prefer the fields." He sat back in his seat too, face grim and concerned.

Ida didn't look out the window again.

Like the rain, this was part of Happily-Ever-After breaking down—the reversion of carefully choreographed seasons back to their natural rhythm, and like the weather they would be erratic. Long ago, the world had been like this. She remembered all too clearly how the Northern winters could be long and the summers too short for enough food to be grown. There had been nights her belly growled itself to sleep. If Happily-Ever-After broke down altogether…but she wouldn't let herself entertain that possibility. It wouldn't. She'd fix it.

After miles and miles of farmland, Ida was glad when the country took on a wilder look. Wasteland took over; the farms disappeared altogether. When the landscape changed to purple-green bushes and gray grass, broken by glassy mirrors of standing water, the coach stopped.

"We'll camp here," Hector said, standing slowly with a series of musical pops and groans. He lurched to the door, reminding Ida horribly of the scarecrows.

The chill air carried a sulfurous taint of rotting cattails and reeds.

"Be careful," Hector said as he stepped down. "Stick to the hummocks if you need to…relieve yourself. There's mire about."

Oh, joy. Just what she most loved about camping, the chance to get your bare butt bit whenever you needed to take a pee. She climbed down, hoping against hope there was a sweater in her luggage. Hari was usually so good to think of things like that, but he'd been so distressed. Dear Hari. Hopefully he was home by now.

"Smoke and fire!" Hector yelled.

Ida grabbed her wand and ran to the back of the coach.

A very dirty, very muddy, very tired gnome crawled in the roadway. Tinbit bent over him, touching him—

"Hari!" Ida pulled him into her arms.

Hari coughed out mud as green as frogs. "Told you, you're not going anywhere without me," he said. Then he fainted.

"Hari!"

"I'm going to get a fire started," Tinbit said. "We need to warm him up. He'll catch swamp fever if we don't." He ran off, yelling something at the skeleton driver in a language that sounded like fingerbones rattling together.

"What's happened?" The salamander crawled out of their jar in the form of a burning lizard when Ida shook the pot. "Why have we stopped?"

"Hari was on the back of the coach and he's chilled through." She pulled off her robe and tucked it around Hari.

The salamander scurried over the robe, leaving little singe marks where their feet touched the pristine white wool. "I will warm him," they said. "But he is already warm inside."

"You mean he's running a fever?" She felt Hari's forehead.

As the salamander said, he was burning up. "Oh, Hari. Why? Sweetheart, why?" She patted his limp hands, feeling helpless.

The coach door opened again, and in came Tinbit with a brown bowl filled with something hot and steaming. He held it with the pinkest, softest-looking oven mitts—they looked hand-made. He sat down beside Hari and gently slid one of the oven mitts off and put it under Hari's head.

"What's in the bowl?" Ida asked. "It looks like clam chowder. Hari's allergic to fish."

"I know. He told me," Tinbit said, shooting her an angry glare. "This is mock clam chowder. I make it with potatoes, veg-etable broth, and kelp." He touched Hari's cheek tenderly. "Hari? Hari, come on. Wake up."

Like a narcoleptic princess being revived with a kiss, Hari opened his eyes. "Where am I?"

Ida leaned over him. "In Hector's coach, you foolish, foolish boy."

"You should never have left without me." He glanced wea-rily at her. "Go put something on. You don't want his Wickedly Witchness seeing you in your underwear."

"I told you not to come after me." Tinbit shoveled up a gen-erous spoonful of soup. "You didn't tell me you never listen. That wasn't in any of your letters."

Hari halfway smiled. "I left some stuff out."

"You left a lot of stuff out," Tinbit growled. "Like your employer is a good witch. The Good Witch!"

"Well, you didn't tell me about Hector, the wicked old coot." Hari struggled to rise, but Tinbit pushed him back down into a sitting position. "How's that for leaving stuff out?"

"Shut up and eat."

Hari opened his mouth to argue again and got a spoonful of chowder.

"You might want to eat while it's hot, Your Goodness," Tinbit said. "I brought some dry sweetgrass for you," he told the salamander.

They blinked at him with golden eyes. "My favorite. How did you know?"

"Hector thought you'd like it and had it summoned. He's a wonderful witch." This last, Tinbit addressed pointedly to Hari.

Hari choked on his soup. "Did I say he wasn't?"

"You called him a wicked old coot!"

Ida walked out to get dressed, leaving the two gnomes jawing while the salamander looked on impassively, burning sweetgrass blades one at a time and glowing brighter with each leaf.

She found Hector beside the campfire on the side of the road. The skeleton had unbuckled the horses. One of them was limping rather badly. Its front leg shone with silver.

"Will it be all right?" she asked, pulling her sweater over her head.

Hector looked up from stirring the cauldron. "Yes, I've reinforced the bone meld. But when I get home, I'll need to find him a new leg in the boneyard."

"Hari's awake. He's eating."

"Good," Hector said. He ladled out a bowl of the soup and gave it to her. "This isn't my favorite soup. But I know better than to say that to Tinbit."

"He does seem somewhat prickly."

"Well, he works for me," Hector said. "I am sorry about your gnome. If I'd known he was back there—"

"I never should have told him to go home. He's very attached to me. And I to him."

"I can tell." Hector spooned up his soup and carefully blew on it to cool it.

"What's that supposed to mean?" she asked, blowing on her own bowl.

Hector blinked. "You're overprotective of him. Of course, you believe I had a hand in Tinbit's letters—"

"Of course, you had a hand in it. You knew it would hurt him, hurt me—"

"My dear Ida," Hector said with a long, irritated sigh, "if we are to work well together, you must believe me when I say I had nothing to do with it. Did I discourage Tinbit from using a dating service? Yes. I don't trust those things. Was I worried he might find misery instead of bliss? Yes. I care about him. I've known him since he was a gnomelet. Did I attempt to stop him? No. I know better than to order a gnome to do anything he doesn't want to do. You'd have more success moving a mountain, which you should remember the next time you order your gnome to do something. Like seduce mine."

"My dear Hector," Ida said, "if we are to work well together, you'd better quit pontificating like you wrote the rules of magic with the pen shoved up your ass."

He looked shocked. Good. He needed some shocking—the kind a nice lightning bolt called down from the sky would provide readily, were she not a good witch. "For your information, I did everything I could to keep Hari from seeing Tinbit. When you care about a person, you intercede when they are about to make the biggest mistake of their lives! You love them enough to protect them. You don't let them run off and break their hearts because those things can't be replaced, and they never heal. They scar."

Hector's pale, thin cheeks glowed a shade of bright brick. "Where is free will in your kind of caring? Where is autonomy? Where is trust?"

"Where it belongs," Ida said. "In myself."

"Trusting in yourself is what got us into this mess," Hector said.

"Now you're blaming me?"

"Yes! I blame you. You've shown yourself to be irresponsible with magic, and I, for one, don't intend to lose my job and my immortality to your incompetence, woman!"

Ida slapped him.

Hector's spoon clattered to the ground along with his soup. He reached up for his cheek and touched the place as if it actually hurt him.

Ida's face burned. "Call me irresponsible again, I will name you for what you really are—a farm boy with limited magic who gets by on what he learns out of books and prays to the Gods that no one ever finds out he's a fraud."

Hector's voice overflowed with anger. "And I will tell the other witches what I know. You're nothing more than a provincial girl who dreamed of being a princess but you were never chosen. That's why you became a good witch. You didn't have the guts to become wicked like you wanted."

Ida gripped her bowl tightly. "I'm going to eat in the coach. The second this trip is done, you'll go back to your corner of the world, and I'll go to mine, and we will never speak again except in the course of our professional lives."

"Agreed." He turned his back on her.

She stomped off, flushed and furious. She'd never told him anything about her life before she became a witch in her letters. He'd never told her any of his life story either, and yet his face grayed beneath the blush. She'd deduced it from what she knew about him, about his work, and from the way he cited every rule when he was questioned. Had he done the same? Gleaned all that from her letters? Two people couldn't really know each other that well when all they'd done was pour words out onto paper and stick them in the mail.

Perturbed, she closed the door to the coach. Something was going on.

23

Hector

Dear Adair,

I'm disheartened you haven't seen scale nor tail of Alistair yet, but tell Morga not to panic. It's likely he and the princess are still together. I know he said he'd come home, and you're as worried as I am, but we'll sort this out. Regardless of how much trouble he can be, he's a good dragon. More than likely, he's simply making sure the princess is comfortably cared for given the delay.

I'll write to you as soon as I'm home. Best not to try to contact me again while I'm on the road. I had to extract your letter from the stomach of a fire toad when it ate the carrier bat.

Your friend,
HECTOR

HECTOR ATE THE REST OF HIS SOUP BESIDE THE FIRE. Where Ida had slapped him still burned. He'd always considered her temper to be her greatest flaw as a witch—she let her emotions run away with her far too often—but he hadn't expected to feel so angry.

She'd actually wanted to be wicked like him? He hadn't really known. He'd guessed at it, from the way her charms outdid his hexes, always so clever, so innovative. Her ingenuity reminded him of first-rate wickedness. He—well, he'd always need to back up his work with a book. He couldn't even curse without worrying about it. He could almost feel the proverbial pen up his ass after what she'd said to him. His heart was safely locked away under the apple tree at home, but the way he felt now, he could almost believe it was beating in his chest.

Tinbit appeared at the door of the coach, hopped down, and strolled toward the campfire, carrying an empty soup bowl and a spoon.

"Well?"

"I got him to eat," Tinbit said. "Not much, but it was something anyway. I feel awful. He didn't even call out."

"It's not your fault."

The spoon clattered abruptly in the bowl as Tinbit dropped it in the freshwater tub he'd insisted Hector conjure because washing bowls in swamp water was about as unhygienic as it got. "Yes, it is. I told him to go home. At the Happily-Ever-After, he came and found me in the stable, and I told him he had to, there was no other decision to make."

The soft, boggy spot in his chest where his heart used to be throbbed unpleasantly. "Decision?"

"I told him it would be better if he forgot me. He said he'd make that choice for himself, he didn't care who I was or who I worked for, he couldn't forget me, not after we'd—well." He blushed.

"I really am very sorry about all this," Hector said, feeling miserable. Ida's philosophy that he'd so recently dismissed as overbearing manipulation seemed rather sound now that he thought about it. He should have been much more discouraging the moment Tinbit told him he was writing letters. That sort of thing could only end in heartbreak, hurt feelings, and the miserable wish that things could be different. For instance, if he'd never written Ida all those centuries ago, his face wouldn't still sting the way his ego did after her assessment of him. How had she figured him out so well, just from his letters?

"Don't be." Tinbit sighed, almost as if he'd heard Hector's thoughts like he'd heard his apology. "It's not your fault either."

Hector didn't say anything. The unfortunate truth was that Tinbit was wrong. It absolutely *was* Hector's fault. A hearty young gnome should not get swamp fever from a rainy day spent on the back of the coach, no matter how lovesick he was. Pestilence and plague—he knew them well. They were one of his special areas of concern, and among the hardest to mete out fairly. They'd also been one of the most challenging things to control with Happily-Ever-After—even with him handling all the details. If the magic was broken beyond repair…but he couldn't even bring himself to think about that right now. He already felt too unhappy.

Hector slept rather badly.

He never slept well away from home, even in hotels, but something about cold hard ground seeping upward through the thick down sleeping bags he'd conjured for himself and Tinbit added a whole new level of discomfort. The horses, however, woke up refreshed and exuberant, the ground being like the comfort of the grave for them. Napoleon even knocked Hector's hat off with an affectionate swipe of his bony nose.

He stayed for a moment, stroking the hard jawbone of the animal affectionately. He ought to retire the ancient horse, let him live out his magic and turn to dust. Horses weren't meant to live forever, not even the undead ones, and Napoleon had outlived so many others because Hector kept patching him up, replacing bones, reworking sinews. His eyes rested on the silver-coated cannon bone. "Old friend," he said, touching the horse's shoulder gently, "some of us might be better off without immortality weighing us down."

The coachman gazed at Hector with impassive hollow eyes, but he gaped in dismay.

Hector laughed. "Not you. I told you centuries ago you could stay as long as you wished. I'm not putting my best driver out to pasture."

The skeleton raised himself on his toes, squaring his shoulders proudly, and went back to harnessing the other horses.

"We'll go easier on Napoleon this time," Hector said. "I want to stop in town and give him a good twelve hours rest before we set off again."

The coachman nodded.

The door to the coach opened and Ida stepped out into the morning sunshine.

She wore a silk blouse, red, with ruffles Hector would've considered a laughable flamboyance, but on Ida, it looked natural, like the plumage of some bright bird. She'd belted the long, silk tunic around her midsection with a bright purple sash bound with a gold clasp at her hip. She was brushing her hair as she stood outside the door, fiddling with a clip and the brush at the same time, a curiously determined expression on her face. The tip of her tongue stuck out the side of her mouth as she pulled a vast quantity of unruly waves and curls into her hand and bound it into a single ponytail, then flipped part of it back through the barrette, to give it a softer look. In the dawn light, her hair was almost the color of bright blood, with streams of bone silver running through the red. She startled when he approached, and her lavender eyes flashed dangerously.

"How's Hari?"

She tucked her hair brush into a handbag she'd set on the steps behind her. "A little better," she said. "He's asking for breakfast anyway, which I take to be a good sign."

"Tinbit is working on it, I believe," Hector said, like he didn't know that Tinbit had risen before dawn to gather early swamp huckleberries for a complicated clafouti involving eggs, honey, and rose water.

"I appreciate that. He's been attentive and kind."

"He's a good gnome. He takes the best care of me and my house."

"Hari is the same way," Ida said. "I understand, perhaps better now, why they would find so much in common." Her eyebrows pulled together in a grimace of pain. "Hector, can we walk? I need to speak to you."

"Of course." Hector gave Napoleon a final pat and the coachman led the horse away to harness him with the others. He joined Ida on the path, walking into a dawn turning the mist the color of gold.

Ida put her hands behind her back. "I shouldn't have slapped you last night. I'm sorry."

Hector paced beside her, facing the bright eastern sky,

unwilling to trust his face. "I deserved it. I shouldn't have said what I did. I'm afraid I'm not accustomed to company or with-holding my opinions when I ought to. My mistake. We need to work together."

Ida stopped in the path. "We do. And I forgot that last night. I was angry—with you, with myself, and I'm still worried about Hari. But I will not let my emotions get the better of me again."

"The fault was as much mine as yours. I mean—it was all mine, and—"

Ida laughed. It sounded like summer birdsong; it made him want to smile, to laugh back. He had the most horrible sensation in his chest again—not the squashy, squelchy feeling he'd had with Tinbit, but something light, dancing, effervescent.

"You never could apologize properly," Ida said.

He laughed back. "No, I suppose I never could. But I accused you of something you would never do. I blamed you for setting up my gnome to fall for yours, and for that, I apologize." He bowed slightly.

"I can forgive you if you can forgive me." She smiled. "After all, I thought the same thing."

He resumed walking, and she matched him stride for stride. "I suppose the question now is what we're going to do about it."

She nodded. "I was up most of the night with Hari thinking about that. The thing is, I'm not entirely sure there isn't magic involved here, and they have to be told."

"But you just said—"

"Oh, I didn't do anything and neither did you. I can willingly believe that they simply connected over shared interests, but if you'd heard Hari last night—"

"Heard what?"

She glanced over at him. "He's in love with Tinbit."

He gaped. "Surely not. You must be mistaken. They only just started writing each other—it's not been long enough."

"I'm not," she said. "And from the look on your face, you believe Tinbit is in love too. Now, you tell me, is that possible without magic?"

"I wouldn't know. That's not really my province." He pointedly stared down at his feet, shuffling the muddy grasses aside.

"Well, it is *my* province, and I've been thinking about something ever since I saw the scarecrows. Happily-Ever-After is…" She hesitated.

She didn't want to say the word any more than he did. Broken. Shattered. Fractured. Whatever one called it, it wasn't something either of them wanted to face yet.

"Well, something happened with it and things aren't behaving the way they should be. I think it's the love magic. It's gone wrong along with everything else, and I think it's affecting Hari and Tinbit."

"You're certain of that?"

"People can't fall in love in a week! That's not natural."

"I suppose—"

"Which means we need to find Amber and the dragon as soon as we can. If we can get everyone back together where the magic went awry, we might be able to fix this for everybody, including Hari and Tinbit. But the longer they think they're in love, the worse it will hurt when magic ends. We need to hurry and get this sorted out."

"You'll get no argument from me there."

"They have to be told, of course." She sighed.

Not something he was looking forward to. "Yes, I think that

is probably best. It may help with the aftermath. I only wish it hadn't happened at all. Tinbit is rather prone to falling in love. He will take it hard."

"Hari, too, but it wouldn't be fair to let them think it's real." Ida sounded sad. "It's depressing, really. I'd like to see Hari settle down with a nice gnome."

"I've wanted the same thing for Tinbit."

She smiled. "Well, we have that in common. It's a good thing you and I can't be affected by love magic or we might find ourselves in the same predicament as our gnomes."

He snorted. "Impossible."

"I'd like to press on to your castle today. If you think your horse can't make it, perhaps you could leave him there and we can hire a coach in the village."

She had good sense, and if he hadn't been so concerned about Napoleon, he might have agreed. He certainly would prefer to clamp the lid on this disaster before things far worse than love magic leaked out. "I wish we could, but hiring a coach isn't a good idea."

"Why not? Don't they have stage service in the village?"

"Oh, yes. But they rob them in the Fearsome Forest and leave the bodies for the trees. It's part of the service they worked out with the dryads. No, I think it's probably best we stop for the night there and continue on tomorrow morning."

She gaped. "And you mean to stop there for the night?"

"It's far easier to hex the doors of a hotel room than to fight fifty armed bandits in the woods. That gets messy. One night and Napoleon will be fit to make the rest of the journey without another break, providing nothing else does. And Hari could use the rest. You know as well as I do, this isn't a natural swamp fever."

She regarded him quietly, deep lavender eyes squinting as if she was considering his confession and deciding what to do about it. He'd never noticed how brightly they sparkled or how deep they became when she was thinking. "All right," she said finally. "One night. No more."

"Agreed."

Hours later as he rocked and ruminated in the coach did he reflect that he and Ida had agreed on more in the last twenty-four hours than they'd agreed on anything in the last nine-hundred years.

Something was going on.

24

Ida

Dear Malia,

Hari is with me. I'm sorry, I've been on the road and haven't been able to write. I hope this letter doesn't take too long to reach you. I had to grab a stray bat last night to deliver it. I hope it didn't bite too hard—I checked it with a spell and it's not a vampire. Rest assured, Hari's quite well and safe.

Don't worry.

IDA

HARI *WASN'T* DOING WELL AT ALL.

The gnome ate breakfast, but he did it to please Tinbit, not because he was hungry. If Tinbit had served up frog spawn and swamp water instead of huckleberry clafouti and hot tea, Hari would've gobbled it and called it the best meal he'd ever eaten. But Cear crawled over Hari's forehead and pronounced him still on fire before they retired to feed on the sweetgrass in their firepot. The whole coach smelled like burnt vanilla pudding. Hari lay in the seat, head in Tinbit's lap, wrapped in Ida's wool robe, shivering uncontrollably.

"Are you doing all right?" Tinbit combed his fingers through Hari's thick hair.

Hari's smile was a wan moon. "A little uncomfortable."

"Next stop, you can rest," Tinbit said. He'd been saying that every fifteen minutes since breakfast.

Ida glanced at Hector. "How much farther?"

"Another three hours." He regarded Hari, and after a moment, he reached out and adjusted the wool robe to cover Hari's feet. He was surely worried about his own gnome and if the swamp fever would get him next. She would keep telling herself that because she'd started to believe he actually cared.

It seemed like he cared. And it had sounded like he cared this morning, walking side by side with her in the mist, his tall frame slightly stooped, salt-and-pepper hair catching every drop of light like a prism and turning it into rainbows.

Stop it. Stop it, woman. You are immune. She ought to be anyway. True, she'd never destroyed her heart, but having a heart had never been a real drawback before. She rather thought it gave her an edge. Well, she knew about the love magic's effects at least, and she could combat them.

She leaned across the coach to take Hari's hand. "Sweetheart, do you need us to stop for a minute?"

"I think…I think so," Hari said faintly. "I don't mean to complain."

"You aren't complaining," she said. "We'll see if we can make you more comfortable."

She consulted with Hector standing outside the coach while Tinbit went through their luggage, searching for anything soft they could use to make a bed for Hari on the coach seat.

"I don't mean to fault your horse, but I would beg you to

have your coachman push him more," Ida said. "The sooner we can get Hari to the inn, the sooner I may be able to effect a cure for him both for this damned fever and the damned love magic."

"I don't think you'll have any trouble finding what you need for the Heartsease in town, but we may be hard pressed to find everything we need for a tonic. There are no herbalists or apothecaries, only poisoners and would-be poisoners. They don't carry anything that isn't lethal."

"I can work with lethal." Ida folded her arms over her middle. "My stepmother was a hedge witch. She taught me herbs."

His eyebrows lifted. "A wicked witch?"

"It was a long time ago. No one cared back then whether a witch was good or wicked as long as they could help. My stepmother was a wise woman, a healer."

"We'll see what we can find on the way. I think I know which ones you need."

"You do?"

"I know my herbs, too. It's quite difficult for a giant to get to an herbalist when they are ill. I go to them."

Another unpleasant jolt of surprised admiration. *Nope. It's not caring, no. He just wants his giants healthy so he can send them to step on people.*

She cleared her throat. "Marshmallow would be appropriate, and perhaps horehound."

He nodded. "Marshmallow may be blooming now. We should be able to spot it from the coach. Horehound will be more difficult, but I'll watch from this side, and you from the other, and if you see a pale white flower growing in a clump, yell and I'll alert the driver."

Hari muttered something unintelligible as Ida climbed back into the coach. Tinbit gave her a nervous look. He didn't need to say anything. The sooner they got to the inn, the better.

Ida was completely worn out with worry when they reached the town, and also muddy up to her armpits. A light rain was falling, turning everything cold and wet, inside the coach and out. While pursuing a clump of marshmallow down to its roots, she'd inadvertently stepped in a pit with a mire imp. Only a fast jab with her wand and screaming her head off kept her from going under. Hector had come to the rescue, thumping the creature between the ears with his staff before he pulled her out, apologizing profusely.

"They're not truly evil," he said, "just…somewhat unfriendly."

"It said it would eat me, saving my internal organs for last so I would live longer." She spat mud.

"Oh, they all say that." Hector waved her concern off. "It would've stopped with one foot and decided you weren't worth the chewing—humans aren't their favorite prey. Prefer Will-o-the-Wisps."

Ida scraped as much of the mineral-laden mud off her shoes as she could. Clothes and all, she glowed like a bioluminescent animal. "Perhaps you should put up warning signs for travelers. The heroes will go on undaunted, but perhaps there won't be quite so many peg-legged people stumping around this town."

A surly pirate type gave her a stern glare as he passed, heading into the inn.

"I thought you said this was the best hotel in town. It looks like a dive."

"It is," Hector said in a weary tone, leaving her to decide which description was accurate. He scooped Hari up in his arms and carried the gnome into the inn, a worried Tinbit at his side.

The inside of the building did nothing to make Ida feel better. A gritty barmaid with a knife in her hand threatened a nonpaying customer while a pickpocket worked the room with his sad ragamuffin face and sticky fingers, right up until he tried the barmaid and she boxed his ears. But when the innkeeper saw Hector, she froze right in the middle of a gut thrust into the abdomen of a cutthroat who'd had his purse belt slit and was giving her grief about it.

"Your Wickedness! What can we do for you?" She wiped down her knife and bustled toward Hector.

The cutthroat tried to sneak off.

A quick throw by the barmaid pinned him between the shoulder blades.

"Gods!" Ida cried out as the man crawled a few inches toward her feet and then collapsed.

"Pay him no mind, Your Goodness," the innkeeper said. "He's a zombie. We do this every week. What's wrong with the gnome?"

"Swamp fever," Hector said. "Deadly. Contagious too. It will kill anyone who catches it in three days or less."

The inn emptied like a burning building, all but the innkeeper. She grinned. "Well, then, you'll be renting the whole inn, won't you, for bringing such a devastating sickness into my house?"

"Naturally," Hector said.

"Lovely, lovely. I'll go put the plague signs on the door right after I show you to your rooms."

"Oh, Belinda, that won't be necessary. I know I'm putting you out two week's earnings and—"

"No apologies, Your Wickedness," she said, wiping her blood-stained hands on her apron. "You know I'm always glad to help my old boss."

Hector glanced at Ida. "Belinda's mother worked as a hired assassin for me for years—one of the best. So did Belinda—"

"Then I got married and had a kid," Belinda said. "After that, I had a family to provide for. No more murder for me."

"Where is your son today?" Hector asked.

Belinda smiled with pride. "Out robbing the stage with the boys. He'll be back this evening." She wiped a tear from her eye. "They grow up so fast. One day they're picking pockets and the next day they're a hired hit man." She handed Hector a skeleton key. "Here you are, Hector. The best room in the house for you and your lady. I'll bring up hot water for the bath in a jiffy."

Ida glared at Hector as they climbed the stairs. "*Your* lady?"

Tinbit unlocked the door, and Hector laid Hari down on a rough but serviceable couch. "They are evil-minded, my dear Ida—the bed is yours. I'm quite used to sleeping on the floor."

"Oh, no, you don't," Ida said, eyeing it with great dislike. "I wouldn't be surprised to find rats nesting in it. I'm taking the floor. You get eaten."

"Can you both quit arguing?" Tinbit grumbled. "I'll bathe Hari for the fever while you two get started on a potion."

"I'll go purchase the herbs," Hector said. "Far safer for me to do that. You stay here and help him, Ida."

Ida sat on the end of the couch and unlaced Hari's long,

stylish boots, irreparably damaged, probably from dragging the ground as he clung to the back of the coach.

"He's going to be okay," Tinbit said stubbornly.

"Yes," she said. She wouldn't forgive herself otherwise.

25

Hector

HEARTSEASE REMEDY

To break two hearts, take one black rose,
Ten petals to each glass,
Fumitory for the will,
Use cohosh for a lass.
For a swain, take moonseed sap
A drop, no more, to join
Sun's-Own-Son, to ease the grief,
Vitex for the loins.
Pine rosin will relieve their guilt
Hawthorn lends its healing,
Violet soon doth soothe the hearts
Red rose will bring their mending.

HECTOR GRIPPED HIS STAFF TIGHTLY AS HE SET OFF down the muddy main street. He'd always been proud of this place until Ida called it a dive. Now the whole town looked dark, dreary, and miserable. He ought to be proud. It wasn't every wicked witch who could boast of a whole town full of outlaws—a model city of villainy.

"I am wicked," he muttered. "I should never be ashamed of it." But the mantra sounded wrong today, and it felt even more wrong when he reached his favorite poisoner's shop and was informed by the landlord the man had died of an overdose of amanita mushrooms two days earlier.

"Well, I'd like to purchase his stock," Hector said.

"Can't allow it, Your Wickedness," the landlord whispered through the crack in the door. "Whole thing belongs to the guy who killed him and I don't want to be next."

"I'll give you my protection."

"You'll be gone in the morning. What good will that do me?"

It occurred to Hector to hex the man's nose into a sausage, but his heart wasn't in it. He turned away and headed down the alleyway connecting the backstreet to a more unsavory shop, dispatching one would-be-murderer with a sleeping spell and his accomplice with a far more painful crack over the head with his staff. While he appreciated the treachery, he didn't have time for backstabbers today.

It took him the better part of three hours to obtain the right ingredients for heartsickness and swamp fever. By then it was raining hard, he was chilled to the bones, tired, and his back hurt. He wished he hadn't said he'd sleep on the floor. It seemed more like foolishness than chivalry.

"Is this all you could find?" Ida sounded disappointed.

"Yes." He set the herbs down on the table next to the muddy marshmallow roots that had nearly cost Ida an arm and a leg literally. The flames sputtered unproductively in the room's fireplace, barely giving off any heat. The salamander had done their best, but a smoky, miserably cold fire was standard in the hostile hostel business—building code in fact.

"I needed feverfew."

"There wasn't any, but I got willow," he said in a deliberately calm voice. "Where is Tinbit?"

"In the bathroom watching Hari. He was worried that if Hari fainted, he might drown, and I agreed." She sighed.

Hector nodded. "He's a good gnome, a sensible man."

"Yes, he is," Ida said, sorting through the roots and pulling out the moonseed. She held the plant up, set it down next to the fumitory. "I almost wish we didn't have to tell them."

Hector sighed. "So do I. But it will hurt less if it comes from us."

Ida conjured a knife and a bowl and cut up the marshmallow root while Hector, freezing but unwilling to let Ida ogle him in his underwear, sat at the table with her in saturated robes. She handed him the licorice leaves and the knife.

"It's for the best," he said, mincing carefully. "Tinbit would never leave me, and I don't think Hari would leave you."

"He wouldn't," Ida said, jaw firming as she smashed roots in a stone bowl she must have borrowed from the kitchen. "It's for the best," she repeated.

Hector helped Tinbit get Hari out of the bath. The young gnome looked as pale as death's horse, but he seemed more alert. Also aggravated.

"I'm sick and you drop me into ice water?" he asked, shaking as Tinbit wrapped a towel over his shoulders.

"You had a fever," Hector said.

"It was cold!"

"Well, at least you can talk sense now," Tinbit retorted. "You've been singing the most damned awful ballads for the last hour and a half."

"I was not! Was I?" Hari let Hector dress him in a clean shirt of Ida's, well-worn and soft.

"Off-key," Tinbit said. "I'm going to go see to the horses."

"Wait a minute, and I'll go with you. Here, Hari, go lie down on the couch by the fire. Ida and I have made a tonic that should make you well."

Tinbit stared curiously after Hector as he walked out. He had every right to be suspicious. Hector and Ida had talked it over while they pulverized roots and leaves and composed the magic to make the Heartsease potion for Hari and Tinbit. It had been Hector's decision to mix it in with the fever tonic for Hari, although Ida objected strenuously.

"If he doesn't know about it, it won't be as effective."

"Who said anything about hiding it? You tell Hari; I'll tell Tinbit. Not that he'll be accepting. He's far more attached. Once he takes care of someone…"

Ida glared him into silence. "But I'm not sure how Hari will take it either. Knowing he's drinking something to make him forget about his feelings for Tinbit might depress him more than the violet could help, and with him already feeling so bad with swamp fever…" she bit her lip. "But you're right. We might as well get it over with. But you be sure you explain it to Tinbit properly. Otherwise he'll be brokenhearted, and I don't want that any more than you do."

"Don't worry, I will." Hector touched the vial in his pocket. But he was worried. He'd have to be brutally honest with Tinbit. He didn't know how Tinbit would take it.

Quite badly, as it turned out.

"You want me to drink what?" Tinbit attached the feedbag to Napoleon's halter. "No way. This is what you get for traveling with a good witch—she's totally messing with you. It's just her way of making sure she doesn't lose her…fucking gnome." He jerked the bag straight and Napoleon settled in munching his chaff happily, standing comfortably on his injured limb after Hector's cursory exam—his silver mend had melded properly with the bone. The horse would make it home easily now.

"That's not true—"

"Like hell it isn't."

"It's for the best," Hector said, keeping a tight hold on the vial containing the evil-scented concoction. Tinbit looked ready to throw it at his head if he gave it to him now. "With this love magic running wild, you might have, theoretically, fallen in love with him by accident."

"I'm not in love with him." Tinbit looked at him like he sprouted horns. "Anyway, we talked it over, like I said. He's not leaving her, and I know I can't leave you, if that's what you're worried about."

"I am not worried about that," Hector said, feeling annoyed. "But you're taking care of him, and I know what that does to you."

"I'm taking care of him because he's ill."

"You washed his hair, Tinbit."

"It was filthy."

"You were out in the swamp before dawn to pick huckleberries for that clafouti."

"I happen to like huckleberry clafouti."

"You gave him a foot rub."

Tinbit flinched. "So what? I used basil oil—draws the fever out from the feet. That was a strictly therapeutic foot rub."

"Tinbit—Hari's going to take the potion."

Tinbit scowled. "Willingly?"

"Of course. Please." He stared directly into Tinbit's eyes. He couldn't watch Tinbit drag it out, dying a little more inside with every lovesick sigh. "I wouldn't ask if I didn't care so much about you. You're such a good man, a kind man, and you deserve happiness. I wish things were different. I like Hari too. But it can't be. And I think, deep down, you know it. You would never ask him to leave Ida."

Tinbit stared at his booted feet, face stony. "He would for me. I know he would."

"When he feels the same way about her as you feel about me? What would you tell him if he asked you to leave me? Could you tell him the truth?"

Tinbit let out a painful moan.

Oh, Gods. Ida was right. He *was* in love. Hector handed Tinbit the flask. "This will help."

"I don't want to take it."

"I know. But do it for him if you can't do it for yourself."

Tinbit put it to his lips. Paused. "Hector, if I ever fall in love again, just let me die. I can't stand this anymore. For Hari." He drained the flask. Grimaced. "Gods, Hector, is there demon piss in there or something?"

"It's a bit bitter," Hector said. "My apologies. They didn't have any honey in the kitchen."

"Not half as bitter as I feel," he said. "Go back and take care of Hari for me. I want to stay out here with the horses for a while, at least until I don't feel like such a horse's rear end."

Hector obeyed. He felt a lot like a horse's rear end himself.

He met Ida in the empty main room of the inn. Belinda was in the kitchen, talking in low tones with her son. He sounded disappointed. Probably they'd not given him a proper share of the loot.

Ida sat by the fire in a low armchair, a cup of strong tea at her elbow. She held Hari's dirty smock in her lap. "I thought Belinda might have a washtub. But she said she'd wash it. Wouldn't hear of me lifting a finger."

"I hope you didn't argue with her," he said, taking the other armchair. "Hotel laundry is a lucrative side business."

"I didn't argue."

"Hari is resting?"

"He took his potion and went to sleep," Ida said. "He…he cried a little."

"Did you tell him?"

"Yes." She twisted the smock into a knot. "He didn't want to believe me."

"Tinbit didn't either." He leaned back, staring up at the smoke-tinged ceiling.

"I feel like shit, Hector. He was so sure it was real, and he almost got me believing he might be right. If I didn't know better—"

"That makes two of us. If you asked me two days ago about what I believed was better—falling in love or a scarless heart—I wouldn't have hesitated. A heart, well-protected, safe, happy in its own way, contented, is always preferable, but…"

"It's a good thing we don't have them anymore." She laughed, but it sounded harsh and sad.

"Good thing."

Ida reached for his hand. He twined his fingers through hers, and together, they watched the fire crackle in silence.

 **26**

Ida 

There's Only One Bed Charm—used in the latter half of the Happily-Ever-After spell to instigate emotional and physical bonding. Use when the bonding at the Rescue is weaker than anticipated.

MAGIC AND MISCHIEF—A THOUSAND YEARS OF HAPPILY-EVER-AFTER: A MEMOIR

IDA NORTH

HARI DRANK THE POTION IN GOOD FAITH, TRUSTING her to cure him. Then he'd heaved, and grabbing his chest, he began to sob, a dreadful brokenhearted sound, and the tears—so many tears. She'd rocked him like she used to do when he was a tiny gnomelet, sweet and furry as a kitten in her lap.

He didn't know why he wept. She did. His love for Tinbit was strong, even if it wasn't real. But some things weren't meant to be. Hari didn't want to leave her. Tinbit certainly wouldn't leave Hector, even if Hari had asked him to. At least this way, they'd never have to endure that heartache.

A pine log snapped in the fireplace, shedding bark. She stirred and picked up her tea cup. Grit polluted the bottom now that the tea leaves had settled, and it tasted dirty, but at least it was hot. Belinda offered it as Hector's favorite.

"Well, it's over now," Hector said. "We can concentrate on what we're going to do once we find Alistair and the princess. To be frank, I'm disturbed by how upset Tinbit was about taking the potion. The dragon and the princess may have also been affected in the same way. And if they're anything like Hari and Tinbit, we may have difficulty in getting them to understand."

"This potion, could we use it to—"

"No." Hector shook his head. "It might work on the princess, but not on Alistair. Dragons are largely resistant to potions. The fire in their bellies deactivates everything."

"Even when they're human?"

"They're not human, no matter how much they look it. And most of them don't look it very much. Alistair can pass because he's only around seven feet tall, but he's young. He's not attained his full growth. His father is over ten feet tall, and his mother is taller—the females usually are. For him, at least, I must unravel where the magical threads got tangled and cut him out of it. I can't help but think how much of this is my fault for not listening to him. He didn't want to be the chosen dragon this year, and I blew him off. I thought he could separate his personal feelings from the theater of it, but I was wrong. Perhaps if I'd been more understanding, he wouldn't have overreacted."

Not in another ten centuries would she understand the man. What on earth was he trying to do? Earn her sympathy? Assert his own guilt? Or something entirely different—like getting her to play along and blame herself for the princess? She'd already done that in her own mind, thanks. She wouldn't play games with Hector West. And yet—he seemed entirely honest when he leaned forward, clasping his bony hands over his equally bony knees.

Odd, she'd never thought of him as a man. In her mind's eye, she'd always imagined him the consummate wicked witch, strolling around his castle in long black garb, stiff, stained, and forbidding. But in these worn, faded trousers with the odd patch in the left knee and a button-up plaid tunic dug off a goblin-resale rack, he appeared utterly ordinary, like someone's stray husband forgotten on a park bench in autumn.

"We'll find a way to sort it out," she said quietly.

His fingers closed over her hand. "Thanks for the confidence."

"It's not confidence," she said, staring at his hand. "You don't want Happily-Ever-After broken any more than I do, and that's a strong motivation to work things out. I think I'll go upstairs to see how Hari is doing. And then we need to fix the sleeping arrangements. With a whole inn to stay in, I believe I'd like a room down the hall for myself and Hari. Now that they've taken the potion, it would be better to keep them apart. The love magic is still active after all."

"I wish I could say that was a good idea," Hector said. "But I recommend we all stay together. It's only for one night, and while I can safely say I can keep the inn from burning down or being stormed by bandits, it's harder to put safeguards on more than one room at a time. The bed isn't full of rats—we had a piper through last year. And the bedbugs are easily repelled with a burning hex. Please. I insist. You and Hari take the bed."

But Hari didn't want to sleep in the bed. He lay curled up on the couch, back facing Ida, when she came in and gently asked him if he might be willing to eat dinner, provided she found anything edible in the kitchen.

"I don't want to eat. I want to be left alone."

"You'll feel better if you eat something," Ida said kindly.

He rolled onto his back and stared up at the ceiling. "I thought the potion was supposed to make me feel better."

"It will," Ida said. "Your fever's come down already."

"Not that part of it. The other part. But I don't feel better. I feel empty."

"That's why you should eat."

"Not that kind of empty. I want something—I really want it—but I don't know what it is."

"Well, I'll bring you some stew anyway," Ida said. "Then you should get some rest. I'll pull down the sheets and make sure Hector got rid of the bedbugs—"

"I'll eat. But I'm not sleeping in the bed. I want to sleep here. Alone."

She didn't argue with him. Hector and Tinbit could share the bed. She'd drag in a mattress from one of the other rooms and sleep on the floor. Of all the foolishness. She often cooked this up into a spell for the happy couple after the Rescue—a room in an inn with one bed where the lovers must shed the last of their reservations about each other and give in to the magical experience of acting on their passion. But this was ridiculous.

Tinbit opened the door tentatively. "Your Goodness?"

Hari jerked around like he'd been stung.

Tinbit glanced at him, and a red blush bloomed in his pale cheeks. "Hector asked me to ask you if you want to eat in the dining room with him and Belinda or if you'd rather I bring dinner up here."

"Here, I believe." She watched Hari's face closely. He looked hurt but not distraught. She could breathe easier now. It would be all right in the end.

"Very good," Tinbit said. He glanced at Hari. "I'm glad you're feeling better. You…you are feeling better?"

"Much better." Hari flushed slightly. "Thank you for taking care of me."

"My pleasure," Tinbit said with a completely friendly, non-romantic smile. He backed out the door.

Hari sat up, twisting the blanket between his fingers. He grimaced. "Ida?"

"Yes?"

"He's the empty place," Hari said faintly.

"Lie down," Ida said, feeling sick. "You're still weak. Once you've eaten, I'll give you something to help you sleep."

Hector brought the stew. "Tinbit made it, so it won't kill you, although I can't vouch for the quality of the ingredients. How's Hari?"

"Still tired," she said and sampled the stew. To her great surprise, it tasted good, although perhaps a bit smoky and mushroomy. "He just needs time."

"I told Tinbit I'd make him a sleeping draught tonight. You'll want the same for Hari, I suppose."

"Yes," Ida said. "Thank you."

"It's nothing," Hector said. "I'll get the belladonna."

When Hector and Tinbit came up the stairs to the bedroom, quite late, darkness had fallen. Ida stood by the window, watching the lights come on in the town. Faintly candling beyond the range of torchlight, Hector's wisps floated through the swamp to be gobbled up by mire imps.

Hari snored on the couch, a light blanket pulled up almost to his chin. In the firelight, he looked almost like himself again—brown, small, a slight smile curving his mouth, reminding Ida of his laughing face every time he woke her in the afternoon and said good morning.

She yawned. The trip and the week of forced early rising were wearing her down. She ought to be wide awake at this hour. Instead, she felt ready to drop on the straw mattress Belinda brought in and draped with a rough blanket. But she dreaded the bug bites. Cear had offered the help of a magical barrier of fire, but the idea of sleeping on a straw mattress surrounded by flames, even magical ones, unsettled her.

"He's sleeping?" Hector said.

"Like a child," Ida said.

"Good," Tinbit said grumpily. "I'm about to join him."

Ida froze.

He glared at her. "I meant in sleep," he said.

"Of course," Ida said.

Tinbit kicked off his boots and with a grumpy sigh, he lay down on the mattress on the floor.

"Uh—" Ida started.

"Tinbit, you and I will take the bed," Hector said.

"No, we won't." Tinbit folded his hands over his chest. "I want to be alone. You want me to be alone. You want Hari to be alone. Well, we're alone. You and her Goodness fight it out for the bed. I'm tired, I'm mad, and I'm going to sleep. Night."

Hector glanced helplessly at Ida. "I'll go back downstairs."

"You said you didn't feel it was wise to be separated."

"It's not, but—"

Ida looked at Hari's face. Thin silver streams of tears trickled down his cheeks and his shoulders shook. Not asleep after all then. She sighed. "We'll share the bed, Hector," she said.

"You can't be serious," he stammered, going as red as any one of her roses. "I mean—you…and me…and…" he trailed off, obviously too flustered to go on.

"For pity's sake! It's not like we'll be naked! Put your pajamas on—but I'm warning you, I will smother you with a pillow if you snore."

27
Hector

Dear Sebastian,

I require overnight lodging in your establishment Rainsday evening. Please prepare my usual room, and another for a friend of mine. Not the Honeymoon Suite.

I also have a matter of business that I must speak to you about regarding an item I need to dispose of safely.

Yours sincerely,
Hector West

HECTOR EYED HIMSELF CRITICALLY IN THE MIRROR. Of all the foolishness, this was the worst. Ida didn't care what he looked like. So why did he? He wished Heartsease potion worked as a preventative against this overactive love magic—he'd have guzzled a whole bottle of it, just in case. His damned heart. He ought to have gotten rid of the thing long ago. At least in another two days, he'd have nothing more to worry about. He'd sent his missive to Sebastian by high-speed vulture. The ghoul wouldn't ignore it. And after all, it was only one bed, not Only-One-Bed magic. He'd manage.

When Hector came out of the garderobe, having brushed

his teeth down to the gums, he found Ida on the right side of the bed, clad in a low-cut blue silk nightgown, glasses perched on her nose, reading.

He coughed, feeling self-conscious. He'd donned his favorite nightshirt, the red one missing a button at the top, but it was short, falling partway down his hairy thighs in the front and barely concealing his backside. He wished he'd brought a bathrobe, but he didn't own one. Tinbit didn't care if Hector walked around the castle naked, and the skeletons were too polite to laugh. With as much dignity as was possible in a threadbare flannel nightshirt missing one button, Hector paced to the bed, pulled the covers down on his side, and slipped in.

Ida closed her book. It winked out of sight along with the illumination.

"You didn't need to stop reading," he said. "I don't mind."

"I was done with the chapter," she said.

"Is it a book of spells?"

She narrowed her eyes. "Is that what you read before bed to help you go to sleep?"

"Well, no," Hector said. His sleeping aid was a genealogy of the kings and queens written in the ridiculously begat-begot style. He never made it past the fourth page. "But if it was a book of good spells, pertaining to Happily-Ever-After, I should like to read it."

"Should you?"

"I'm not familiar with your end of the magic—at least not the application. I'm comfortable enough with the theories."

"I'll find one for you," Ida said. "But I wasn't reading spells. It was simply a good book."

"A romance?"

Ida glared at him. "No, a thriller. I deal with romance enough in real life. Now, I suggest we both get some sleep."

"I agree." He closed his eyes, turned onto his side, and flopped into a trench in the center of the bed. Ida crashed into him a second later.

"Oh, for the love of magic!" She thrashed and clawed her way out while he fought to get back on his own side of the bed. "There must be a weak spot in the middle. Perhaps if we balance—"

He positioned himself on the extreme edge of the bed. Ida did the same. One shift—back in the trench.

"Well?" Ida's nose bumped his.

"I could sleep on the floor—maybe Tinbit would let me…"

Ida wriggled around and put her back to him. "Just don't kick me. Please."

"I won't." He'd break if she moved against him, he was so tense now. He hadn't touched another person like this since—since never. Her hair tickled his neck, tangling on his remaining buttons. Her slick nightgown brushed his thighs. If he moved at all, her hips would be touching him much more intimately.

Well, he simply wouldn't move or sleep. His entire body was on high alert, every sense heightened to an almost hallucinatory degree. With each breath he drew in her scent—sharp and clean, like lavender soap mixed with basil. How had she managed to find soap in this inn?

Ida moved. He gasped as her shapely rear end rubbed suggestively against his nervous penis, only not so nervous now, more intrigued by this new and strange development. *Oh, Gods.* He had to get out of this bed. "Uh, Ida?"

"What?" she muttered.

"I really should sleep on the floor."

"Hector, I don't like your cock on my ass any more than you do," she said sleepily. "Please relax. I am quite familiar with what happens to a man when he's pressed, so to speak."

"I do apologize."

She half-turned. "What on earth for?"

"For this," he said. "For…well, maybe everything. That candor curse was over the top."

Ida made a noncommittal sound in her throat. "I'm as much to blame as you. I sent you the laughing charm. You retaliated. I ought to have expected it. You always do. In fact, I admit, I did it to get back at you for the pumpkins. Isn't that stupid?"

"I sent that because of your infernal dandelions."

She shifted until she was facing him again. "You told me you had them under control!"

"My lawn is probably a carpet of them by now." He smiled sheepishly.

Ida laughed softly. "You're horrible."

"And you're detestable." He hesitantly draped an arm over her.

She flinched.

"Shoulder," Hector explained. "A giant dislocated it a few centuries ago—it gets stiff if I don't stretch it out."

"I broke a hip riding four hundred years ago. I don't like sleeping on my right side. I prefer my left. But I'll be facing you all night."

"I don't mind."

Her lips brushed his beard—her breath tasted of wintergreen. She pressed her cheek against his shoulder. "I begin to understand the purpose of this spell."

"Oh?" He was dreadfully afraid he did too. His body did at least.

Ida sighed. "There's something disarming about sharing a bed with a person. I can almost believe you aren't half as wicked as I thought you were."

Oh, Ida, not the half of it. He was feeling very, very wicked indeed. He'd like to plant a kiss on her lips, move himself into position, slide her nightgown up along with his nightshirt and see if she felt wicked too. But he said nothing and lay quietly while Ida relaxed against him. Her chest rose and fell evenly, and to his great surprise, she let out a sudden, ridiculous snore that rivaled Tinbit's.

Gently, so as not to wake her, Hector tangled his fingers in Ida's hair.

28

Ida

The Morning After—critical to establishment of a fidelity bond, the couple may engage in an initial pulling away from each other as they grapple with their feelings about what has occurred. It is critical they come together again after this initial "running away from their feelings."

Instruct hotel staff to deliver breakfast to the room quietly. Include red roses and strawberries for love, cream and honey for home and hearth. Hot tea.

MAGIC AND MISCHIEF—A THOUSAND
YEARS OF HAPPILY-EVER-AFTER: A MEMOIR

IDA NORTH

ON NO ACCOUNT SHOULD THE MORNING AFTER EVER involve a woman waking up in a man's arms with his morning breath stinking in her face and feel like she wants to laugh at him, yell at him, and make love to him all at once. But that's exactly how Ida woke up, and the urge to make love was unpleasantly strong.

Maybe it was because Hector had indeed been "pressed" and what had pressed out was highly respectable. Maybe it was because sleeping tangled up in his arms had caused a series of vivid dreams in which she was waltzing in her castle with the most beautiful man in the world. He had expressive eyes of purest green and long black hair. When he danced, he moved so divinely that roses bloomed, sending their heady fragrance washing over her. Like so many erotic dreams, this one ended with her lying on satin sheets in her own garden, with him naked and easing into her, his kiss burning her lips, the sound of his breath in her ears, and the heartbreak of waking, wet, ready, and empty.

Hector lay curled, one arm draped over her, the other thrown up on the pillow above her head, fingers resting somewhere around the vicinity of her right ear. His eyelashes fluttered, and his mouth moved softly. In a sleepy way, he asked Tinbit for a watering can. In his dreams, the clearly heartless Hector West was working in his garden, oblivious to the intoxicatingly suggestive effects of love magic running wild, the lucky asshole.

Trapped against his chest, legs tangled in his, Ida thought about every Morning After spell she'd concocted for toast and tea to deal with all the angst from baring one's body to another. How ridiculous. Waking up after sharing a bed with the worst man in the world didn't make her feel one jot angsty. Instead, she felt oddly comforted and the scent of sweet, dark roses bloomed in her mind.

With a soft sigh, Hector muttered something unintelligible, then sighed, pulling her closer, a smile on his lips.

This happy feeling was magically induced, certainly, but right now she found she didn't care. He was warm, and she snuggled into his arms, and gazed around the room, feeling less disgusted than before.

To her great surprise, the balky fire had burned down in the fireplace; the salamander's pot glowed with life but not heat. Hari and Tinbit lay curled up together on the mattress on the floor, with Hari's blanket thrown over them, their hands in front of their faces, fingers locked together on the single pillow they shared.

Shit. She wriggled, struggling to get out of the trench.

"Mm—Tinbit?" Hector jerked awake in a few sharp twists. He looked surprised to see her so close to him, and his arm, which had been happily engaged in petting her, froze.

"He's with Hari," she whispered.

"Ah," Hector said. He regarded her for a moment, then took his hand from her back and touched the dried-up corner of his mouth and a patch of sticky beard. "Well, it was cold last night. Tinbit probably wanted to be sure Hari stayed warm."

"It's still cold."

With a grunt, Hector shifted to get out of the trench, but he didn't throw the covers off. Instead, he pushed them gently around her while he got out of bed, with a soft creaking and snapping of joints. He shuffled across the room and picked up the fireplace poker. He stirred the coals, squatted slowly, and fed the fire a few pine sticks and bits of cedar wood. A warm resinous smell filled the room. He added a handful of sweetgrass to the salamander's pot, quietly asking if they would like a pine knot as well, and handed it to them. The happy feeling shuddered over Ida again as Hector, shivering, returned to the bed and eased back in, careful to keep his icy feet off her.

"I don't mind," she said generously, setting her feet on top of his. "You should wear wool socks like me."

He settled on his back until the bed forced him next to her again. "Be warm soon."

"Hector? Put your arms around me. I'm cold."

He obliged and shivered against her as she snuggled next to him.

"It's been a long time since I've had anyone in my bed," she said, speaking quietly so the salamander would not hear.

"That surprises me."

"Way to call me unprofessional." She snorted.

"I didn't mean it like that! You were a very attractive woman—I mean, you are a very attractive woman, and I—"

She giggled. How on earth did he deal with dragons if he always spoke his mind without considering how it might sound? And why did she suddenly find that charming? She patted his cheek. "And you're an attractive man. I've no doubt you've had a paramour or two in your centuries."

Hector twisted a fold of her nightdress between his fingers. "I never…I never took one," he said. "I considered it when I was younger. But I didn't think I could keep an emotional distance."

"You didn't destroy your heart soon enough," she said.

His mouth twisted in a thoughtful expression. "I did it when it seemed right to me, as I'm sure you did with yours."

She pressed her ear against his utterly silent chest. "Yes, of course I did," she said quietly. "But there are still times when, if I'm honest, it might be nice to wake up with someone who mattered, to share the warmth and then a good breakfast."

"You should get a dog," he said.

She laughed outright. "You are lying in bed with a very attractive woman who says she finds you pleasant to wake up with, and you tell her to get a dog."

He blinked, and the gray fringe brought out the intensity of his green eyes in the shadows of the covers. "I'd be frankly envious of that dog."

She touched his cheek gently. "Would you?"

"We should get up. I need to order breakfast—it won't be good, I'm afraid—and get my coachman out of his coffin box to harness the horses." But he didn't move.

Neither did she. The room was still and quiet, and he was so warm and comforting. His throat bobbed as he swallowed. His hand trembled as he touched her breast.

"Ida?" Her whispered name was soft and gentle on his lips.

She gulped. "Hector?" All she had to do was guide his fingers over her nipples. She wanted to. The dream throbbed in her mind, and the cleft in the bed was deep enough that should he take her quietly from the top, no one would even see the covers move.

A snap of a pine knot breaking, and the fire crackled.

"You're right. We'd better get up." She shoved his hand away, crawled out of bed, and fled to the bathroom.

There was no hot tea. Belinda came knocking a half hour later and delivered a pan of greasy meat gravy, a few hardtack biscuits, and something that might pass for coffee, if one was drunk. By then, Ida had composed herself.

Clearly, she wasn't as immune as she'd hoped to be. But it didn't matter. In a few days, all this would be over and she could go back to her regular schedule of hating Hector and hexing him by mail, not wishing that the distance between them could be like that bed instead of the wide gulf dividing good and evil. She'd have to remember it existed the next time she faced him alone again, which hopefully wouldn't be soon.

Tinbit and Hector were gone. Cear, in salamander form, sat

on the edge of their firepot, preening their bright coal-red skin with a delicate orange-colored tongue. Large eyes as blue as the deepest part of a fire gazed at Ida reflectively for a moment, and blinked. Hari sat on the couch, wrapped in a blanket.

"Did Tinbit go with Hector to see to the coach?" Ida picked apart one of the biscuits, searching in vain for butter or lard to make it more palatable.

"A few minutes ago," Hari said.

"Are you feeling better?"

Hari made a sound like a sob crossed with a laugh. "In myself, yes. In my heart, no. It hurts. It hurts to look at him, to know he doesn't feel that way about me now. I didn't mean to sleep with him last night, but I was cold, and he heard my teeth chattering and asked. I'm sorry." He stared at his hands, shamefaced.

She wanted to pull her neatly coifed hair out by the roots. "He was simply being kind, Hari."

"I know. It's not him I'm apologizing for. It's me. I couldn't lie beside him and not want more. I didn't touch him, Ida, but I wanted to. And I wanted him to touch me. I can't forget the way his whole body trembled when we made love, like I was the one thing he most wanted in the world."

"You'll make yourself sick dwelling on that," Ida said. "Don't."

"I'm trying not to," he said. "Tell me when this is over, we'll go home right away. I can't stand to be near him and not have him."

"We will."

Not only for Hari did she promise. If she spent much more time with Hector, she'd be as unhappy as her gnome, torn between the professional hatred she had to maintain and the feeling that, if it wasn't there, every other barrier would melt away like wax to his flame.

29

Hector

Happily-Ever-After is the most important task a Cardinal Witch oversees. I've been honored to participate in every one of them. The one thing I can say with certainty is they are never the same. Therefore, each obstacle must be tailored to the participating prince and princess and never duplicated. Invention in this case is mothered by circumstance rather than necessity. For instance, I've found great success in creating a deeper emotional bond between the couple by interrupting the honeymoon period known as Only-One-Bed in some circles.

You'd be pleasantly surprised what an attack of bedbugs can accomplish.

A THOUSAND YEARS OF WICKEDNESS: A MEMOIR

HECTOR WEST

HECTOR COULD NOT LEAVE THE ROOM FAST ENOUGH. As soon as Ida left the bed, he bolted, frightened by the thoughts burning through his head and in far more distant locales.

How soft and pleasant she was to hold tenderly, to touch, to feel. When she'd nestled into his arms and wrapped her leg around his, he'd been unable to think about anything but the surging need in his groin. Oh, this wasn't happening. He was a wicked witch. That should make him immune, heart or no heart.

But it certainly didn't feel like it. Ida was right about what he'd missed in those long years alone—companionship. What must it be like to sit down at breakfast with an equal, spend a day in happy magical work together, and fall in bed with them at night, knowing the next day and the next would be full of the same peaceful communion of purpose? A horrible understanding had dawned as he gazed at her. If Ida North had lived closer, he could never have been celibate.

It was lust. Only lust. That at least was a wicked feeling. He stomped the others out of himself as he descended the staircase. Ida might soften at the touch of magical love, but not him. A squirming, pleasurable feeling twitched through his unruly body. *Oh, no, my man, you certainly didn't soften.*

"Gods save me." He crumpled the reply he'd received from Sebastian as he went out to the stable. What did he mean, "I've only the Honeymoon Suite available at such short notice"? It was the old ghoul's attempt at a joke certainly and in very poor taste.

Well, if he wasn't immune, he'd simply have to fight it. Love had always been for others, never for him. There could be no ever-after when one outlived one's lovers by centuries, and no happily with inequality. The idea that he'd even considered, if only for a moment, that after all these years, he might actually have found someone who he could consider his equal made him almost as queasy as the time a venerable gentleman dragon insisted on serving him a special meal of rare knight, roasted over an open flame.

He didn't wait for the coachman to oil his bones. He went

out and started harnessing the horses himself while the old skeleton fixed his trick knee.

He was leading Napoleon out of the stall and into the traces when Tinbit appeared, groggy and miserable. Wordlessly, Tinbit readied the feed bags for the horses already in harness, and fixed them in place before grabbing the seat brush to clean out the coach for the day's ride.

"I'd like to reach the castle by midafternoon," Hector said when he'd finished harnessing Napoleon.

"Then don't stay for breakfast or we'll be stopping every half hour," Tinbit said. "I smelled it cooking when I came downstairs."

"I ought to at least sample it. A thumbs-down of mine carries a lot of weight."

"It's your stomach," Tinbit said. "I'm waiting until we get home, and then I'm making a roast beef sandwich bigger than my head and some deviled eggs. Hari could use the protein."

"Hari can't stay, Tinbit."

"I know." Chaff showered Hector as Tinbit shook out an empty bag. "But I'm not sending him home without a good meal and plenty of hot soup. He's not well yet."

"If you keep taking care of him, no amount of potion—"

"You think I don't know what I'm risking? But if I can't love him because he can't love me, can't I at least call him a friend? Even you'll get to write to Ida when this is all over—I half think she'd actually like you to write more often than once a week if I read her right—but women aren't really my province."

"Ida does not consider me a friend," Hector said. "We are professional enemies."

"Right. And you pillow talk all your enemies, do you?"

Hector's face burned. "That wasn't pillow talk!"

"Could've fooled me. Face it, Hector, you feel something for her, and it's bugging the shit out of you."

"What I feel—and I'm not saying I do—is a normal physiologic response, explainable by proximity and an extremely minor reaction to love being unfortunately 'in the air' at the moment."

Tinbit smirked unpleasantly. "Yesterday, I might've had some sympathy. Today, it's not happening. I hope you get blue balls and don't know what to do with them."

"You are the most disrespectful butler in the kingdom."

"You're lucky you have me," Tinbit growled back. "Now go in the far stall and jack off. Trust me, you'll feel better."

Thoroughly chastened, Hector fled.

Ida was helping Cear with ash removal when Hector returned to the room. The breakfast tray, largely untouched, sat on the battered oak table.

"Did you eat?" he asked.

"No, it looked too dangerous." Ida used the gravy ladle to clean the firepot. "Hari is packing your things. I hope you don't mind. He said Tinbit went to help you."

"I don't mind," he said, although he very much did. But at least they'd be ready to leave sooner rather than later. He sat at the table and tore off a piece of hard, dry biscuit and dunked it in the dubious gravy.

Ida stopped shoveling. "You're going to eat that?"

"It's part of my duties as Wicked Witch. I rate the cooking at various hotels in this town. The worse, the better."

Ida blinked. "It's your stomach," she said, echoing Tinbit.

The breakfast was truly terrible. Salty gravy, rancid mutton, and biscuit hard enough to break the teeth of a mountain troll. Five stars in his opinion.

It would be good to get home, to spend a night in his own bed—alone—to eat a good meal, walk his garden—alone—and try not to think about Tinbit, Hari, the princess, the dragon, or Ida. He shoved his plate aside, rose, and carried his own luggage and Ida's down to the coach.

Trees made a welcome change from the fens of yesterday. Hector loved the Fearsome Forest, with its dark emerald shadows, dangerous dryads, and no shortage of carnivorous animals with which to threaten questing heroes. But today, even the bucolic sight of a lovely mother manticore and her three fluffy kits feasting on a deer couldn't cheer him up.

Hari also stared out the window, elbow against the glass. His eyes were red and slightly swollen. Tinbit had elected to ride with the coachman, something Hector wished he could do himself. Being stuck in a coach with a sad gnome, a watchful salamander, and a scowling witch he'd wanted to kiss that morning put him dreadfully out of sorts, even more than the rotten meat he'd eaten at the inn.

"I thought we might discuss setting out to reach the dragons this afternoon instead of in the morning." Ida's mouth was drawn in a firm line, her gaze lofty and cold. Good. He preferred it to the soft—perilously soft—way she'd looked at him in bed.

He cleared his throat. "It's unwise to start out too late in the day when hiking into the mountains."

"Because of dangerous creatures?"

"No, it's the terrain. We want to reach the hostel before dark."

"You stay at a hostel when you visit the dragons?" Ida sounded surprised. "I thought we were taking a giant."

"I've been thinking. Every dragon in the mountains will know we're coming if we take a giant. If Alistair acts like a proper dragon, he'd simply move his princess to another cave and we'll not find him. The key to finding his lair is secrecy. Also, I need to talk to his parents."

"He has parents?"

Hector laughed. "Well, of course, he does. Did you think dragons hatched out of eggs alone?"

Ida's eyes widened. "They hatch out of eggs but they are… men?"

"Not men, but yes, they hatch from an egg. Alistair is the only egg of his mother and father, and he's very special. Not every egg can grow to be a Flamelord."

"Are you saying Alistair isn't just a dragon, he's a prince of dragons?"

"Yes," Hector said.

Ida's face paled to cream.

"What?"

"I didn't know he was a prince!"

"He's not a human prince—"

"For your information, I don't explicitly state 'human prince' when I compose the set-up spell," Ida said. "You never told me. All these years, you've been sending me dragon princes?"

"I didn't think it mattered. After all, the dragons have their own traditions in this matter."

"Well, it would've been nice if you'd said something!" Ida folded her arms over her chest. "I stipulated the prince should fall in love at first sight with the princess, and damn it, if your dragon prince didn't arrive first on the scene. This could really complicate things if they've accidentally fallen in love."

"It wasn't my fault! Your princess should've been out on the field with her prince long before Alistair got there."

"Oh, for magic's sake—"

"Please don't shout," Hari said in a dead, dull voice from his corner. "My head hurts."

Cear emerged from the firepot as a salamander. They perched on the edge of the pot, staring at Hector with a curious expression.

Hector composed himself. "Do you have a question, Cear?"

"Yes," they hissed from the flames. "Is it customary for creatures in love to fight as you and Ida are fighting?"

A horrid flush warmed his cheeks. "You mean, as part of the setup when the spell is prepared?"

"Yes."

Ida pursed her lips and nodded. "I see what you are getting at, Cear. You want to know if their argument at the beginning increased their initial attraction?"

"Yes."

Hector tried not to breathe a sigh of relief. Who ever heard of people falling in love when they quarreled? "That kind of thing doesn't happen in real life, Cear. Only in books."

"You might be surprised," Ida said, eyeing him over her glasses. "But no, I didn't set the spell for initial animosity. Not on purpose, anyway."

"Not on purpose?"

She looked uncomfortable. "When the kingdom had families who didn't like each other very much, it wasn't uncommon for a princess or prince to deeply despise the person—"

"You mean this foolishness *is* part of your spell?" Hector asked. "You didn't tell me?"

"Well, I assumed any Cardinal Witch would have a good grasp of history! Love at first sight is one of the best ways to counter initial dislike—it's like getting a person to eat that dreadful inn breakfast by starving them first! They'd never do it if they weren't sure they'd die of hunger if they didn't. They'd be more logical about the whole thing."

"What about that?" Cear asked. "Could the logic of their choice be used to separate them as their love cools? A human may not bear eggs. A dragon may not give seed for a child."

Ida sighed. "When people fall in love, it takes a great deal to convince them it isn't wise, even when it's not caused by magic."

Hari shuddered.

Cear fell silent.

"But that's what we will do," Hector said.

Ida's eyes met his, and in her gaze he saw the same concern. What if they couldn't separate Alistair and Amber? What if they had fallen victim to the same love magic that had caused Hari and Tinbit such grief? He could comfort Tinbit like she could comfort Hari, but he somehow doubted that talking a dragon out of a strong magical infatuation would be a safe and rewarding experience for anyone. But he'd have to find a way. If he didn't, he was as doomed as Happily-Ever-After.

 # 30

Ida

Following the Morning After, there may be a lull in the couple's romantic feelings for each other. This is normal and an encouraging sign. Initial obsession and magical attraction must give way to a more permanent and lasting affection.

The real magic of Happily-Ever-After isn't the spells and manipulations of Witches. It's the moment when a couple looks at each other and decides to go forward into the unknown together, not through the compulsion of magic or the desires of their own bodies, but by the desire of their hearts—to discover each other purely for the pleasure of the adventure.

(Editor—redact last paragraph. I'm wallowing in my feelings again.)

*MAGIC AND MISCHIEF—A THOUSAND
YEARS OF HAPPILY-EVER-AFTER: A MEMOIR*

IDA NORTH

IDA HAD EXPECTED A TRADITIONAL DARK TOWER, A crown of thorns building designed to repel all invaders with a few pokey windows in a black granite keep—a true fortress of evil. It didn't disappoint.

Hector's castle stood in the foothills of the Dread Mountains, and if it wasn't on a barren plain full of fuming pits and bare rock, it was at least flanked by deep, dark pine forests on a verdant hill overgrown with brambles and thorns.

"How forbidding," she said, seriously impressed.

Hector blushed. "Thank you. I've worked hard to make it so."

They passed under the arch and into his courtyard. A canopy of black flowers with thin gray leaves and footlong thorns covered the stone walls. A strong rose odor filled the coach when Hector opened the door, overpowering in its intensity.

"The black rose?" Ida stepped out of the coach on her own, refusing to take the coachman's helping hand. He looked so old, she feared his fingers might fall off.

"They've naturalized here now," Hector said. "Locals call it Skeleton Rose. They make a formidable barrier plant—the thorns are tipped with poison and the roses emit a sleeping draught when they open at night. Most useful for insomnia in the summer. And of course, the fragrance can be concentrated into a very useful forgetfulness spell. Can turn a knight right around and make him forget all about why he decided to storm my castle. I haven't needed 'no trespassing' signs in an age."

"They're beautiful." On their long, silver stems, the tiny roses glittered like obsidian droplets, and she breathed in the fragrance, feeling the sleepiness Hector had spoken of, but something else too, a deep sense of peace and pleasure, not unlike the feeling she'd had in his arms. Guiltily, she glanced back at Hector. "In a completely horrible way, of course."

"Horribly beautiful is the very essence of wickedness. Shall we go in?" He offered her his arm. When had that gone out of style? Eight hundred years ago?

She took his arm anyway.

Inside proved no less dark and devastating than the outside. Long torches of everlasting flame lit the hall with a smoky light, reflecting in the black stone and creating a sense of disorientation. Two shining skeletons waited, both with identical welcoming grins, one holding a tray with a flask and two silver cups, the other with hands folded in front of its pelvis. It bowed to Hector as he came in, and he handed it his staff. "Thank you. The place looks wonderful," he said.

Skeletons couldn't show much in the way of appreciation, but Ida swore the red light in their eyes warmed. The first poured two glasses full of the liquid from the flask and handed one to Hector. It gave the other to Ida with a respectful dip of its head.

"Oh, I'm sorry, my manners," Hector said, waving his free hand in Ida's direction. "This is her Goodness, Ida North."

A grating, spine-chilling noise came from the first skeleton's teeth. Ida almost spilled her drink.

Hector nodded. "Yes, the guest bedroom overlooking the gardens will be perfect. Spiders in the bed won't be necessary—you may dismiss them."

Both skeletons rattled away.

"Who are they?" she asked.

"My housekeeper and steward," he said. "Dead long ago."

"Which is which?"

Hector frowned. "I don't remember. For several centuries after I raised them, I could tell them apart by their teeth. My steward had a gold tooth in the right maxilla, but teeth fall out over time, and he lost it."

"Do they answer to their names? Like your horse, Napoleon."

"Not anymore. Neither does Napoleon. You must forgive

my idiosyncrasies—he doesn't need a name, nor does he want it, but it's my foolish desire to hang on to the memory of a nice black horse that wandered into my castle courtyard one day dragging a dead knight with him. He was always something of a pet." Hector sipped his glass. "Do try this—it's spiced wine. It will take off some of the sleepiness the roses induce. As soon as you're rested and we've eaten, I'd like to go to the library and work for a few hours. We need to decide how to handle this situation and quickly."

"No tour?" Ida said.

Hector looked surprised. "My torture chambers aren't ready for guests. My staff cleaned them recently."

"I could skip those, but I'd like to see your gardens."

Hector smiled, his green eyes shone, and Ida shivered. He was horribly beautiful too, and she was finding him far too hard to resist. Perhaps she should forego the gardens.

"I'd be delighted to show you later," he said.

"Where's Hari?"

"He said he felt well enough to help with the luggage. I don't think Tinbit will let him overdo it."

The coachman carried Cear's firepot in, past them, and into a doorway on the left.

"Go with him," Hector said. "He has orders to take Cear to the library and build up the fire. I'm sure they want to stretch their legs after living in that bucket for the last three days and you might want to do the same after the coach ride. I'll be along presently." He swept his travelling cloak around him and strode back outside, leaving Ida with the skeleton.

"Lead on," she said, as it gave a grating sound that set her teeth on edge. How Hector had made a language out of it was a mystery she'd rather not be privy to. Probably involved magic spells composed of entrails, blood, and the distillate of shadows.

Ida tried to keep up with the number of twists, turns, stairways, and hidden doors, but soon lost count. This was the sort of place requiring a trail of breadcrumbs or lentils, but she had neither, and anyway, Hector wasn't trying to confuse her on purpose. When she entered the library, she decided Hector might be the most wicked witch in the world, but his inner sanctum was the kind of place she'd be happy to stay in for hours.

It was the brightest, airiest room imaginable, and the fact it existed inside his dark, forbidding castle, seemed as incongruous as a delicate fern on a stand that reached out for her, tangled a frond in her hair, and withdrew it at a soft grating command from the skeleton.

The tall bookcases spoke of a place of study, but most of the room resembled a makeshift conservatory. Along with heavy leather reading chairs and walnut tables, there were multiple plant stands and a wrought iron potting bench next to a sunny window. A tray of small plants sat on it, all of them about to outgrow their pots and reeking like young skunks. Beside a pile of unshelved tomes, a vampire bat lily flapped excitedly at the sight of her, realized it couldn't take off from its stalk yet, and subsided, closing its sepals around itself.

Ida paced the well-worn stone floors, hands behind her back, looking at everything—the cluttered tables, the leather pillows, open bags of potting soil and plant food, the books, a black wool blanket folded carefully up in a seat, and a pair of well-worn house slippers resting below an ottoman. Another horrible grinding sound came from the skeleton as he set Cear's firepot on the hearth.

She resisted the urge to cover her ears. "No, I require nothing. Tend the fire for the salamander and you may leave."

The skeleton shrugged its clavicles and started to pile the kindling in the fireplace. She'd only guessed at the question—probably something like whether she needed refreshment or the card catalog. Any answer would do to make it quit grinding its teeth.

The fire was soon leaping in the grate. The fern, now dropping long tendrils and attempting to walk across the room toward her, saw the salamander crawl out of the pot and retreated, drawing its fronds up fearfully. The skeleton walked out of the library, leaving Ida alone with Hector's strange plants and Cear, taking a human shape as they stood in the fresh flame, dusting ashes from their legs.

"He asked you if you were Hector's friend," the salamander said quietly.

"I don't know if I'm his friend or not," Ida said. "He is not what I expected."

"Nor are you what he expected," Cear said. "You surprise him and interest him too."

"I suppose." Ida picked up a book and prepared to whack the nosy fern with it. "What is this infernal plant doing?" she asked as Hector came through the door.

The fern retracted all its feelers and froze, a rigid plant on a stand. Hector eyed it in surprise. "Why, what did it do?"

Ida set down the book. "It crawled out of its pot and tried to get in my hair."

Hector gently brushed the fern's curling leaves. "There, there. She wouldn't have really hurt you."

It wilted.

He sighed. "It's a sensitive fern…a relatively harmless species. It only kills people when it's been slighted."

"Oh." Ida gave it the side-eye. "I'm terribly sorry," she said, but it had already curled itself up into a ball. "Your library is magnificent, Hector. Any fern would be comfortable here."

"It actually prefers the greenhouse," Hector said, stroking its curled leaflets. "But it had a falling-out with a man-eating Venus flytrap, and I caught it trying to fertilize it to death. I decided I'd better keep it here until the drama dies down." He bent over the fern. "And yes, pet, I know it didn't properly appreciate you, no one does, but I love you, yes, yes, I do—"

Ida watched him, unsure if she should laugh or shake her head.

"I came to escort you to your room," he said. "My housekeeper is taking down the cobwebs now, and I thought you might like a hot bath before dinner. Then, if you are willing, I'd like to discuss the spellwork on your side of the Happily-Ever-After and answer your questions about mine. I know it's not done—discussing our magic with each other—and I fully expect you to take advantage of me the next time, but I can assure you, I won't be doing the same things next time."

"I wouldn't expect anything less," Ida said. "Rest assured, you won't get any advantage over me, either. But this has to be solved together, I agree."

"Splendid. Shall we?" He offered her his arm.

Well, it was his castle. She'd indulge him.

Hector led her up several flights of stairs, each gloomier and darker than the last. Long strands of blood-colored moss hung from the ceiling, torches burned fitfully, spluttering and casting creepy shadows on the walls, and once, a hellhound jumped out of a hidden alcove and attempted to lick her to death before Hector told it to settle down, she was a guest and not to be eaten. It stalked after them both, drooling flames happily.

Hector opened a set of large, frightfully squeaky doors. He stepped aside for Ida to enter. "You can go right in. I've disarmed the trapdoor." The dog frisked around him, and he scratched behind its ears. "No, Spot, she doesn't want you on her bed to warm it."

It whined.

"Oh, I don't mind," Ida said. "As long as it doesn't shed too much brimstone."

With a happy bark, the massive animal jumped up on the huge, forbidding bed and wallowed around, black and red fur turning golden with heat.

"Spot?" she raised an eyebrow.

Hector watched, amused. "When the dog first came, Tinbit didn't like her because she wouldn't stay off the furniture. He took to calling her 'out, dammit' and I added the 'spot.' I didn't know you liked pets."

"I've had pets before. Once, a lovely Cheshire cat moved into our stable and had kittens. Of course, they all vanished as soon as they grew up, but the mother stayed with me in the castle for many years until one day, she remained visible while sleeping and I realized she was dead." Ida stopped. She'd wept for weeks after that cat died. She didn't keep pets after that. It was too hard to say goodbye.

The hellhound winked out, leaving a distinct smell of sulfur, a parting fart perhaps.

"I must see to supper, but if you would like to visit the gardens, I'll accompany you later."

"No. I think I'll rest," she said quickly. "I didn't sleep very well at the inn."

Hector drew a deep breath. "Ida, I must say it. I'm sorry—I never meant for it to go so far, and I deeply regret my actions. It won't happen again, I assure you."

She clamped her eyes shut. "Don't apologize, Hector. The feeling is completely mutual."

"Good, good," he said, suddenly brisk and professional, not at all like the man who coddled sensitive ferns and let hellhounds hop on his beds. "I'd hate to think you saw anything untoward in what I did. I didn't mean to…uh…touch you."

"And I didn't mean to enjoy it—" She cut herself off sharply. "Perhaps it would be better if we said no more about it."

"I agree." He turned his back on her. "Dinner is at six. Any skeleton can show you to the dining hall."

Then he was gone, shutting the door behind him.

31

Hector

When I think back over the number of years spent in these mountains, I am humbled by people traditionally consigned to the lexicon of monsters—dragons, giants, goblins, even gnomes to a lesser extent. History may record I did a great deal to advance the protections for the folk in my care and improved their lives, but it wouldn't be honest.

In so many ways, they've taught me my own insignificance as a human, reminded me a millennium is not enough time to even break the surface of the great mystery of magic, and have changed my life in ways for which I am profoundly grateful.

(Editor: redact whole passage. Entirely too personal.)

A THOUSAND YEARS OF WICKEDNESS: A MEMOIR

HECTOR WEST

HECTOR HESITATED BEFORE OPENING THE DOOR TO the skullery. Tinbit hated it when he looked over his shoulder or made any kind of suggestions regarding dinner, how he'd like it to be served, or even what he'd prefer for breakfast in the morning. As a wicked witch, Hector knew he should expect total and complete control over his employees, but then, he doubted any wicked witch ever had an employee quite as stubborn as Tinbit. Or one he considered so much a friend. He took a deep breath and pushed the door open.

Tinbit glanced up from the crabapple pie he'd plated. "Her Goodness is settled in?"

"Yes."

Three skeletons prepared dinner, bustling about with a happy clicking and clattering. One tossed greens and flowers with a vinaigrette, another basted the haunch of venison in the oven, and the other tended a pot of soup over a raised burner, maintaining a delicate simmer. A warm, oniony aroma drifted from the pot.

"I moved dinner to five, not six," Tinbit said, artfully applying a generous portion of whipped cream over the pie. "I thought you and Ida might like a walk in the gardens afterward before you retire to the library, or the bedroom." He left off swirling with an angry jerk.

A retort formed in his mouth, but he thought better of it. "Is that for Hari?" he asked.

"Yes," Tinbit said. "I took him some potato and leek soup. He ate it all and he's feeling much better, so I thought he might like dessert."

"Good," Hector said. "I'm sure Ida will be pleased that he'll be well enough to leave for her castle in the morning."

Tinbit huffed. "He's not well. And neither am I."

"It will pass," Hector said. "Ida and I will find the dragon and the princess and sort all this out soon. I don't know when we'll be back, but I really think you might be better staying here at the castle."

"That won't suit." Tinbit jabbed a fork in the pie slice. "I'm going with you. And Hari is going with Ida. He's her gnome and he'll want to go with her. It's no different than me saying I'm going to the mountains with you. You need me."

"I go to the mountains without you all the time—"

"In a giant's knapsack," Tinbit said, glaring. "I trust Pocket to get you out of trouble if you get yourself into it. But you aren't taking a giant this time. I'm coming. Besides, someone has to take care of Hari."

"That's not a good idea, not with the love magic still running rampant."

"Maybe not. But we're all in this fuck-up together now, Hector, whether you like it or not, and we'd best sort it out together too." Tinbit picked up the plate and left the kitchen.

Hector flopped into the chair Tinbit had vacated. He'd call it a magical cascade failure rather than a fuck-up, but Tinbit had a point.

It was one thing to know that his own feelings were the reaction to Ida's obnoxious love magic, but it was another thing to believe it wasn't more than that. He enjoyed her company, and when he thought back over the last thousand years, he always had. He liked their conversations. They'd always been stimulating, thought-provoking, and when it came right down to it, fun. Her mind engaged him, her temper provoked him in the best kind of way, and when he remembered how the light hit her hair as she stood, bathed in the hellhound's flames, he burned inside. If she'd asked him to take up where he'd left off that morning, he'd have been out of his robes in a hot second. It was enough to make him question his proposal to Sebastian.

He groaned under his breath. Tinbit was right. Love magic or not, this *was* a complete and utter fuck-up.

He rose and tapped the skeleton stirring the soup on the scapula. "Serve dinner on the tea table in the library instead of the great hall, please. Send someone to tell Ida to meet me there. And bring a platter of fresh-cut sweetgrass to the table as well."

At least in the library, Cear's presence would keep him from making any more mistakes.

He found Ida waiting for him in the library dressed in her white robes. She'd taken the sensitive fern from its stand and was telling it how green and robust it looked while it curled its fiddleheads in happiness. Hector watched quietly from the doorway, curling in happiness himself. How could such a robe, decidedly unrevealing and covering every inch of Ida's body, thrill him like a boy at Midwinter Feast, eager to open a present? He swallowed hard, and stepped aside to let the skeletons set out the repast on the small table where he often took breakfast.

Cear rose in human form on the hearth as the skeletons brought in a wrought iron balcony chair and table for them to use. The fireplace glowed with a warmth in keeping with the evening chill, but Hector sweated uncomfortably around the collar as he entered, coughing to announce himself.

Ida turned around and smiled. Her cheeks colored red as poppies in the firelight and her lavender eyes shone, changing almost the same way her hair did in different lighting.

One more day. One more, and he'd be done with this nonsense. He took his seat across from Ida. "I see you've made a friend," he said, nodding to the fern.

"It really is charming," she said, petting it gently. "If it ever sends out runners, I'd like one." She set the fern gently on its stand

and took the seat the skeleton pulled out for her. "Thank you for serving dinner here instead of the grand hall. While I applaud your attention to evil detail, blood moss, damp stone, and guttering torchlight isn't my idea of a tasteful dining experience."

She was being professional. Good. Professional would help. "Nor mine. The last time I served guests in the main hall, I hosted a masque for the fae university. I didn't think we'd ever get the smell of mead out of the magic carpets." He tucked his napkin into his collar and sat back as the skeleton set a bone-colored porcelain bowl of greens sprinkled with borage flowers before him and drizzled it with creamy poppyseed dressing.

"This is lovely," Ida said, gazing at the bright safflower petals and nasturtium blossoms in her bowl. "From your gardens?"

"Oh, no. Most of mine are devoted to magical plants," he said. "Tinbit grows the edible flowers at his house."

"Where is Tinbit?" Ida asked, sampling the soup. The skeleton clattered over helpfully with the pepper grinder. She waved them away.

"He never eats with me," Hector said, waving the skeleton with the main course into the room. "He considers it inappropriate. He'll eat in his house. Indeed, he took a bowl of soup to Hari earlier—you don't need to worry. He'll take good care of him."

"It's not *that* I'm worried about," Ida said, frowning.

"I know," he said. "Perhaps if they took the potion again—"

"You know as well as I do, it won't keep them from falling back in love with each other," Ida broke in, tearing open a roll to dip in her soup. "Separation should help, but—"

"It's the love magic," Hector finished. "As long as it's spreading, it's a factor."

The skeleton served the venison next, hot, buttery, and

redolent with rosemary and juniper berries. Hector complimented the chef after tasting it. Skeletons as a rule weren't as temperamental as gnomes, but any chef, even a dead one, likes to hear their work is exemplary. The skeleton blushed blood red to the marrow as he retreated.

"Perhaps it might be best you first tell me everything you can about how you conduct your end of the Happily-Ever-After before we meet with the dragons. The more I know about how Alistair is involved, the sooner we can counteract this magic," Ida said, cutting her venison into small portions.

Cear, having finished their sweetgrass, gazed at the table with interest, but their plate of food, which Hector had insisted on serving, remained untouched. "Everything about Happily-Ever-After would take a long time to explain, would it not?"

"Not really." Hector pressed his fingers together. "The tradition has evolved somewhat over time, of course, but the magic itself hasn't changed in centuries. Once upon a time, the knights were chosen to compete for the hand of the Common Princess since, at the time, there were no true royalty—just warlords. Even before Happily-Ever-After existed, dragons considered roast knight a delicacy. Cooked in their armor, which acts like a cast-iron pot, great tenderness could be achieved, and with a little sage and thyme added—"

"We're eating, Hector," Ida said, taking a long gulp of wine.

"My point is dragons have always kidnapped princesses to attract knights. In fact, many of them used to collect princesses much as an angler collects their favorite lures. That made dragons a natural choice for the event. Of course, now that they don't have to eat knights, there's little need to collect princesses, but they are still avid collectors—it's a matter of what and to what extent. Adair, Alistair's father, collects folk art. Alistair is slightly unusual in that he collects what he makes. He's a sculptor."

"With what would a dragon sculpt?" Cear asked.

"What he has in abundance. Fire."

Cear's breath smelled of hot wind, cinders, and sweetgrass "How unique. I long to see it."

Ida sipped her wine. "So when you give a dragon the black rose, it makes them want to collect princesses instead of what they usually collect."

"Yes. I prefer to influence the natural instincts of my…monsters, as you would call them. But Alistair was reluctant from the beginning. He said Happily-Ever-After was demeaning to both dragons and princesses."

"Demeaning?" Ida leaned forward. The fern crawled down from its stand, up into her lap, and tangled its fronds in her hair. "Why?"

"Alistair is a dragon of strong, often controversial, opinions," Hector admitted. "He felt quite strongly that the whole thing left him no choice, and the girl had less than he. Went on about it for some time. Of course, both his parents and I explained to him the significance of Happily-Ever-After and that the girls actually compete to be princesses. I seem to remember that you have fairly extensive preparation trials—"

"He didn't come to kidnap the princess," Ida said, eyes wide. "He came to make a point." She sat back in her chair, hand absently curled in the fern's fiddleheads.

Hector irritably set his wine glass down and reached for the water. He hadn't meant to divulge that much, not in front of Cear. "Perhaps, but in the end, he accepted his role." At least he'd thought so. "There's nothing wrong there. Perhaps something was wrong with the princess. She shouldn't have even wanted to defend a dragon."

Ida reddened and set down her wine glass too. "Like your dragon, Amber has strong opinions about fairness and right. But like you, I hadn't changed my love charm since it was handed over to me by my mentor. Once the princess takes the rose, she becomes open to love. It's as simple as that. When she meets the prince, who has had his heart opened by drinking a potion containing the petals of that rose, she falls in love with him and he with her, and they live happily ever after. After the dragon comes, kidnaps the princess, and the prince goes on his quest to rescue her, of course. Which clearly doesn't appear to be going according to plan."

"Alistair did kidnap the princess." Hector glared at Ida.

"Looked more like a rescue to me," Ida said. "But, Hector, we're never going to get anywhere arguing about *who* went wrong."

She had a point. "If there's nothing wrong with my dragon or your princess, could it be what we did at the end—you tried to protect your princess and I tried to protect my dragon?"

She shook her head. "I don't think so. We shouldn't have needed to protect either of them. The mistake must have happened before then."

He cleared his throat. "Well, let's go further back, to the choosing. As I told you, Alistair is a prince of dragons. They've built their entire royal hierarchy around Happily-Ever-After, with their king-eggs all descending from Flamelords who have fought princes from the beginning. So how did you come to choose this princess?"

"Are you insinuating that I picked the wrong girl?" Ida tossed her napkin on the table.

So much for not fighting. "I'm not insinuating anything. But Amber does seem a little—unusual—I mean, compared to your previous selections."

She huffed. "I could just as easily say maybe you picked the wrong dragon! There's never been any need for the dragon to be a prince."

"It's traditional."

"Well, maybe I picked the Common Princess in the traditional way!"

"Very well then." He sighed. "Let's look at the Prince. You said you brew the potion with the petals of the red rose. Did something happen with that?"

"You were there, Hector. Aside from the theatrics of the thing, it went according to plan." She rolled her eyes.

"I'd hardly call anything about that night according to plan," he said.

She smiled slightly. "You still owe me a new wand."

"And you owe me a new jersey. Tinbit couldn't get the stains out."

"So what? It will match the rest of your clothes."

She was smiling now, and curses, the feeling he'd had—that he'd touched on a sensitive spot by attacking her choice in princesses—vanished in a pleasant bubble of wishing she'd smile at him that way all the time. He popped it with a forced frown.

"Walk me through the procedure anyway."

She brushed an inquisitive leaflet out of her face. "Very well. The spell is steeped in golden wine along with the rose petals for three days. It's served at the Prince's Dinner as the traditional toast to the happy marriage. I made it the way I always do, and the captain of the guard—that Caedan fellow—served it to the prince. I gave it to him as soon as I got there."

Hector stifled an unhappy burp. He regarded his untouched crabapple pie, appetite vanishing in a dreadful sense of foreboding.

The captain of the guard had been with the prince at the game. Then he'd been on the field when Alistair landed, getting in front of the prince to defend him, and then there was Rupert's cryptic comment about how he'd like the young man to be eaten by a griffin. "Hypothetically, if the prince didn't drink that potion, what would happen to your love magic?"

"Nothing. With no love interest available, the princess wouldn't fall in love. The spell would remain incomplete until she found a person with whom she might be naturally compatible. Oh, Gods." Ida leaned back in her chair, face draining of color. "Do you think that—"

He nodded. The crawling, burning, and freezing sensation of doom had just galvanized into a horrific certainty. "Yes. The prince never took that potion. The captain of the guard made sure he didn't. Archibald Quentin Rupert II is gay. And he's already in love."

32

Ida

One of the things I most admire in gnomes is their deep commitment to each other. They are attentive to the wants and needs of their partners in a way that might make me jealous if it didn't give me the wonderful opportunity to study natural Happily-Ever-Afters. There are no happier couples than gnomes who may stay together for a century or more.

The only problem I've encountered in their community is the ostracization of those gnomes who find it hard to settle, who don't make the familial bonds expected in their rigid social structure for one reason or another, a failing that sometimes distresses me as it has affected a dear friend of mine.

*MAGIC AND MISCHIEF–A THOUSAND
YEARS OF HAPPILY-EVER-AFTER: A MEMOIR*

IDA NORTH

"You can't be serious. Oh. Oh, Hector!"

She balled her hand and pressed it to her forehead. In all the years of royalty marrying commoners, it hadn't occurred to a king, queen, or member of the selection committee that a prince might not wish to marry a common girl—he might prefer a common man. But it should've occurred to a witch.

Hector rested his elbows on the table, rubbing his forehead like the evening's wine had given him a tremendous headache. She certainly had one, but it wasn't the wine.

"What do we do?" She barely trusted her voice. She'd met the man, Caedan, at the Happily-Ever-After, felt that little niggling sense that perhaps he cared more for his prince than the average knight, but she'd been so focused on Amber and the botched selection process, she'd not given much thought to the prince.

"I don't know," Hector said, looking up. "I must confess—I might have had some inkling—"

"When? Hector, when did you have an inkling?"

"At the game. Rupert told me he wasn't happy about Caedan's influence on the prince. He talked about sending him on a quest, and he mentioned something about hoping he'd be killed—"

"Gods, Hector! You could have told me. I was right there!"

"Since when did I ever interfere with your side of the magic?" he asked, sounding annoyed. "And I had no reason to believe it was anything more than Rupert being Rupert. He's never been a pleasant person—you should have seen what he did to my poor troll at his Happily-Ever-After. And he wanted Archie to kill the dragon. He's about as trustworthy as that disreputable rag, the *Star!*"

"Which got it right." Ida leaned back in her chair, arms folded over her chest.

"Since when did that infernal tabloid ever get anything right? They predicted the end of Happily-Ever-After last year based on a comet!"

Cear, standing by the fire, folded their hands in front of them. "Correct me if I'm wrong, but if the spell was not concluded as written, shouldn't it dissipate? Why did the dragon kidnap the princess? Why would he not immediately leave the field? Why would the princess not simply go home? They aren't compatible at all."

Ida squirmed, horribly uncomfortable now. The princess should have left—she'd wanted to from the very beginning. But Ida'd had to go and insist that the magic itself had chosen her. How could she have been so foolish? Hector and his candor curse couldn't fully account for that. She'd just been so angry, so upset with the way Happily-Ever-After had been corrupted, how she'd not stepped up and said something, all because that would have meant admitting her mistake to Hector. But wouldn't the magic have gotten it right? It clearly hadn't.

"Well, that's neither here nor there," Hector said, drumming his fingers on the table. "The fact is, they didn't run, and even if they are accidentally in love, the spell didn't stop with them. And it's not just the love magic that's still spreading: Everything is coming out through the cracks. First the scarecrows breeding out of season, crops ripening before they're ready—I shouldn't be surprised if we don't hear of floods in the south and forest fires up north soon."

"What I'd give for a copy of a paper right now," Ida murmured. "I don't suppose you take the *Star*, though."

"I don't get any papers out here. Eagle delivery is outrageously expensive. Too many of them get eaten by griffins."

"What if I wrote Annabeth tonight, confront her, see how Archie is doing—"

Hector's hands curled slowly into fists. "No, no, no—we talked about this. We can't have anyone going to the papers, and you know she will."

"Unless she staged that party specifically to refute the paper's allegations," Ida mused. "I wouldn't put it past her."

"I'm almost positive Rupert knew they were true. I only wish I'd suspected sooner. Maybe we could have countered this then, but what do we do now?" Hector pushed his chair back forcefully and rose. He left the table and crossed to the window that overlooked the courtyard of black roses.

Ida joined him. The roses were silver in the dusk, lighting up as if from moonlight within, but when she looked closely, one of the white lights left a rose and drifted to the next—lightning bugs. Probably poisonous. She pulled her robe tighter around herself. She wanted Hector to put his arms around her like he had at the inn, to squeeze her hand, tell her it would be all right, they'd figure things out, they'd make it right. But how could it ever be right again if it had always been wrong? Somehow, she had to make Hector see that. She had to let him know what had happened at the choosing, what she'd done. He'd never be able to understand if she didn't.

"Hector, I…"

"Yes?"

No. She couldn't do it. She didn't want him as her enemy again. "I…I think I'll go check on Hari and try to get him to go home if I can. There's a possibility that the love magic may intensify as we get closer to the princess and the dragon, and I don't want any distractions. We'll need all our wits about us to solve this. And after that, I think I'll read for a while and see if there's anything in my books regarding dragons in love. Perhaps, you could get my library for me—I'll give you the location if you could transport the books to my room."

He shuddered, as if he'd grown cold, although the breeze was unusually warm for this time of year. More climate change.

"I'll have them sent to the dining hall," he said. "If your library is anything like mine, I doubt your room would hold them all."

"Thank you. It was a lovely dinner."

"Ida?"

Her hand was on the doorknob when he spoke. "Yes, Hector?"

His green eyes shone with steadfast determination. "We will fix this. I promise."

"Of course." She inclined her head and shut the door quietly behind her.

Hari, as it turned out, was not in the castle at all. A skeleton directed Ida to the courtyard and pointed out an arch in the rose hedge that led to a house that looked so different from Hector's castle, Ida automatically knew she'd entered a different and somehow forbidding world. A gnome's world.

This was Tinbit's domain, and everyone from the skeletal housekeeper to a squat frog carrying a mouth full of keys that he used to open the gate for her looked like they didn't belong there either. She hurried across the tiny courtyard filled with small potager gardens and a fountain that fed a small pool full of—

"Are those razor-toothed redfish?" She gazed into the water where tiny crimson fish happily fed on what looked like a chicken leg.

"Don't tell Hector. They're his birthday present." Tinbit rose from behind a boxy rosemary he'd been trimming. "You're here to see Hari."

"Yes."

Tinbit snipped a few green leaves and tucked them in a small handbasket. "He's fine, you know. I fed him and put him to bed. I can take care of him."

"I know you can."

Tinbit fixed her with a curiously intense gaze. "You think that if I could take him away from you, I would. Well, you're right." He snipped a few more leaves. "I would. In a heartbeat. But I won't. I wouldn't hurt Hari for all the world. Go in the house, turn left past the kitchen, and he's in the third room on the right. It was my bedroom when I was a boy."

"I wouldn't want to disturb your family."

"No one else lives here now. It's just me." He returned to barbering his rosemary.

Ida crossed the paving stones, weaving her way through more rosemary, lavender, scented geraniums, and roses. These weren't the black, thorny things she'd seen in Hector's courtyard, but little tiny musk roses—pink, white, yellow, and even a soft, summer orange variety. They'd escaped their trellises, almost covering the low, one-story house sprawled in the evening mist beyond the garden. She ducked to enter the arched doorway.

Tinbit's gnome home was as cozy a place as Ida had seen, although the décor was quite different from what she was used to at Hari's mother's house. Hari's mother loved the clean, airy, modern style of minimalism. If there was a coaster or a doily, it was meant to be used. But Tinbit seemed to positively delight in useless bric-a-brac.

It was gloriously cluttered with everything from decorative

flowerpots to bird skulls. Hari would have the time of his life in this place where there would never be any end of things to clean up, organize, and put away. Tinbit evidently shared Hari's fascination with clothes, which surprised her because he seemed to prefer dressing plainly, wearing only a cream-colored shirt and dark gray overalls with red-and-gold embroidery. But from the number of items lying around in various states of alteration and mending, it appeared Tinbit once had a thing for red velvet with black filigree, and he was also fond of satin waistcoats in vivid patterns. But they were all incredibly old. Many of them appeared to have been eaten by moths. If he didn't wear them, who had?

She passed through the sitting room, ducking to avoid the hanging light fixture, and entered the small kitchen. She'd expected this to be largely unused since there was a kitchen in the castle, but on the stove, a bright copper kettle glowed with a warm look, and steam rose delicately from the spout. He must have just made a cup of tea for Hari before going out to gather herbs. A basket of eggs sat on the counter along with a block of fragrant cheese and two gray shallots. Omelets for breakfast. Hari loved omelets.

There was no one in Hari's life, other than Ida, who doted on him like this. His mother loved him of course, but she'd always been the housekeeper, far too busy to indulge her offspring in anything. Hari had grown up learning how to carry a tray to Ida's room, lisping politely, "Your Goodneth?" until he'd earned a place in her heart that she'd reserved for him for his lifetime. But he'd never been…worshipped.

Tinbit would worship him.

"Oh, Hari," Ida muttered, easing through the narrow archway

into the hall. She knocked timidly on the little oak door at the end of the corridor.

"Come in," Hari said.

He was sitting up in bed. The brightest, most amazingly alive look was on his face, but it vanished as soon as he saw her. "Oh. I thought you were with Hector."

"What's that supposed to mean?"

"Nothing—just I thought you might be planning. Big day tomorrow and all."

"Oh. Later. He's getting my library for me." She moved to the side of his bed and chose a chair that had been pulled up to a comfortable distance for talking. Or rubbing someone's feet. "I just wanted to see how you were doing."

"Tinbit is taking good care of me."

"I see that." She glanced at the bedside table, where an empty tea cup kept company with a soup bowl, an empty plate, a saucer, and a cluster of multicolored roses in a vase. "But you have to leave early tomorrow," she said, touching the tea cup. "You probably shouldn't be drinking tea this late."

Hari gazed past her at the open doorway. "I'm not going."

"Hari, you specifically asked me if you could go home!"

"I've changed my mind. I'm well enough to go with you to the mountains. I want to stay with you."

"Why?"

He bit his lip. "Because if I try to go home tomorrow, alone, I'm going to get off at the first stop and run right back here. To him." He slumped in the bed. "I can't help it, Ida. I'm trying, but—"

"Tinbit is coming with us," Ida said softly. "Hector told me."

"Oh," he said quietly.

She nodded. "That's why you can't come, Hari. It will only make things harder for you. For both of you."

Hari bit his lip. "I know. But I'll have you and he'll have Hector and work always helps. If I'm focused on caring for you, making sure you have everything you need, I won't be thinking about how he's everything I need—Oh, Gods." He covered his face with his hands. "Why does he have to be everything I've always wanted?"

Ida held Hari close while he sobbed. "If I'd known how much this would hurt, I'd have burned his letters and let you hate me."

"I know it's not real. I know I'll have to take more of that damned potion and it burns and makes me sick, but I can't help it. He looks at me, and I love him. He smiles, and I melt. He sets a vase of roses down beside me because he thought I'd like the way they smell, and all I can think about is how he smelled when he was in bed with me—spicy, dark, and warm—and I want him. Oh, Ida, if he told me to walk off a cliff with him, I'd go."

She rocked him in her arms like she used to do when he was a gnomelet. Of all the miserable revelations she'd been through this evening, this might be the worst. Yes, love magic was running amok; yes, Happily-Ever-After had broken and she was pretty sure that was all her fault now, but if it was wrong, if they were wrong all along, maybe they'd been wrong about this too.

"You're stronger than that," she said, stroking his hair. "If he took you to a cliff, you'd pull him back from the edge and take him home with you."

He sniffed. His eyes filled with confusion. "Ida?"

She stroked his hair. "I'll talk to Hector. If you really feel that strongly, maybe I'm wrong and there's something real there. I'll ask him if he could use another gnome."

He sat up, horrified. "But…I can't leave you!" He covered his face with his hands. "I can't let him see this."

"I'll let Hector know. He's a witch; he'll keep your secret safe if that's what you want."

"No." Hari's jaw tightened. "No. I can't. You're right. It's not real."

"Honey—"

"I'll fight it. Besides, you're going to fix it, and it will be over then."

She patted his hand. "It will be over. But Hari, if there's anything still there, you have my permission to follow it as far as it leads. I won't interfere. If you won't leave me, perhaps Tinbit might come back with us."

"He won't," Hari said stubbornly. "And I'm not going to make him." He lay back against the pillow and closed his eyes. "Go. I can handle this on my own."

Feeling terrible, she shut the door to the room gently and let herself out.

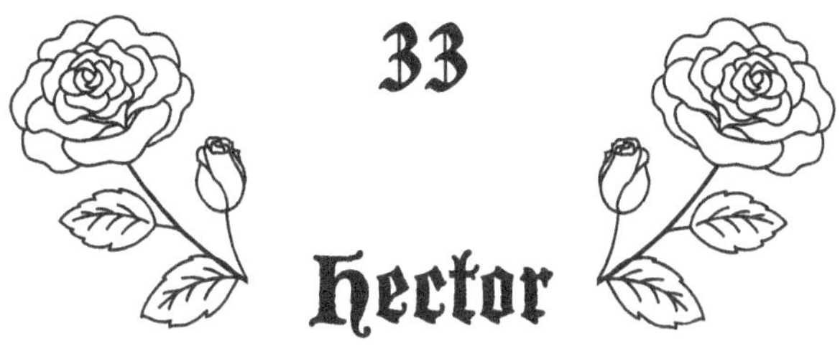

33

Hector

Among the most important things a Wicked Witch should consider when designing their evil lair is to include a space where they can reflect on their plans and schemes when things go awry. It's better to break a flowerpot than someone else's head.

A THOUSAND YEARS OF WICKEDNESS: A MEMOIR

HECTOR WEST

CEAR VANISHED FURTIVELY INTO THE COALS AFTER Ida left. Hector was glad. He didn't want to hear any further questions that he didn't have answers to. After a while, he left the window and went to his desk. He pulled an ancient parchment folio from the drawer he'd bewitched into a never-ending file cabinet. He opened it hopefully, but it was nothing more helpful than his mentor's treatise on slugs and how to eradicate them from one's flowerbeds without resorting to inviting a murder of crows every day for breakfast. He put it back before it crumbled to dust in the modern air of his library. There had to be something he could do to save this situation. He hadn't given up his own life and chance for love to let everything he'd worked for crash down in ruins a thousand years later.

He didn't like to think about that, but it was foremost on his mind now along with all the horrors he'd grown up with. He picked up another folder of his mentor's old writings, a collection of her gingerbread recipes. There was a time when nothing would grow in the polluted land, and families like his, with too many mouths to feed, sent their surplus children out the door with nothing more than a crust of bread for lunch and told them to get lost in the woods. And sometimes that was a far better option than going home…

He sighed. Even after Happily-Ever-After, healing the land had taken a long time. Fields flourished, but without a population to work them, food was scarce. Plague became a thing of the past, but so many people had been wounded or were already ill from the wars. They died by the thousands. People blamed his monsters for their continued misfortune. And they died by the millions.

He rose, walked to the table, and poured himself another glass of wine. This made three, and he seldom took more than a half glass with dinner, but tonight felt like it called for more. The anger Ida had directed at him for not talking to her earlier rankled. True, maybe he should have been more suspicious, but love wasn't something he dealt in, only in ways to delay it, hinder it, to thwart it as much as Happily-Ever-After called for, and all in carefully measured and precise ways. He deeply resented having it all upended like a cart of compost, especially by the prince. *That spoiled-rotten rich boy with a bad mother and a worse father, he's the one who gets a choice in his life now? I never had one.*

"Cear, I'm going out for a walk," he said to the flames. "I'll send someone in to bank your fire before bedtime."

Hector's gardens had been his sanctuary since he'd first moved into the castle, back when it was little more than a round tower built on very structurally unsound foundations by a former sorcerer who thought it had been a good idea to make his life force the cornerstone. Along came a freelance hero with a second-hand magical sword and boom, there went his "fortress of adamant." But the location was ideal, nestled in the bosom of the mountains, and when he'd seen the backyard and the lovely bog in the corner, he'd been sold.

Just past the stable and the field where the bone-horses frolicked, he'd planted his poisonous plant garden, a full half-acre of the most dangerous and deadly herbs and flowers from around the world, each one given its own favorite habitat. It had taken him the better part of three hundred years to accumulate all of the seeds and raise the plants. The corpse flower alone required regular applications of bone dust. Whole graveyards full of it, for centuries. He'd been so proud when it finally bloomed, even if Tinbit had walked around with a clothespin on his nose for a week.

After the garden, he'd built the greenhouse. This was his pride and joy, where he bred sentient species of plants, like the sensitive fern. His young bat lilies were there, fluttering around and eating insects, the carnivorous sundews were happily eating careless bat flowers, and the man-eating flytrap—well, he'd probably need to see if the kitchen had a leg of mutton lying around because it might be a week before he fed it again, and maybe more than that if he didn't come up with a way to fix Happily-Ever-After.

"Hector?"

He turned.

Ida was coming out of the rose gate that led to Tinbit's house.

He forced a smile. "I was just going for a walk before I turned in. Early start in the morning."

She pulled her robe tighter against the chill. "Do you mind if I walk with you? I have something I need to talk to you about. Maybe a few things."

"All right," he said. He almost offered his arm, took one look at her tilted eyebrow, and decided against it. "I did promise to show you the gardens after all."

"You did," she said. She folded her arms behind her back, pacing beside him.

"What would you like to see first? The poison garden? The greenhouse? My updated bog?"

She smiled slyly. "You were going to enter your bog into *Witches' Weeds* contest, weren't you? And here I thought it was going to be your front flowerbeds with the three-foot sword thorns."

"Maybe," he said. "But that was before your giant pumpkins caught my attention."

She snorted. "To think, losing that damned contest to you was all I was really worried about two weeks ago."

"Things change."

They walked on in silence for a while. "Hector? Do you think anything like this has ever happened before?"

"I don't know," he said heavily. He opened the door to the greenhouse. "I hope not."

"I don't think it has," she said, picking up a fledgling bat lily and setting it on a plant bench—not the one with the sundews, curling their leaves in excitement. "But that might be wishful thinking on my part."

"Have you ever had a princess who hesitated before?" He surreptitiously nudged an open sack of freeze-dried mice out of sight.

Ida's cheeks blushed pink in the sunset rays coming through the panes of the greenhouse. "Not…not that I can recall. What is that? The thing with the beetle-shaped blossoms."

"Oh. That's a bugainvillea—I got it to feed the bat lilies. Don't worry—it isn't spawning at the moment. Or it shouldn't be." He surveyed it with some anxiety, but the buds didn't look more swollen than usual. "There's always a first for things. I've never had a dragon as reluctant as Alistair, although Adair did insist on writing a poem for his event—he was nearly late because he couldn't get that sixtieth stanza just right."

"I remember," Ida said, smiling. "Annabeth yawned."

"Rude. And he was being nothing but polite."

"*She* was only polite when it was in her best interest. She's nothing like Amber."

"I'd still like to know more about that girl," he said.

She set down the pot of serpent moss she'd been examining. "What about her?"

"Only—only that she seems a remarkable woman," he said, surprised by her sharp tone. "I can see why you chose her. She has a wonderful sense of duty and honor."

"Oh," she said, reddening further. "Pity it wasn't Caedan who I picked."

"Perhaps after this, you can simply recruit as many men as

women to select as Common Princess. Prince. Although, I must say, it would have been more helpful to have known the prince's inclination before all of this." He picked a stem of blood orchid and handed it to her. "Don't bring it too close to your robe—you'll never get the stain out."

She just held the blood orchid like she thought it might bleed all over her hand. "Well, why didn't we?"

"I beg your pardon?"

"Why didn't we?" She gazed out through the windows at the mist gathering over the bog with a disconcerted and pained look on her face. "A thousand years we've been in charge of Happily-Ever-After, Hector, and we didn't even bother to find out if the prince was gay. Who's to say whether we've made mistakes like this before? We may have made hundreds of them. Thousands of them. And not just in matters like this."

"No one said we were infallible—"

"But isn't this magic supposed to be?"

"Yes," he said, dragging out the word. He'd seen her take this line of questioning before, in Council, usually when she wanted to get Tara on her side to go against him—Agatha nearly always sided with Ida as a matter of rivalry. He turned to snap a few dead leaves from his vicious ficus, crooning a few words of calming to keep it from lashing out at him with all its branches. "The magic can't be wrong. But traditions should change, and it's entirely possible I have been…a bit absent in this respect—something I intend to rectify. It won't be that difficult to make sure we keep up with the times. I'm quite sure many common men would jump at the chance to wed a prince in the future. You could send them on quests to test their worth, like you test the princesses."

She blushed, and he thought the beauty of her face outshone

the sunset. A sudden impulse seized him to pluck a flower from his blooming moon-star cactus and twine it in her hair. He shoved both hands, full of dead ficus leaves, into his pockets.

"I'm quite sure common men will jump at the chance. What I'm not sure about is how the committee will feel about it."

"Committee? What committee?"

She set the blood orchid bloom down on the bench as it had started to drip. The fledgling bat lily bud crawled over from behind a weeping fern to investigate. "Do you remember when I brought that petition to the Council about the commoners wanting to streamline the process of choosing the princess?"

"Vaguely. I believe there was something about the whole picking up grains of wheat and your enchanted mice being a little frightening?"

She waved her hand dismissively. "They set up a committee to process applications and added a long questionnaire I wrote up, yes. But it didn't stop there, Hector. For the last few Happily-Ever-Afters, the committee has chosen the Common Princess."

"I see." He rocked back on his heels. "Well, I wish you'd told me, but it actually might make our explanation to the Council easier, if common people, and not you, chose Amber. She's the wrong princess."

"No, no, no, Hector. She's not the wrong princess. I wish she were." She folded her arms over her chest and turned away, as if she couldn't bear to face him. "I let the magic choose, and it chose Amber. The magic itself chose the princess."

 **34**

Ida

There are times when turning someone into stone would solve so many problems.

MISCHIEF AND MAYHEM: A THOUSAND
YEARS OF HAPPILY-EVER-AFTER

IDA NORTH

HE OUGHT TO SCREAM AT HER. HE OUGHT TO AT LEAST step back as if completely stunned. Or look outraged. Anything besides just staring at the pea-gravel floor with both hands jammed in his robe and ficus leaves poking out of his pockets. His mouth worked for a moment, like he couldn't decide whether or not to curse. He'd obviously come to the same conclusion she had and didn't know how to process it. But she already had come to the inevitable answer.

"It's not that our choices alone were flawed," she said quietly. "You yourself said we were fallible, and for that, we could make amends. We could get the princess, the dragon, and all go back to the castle and sort things out, that's true. I'm even willing to bet that if the prince marries his Common Prince, the magic will be fulfilled and we can go on thinking everything is right. But it's not. If the magic can't make mistakes, then how do you explain Amber? I can't. And it absolutely chose her, Hector."

"I don't see that you gave it much choice," he said.

"If that's so, why didn't the rose simply wither in my hand? The magic made a mistake—and if that's the case, what if we haven't been monstrously wrong all this time? We've been insisting that the prince marry a commoner since the very inception of Happily-Ever-After—two hearts for the peace of the world—because it seemed right to us and because magic of this nature requires constant maintenance. But we manufacture that love—you with your monsters to test the courage of the royals, and me with my potions and charms to make everything end happily-ever-after for the common people. Without that, do you seriously think that any prince we've ever married to a Common Princess would have chosen that union?"

"Of course not. That was the whole point." Hector jerked his hands out of his pockets and leaned on the orchid bench, staring into the forest of green leaves and crimson flowers dripping that deep purple-red nectar all over the ground below, creating a slick of blood that pooled around his feet. "We couldn't count on anyone to do the right thing but ourselves. The royalty had practically salted the earth—you haven't forgotten that and neither have I. They deserved to have their choice taken away from them!"

"How was that fair to the common people?"

"Happily-Ever-After wasn't ever intended to be fair. It's there to hold the world together, to keep the peace. What's not fair is to ask an entire world to suffer because two people object to being in love." His voice carried a distinct chill.

He was angry. Well, so was she.

Ida pulled her arms tighter around herself. "Three objections now. I'd hoped it would be four. Can't you see how wrong it is? I thought you were better than that, Hector."

"Better than—Ida, I was there when we cooked that magic up. Believe me, there was no doubt in anyone's mind—including mine—that it was necessary. Why else would we Cardinal Witches give up so much for it? Don't presume to lecture me about sacrifice. I know what I lost, the same as you do." He leaned heavily on the bench, long dark hair sweeping into his salt-and-pepper beard like the night sweeping into the stars ahead of a storm. She'd never thought of him having any regrets about a life without love, without family—a long life of loneliness. She'd always thought he might as well have been born heartless. A sudden sadness filled her. He'd missed as much as she had.

She touched his shoulder gently. "Well, maybe I think it was all a little much to give up for something that would force people to fall in love where they have no natural inclination."

Hector rounded on her. "The alternative was an eternity of war. I don't think the desire of two people—or one witch—outweighs the need of an entire world for peace. And I can't believe you'd think that now."

She drew back from him in horror. "You would force the prince and Amber to marry?"

"Did I say anything about forcing them to marry? No! We'll find Alistair and Amber, get them all together with the prince and the captain of the guard, and we'll work something out. You can pick a few more roses, put them in the right hands, and we're done talking about this." He turned, heading for the door.

She stalked after him. "No, we're not done talking about it! Just putting people to rights won't fix Happily-Ever-After. We were wrong! The magic itself is wrong! You can't ignore that, Hector." She grabbed his arm, stopping him.

He was breathing through his nose like he'd just been running from a griffin. "No one is pretending we can't make mistakes, Ida, but the moment you go blaming magic that has worked perfectly for a thousand years—"

"Maybe it *never* did! Did you think about that?"

"Next you'll be saying you think the world would have fixed itself without Happily-Ever-After. After how many people died, though? After how many acres were forever ruined? After the royals hunted every magical creature to extinction, looking for the secret ingredient that would give them a potion that would make them invincible?"

"I'm not saying that at all. What I'm saying is that maybe they're right—the princess, the prince, even your dragon. Perhaps Happily-Ever-After should end now. This isn't the world we grew up in. It's changed. The people have changed. And we need to change too."

"You speak of that time like you never lived through it."

"I lived through it," Ida said quietly. "And I remember it as well as you do."

"We can't let that happen again, Ida. I promised myself—no war, no starving people, no plagues that kill whole cities. Never again. No one else should ever have to go to the graveyard and watch their mother weep for her dead father and brothers. No one else should ever have to come home and drink himself to death in a ditch because he can't get past what he saw in war. No one else need ever stare at their fallow fields, knowing they'll never yield grain again while their children starve in front of their eyes."

She set a hand on his shoulder. "We're not going back there, Hector. People aren't that way anymore, they aren't consumed by the need for power—"

"You can say that, when a king and his son wear dragon skin and threaten to kill a boy you've known since he was a dragonet—"

"Did the prince say he wanted to kill Alistair? Did he?"

Hector said nothing.

Ida drew herself up. "We find the princess and the dragon. They didn't deserve to become mixed up in this, especially Amber. And we'll make sure the prince and his captain of the guard wed, if that's what they want. But when this is over, we need to go to the Council and tell them the truth. Happily-Ever After has to end."

Hector looked up, eyes smoldering. "Are you serious? You want to undo the only thing that has held this land safe and happy for a thousand years? We can't just abdicate our responsibility like that. I won't let you. We will fix Happily-Ever-After, not abolish it. We will recruit common men as well as common women for the princess, I mean the prince—"

"And how do you think the world will react to that? Some of them will understand, certainly, but others will not—they'll want to know why we haven't been doing that all along—"

"Ida, I am way beyond caring what anyone thinks at this point! What's important is preserving the magic."

"You honestly think that people won't ask questions? The *Star* is—they've already called Amber's selection into question. How long do you think it will be before they're demanding more transparency in the process and all this comes out?"

He rounded on her, tall, furious, and his green eyes shone

with a vivid, almost yellow light in the darkening garden. "What you want is for me to tell you you're right and Happily-Ever-After is wrong. I'm not going to say that. I don't agree. And I'm not going to let the world fall apart because you can't get past your little fit of conscience. Like it or not, your slipup caused this whole disaster."

"It was your candor curse that gave me that 'little fit of conscience,'" she said, staring up at him, her temper building to a mountain of wrath. *He,* of all people, should have understood. She knew he was stubborn, but she'd never thought he was stupid.

"I'm not forgetting that," he said. "But you wouldn't have had one if you hadn't outsourced your responsibility in the first place."

"Of all the—" She stormed after him as he stomped off toward a beautifully constructed arbor of sleeping pea plants, all drowsing comfortably in the rising moonlight. "I didn't outsource my responsibility. I let the magic choose, as I should have done all of these years, and it picked the wrong person!"

"More evidence that you shouldn't have ever been in charge of Happily-Ever-After in the first place."

Had he slapped her, it couldn't have hurt more. She stopped where she stood, frozen in fury. "Fine," she said, finding her voice although it broke against the torrent of things she wanted to scream at him. "Fire me, revoke my immortality, whatever you want to do when we get back. But the truth will get out. I'll make sure it does."

He glared at her, face twisting in rage. "And I'll make sure no one ever suffers because of you."

She fled toward the castle, blinking away angry tears.

35

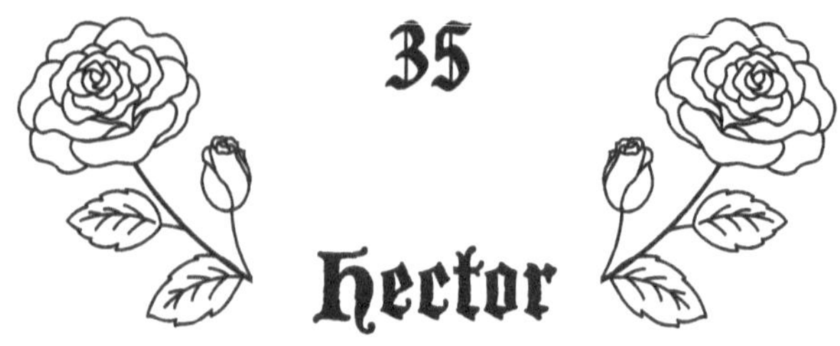

Hector

DRAGON KIDNAPS COMMON PRINCESS;
PRINCE REFUSES QUEST!

Queen Annabeth and King Rupert are said to be recovering at a resort spa in the coastal village of Serenade-By-The-Sea following the unexpected refusal of Crown Prince Archibald to leave on his quest to rescue Common Princess Amber Smith from the clutches of the vile (and incredibly sexy) dragon who carried her off to his evil lair.

The prince first claimed his best horse foundered, but this paper has obtained information from the First Stableboy that the horse, a gray destrier named Champion, is healthy as any horse and has suffered no lameness. The prince remains in the castle with the Captain of the Guard. Are wedding bells soon to ring for the prince and his paramour? This paper says yes!

Council Set to Burn Witches Over Magical Snafu. Is Happily-Ever-After Dead? Juicy details on page four!

—THE SORCERER'S STAR

A DISTANT THUD FROM THE DIRECTION OF THE CASTLE let Hector know Ida had reached it and that she was still in a towering temper. He turned and walked off in the direction of the bog garden.

This was his favorite place, and one he'd wanted to show Ida especially. Here, a peace descended with the mist that brought him comfort on restless nights. It had always brought him comfort on the nights when the belladonna failed to keep the insomnia away. He loved to walk the paths he'd raised between the pools, where his tame mire imp might be snacking on stray Will-o-the-Wisps, to smell the skunk cabbages reeking, and listen to the fire-toads croaking in the mist. And he loved to gaze at the dangerous snapdragons devouring gnats, the ghost lilies floating on the water—here one minute and gone the next—and to hear the stray plop-fizz when a firewort shot off a volley into the murky water. But he found no peace tonight as he made his way, a garden trowel in hand, to the lone tree on an island hidden in the middle of his sanctuary.

How could she be so foolish? He'd had his differences with her, which was understandable when he was wicked and she was good, but he'd always found it reassuring to have at least one person in the world who knew what he'd endured in the past. Granted, the Northern Mountains had never seen the kind of devastation he'd witnessed in what had once been the breadbasket of the kingdom, but still, she should remember how hard it had been waking up every morning knowing there was no breakfast, wondering if the smoke on the horizon was a charcoal burner taking advantage of a destroyed forest that some giant had knocked down or if it was a warlord's army on the march and no one in his family would survive to eat dinner, if that existed anymore.

He could not—could not!—allow that to happen again.

Happily-Ever-After must be saved. The warning signs that the fractures were spreading were obvious even here, when he saw the tiny fruits swinging red and wrinkled on an apple tree that was just beginning to flower. He knelt in the grass, parting it until he found the stone that marked where he needed to dig.

He didn't have far to go. His shovel struck a box after only six inches of earth had been removed. He knelt and carefully dug it out of the damp soil. He didn't need to open it, but he did anyway, fitting the silver key that he'd taken from the library desk drawer. Inside, his heart beat, an organ darker than the velvet night settling over his castle.

He should have done this years ago—a thousand years ago to be precise. Ida had clearly done away with hers, probably the day he'd sworn her in as a Cardinal Witch, or she'd have never been able to condemn an entire world to destruction just to salve her conscience. The worst part was that the moment she'd said it—Happily-Ever-After was wrong—he'd actually *wished* she might be right.

That was pure selfishness—the selfishness of an eighteen-year-old boy holding a black rose seed and thinking that running away from home might have been a mistake after all. His heart had helped him then, giving him the courage to face what he would have to do to preserve everything the world needed. But it was a hindrance now.

He filled in the hole.

The box, he carried back to the castle.

The next morning dawned misty, but by the time Hector led Ida into the foothills of the Dread Mountains, a sun as hot as summer could make it had baked the sky dry. He sweated under his robe as he took the lead onto the path that would take them to the Flamelord's lair.

He hadn't been this way in probably six hundred years—not on foot anyway. But when he was younger, he'd hiked his way through these mountains, starting when he was an apprentice and his mentor sent him out for a six-month quest to discover the people who would be part of his life as their Wicked Witch. He'd enjoyed it: meeting giants, making friends with the dragons, getting nearly seduced by an attractive chimera who seemed to know he liked men as well as women, and making the acquaintance of Adorphus, who strung him up by his toes for filching pickled eyeballs before deciding he wasn't such a bad sort...for a human.

Ida hiked behind him, wearing a set of his boots she'd enchanted to fit her feet. She'd not said a word to him that day except "good morning" and "did you pack an extra umbrella" since they'd left the castle. Beside her, Tinbit led a furry goblin pony carrying their baggage—warmer clothes for the mountains mostly, but food as well, and Tinbit's cooking gear. Hari perched on top, looking much better but still pale.

Hector cleared his throat. "When we reach Wyrm's Pass, we'll call it a day. Sebastian is expecting us."

"Oh, joy," Tinbit said in a tone that implied he was anything but joyful about the prospect.

Ida said nothing, merely leaned on the spare staff he'd loaned her.

"Why is it called Wyrm's Pass?" Hari asked.

"For the worms, of course," Tinbit said. "Nasty things. They burrow under your skin and cause a horrible rash. Hector read about them in a book and thought they sounded fun."

"I did not think they were fun. They sounded like a good, solid obstacle for questing knights. It's important a man face his own mortality with a good case of uncontrollable itching. So much more useful in building character than slaying the blind worms who used to live here. Extinct long ago. The king used to send his knights to fight them for sport. That's royalty for you."

Ida's shoulders went up an inch.

"How long to reach the dragons?" Hari asked.

"We should reach the Flamelord's home tomorrow evening. After that, I don't know. It will depend on whether Alistair told his parents anything about his lair. His mother at least will have some idea of where it is. It may not be accessible by foot. Dragons fly from cave to cave far more than they walk. His parents may need to give us a ride." Not exactly something he was looking forward to, either. Dragons were not for riding.

Ida said nothing.

Hector glanced over his shoulder and caught Tinbit's curious look. He faced front again, squaring up to the task ahead of them. The less the gnome knew about his falling out with Ida, the better. He'd been worried Cear might ask, but since they'd set out, the salamander had not left their firepot. "We'll get an early start in the morning, as long as I can convince Sebastian not to make a big deal over our visit. He's prone to going overboard for things like this, and—"

"You rang?"

Ida yelped as a head popped up next to her elbow.

The grotesque thing turned toward her with a grin. "Her Goodness, Ida North! My, my, this is an unexpected pleasure. Shall I put on a spider pie and a cup of mud for you both? Delighted, delighted—"

Hector shut him up with a well-placed cork.

The ghoul spat it out and glared at him. "That was uncalled for, you mean thing."

"So was spider pie and a cup of mud. All I require are rooms for the night. No spider pie. No mud. And no popping out of the sheets as a cut up corpse. We're here on business, not pleasure, Sebastian."

"After the prodigal dragon, are we?" Sebastian grinned and rolled his bloodshot eyes.

"What makes you say that?"

Sebastian popped his eyes out at Hector. "Why, it's all over the papers. Didn't you hear?" He manifested a pair of bony arms and put on a horrible, cracked voice like a crystal ball broadcast when the magical connection was a bit staticky. "Dragon Kidnaps Common Princess; Prince Refuses Quest. Council Set to Burn Witches Over Magical Snafu. Is Happily-Ever-After Dead? Details on page four!" He cackled and his teeth clattered to the ground.

"That's disgusting." Ida shuddered.

"Oh, do you really think so?" Sebastian's eyes leaked tears. "How nice of you to say that. Isn't that nice, Tinbit? You're never nice to me."

"That's because you're a total ass, Sebastian," Tinbit growled.

"Takes one to know one, Tinhorn." The head floated up over the goblin pony and circled like a bat, complete with wings where ears should be. "Who's the cutie in the baggage? I approve, I really do. Much better looking than the last clotheshorse you were with."

"Shut up." Tinbit picked up a rock.

Sebastian stuck out his tongue and waved it around. "Oooooo, look who's talking, the guy who can't close it with anyone, not even if they come ready-packed in a casket. Does your sweetheart know all about your past romances? No? Dear me."

"You're asking for it!"

"Enough," Hector said, pulling another cork out of the air and holding it up as a warning. "See that our rooms are ready. No booby traps."

"Oh, you're no fun." Sebastian fluttered his eyelashes at Ida. "I'm sure the lady would love to see how beautifully I haunt."

"No."

"One tiny booby trap? I promise no one will die! No one will even be maimed, only terrified."

"Sebastian." Hector raised his staff.

"Fine." The ghoul popped out of existence. "I'll go turn down the bedsheets and hold the flesh-eating beetles. Poo." Then the voice was gone too, and all that remained was the goblin pony's exasperated huff.

"Flesh-eating beetles?" Ida said, and for a moment, she sounded almost like herself.

"He doesn't get a lot of visitors, except for questing knights," he explained. "The ones that get this far usually deserve the beetles."

"Naturally," she said with frost in her voice. "Just another one of your servants, I suppose, doing your bidding because you say it's the right thing to do?"

Tinbit almost choked.

"He isn't my servant," Hector said. "Sebastian needed a place to live. His house burned down in town and left him half the ghoul he used to be. Somewhat literally." He turned his back on her and resumed walking.

Servants indeed. He'd never felt angrier in his life, and it wasn't his sore feet. Didn't she know how hard he'd worked to improve the lives of the people under his protection? He ought to throw something back at her—something about how her whole "Save the Unicorns" campaign had worked out—but he didn't want to get into a yelling match with her in a mountain pass where every one of their arguments would be broadcast from rocks and cliff faces for the entire Dread Mountains to hear, let alone a salamander snoozing in a firepot. But underneath the anger, a tremor, like the voice of his eighteen-year-old self, manifested itself with horrible clarity—yes, he had indeed thought it was right.

It was right that the dragons stopped cooking and eating knights and had contracted with the goblins to raise cattle in the mountain valleys. To pay for that, the dragons looted every dwarf mansion in the Dread Mountains. In protest, the dwarves moved north and eradicated the dragons there. Was that right?

What about the giants? Hector had found their hearts to be gentle, and he'd encouraged them to cultivate their skyfields and be the peaceful people he knew they could be. Then he'd had to erect a massive wasteland of thorns around the mountain roads that led into the clouds because the more cowardly of the king's knights chose giants for their quests to prove their valor. Catch and release, but still.

Then there was Tinbit, who had once been like any other gnome, but now—

Hector gripped his staff firmly, stomping ahead faster than before. He'd never questioned his motives before. He'd never questioned Happily-Ever-After. The thing was done, and for the best, and it shouldn't matter that he'd traded life, love, and happiness for the chance to make things better. Tucked in the folds of his too-warm robe, his heart thudded unhappily in the box. It would be a relief to be free of this ridiculous feeling that Ida truly might be right about things after all.

36

Ida

Following the Morning-After, the Happily-Ever-After is concluded. The obstacles to love have been surmounted. The couple have indulged their carnal desires. They have reflected on the choices that led them to this place in their lives. But it would be premature for the witch to congratulate themselves on their success. Your love magic must be strong enough to combat a lifetime of argument, misunderstandings, and occasional just plain meanness.

True love can't be a hothouse plant—sensitive to everything from a light frost to heavy rain. It must be more stubborn than a perennial weed.

MAGIC AND MISCHIEF—A THOUSAND
YEARS OF HAPPILY-EVER-AFTER: A MEMOIR

IDA NORTH

SHE DIDN'T KNOW WHAT SHE'D SAID. BUT WHATEVER it was, it had shut Hector up. What was it about men and their mouths? When you wanted them to talk, you couldn't get a word out of them. When there was nothing to be said, you couldn't shut them up. He had nothing to say that would erase what he'd said last night, and it had better stay that way, because she'd been up all night thinking about it, crying, and then kicking herself for caring. He was a wicked witch. Of course he was going to do the wrong thing. She just hadn't expected it to hurt quite so much.

She took the bowl of stew Tinbit handed her, keeping one eye on Hector, wearing that ridiculous black wool robe, pacing just beyond the shadows at the fire's edge. And here she'd thought she could trust him to listen, that he would pay attention to her concerns because he *cared*. That was the foolishness that came with having a heart, she supposed. Or maybe it was just the lack of sleep making her morose.

"I thought we were staying at the hostel," she said. "Why aren't we pressing on?"

Tinbit stirred the pot. "We are staying there. But you don't want to eat anything in that place. Sebastian is famous for disguising three-day old dead man as pot roast."

"How long has Hector employed Sebastian?" she asked, picking dubiously at the rabbit now that Tinbit had brought up cooked corpse.

Tinbit blew on the ladle before he refilled Hari's bowl. "It's been three hundred years or so now, I guess. He used to own the inn in Thieves' Town. Some guy came through bragging about never knowing fear, and he was told to stay there so he'd learn. Anyway, Sebastian scared the piss out of him, so he decided to burn the place down rather than show his dirty underwear. Hector needed an innkeeper for this hostel, and he gave Sebastian the job. He's a soft touch for ghosts who pop their eyeballs and their teeth out at him."

"You don't like him." Hari took a biscuit and sopped up the broth with it.

"I think he's a perfectly fine ghoul." Tinbit jabbed the ladle in the stew pot. "He's just the kind of person who always speaks his mind. If he had a mind to speak with, I wouldn't object. But his brains are mush—and he likes to demonstrate—so everyone better digest that stew or it will be coming up later." He got up, grimacing, and left the fireside where the salamander roasted in the coals, devouring dry sweetgrass and a few oak leaves Hector had gathered on the way as a change of diet.

Hari blew out his cheeks. "Well, I don't understand every-thing the ghoul said to Tinbit, but it messed him up," he said to Ida. "What do I care if Tinbit has been with people before me? It doesn't matter." He wrapped a green velvet jacket Tinbit had given him tighter around his shoulders.

"You shouldn't have come with me. You should have gone home like I told you to."

"I told you, I'm not letting you go anywhere without me. And the back of a pony beats the back of a coach. At least it's dry."

Perhaps too dry. Hector was worried about the climate change. Well, so was she. She'd seen everything he had—the scarecrows, the browning trees, the grain ripening before it was ready. Did he think she didn't care too? But what was that compared to the use of Happily Ever-After to marry off a prince to a princess with no considerations for their desires, their needs? And without the magic, things would go back to normal in time. Normal hadn't been bad—well, except for the famines.

"So how was dinner?" Hari asked.

"Delicious, I'm sure." She picked a bone out of the stew. "I'm just not very hungry."

"No, the dinner with Hector. Tinbit said you were there for hours."

"We were discussing the situation with Happily-Ever-After. What is wrong with that?"

Hari's eyebrows went up. "You fought with him, didn't you? I thought something seemed off today."

"We didn't fight. We argued, Hari, like we always do. I don't want to talk about it. Why don't you go help Tinbit with the pony?"

"Okay, but remember I'm here for you when you want to talk." Hari shrugged and took her bowl.

Ida settled down beside the fire with a pained sigh. Even after custom fitting Hector's boots for her feet, her socks weren't up to the task of protecting her toes and heels from discomfort. She hoped that however horrible the hostel might be, there might at least be some reasonably clean water for a soak in lavender salts, if Hari had remembered to pack them. They'd been in something of a hurry that morning; she wasn't sure if bath salts survived the cull when he'd gone through her luggage to select only the essentials to pack on the pony.

Cear stretched out, salamander style, on the nearest log. "Hector is not a bad man. He's only a wicked witch. He does not enslave his creatures."

"That is *not* what I said." Ida grabbed a handful of sweetgrass and placed it near the salamander for their consumption.

"Nevertheless, you thought he had. Do you really believe he never had the best interests of these people in mind when he became a Cardinal Witch?"

"Of course, I don't. I'm sure he had their best interests in mind," Ida said. "They're his monsters. So naturally, he would improve the lives and health of everything under his care."

"As have you, Ida North," Cear said. "And yet, have you never questioned your own wisdom the way you questioned his?" Their fathomless eyes were piercing in their intensity.

She fell silent. Nearly every witch went through a mid-life crisis at some point in their long lives, and she'd been no exception. The unicorns died out, despite her best attempts to facilitate the breeding program. And she'd had to order the removal of the last unicorn's horn to keep it from killing itself. She'd brokered a peace treaty to resolve a centuries-old conflict between the pixies and the fairies, and watched it fall apart ten years later when one pixie insulted a fairy and the war began again. She'd discovered the oak dryads were quietly murdering pine dryads who infringed on their territory, and yes, it had occurred to her then to wonder if she could change behaviors to protect creatures with their own ways of doing things. And what about the commoners? She gave them their committee with the best of intentions, and they'd turned around and used it to elect princesses whose daddies would buy them a tiara. Left to their own devices, people didn't always do the right things.

Suddenly she had a very great desire to go pack the pony with Tinbit. "Someone has to be in charge, I suppose. Whether that was wise or not, it was done. I'll go get your firepot. We should be getting on before it gets dark."

She rose and walked away from the fire, leaving Cear curled up in the coals. She wasn't about to sit here questioning every last one of her decisions. And she damned well wouldn't even entertain the idea of trying to fix a system that had been broken from the beginning, no matter how much it mattered to one Hector West, formerly Hector Prim, stuck irrevocably in the past, and no matter how much he might, after all, have a point.

The hostel lay at the end of a particularly steep section of trail. A narrow path dropped off on one side into a dark ravine with water running far below. On the mountain side, the rock outcrops grew strange, angular cactuses with particularly sharp spines. They stuck out everywhere. Hari got one in his hand, which immediately swelled to three times its usual size.

"What are these things?" Hari grumbled as Tinbit pulled the thorn out.

"*Artemisia horribilius,*" Hector said. "The locals call it the Boot-ripper. Lovely yellow flowers in the summer."

"Another one of Hector's mistakes," Tinbit grunted, bandaging Hari's hand. "It's not native."

"It's naturalized," Hector said. "And I didn't introduce it."

"Yeah, but you didn't eradicate it either." Tinbit resumed his place in front of the pony. It eyed the prickly plant with a hungry eye.

"How much farther?" Ida yanked a thorn out of her boot before it worked its way through the leather.

Hector pointed upward toward a faint star of light gleaming out in the mounting mist. "Tinbit, take Hari, Ida, and Cear inside when we get there. I'll stable the pony—"

"Oh, no, you don't," Tinbit said. "That's my job, thank Gods. You get to make a deal with your ghoul for a good night's sleep. I'd probably tell him to go boil his head, and that would be disgusting." Before Hector could protest, Tinbit swung up on the saddle behind Hari, put his arms around him, and spurred the pony to a gallop. They were soon out of sight, although the noise of clipped little hoofbeats echoed on what sounded like a well-groomed gravel path.

Hector turned to Ida. "Well, shall we?" He offered her his hand.

After a moment, Ida took it. The path was in complete darkness now, and he probably knew these trails from old.

"I wish I'd worn chain mail instead of my robe," she grumbled.

"The thorns are only thick on the paths. The ponies keep it well grazed out in the mountain valleys, and beyond that, the dragons burn it. In the colder regions where the giants live, it won't grow at all. In fact, they make a soup called Artemisia Delight featuring imported plants. It's quite delicious, or so I'm told."

"You haven't eaten it?"

"No. It's poisonous to humans."

"Which was why you didn't eradicate it, of course."

"A knight or two has boiled it down to his demise, I'm sure, but anyone here would tell them not to. They just never ask. Mind your step. Sebastian likes his little tricks." He guided her around a stone that opened its maw hungrily and glared up at her with a hurt frown when she stepped over it.

Sebastian—well, Sebastian from the neck down—waited at the front door of the inn. He waved at them, beckoning them on.

"Where's his head?" Ida asked.

"At the front desk, let us hope," Hector said. "He often leaves his body to wait tables and greet the guests."

The headless corpse bowed animatedly to them as they entered. Ida thought it reflected the head rather well, being jumpy and vigorous as it bounded from table to table, pulling out chairs, and menus, which Hector declined by pushing the hand away.

An appetizer appeared hopefully on the table—a large bowl of pickled eyeballs rolling around to wink at her.

"What did Tinbit mean, make a deal for a good night's sleep? It can't be guessing his name." She glanced at the bright sign full of pixie-light on the wall. Sebastian's Place flashed in brilliant neon over the bar. "I presume he doesn't want a first-born child?"

"Nothing so severe, my dear lady!" Sebastian's head bobbed happily up from behind the counter, and she jumped. "What did you do with your sweet little gnome? Didn't hand him over to Hector's hardluck case, I hope?"

"I need the key to the room for Ida and her gnome," Hector said. "No room service or wake-up call, please."

"The Honeymoon Suite is prepared," the head said. The body handed over the keys to Hector with a flourish and a complimentary spider, which Hector released on the counter.

"And for your gnomes, my delightfully austere Wickedness, the Presidential Suite. All the floating heads of the last century at your beck and call, skeleton keys to go with the skeletons in the closet. Only the best for the boss's boy."

"No suite. I want a regular room, again, for me and Tinbit."

Sebastian's rolling eyes glinted. "Are you sure? I thought you and her Goodness might prefer to be alone to do the dirty."

Hector's voice dropped by an octave, and the temperature in the room went down by ten degrees. "That's uncalled for, Sebastian." He took a black box from beneath his robe and set it on the desk.

Sebastian's eyes took on a surprised and then malicious red glow as his gaze raked Ida's face . "Oh. Oh, oh, oh, oh…Hector. My, my, how the evil have fallen. Don't worry, my dear. You won't miss it when it's gone. And when it is, you'll feel so much better, I guarantee it! Got rid of mine with a side of fried poison apples and see how happy I am!" With an explosive pop, the head vanished.

"What was that about?" Ida raised her eyebrows.

"His idea of a joke," Hector said, glancing at the neon sign now advertising cocktail hour at nine, complete with cocks. "I didn't hire him for his sense of humor, obviously." He was red in the face, and now she was blushing too.

"Go on up to the room. I can almost promise you a skeleton won't jump out of the bed, but you might want to draw your wand anyway. I'll send Hari up when he and Tinbit are done seeing to the pony. Would you kindly see if Cear would like to stay in the lobby's fireplace? It's roomier than the ones upstairs. And probably less vile." Hector turned away from her.

Ida carried Cear past the table and into the main room, but glanced back down in time to see Hector pull a small key from his pocket and set it on the counter. An uneasiness settled in her stomach that didn't feel like the natural reaction to staring at pickled eyeballs.

She didn't like the way Sebastian had looked at her when he said, "Oh."

37

Hector

I have an unfortunately soft heart. I first noticed it when I cut it out after the horrible night I spent by his bedside, wishing I could've been anything but who I was—Hector West, a witch, no fit companion for anyone.

It hurt, of course, like everything that bleeds must hurt. But when I went to set it in the box, still thumping hard in my hand, it slipped, and fell in the garden. It felt very smooth under my fingertips, but malleable, far too weak for the work I needed to do, and I was glad it was gone. Finally, I'd taken the first step every witch must take if they hope to keep their feelings under control.

I buried it under the apple tree in my garden, where I would've buried him.

(Editor: Redact entire passage—too personal)

A THOUSAND YEARS OF WICKEDNESS: A MEMOIR

HECTOR WEST

"Believe me, it's for the best," Sebastian said. "But are you sure you don't want to consult with the lady first? You could let her know she's not getting stuck with the thousand-year-old virgin, which should cheer you both up."

Gently, Hector took his heart from the box. Dusty, covered in a faint crust of earth, it still smelled faintly of roses and blood. The dark red organ beat patiently in his hand, a little unhappily, reminding him of what he was giving up, whether it brought him relief or not. If he kept it any longer, he felt he'd never let it go, and he had to. The next time Ida looked at him with that hurt, angry expression on her face, he'd drop at her feet and tell her she was right, that Happily-Ever-After had to end, and then they could be together.

"That isn't necessary," he said, holding it out.

Sebastian took it from Hector's hands and set it back in the box. "You should've given it to me long ago. Well, better late than never."

Hector couldn't shake the feeling it was probably far too late.

Sebastian gave him a regular room, and to his surprise, he found only one skeleton in the closet. He broke its fingers for trying to throttle him, and told it to find Tinbit and give him the room number while he got a bath. He settled in the large tub that decided not to eat him after he fed it a few cakes of liver-scented soap first. He wondered how Ida was coping with the Honeymoon Suite.

He lay back and stared up at the blood-tinged ceiling. At last, it would finally be over, and good riddance. He was heartily tired of fighting the feeling that the best thing he could do right at this moment was to run to Ida's room wrapped in a towel and apologize. Or better yet, save her from a bloodthirsty skeleton, embrace her like a knight rescuing his damsel in distress, and then maybe fall into the bed for a whole different kind of activity involving bones. With a groan he submerged in the hot water, gripping his cock. The sooner Sebastian ate his heart, the better.

Tinbit dragged in a half hour later.

"What took you so long?" Hector snapped. The bath had not helped. Neither had taking Tinbit's suggestion of what to do with unwanted sexual energy. He sat at the desk now, poring over his books, empty, aching, miserable, and confused. This should be over by now. How long did it take a ghoul to eat a heart?

Tinbit slammed his boots off by the door. "The pony had a thorn. You try putting a poultice on one of those demons and see how long it takes you." He glared at the eager skeleton who politely hung himself in the closet. "You didn't need to send that awful thing for me. It mooned me with its pelvis before it gave me your message."

"And what was Hari doing during all this?" Hector said.

"He put a twitch on the damned thing until I could get its leg wrapped and then he trotted off to bed."

"Nothing else?"

Tinbit folded his arms over his chest. "Meaning did I strip him, suck him, and tumble him in the hay before sending him back to Ida?"

Hector's cheeks warmed. "I…I didn't mean—"

"Actually, you did," Tinbit said, rolling his eyes. "You're just too much of a prude to say it. And since you asked, no, I didn't. The thought didn't even occur to me. Hay isn't all that fun to roll around in—sticks you in the worst places. Almost as bad as that pea gravel in the greenhouse." He sat down beside the smoky fire to peel off his boots.

"What on earth are you referring to?"

Tinbit glared at him. "You think I didn't see you sneak out with Ida last night?"

"What? I didn't—we were touring the greenhouse, not—"

"Fucking?" Tinbit raised an eyebrow.

"No." Hector turned back to his books, face on fire. "We were talking about this unfortunate…situation."

Tinbit had been taking off his socks, but he stopped and stared for a moment before resuming. "Huh. So she's pissed with you. Well, that explains a lot. She didn't talk to you practically all day. I thought maybe you just had been that bad."

"Oh, balls." Hector turned away.

"Yeah, you have them. I'm sure there's a spell for cutting them off without pain and stuffing them in a box. Maybe you could try that next."

"Meaning what, exactly?" He set his pen down.

"Meaning it's not going to be any better lacking a beating heart. Trust me on that." Tinbit laughed harshly.

"I don't know what you're talking about. I'm perfectly fine." Hector rose, pulling his robe tighter about himself, and limped to the dresser where he'd put the few clothes Tinbit had packed for him. The bulk of what he'd brought were books, but perhaps there might be a pair of wool socks in there. His feet were cold.

"Sure you are," Tinbit scoffed. "Did you get a bath yet?"

"When I got in."

"Good. Sit on the bed. I need to dress your feet before you make more of a mess of them," Tinbit said. "You're not getting far tomorrow with those blisters unless I poultice you next."

"I'll do it myself."

"Sit!" Tinbit yelled. "I'm offering to help. You damned well better take it like a man and quit pretending you are infallible and indestructible. You're not. You can't even fight off your own damned magic."

"Is that the same salve you used on the horse?"

"If it works on horses, it will work on horse's rear ends."

Hector snorted. But he sat. The salve did feel nice, and Tinbit's hands felt good on his feet. "You weren't supposed to know about my heart."

"Hector, we've known each other a very long time. How could I not? You take care of that nasty old tree like it was your child. It always blooms first in the spring and you talk to it."

"I talk to all my plants."

"Not like you talk to that tree."

"It was as good a place as any to put it at the time," Hector said.

"You know, I've always thought it was a bad idea, witches taking out their hearts. Makes them not as careful with other peoples'." Tinbit capped the bottle and stared up at him. "How's that?"

Hector flexed his toes. "Much better."

Tinbit grunted his approval. "Now you can sock them up and get back to work." He tucked the salve back into his pocket.

Hector rose and went back to the desk.

"How is it going, anyway?" Tinbit asked, poking the sulky fire and only coaxing a few tired-looking sparks out of it. "Not going to push you or anything, but I really don't want to have to take that potion again. Although, it looks like you might need it more than me."

"It's going well enough," Hector said. "And I don't need a potion."

"Oh, really? You could have fooled me. So, if it's going well, what's Her Goodness angry about?"

"I don't want to talk about it. It doesn't matter anyway." He opened *Dragons: Their Ways, Their Wounds, and Their Weirdness* and took out his quill to take notes. Tinbit was right. Work was the answer. As long as he could stay focused, he wouldn't be thinking about things like Ida's heartbroken face when she told him to fire her, revoke her immortality, do whatever he had to do, she was still going against him and all of Happily-Ever-After. That ought to make him angry all over again. But it hurt. How could she not know that he needed her to be with him on this? No one else could understand the importance of this magic like she could, and yet, she hadn't. That had to be his fault. He hadn't articulated his reasons well, perhaps. He'd become too emotional—his damned heart probably—

"Must have been bad," Tinbit said, setting the poker down. "If you won't talk about it to me."

"A minor disagreement, that's all. It's nothing to worry about."

Tinbit stared at him for a long moment. "All right. If you say so. If you don't need me, I think I'll take a bath before I go out to make sure the pony hasn't kicked that poultice off."

"I'm fine," he said. "Go on."

"Hector?"

"Yes?"

The gnome stood in the doorway, jacket down to his elbows. "You…you didn't bring your heart with you, right?"

He laughed. "Why would I do that?"

Tinbit shrugged off his jacket. "Because you're weird about it. You never had to hide it from me, but you did. You never had to bury it, even if it was a sentimental kind of thing. You could have kept it in the castle. I'd have taken care of it for you."

"It wasn't your burden to bear, Tinbit," he said softly.

Tinbit shook his head. "Hector, you're such a great witch in so many ways. But you really don't know a damned thing about love, do you?" He walked into the bathroom and shut the door behind him.

"No," he said quietly. "And it needs to stay that way." Hector returned to his books, determined to find the answer, for all their sakes.

 **38**

Ida

Those who seem to have the largest hearts often just have a big hole in their chest, while those who seem to have no heart often have the biggest hearts of all. They've simply hidden them away against those who would steal them for their own.

*MAGIC AND MISCHIEF—A THOUSAND
YEARS OF HAPPILY-EVER-AFTER: A MEMOIR*

IDA NORTH

IDA HAD SLEPT IN MANY PLACES OVER HER CENTURIES of travel: posh hotels, enchanted forests in glamping tents, gnome homes, dwarf mansions, elvish tree houses, even in a farmhouse one night when her carriage broke down. All of them had some redeeming quality.

Not this place.

Never had a hostel felt more hostile, starting with the skeleton she subdued when it popped out of her closet and tried to confine her in an elaborate ballgown made of blue satin with a million golden flounces.

"The audacity," she complained to Hari, shutting the last of the angry bones in the chest of drawers in the corner. "Now, let me tend to your hand."

"It's fine," Hari said. "Tinbit dressed it. He's very good. You should've seen how he took care of the pony, and it tried to kick the snot out of him too."

Ida placed the pouting skull on the dresser and lectured it. "You'll get your spine back in the morning if you behave yourself. I agree, he's good, but the thorn was poisonous, like everything else in this part of the world. Let me see it."

Hari unwrapped his hand. The puncture wound barely oozed, and a fresh smell of sage and the bitter reek of goldenseal soaked the bandage. No doubt about it, Tinbit knew his herbs and poultices. She rewrapped it, adding a healing blessing.

"I wish I could've talked you into going home," she said when she finished. "This is my fault."

Hari laughed hollowly. "What's your fault?"

"You're more in love with him today than you were yesterday."

"Well, I have news for you," Hari said, getting up and going to unpack her valise. "It's absolutely *not* your fault this time."

"The magic—"

"Happily-Ever-After magic be damned. I liked Tinbit before I even met him, and I'm going to love him whether I want to or not, even if it's doomed."

"I won't hold you back," Ida reminded him. "If you want to be with him—"

"We've been through that." Hari took out her nightgown and laid it out on the bed for her. "Do you want a cup of tea from the kitchen tonight, or do you want to brew it here in the fireplace?"

"Here, I think," Ida said. "I don't want to see that obnoxious ghoul any more than I must."

"Who's an obnoxious ghoul?" Sebastian's head popped through the floor at Hari's feet. "Is it me? Please say yes."

Ida yanked her dressing gown around herself and glared at the head. "Is this how you treat all your guests?"

"No, dear lady," Sebastian said, bowing in midair. "I'm much more horrible, I assure you. I beg your apology for the intrusion, and I know it's late, but I've a business proposition for your ears, Your Goodness, and your ears only. Toddle off to the kitchen, you dutiful little gnome. I'm going to be a while here, so there's no rush on the cuppa. Why don't you send a skeleton to tell your dearly beloved Tinbit the pony is having a bellyache, and when he comes running, suck him dry in a quiet stall? It works for the vampires."

"Ida—" Hari protested.

"It's all right," Ida said. "I'm sure this won't take long."

Hari left, not without an angry backward glance at Sebastian's grinning skull.

Ida turned to him. "What do you want?"

Sebastian coaxed his body over with a click of his tongue. The body came over, carrying a box, and handed it to Ida. "Present for you."

Ida narrowed her eyes at him. "What horrible, terrifying thing is in there? A large spider? A vampire bat? A thousand trapped souls screaming in torment?"

"Far worse." Sebastian giggled. "Go ahead. Open it. You're probably the only one who can handle it, really."

She did. Carefully. "Gods!"

"Not quite," Sebastian said. "Just the dirty old heart of a man who can't bear it anymore."

Ida stared at it in shock. She'd thought Hector as heartless as any witch should be. He'd kept it. All through the centuries, he'd kept it, just like she had. She took out the heart reverently, dirt and all, and set it in her lap.

"Interesting, isn't it?" Sebastian's hollow eyes glinted. "That old softie. Some people don't know what's good for them. And they're so rich in iron. I was going to sauté it up with some onions and thyme, but I could be persuaded to part with it—for the right price."

"I make a point to not buy organ meat of dubious origin, and you should be more careful too. I'd suggest you return this to the witch you took it from before it poisons you."

"That's out of the question," Sebastian said. "Have you ever woken him up once he's gone to bed at dusk like a good little morning lark? He's liable to turn me into stone."

It was a much larger heart than she'd expected, glistening, red, beating softly beneath her fingers. "He sold it to you?"

"Gave it to me in exchange for the rooms. I believe he was glad to be rid of it. Of course, I never would've made the trade if I'd not had a buyer for it." He pulled up a chair and sat, setting his feet on the coffee table, one at a time. "As you might imagine, good magic in this part of the world is hard to find. Hector can't do good to save his life. I can make a tidy profit selling bootleg good magic. How about it? You get the heart and I get a few canned spells for love and money."

She covered the heart in the folds of her nightgown. "Love and money?"

Sebastian grinned. "Think pleasure instead of love. It's an easier sell."

"Pleasure, you say?"

"We get quite a few questing knights through here, and they like to cut loose when they are in dragon country. A few lovely virgins who dissolve into mist in the morning would be perfect."

She ought to sew up his mouth and box his ears. "And when would you want these spells?"

"Ah, ah! Payment due on receipt of goods delivered. That's my offer. Take it or leave it."

Well, she certainly wouldn't leave it. *Hector, you fool. You really need to do a better job of vetting your hard-luck cases.* "Very well. One heart for four pleasure spells. I'll have them made for you by morning."

"Five."

"Four," Ida said.

"I won't take less than five."

"Perhaps you can sell it to the next good witch who comes to stay at your hostel. I'm sure you get so many here."

"Ha!" Sebastian grinned so wide, he split his skull. He held the jaw and moved it with his hands to finish his sentence. "You drive a hard bargain, Your Goodness. But I think I hear your gnome gnashing his teeth outside the door, so I'll take it. I keep the heart until I'm satisfied."

"Hector's heart stays with me, or you'll find your pleasure spells won't work."

"My dear woman, you are a formidable negotiator, but I'm sure I could find a wicked witch who'd love this heart—roasted, on a spit. Agatha East, perhaps?"

"I wonder how much salt it takes to melt a ghoul." She leaned forward, hissing through her teeth. "I've always wanted to find out."

"Fine." Sebastian stuck the first cervical vertebral body out of his mouth like a tongue. "Keep the blasted thing. But I want those spells first thing in the morning." He rose and carried his head out of the room.

Ida breathed a sigh of relief. "You can come in now, Hari," she said.

Hari did, slamming the door behind him. "Ugh. He spilled his guts in front of me, anus first." He shuddered. "Gross. I hope you didn't give him what he wanted."

Ida dusted the fragments of earth from Hector's heart. "I gave him what he deserved." For the most part, it seemed as if she'd been wrong about Hector and his people. Now that she'd met them, she felt she'd misjudged their hearts and Hector's too. But this ghoul! It looked like Hector actually *did* have one truly evil creature in his employ. It was oddly satisfying to think she was the one who got to dispense a fitting punishment. But for now, she needed to find a safe place for Hector's heart.

She thought of her own heart tucked safely away under her bed at home. That would've been the best place to keep Hector's heart—locked away with hers, where nothing could touch it. But hearts weren't books. A witch couldn't send a heart across time and space—anything might happen to it. There was only one thing for it, only one place it would be safe no matter what happened.

She put it in her chest.

39

Hector

My dear Adair,

I plan to be at your home by Sunsday evening at the latest. Hopefully we can sort out this situation before more harm is done. Please don't write back—this left the castle shortly before I did. I don't trust delivery at Sebastian's. His bats are all vampires. What I need most from both you and Morga is patience, and probably a flight to Alistair's lair. I hate to ask, but I see no other alternative.

Your friend,
HECTOR

HECTOR LEFT TINBIT CURLED UP IN THE HEAVY quilts on the sleeping sofa and donned his black wool robe. Mornings in the mountains could be chilly, and he wouldn't take a chance on Sebastian's kitchen providing a decent cup of coffee or tea. Tinbit had probably packed a coffee press. If he was lucky, he'd find his tea too.

It was cold outside, and he pulled his robe tighter around his shoulders as he gazed out at the sun-kissed snowy peaks. The valleys were dark. Even the knob where the hostel stood wouldn't be in the sunlight for a few more hours. He shuffled into the stable, lifting the latch with chilled fingers.

Horsey warmth spilled out as he walked through the door, and he shut it quickly to keep the heat inside. The pony, a shaggy black creature not much taller than Spot, greeted him with a hungry whinny. He ignored it and turned his attention to the packs slung over the dividing wall.

Another gust, cold and smelling of meltwater, and the door shut.

"Tinbit? Is my tea in here?" he asked, digging out the coffee press and setting it aside.

"If you find it, I wouldn't say no to a cup," Ida said. "Even if it's that smoky stuff you like so much."

He straightened, bumping his head on the saddle rack. "Good morning."

She came around the corner wearing a pair of green pants and her thick gray sweater. "Morning."

"You slept well, I hope?"

"Tolerably. But I won't be sorry to leave the hostel, no offense to your innkeeper."

"I'm quite sure if you wished to leave him a bad review, he'd weep tears of joy," Hector said.

"And send me a box of chocolate-covered spiders for Midwinter's Eve—no thanks," Ida said. "I saw you passing from my window and came to see if I could help. How's the pony?"

"There's no sign of lameness," Hector said. "Tinbit's salves work well. When I had the dragon burns, he fixed me with a wonderful tincture of calendula and lavender."

Ida's mouth quirked at the corner. "I hope you remembered to pack it."

"I'm hoping we won't need it." He dug deeper into the bag and found his box of loose-leaf tea. "Ah. Let me find a pot and some fresh water, and if you could conjure two cups—"

Ida did while he boiled the pot of water with a spell—this being a stable, he didn't want to start a fire. The hot scent of tea leaves added to the water steamed a wide-awake fragrance into the air. He watched Ida strain the tea at the small farrier's table among the bridles and broken leather straps, hoping he wouldn't struggle against these feelings much longer, because right now, he fully appreciated how enchanting a beautiful woman wearing a baggy sweater and canvas pants in the morning could be.

She'd braided her hair. The humidity had loosened enough to frizz around the knots like a soft mist. And when she glanced up at him from under a soft fringe of honey-colored eyelashes and her lavender eyes flashed over her tea cup, he wanted to discard Tinbit's advice about making love in haystacks.

"I've been thinking," he said, taking a sip of the tea to steady himself. "I believe I should go to the dragons ahead of you. I'm not sure Adair and Morga will be prepared for all of us to arrive asking questions. Dragon mothers, when upset, can be…reactive. I'd like to prepare her first."

She pursed her lips. "I see."

"It's not a long journey to the Flamelord's cave from here, and Tinbit knows the way. And it would give Hari a chance to sleep in. You can bring Cear along when you come. You'd be there by midafternoon if you left in an hour or so. Perhaps later, if you happen to run into a hungry manticore or a playful chimera, but I'm sure you can handle those."

"How touching that you have such faith in me," she said.

"What you really want is to talk to the Flamelord without Cear listening in."

He glanced down at their makeshift tea table. "That's partly it, yes."

"Well, I for one would also like to find out what happened with Alistair and the princess without anyone else asking questions. If Tinbit knows the way, I'm sure he can handle manticores and chimeras as well as I can. There's no reason for me to travel with them. I'm coming with you."

"Ida—"

She raised her eyebrows. "Yes, Hector?"

"I really think it's better if I go alone."

Ida sighed. "Hector, may I speak frankly?"

"Do you ever do otherwise?"

She smiled. "I know we're not supposed to be friends. You're wicked and I'm good, and those two things don't mix. But surely, we're both big enough to admit when we're not on the same side and still be professional? I know you're not about to change your mind, and you can't change mine. But your dragon and my princess are more important right now than our…disagreement. I'm not asking for your forgiveness or for you to reconsider what I've said. What I am asking for is a truce—just long enough for us to finish what we've started. Fair?"

"Oh." He could breathe again. He'd been afraid she was about to reveal feelings for him. "I…I absolutely agree! Truce." He laughed and was horrified to hear how ridiculous he sounded.

Ida laughed too, high-pitched and nervous. "You've no idea—I wasn't sure how you'd take that. I've been up hours practicing that speech."

He took her hand. "You didn't need to. I…I was thinking

about asking you the same thing, but in the end, I thought that maybe it was simply better if we, well."

"Didn't see so much of each other?"

"Exactly! That's exactly it. I'm glad we got this cleared up. And as for our disagreement—"

"We'll just not talk about it," Ida suggested.

"Yes! Absolutely!" He was nodding like an absurd lizard, but his heart was a giant sigh of relief. No. Not his heart. He didn't have one anymore, thank Gods. Maybe in time she would come around to his way of thinking. When he imagined sitting in Council and seeing another witch sitting in Ida's chair, he wanted to cry. He'd convince her. She'd see how dedicated he was to dispelling any of her reservations about Happily-Ever-After and everything would be fine.

"Um, Hector? You can let go of my hand now."

"Oh—sorry." He let go quickly. "Just—I was thinking, you may need warmer gloves than what we brought. I'll—I'll just go…uh…fix yours. Add a warming spell."

"That's…thoughtful of you. I'll just…go back to the hostel. Leave a note for Hari with the spider at the front desk."

"Can you leave a note for Tinbit as well? I'll get everything we need ready. You can use my staff as a walking stick if you like."

"No—once we reach the woods, I'll beg a walking stick from an oak."

"Okay. Hurry back."

She flushed. "Okay. Early start, I get it."

"Yes. Exactly." Maybe he should have gotten rid of his tongue along with his heart. He doubted he'd ever sounded so ridiculous in his entire life, but despite it, he bounced back to the pony's stall, whistling.

The pony didn't seem unhappy to see Hector back, only a little miffed. It cheered up immediately when he refilled the hay bag and gave it a handful of grain. Then Hector dug through the bags Hari and Tinbit had stacked in the tack room and found Ida's wool coat and a bright green scarf to match her pants. A pair of thin white gloves sat on top. She'd worn them to the game. How long ago it seemed now. Hector set them aside. They weren't suitable for shaking hands with a dragon. He found a pair of his dark leather gauntlets and stuffed them in his pack for her, complete with the warming spell he'd promised.

When Ida returned from the inn, she was carrying two pairs of boots.

"You didn't summon seven-league boots, I hope? If you take a bad jump, you could end up in the air over a ravine."

"No, they're ordinary boots. I pilfered them from Sebastian's cloak room. Mine were full of cactus spines. I imagine yours were too."

He took them gratefully. "How thoughtful. Thank you." He dusted the hay from his robe front. "Personally, for myself, I think I should've taken more socks. I ripped all mine up on the cactus."

"Tinbit will patch them, I'm sure."

"I'll patch them myself. I knit a lot in the winter—sweaters, hats, oven mitts—it's too cold to do much else." It would be something for him to do every day in his retirement if he didn't fix this. But he was going to fix it. No. They were.

"Shall we go?" He offered Ida his arm.

She took it. "I'm ready when you are."

Two hours into the hike, Hector's stomach growled to him about breakfast, but although the mountain path boasted large stands of wild blackberries, none were ripe. He passed the green and red fruits, wishing he'd taken a few slices of bread from the pack, but Tinbit and Hari would be hungry, and Sebastian wouldn't serve anything edible for breakfast.

Ida walked behind him, the path not being wide enough to take more than one person at a time. She must have been as hungry and weary as he, but she never slowed down, never paused, never complained, but limped after him leaning on the staff she'd asked from a gnarled mountain oak at the head of the pass. Her feet must have been as blistered as his.

"It's a lot farther from the city to the mountains than I thought," Ida said. "I'm trying not to think how airsick the princess must have been, flying all this way."

"It's not so bad, flying by dragon. A bit hard on the tailbone, considering the spikes, but not much worse than a broom."

"And how were you after your first flight on a broom?"

He frowned. "Decidedly queasy."

"So was I," Ida said. "I hope—" She went quiet.

"What?" He turned around, staff up, in case of a manticore, but there were no fantastic beasts there, only Ida, standing on one leg, dumping a rock out of her boot.

"I hope she wasn't too afraid," Ida finished. "I would've been, going with a man I'd never met, with no idea what he's like, or what to expect. Of course, I always consider that when I compose the love spells, but…"

She trailed off, and Hector thought uncomfortably of what he'd said to her about abdicating responsibility and incompetence and felt rather worse than queasy. How could he have been so cruel?

"What kind of man is Alistair?" she asked.

"He's not a man. He's a dragon—"

She rolled her eyes. "You know what I mean. What kind of person is he?"

"A young one," he said after a moment. "Impulsive, artistic, hotheaded, but kind and thoughtful. He would never hurt a princess. Do you need to rest?"

"Perhaps for a moment." She chose a rock beside a small stream and sat, stretching out her legs. Hector knelt and drank, and seeing him drink seemed to make her feel more comfortable. After a minute, she knelt and drank too. "If Amber wanted to leave him, would he let her go?"

"I suppose it depends on the strength of his need to retain his prize," Hector said. "But I think he would. He didn't wish to participate in the Happily-Ever-After, but he did come. And when I asked him to remember his role, he did—albeit a bit belatedly, and he didn't do it the way I expected. He's always been more difficult to read than his father. He's so locked inside himself all the time."

"He's introspective."

"Yes."

"Like you."

He laughed. "Perhaps so. But I know other people depend on me to do my duty. I can't let them down, now can I?"

She gazed at him. "No, I don't suppose you could. And that's what I'm worried about. If he believed his whole world depended upon him retaining the princess, would that be enough to override his thoughtful nature?"

It sounded like she was confronting him, but they'd agreed not to talk about it. He glanced up at the mountains above them.

"I don't know. I confess, I hoped he'd be somewhat older when the time for this magic came about. He's just a boy, and I don't like that all this responsibility has fallen on his wings. He's my godson after all."

"Your godson?" Ida stripped her other boot and rubbed both her feet, wincing.

"The Flamelord honored me with the role. It's very rare they don't choose a dragon, but the egg was dark."

"What does that mean?"

"They candle the eggs, you know, to sex the child and read their future. When they passed the light through his shell, the yolk got in the way; they weren't even sure it was a boy. Without the spread of the blood vessels, they couldn't tell his future. It was muddled. A dark egg. So they put me in charge of protecting him should things go wrong. And now they have gone wrong, catastrophically so."

Ida touched his hand. "I am sorry. I really am. You must feel very unhappy about all this."

He waved his hand. "The responsibility would still be mine were I not his godfather. Only…"

"Only?"

He sat beside her, leaning over his knees. "Perhaps I would not have thrown a shield so quickly. I would've let him defend himself."

"I know what you mean." Ida stretched out next to him, arching her whole body like an upside-down cat in an explosion of small pops and cracks. "I confess, I felt much the same way about Amber. She planned to kill the dragon to save herself. I swear, for a few minutes, I thought she might. She reminds me of myself at that age. Foolish. Headstrong. Temper like a wildcat."

"The temper and the headstrong, I'd vouch for," Hector said, smiling. "Foolish—no. You were never foolish, Ida. Even if I said so."

"I'm not so sure you weren't right." She sighed. "Have you ever tried to stop a fairy war?"

"No. But I did go spelunking with goblins once, and they abandoned me in the mountain for three days because I was naïve enough to think a troll hunt meant actually hunting for trolls."

She laughed and rolled over to face him, lavender eyes sparkling, pink lips parted. "That's the oldest trick in the book."

"And I fell for it." He leaned over her, hand pressed against her palm. "Ida, I know we weren't going to talk about it, but I have to say something. I deeply regret what I said the other night. You were never guilty of abdicating your responsibility, and you didn't deserve the accusations I threw at you. I will *not* be calling for your resignation, or revoking your immortality, or firing you, because if you accidentally had a role in destabilizing Happily-Ever-After, you never meant to. The guilt is mine. I'm the senior Cardinal Witch, and you were right. I should have been much more involved."

She curled her hand around his. "And I should have told you earlier. I know that now. But what's done is done, as Cear reminded me yesterday. Whatever our differences, we can't let anyone else suffer for our mistakes. But I am worried—what if—what if we're just making things worse? Hari and Tinbit, and now the princess and the dragon—"

"Do you believe we are making things worse?"

"I don't know. And that terrifies me."

He went down on one elbow, chest brushing her arm. "I'm as

scared as you are. But we said we'd fix this together. And knowing you're with me gives me some hope that we can."

"Me too." Her chest rose and fell as she looked up at him, and he remembered that morning with her in bed, when he'd touched her, and desire filled him again. Gods. Tinbit was right about the balls. It would be the simplest thing in the world to lean over her, to kiss those upraised lips, to turn the soft streambank moss into a bed. He wanted to.

"Ida, I—"

"It's getting late," Ida whispered. "We'd better be getting on."

"Yes. Yes. You're right." He rolled onto his back, staring up at the whispering leaves, trying to compose himself. She was right. The sun was already high overhead. Tinbit and Hari would not be far behind.

The Flamelord's cave came into view around noon. It was a far, far steeper climb than Hector remembered. Breathing hard, he stopped at the last place on the trail where he could rest and leaned against a rock to catch his breath.

"Let. Me. Do. The. Talking." With a groan, he leaned on his staff and struggled up the last stretch, hoping against hope that when Tinbit arrived with Hari and the pony, he'd have the arnica tincture. His shins were killing him.

"It's quiet," Ida gasped from behind him. "Are they home?"

Hector drew in a deep breath. He cupped his hands around his mouth and roared a greeting. "Flamelord! It's Hector West! May I come in?"

For a moment, there was no reply. Then a figure came to the door.

It wasn't Adair.
It wasn't Morga.
It wasn't Alistair.
It was the princess.

40

Ida

This just in! Prince Archie marries Captain of the Guard in secret wedding! Wild honeymoon in the Mermen's Resort reported by eyewitnesses. Orgies! Sex parties! Pictures on page seven!

—THE SORCERER'S STAR

GONE WAS THE CHAIN MAIL OVERCOAT. IN ITS PLACE, Amber wore a gray robe, far too long for her. She'd tacked the bottom up so she could walk, and she was barefoot.

"Amber!" Ida cried out. "My poor girl. Are you all right?"

Amber looked surprised. "How did you find me?"

"Well, the dragon who carried you off—"

"Alistair," Amber said.

"Excuse me?"

"His name is Alistair." Amber stepped out of the doorway.

A huge, dark-scaled dragon slithered through the door, shapeshifting into a dark-haired woman as she came out. "Oh, thank Gods, you're here, Hector!" As she reached them, she donned a long silver robe and tightened it around her waist with a golden girdle. She glared down at Amber from her impressive height of twelve feet. Hector hadn't exaggerated. Female dragons were impressive . "Go inside, child. This doesn't concern you."

Amber folded her arms. "The hell it doesn't."

Morga flicked an angry forked tongue at the princess. "Perhaps I'd better start at the beginning."

"Alistair and I are married," Amber said. "And there's nothing either of you are going to do about it." She turned on her heel and walked back into the cave.

Oh my Gods. Ida had about a thousand things she wanted to say, but half of them were curses. Married? Of all the things she'd envisioned finding here, she hadn't expected that. Could the love magic have really hit them that hard?

From the expression on Hector's face, he hadn't expected it either. He turned to the tall woman with the bloodshot eyes and long black hair. "What happened, Morga? Tell me everything."

"Oh, Hector, Hector, you have to do something. Alistair is bewitched. He spends every waking moment with this girl. He refuses to be separated from her. What are we going to do?" Morga blew her nose into her hands, and flames shot through her fingers.

Hector laid a hand on Morga's arm. He looked like a ten-year-old boy guiding a giantess to a stone table in the dragon's cave. "We'll sort this out, I promise."

The dragon sobbed. "He's not her mate. I refuse—I refuse to accept her as my daughter!"

"Yes, yes." Hector placed her in a chair. "Morga? Where's Adair?"

Morga wiped her streaming eyes. "In his bedchamber. He tried to talk sense into Alistair, and they fought. I had to get between them before they killed each other. That hateful girl—she tried to hold Alistair back. Hector! What am I going to do? I had such dreams for my sweet boy. I wanted him to marry a nice dragon from the Snowy Peaks, have grand-eggs…"

Hector folded his hands on the table in front of him. "I know this is hard for you, but can you tell us what happened? Anything could be important."

Morga sniffed and glanced at Ida. "Oh, where are my manners. I should offer…you…tea…" She broke off into hysterical sobs again.

"No, thank you," Ida said, squirming in her chair. If she knew where the kitchen in this place was, she'd brew a cup herself and add a shot of something strong to steady her nerves.

Morga choked. "He left on the day of the tournament. We had to make him go. He was angry. We could only hope he would do his duty. When he didn't come back immediately, we thought nothing of it. We knew he had a lair ready. But we expected him to come and tell us how things had gone. After all, what reason would he have to stay? Yesterday he arrived—with her—telling us she was his mate and if the prince came for her, he'd roast the man and eat him. And she was holding onto him like she'd help him do it. I never heard anything so ridiculous in my life!"

Ridiculous didn't begin to cover it. It sounded very much like she'd been right—the open-ended spell had seized on the pair and created the bond it should've made between the prince and the princess. Damn Hector and his dragon "prince." "And… the princess?" she asked in a faint voice.

Morga snorted. "Don't talk to me about that girl! She walked in here like she *was* a dragon. Of course, Alistair told her to act like one and that's all she's done since she got here. I offered her our guestroom. She said no, she would sleep with her mate.

Adair offered to take her home. She told him her place was here, with Alistair. And Gods, the noise they make—the roaring, the panting, the sucking, the moaning—it's every bit as bad as Adair was with me."

Hector turned almost as red as his blood orchids. "Don't worry, Morga, Ida and I will fix this. I'm sure Alistair and the princess will separate, and soon."

"Good," Morga said. "Because if they don't, I'm going to bite that girl, and sharp, right on her round little bottom. Steal my son from me, my grand-eggs—"

"I'd better see Adair," Hector said, rising.

Ida rose too. "I'll go talk to the princess."

Hector caught her arm. "Ida—"

She touched his hand, patted it. "I know, I know! But we'll get nowhere until we talk with the couple. The love magic is my specialty—let me find out what happened."

He sighed. "Very well, but, Ida—"

"Yes?"

"Dragons are possessive of their mates. He may protect her if he sees you as a threat."

"Don't worry about me," she said, smiling grimly. She raised the fold of her sweater, showing him the handle of her wand.

"All the same," he said. "Be careful. Alistair's room is just through there. You'll find it by the smoke leaking under the door."

Ida had never set foot in a dragon cave before today, but she soon appreciated this particular cave was a palace. She wandered through the largest of the galleries, casting curious glances at the strangest folk art she'd ever seen. Once out of the gallery, she passed a smaller cavern with couches surrounding a wall of fire, clearly designed as a family lounge, and a smaller room lit by the afternoon sunlight streaming through a wall of sheet crystal. The light spilled over rows and rows of stone and iron plant benches like the ones in Hector's greenhouses, filled with rare orchids. But these were Dragon Hoards. Look, don't touch.

When she got to the back of the cave, however, things changed.

Here, the halls were smaller, less adorned. The walls were scorched black, and the air carried a distinct odor. She wrinkled her nose. Apparently young dragons, like young men, exuded a rather peculiar aroma—musky, strong, pungent, and mixed with another odor. Smoke.

She crept closer to a faint line of red cracking the blackness of one wall with sudden shattering light.

A hot, roaring sound echoed in the hallway. "They're both here?"

"Yes." A woman spoke, her voice soft and fearful. "You know they're going to try to separate us."

A deep, masculine growl. "I won't let them take you from me."

"And I won't leave you, not if they drag me away—but, Alistair, they're Cardinal Witches. We can't fight them and expect to win."

"Hector won't fight me. He's a reasonable man, for a witch, and he's my godfather besides. I don't know the woman, though."

"Far worse than Hector, believe me," Amber said. "She's rude, condescending, and arrogant. But if she hadn't chosen me, I'd never have met you."

A pleasurable growl, the sound of lips coming together. Gentle sucking sounds followed and Alistair moaned. "I'm never going to finish this sculpture if you keep distracting me."

"Maybe I *want* to distract you."

Ida coughed loudly and pushed the door open.

Alistair gave an annoyed hiss and covered his bare crotch. Amber scrambled to her feet, pulling the ragged edge of her oversized robe up over her shoulder.

Not lips coming together then. Ida blushed.

Amber folded her arms, blushing too. "Well, don't say you are sorry for interrupting," she said in an annoyed voice.

"I'm not going to," Ida said, coming in. "You knew I'd want to talk to you."

Alistair showed his teeth. They were sharp, and black in color, shiny as knives. "Amber is my mate. If she doesn't want to answer your questions, she doesn't have to."

Now Ida could see what Alistair was making. A life-sized statue of a woman stood on a block of stone, carved from magma. Amber's hair billowed around her shoulders in red and gold tendrils, her eyes blazed like those of a salamander from the smooth orange, blue, white, and red face. Hints of purple shown in her naked skin, and her breasts shimmered like golden opals. Clear to see a man had carved it, even if he was a dragon.

"I have no objection to you hearing what I say to your...to your princess," she said, mindful of what Hector had said about dragons being possessive of their mates.

"Yes, she *is* my princess," Alistair said. "But she is also my mate, a mate after my own heart. I knew it from the day we met."

Ida held up her hand. "I understand. That was my fault, and I take full responsibility for it—"

"You don't understand a thing about it." Amber gripped Alistair's hand, pressing her nails into his scales. "You didn't make this love. And you won't take it away from us."

"But I *did* make it." Ida sighed. "None of this is real. There's been a—mistake—with Happily-Ever-After. It's not your fault at all, but it looks like you may have fallen in love with the wrong person. You were supposed to fall in love with the prince—and I'm very sorry about that too, long story—but the point is I'm here to make it all better. So if you'll just pack your things—and Alistair's too, because this certainly involves you, and I'm not forgetting that—we'll all go back to the castle and get this sorted out. You don't have to marry anyone you don't want to, Amber. I'll make sure of that."

"But I am married," Amber said. "To a prince. A prince of dragons. I'm a princess, don't you remember?"

"By magic—and it was absolutely the wrong thing to do—"

"By marriage." Alistair growled. "I have mated with her."

The look that passed between them was laden with longing and hunger.

She needed to put an end to that right now. "Can I speak frankly to you, Alistair?" she said, folding her arms.

His face said no, but he said nothing and she didn't see fire brewing in his throat, so she continued.

"You weren't meant to be involved to this degree. All you were meant to do was kidnap the princess, deliver her to the mountain lair, and then let the prince discover her."

"She is not my prisoner! I offered to set her down anywhere between the city and the mountains."

"Repeatedly," Amber said with a hint of a smile.

Ida held up her hand. "I'm using the word kidnap in terms

of Happily-Ever-After. Amber was to be rescued by a prince, fall in love, and live with him in his palace. That was how the magic was written."

"Alistair *is* a prince! He did rescue me, I'm in love with him, and I will live with him in his palace!"

"It's not that simple," Ida said. "Think about it, Amber. What did you tell me when we met? Your world was the forge, your family business, and that's all you wanted to do with your life. You wouldn't give them up for any man. I was foolish not to listen to you. I'm here to give that back to you. You didn't want to marry a prince—any prince—but certainly not a dragon prince. In fact, you were willing to kill him to avoid that fate only a few days ago. And now you think you are in love with him? Is that logical?"

Amber said nothing.

"Alistair, Hector told me how you hesitated. You didn't want a princess. You only came to the Happily-Ever-After because he reminded you of your duty. And now you want to marry this girl? A human girl? You aren't a man. You can never love Amber as a man."

Alistair's heated breath warmed Ida's face. "I love Amber more than she has ever been loved by anyone. It doesn't matter that I'm not a man. Isn't that the point of your ridiculous Happily-Ever-After?" He turned his back on Ida and walked to the large open window admitting the chill of the darkening mountains.

"The point of this ridiculous Happily-Ever-After was to preserve the peace," Ida said. "Two people agree to an arranged marriage so everyone else can live happily ever after. Whether or not that's right or wrong is beside the point right now—both of you are victims of a misplaced spell. That's why you feel attracted so strongly to Amber. She may even have feelings for her captor; that's not uncommon—"

"First of all," Amber said. "I'd appreciate if you'd stop calling *me* a victim. I said I'd be the princess when you gave me that spiel about duty and honor, didn't I? I came of my own free will!"

Alistair turned and draped both his arms over Amber's shoulders. "I too came of my own free will. Hector reminded me of all the sacrifices my dragon ancestors have made to keep our people safe. It's not just humans who have given up their choice for Happily-Ever-After. Many dragons have died for your peace. I chose to honor that tradition in the end. How could I call myself a prince of dragons and not?"

He turned to Ida. "If Amber wants to go back to her home, I will take her myself. I've always been willing to. But I won't stop loving her, no matter what kind of spell you throw at me. And if you think a potion might change my mind, you can ask Hector what happens when you give one to a dragon."

"What happens, darling?" Amber asked.

"Wicked gas for one thing," Alistair said, grinning. "But the acid in our stomachs generally deactivates anything our venom doesn't."

"I'm sure your venom isn't good for Amber, either," Ida said with a snort.

Alistair burst out laughing. When he collected himself in spasms of fire and smoke, he said, "Put *that* on your list of questions to ask Hector about dragons."

"Should I also ask him about how to get a dragon to be reasonable?" Ida said. "You say you care about your people, and you want to marry a human? How is that thinking about your people and their traditions?"

With a roar, Alistair loomed in front of her, glaring down from his considerable height, smoking at the ears. "You think I haven't been thinking about tradition since I met Amber? I could've kept her at my lair and hidden her from everyone, kept her for myself. Instead, I brought her here to meet my parents, to get to know my people because she's my mate!"

"And that's going so well." Ida scoffed, although she felt like her heart was in her throat and not back in the box at home. "Is that why you bit your father?"

The smoke drifted away. He gazed down at her with more respect. "You aren't short on courage, Witch. But I didn't bite my father out of anger. I challenged him as our tradition demanded. I won. Now I am king." He turned his back on Ida and went back to Amber, taking her by the shoulders and pressing his nose against her neck.

"And I'm your queen," Amber said, nuzzling him back.

"I suggest you both take some time to think about what I've said," Ida said. "Because from where I stand, I don't see a king and a queen. I see two children making the biggest mistake of their lives because of my magic, and I'm no kind of good witch if I let that happen."

Alistair wrapped his arms around Amber. "Maybe you're no kind of good witch if you can't see what it means to love someone so much you'll do anything to be with them forever. I think you'd better leave now."

His voice was soft and nonthreatening, but Ida backed out of the door, far more terrified than she'd been when he blew up in her face.

41

Hector

Queen Annabeth petitions Witches' Council to remove His Wickedness, Hector West, formerly Hector Prim, and Her Goodness, Ida North, formerly Ida Moonshadow, from their positions as Cardinal Witches! No word yet on how King Rupert has responded. Sources say the king is in the counting house, counting all his money to repair his botched nose job, which keeps regrowing as a sausage.

Queen Annabeth has also filed to have Crown Prince Archibald's marriage to Captain of the Guard Caedan Cay annulled on the grounds it was performed by a drunk centaur. Sources say the centaur told the queen to take advantage of her husband's sausage and shut up about everyone else's.

—THE SORCERER'S STAR

HECTOR FOUND THE FLAMELORD IN DRAGON FORM, lounging in a hot mineral bath. He appeared in good spirits for a man whose own son had taken a large bite out of his foreleg and back. The wounds were contracting, black and green in the center. Alistair hadn't restrained his venom. He'd meant business.

"Hello, Hector!" Adair submerged briefly and grinned as he

rose above the surface, showing all of his sharp, red teeth. "How kind of you to come visit me in my dotage." He chuckled.

"I'm sorry." Hector stared stricken at Adair's arm. "Morga told me about the…mating."

"Arrrrragh," Adair sighed. "I've mixed feelings about it. On one claw, it's utterly absurd, even for Alistair. On the other claw, it's the first time that boy has ever attacked me. I was wondering if I'd have to jump him to get him to claim the kingship."

"You're not upset?" Adair had always been protective of his position, almost to the point of arrogance, but here he was, lounging in the bath, looking positively amused by the situation.

"It was bound to happen sooner or later. I'd quite enjoy rolling over and letting him take over the responsibility if it weren't for the girl who's made a lizard out of him. He won't even take dragon form with us now, apart from the day he chewed me up and spit me out, and I don't think he'd have done it if I hadn't challenged him to combat with the girl there. Amber, I believe?"

"That's right."

"She's made of stern stuff for a human," Adair said. "But no dragon in these mountains will stand for it. Sooner or later, he must take her back where she belongs. I hoped the prince would turn up demanding his bride and one or the other of them would come to their senses, but I've given up on that fantasy. Even if Alistair refused to fight, Amber would pick up a sword and go after the poor man. She's utterly smitten with my son. Some sort of fetish, I suppose. I've heard human women go for shapeshifters."

"Those wounds look infected."

"Pshaw. I had worse when I got drunk and flew into a manticore's nest, but to hear Morga talk, you'd think I was dying." He heaved himself out of the bath, and with a grunt, he contracted down into his human form, naked and proud, and strolled over to a shelf of rock for his robe. The wounds looked even worse on human flesh, and from the way Adair moved, they bothered him more than he let on.

"Tinbit will be here soon with the pack pony and wound balm. I'd let him tend those," Hector said. "In the meantime, can you tell me about what happened when your son flew home with the princess? I asked Morga, but she was…understandably upset."

Adair shook his head. "He is our only egg after all. I doubt even a high-dragon from the ancient Silver Mountains of the north would've met with her approval. But then again, I doubt she'd ever expected to get in the middle of a dragon fight with a human by her side."

"She said Amber tried to stop Alistair."

"The child practically jumped down his throat and told him if he bit her father-in-law again she'd kick him in the groin. He stopped in a hurry. I probably ought to thank her. She's the reason I have two bites in nonvital places and not three very vital places." He laughed. "I don't know what Her Goodness feeds princesses these days, but this one grew up on nettles and brimstone. Pity she *isn't* a dragon." He wrapped his robe around himself and took a seat on a large stone chair. He motioned Hector to take a similar chair drawn up to a table where a large flagon of smoking liquid sat next to a large glass. Adair poured the black ale, took a long drink, and set his glass down. "So, Hector. Why have you brought Her Goodness with you? I expected you, but not Ida North."

Hector squirmed. "Well, as a matter of fact there was a little mishap at the start of Happily-Ever-After. Due to some issues with—" He hesitated. Yes, it might have been the choosing, but he didn't want Ida eaten. "Well, never mind exactly what the issue was. It looks like the princess and the dragon fell in love with each other instead of the princess falling in love with the prince as usually happens. Nothing I can't sort out, but Ida deals more with that part of the magic than I do."

Adair's pupils constricted slightly. "A mishap."

"A minor one."

"Hmm." Adair snorted smoke. "Better not mention that to Morga."

"I don't intend to," Hector said. "Adair, I am deeply sorry this happened. You have my word I will make it right."

The Flamelord placed his fingertips together. "I trust you. You've never done anything detrimental to the safety of our nation before. But this can't stand, Hector. She can't be a queen of dragons, no matter how much my son demands we recognize her. I told him if he wanted to have a fling with a human, I'd look the other way, but to have a human wear the mantle his mother has worn since we mated—completely unacceptable." He took another swig of the drink. "That's when he jumped in the middle of me."

"I will—I will fix this," Hector said. "But it may take time."

"And I will give you that time," Adair said. "I owe it to you, both as my friend and as Alistair's protector and teacher. But if my son doesn't divorce that princess, the dragon council will meet and they will choose another king. I don't think either of us want that."

No, Hector most certainly did not want that. The dragons would find Alistair unfit to be Flamelord and appoint another.

Then they would kill him, his mate, his father, and his mother. Hector would be left with a messy diplomatic situation as well as four burials—well, three.

Custom dictated they'd eat the Flamelord.

42

Ida

I am extremely reluctant to take the unprecedented step of removing both of our oldest and most talented witches. I know you feel, as I do, we owe a great deal to Ida North's unwavering commitment to advancing the understanding and perils of good magic—however you may feel about her prickly personality—but we can't simply kick her out of the Council to make a ridiculous queen look less ridiculous. We must proceed carefully here, not just for the optics of the situation (seriously, could Annabeth have made this more awkward!) but for the sake of magic.

There's no doubt this is a magical disaster of epic proportions, with far-reaching ramifications, but I, for my part, would rather fire Hector than Ida. After all, anybody can manage monsters.

Letter from Good Witch Tara South to Wicked Witch Agatha East

DINNER WITH THE DRAGONS WAS A STRANGE AFFAIR. Morga served them at a long table in the formal room with the firewall, clearly determined to extend all the hospitality due to visiting celebrities, but her heart clearly wasn't in it. She wouldn't quit crying, and the hot tears created enough steam to make the whole room feel like a sauna. Ida was glad when Morga finally excused herself to tend to her mate.

"Where are Tinbit and Hari? They should be here by now. Something's happened." Ida tossed her sandwich on the plate, still hungry, but she'd eaten as much chargrilled cheese as was wise. Exactly two bites.

Hector chewed through his sandwich as placidly as a cow. "The pony had a thorn. Tinbit won't push the animal hard."

"It will be dark soon."

"Not for another two hours on this side of the mountain."

"I wish I'd taken my crystal when we left this morning."

"If they aren't here in another hour, I'll borrow a broom and go out and look for them."

Someone must have told the man if he didn't chomp his food into mush he'd choke. "How can you be so calm?" Ida tried to push back her chair but found it far too heavy and stony to move.

Hector finally swallowed. "Because I can't do anything right now. My medicines are on the pack pony. The pony won't be here until Tinbit and Hari arrive, and I couldn't speed it up if I tried—those creatures are simply immune to haste spells." He took another bite of sandwich. "I gather it didn't go well with the princess and Alistair?"

"Horribly," Ida said. "They refused to separate, even to talk."

"That's not surprising. Newly mated dragons rarely leave their cave for the first few weeks. It's essential they have sex almost continuously in order to develop a tolerance for each other's venom."

So that's why Alistair had laughed. Ida blushed. "Well, I'd say they're handling that little requirement quite well."

Hector sipped his tea with an infuriatingly unconcerned look on his face. "Surely the princess doesn't want to leave her family to become a dragon queen. She can't know what it entails."

Ida folded her arms. "She claims she does. It's clear they've talked a great deal about it. He intends for her to be queen. And she feels the same way."

Hector sighed. "I knew about Alistair. Adair told me. But the dragons will never accept it. It may well tear their nation apart."

"I'll let you tell him that." Ida rubbed her temples. "I got nowhere with him, and I used the same argument—he wasn't thinking about his responsibility."

He reached across the table and touched her hand. "You handle the princess. Let *me* handle the dragons."

"Good luck. Honestly, Hector, I don't know if I will get anywhere with her until this earthquake in my head abates."

"When Tinbit arrives, I'll have him mix you a headache cure after he's done with Adair. You should go lie down for a while."

"Hector, you know I want to do as the dragons do for your sake, but I can't sleep on a stone bench with no blankets, no sheets, and a lumpy old rock for a pillow."

Hector laughed. "They keep a guestroom for humans here— quite comfortable. There's even a bed with proper linens and not asbestos."

"I suppose next you'll say they'll give us bear skins and wolf pelts to keep warm."

"Five hundred years ago they would have, but no, I keep them well supplied with quilts. You and Hari can share the guest room. I'll stay with Tinbit in the stable, so long as it suits you."

"What would suit me is a bath," Ida said. "And a fresh change of clothes afterward."

"A bath can be arranged. And Morga probably has an extra robe you can borrow."

"Can you do anything for the Flamelord?" she asked, rising.

"I think so. His wounds are not severe—at least for a dragon. He'll recover. Now go lie down. I'll clean up here."

Ida found the guest bedroom by avoiding doors with scorch marks until she found one without any. It was much smaller than the others too. From this she concluded that at least in this part of the cave, the dragons kept their human shape. From a diplomatic perspective, it made sense. Most humans probably wouldn't be comfortable sleeping where a dragon could enter at will.

A fire immediately ignited in the center of the floor when she walked in, a single jet of flame roaring skyward with a loud whoosh, then subsiding into a merry crackling blaze over a few chunks of reddish-black obsidian, carefully arranged and carved to resemble chunks of wood. Cear would love this. How were they doing, trapped in their firepot, tied on the back of a goblin pony, somewhere in the mountains? What would they say when they arrived? They'd have questions, and of course, she'd have to answer, because Cear would want to stay with her. Not that she blamed the elemental—a stable was no place for a firepot. She set her hands in the middle of her back and stretched, hearing every pop, feeling every tight place. The bed at the hostel had been bad, worse even than the one at the inn. But she'd been less sore after the inn.

She crossed the room to test the mattress, deliberately not thinking about the way Hector's eyes had burned this morning, bright as dragon's fire, when he leaned over her lying on the moss. For a moment, she'd been almost sure he was going to kiss her. And she was absolutely sure she'd have kissed him back if he had. She shuddered. When this was over, she didn't care if she ever spelled a truelove's kiss ever again. She'd swear off romance for her entire retirement; become a grumpy old witch with a little gingerbread cottage, a garden full of nettles, blackberry hedges, and rampion; and keep an evil white goose to bite the backside of any lovelorn fool who came calling.

The bed yielded springily under her hands. She lay down, kicking off her boots, and eyed the large tub in the corner of the room longingly, but until Tinbit and Hari arrived with the pack pony or Morga brought a robe, she only had her dirty sweater and pants. The idea of crawling back into the filthy things again repulsed her.

She stared up at the bright firelight flickering on the ceiling, thinking about Hector's castle, the library, the funny little fern, and the deep, rich scent of the black rose drifting in through the windows, so like the scent of Hector. The vision came to her of that little cottage with the garden and the goose, the smell of flowers drifting through those open windows, over a cozy bed where she lay nestled next to Hector, one hand resting on his chest after making love to him—warm, happy, replete. She could practically hear his soft breathing and see his salt-and-pepper ocean of hair drifting over the pillow, waterfalling into his deep green eyes as he smiled, as happy as she was.

She blinked fiercely. She was too old to think about things like a lovesick princess, believing every problem could be solved by one kiss on some enchanted evening. But she couldn't help but wonder if Hector had been a nice farm boy who'd come calling when she was a girl, whether she'd have heeded her father's advice, or if she, like the princess and the dragon, would have given up everything for one simple lifetime of love.

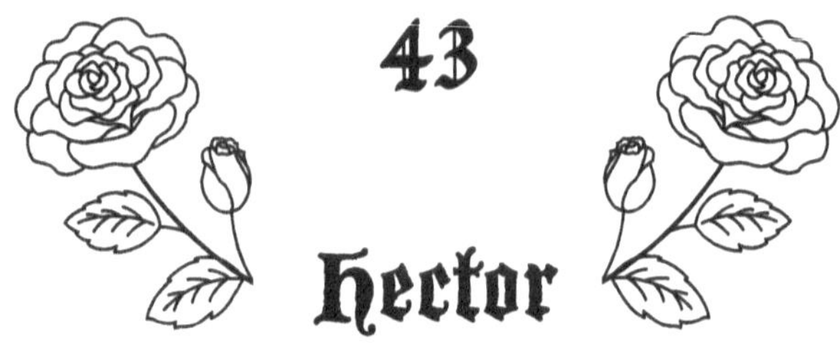

43

Hector

Don't think I can't see right through you, Tara. If Hector goes, I'd have to appoint a young witch to take his place, and they'd have less death magic in their whole body than Hector has in his little finger. I'm not about to let you and Ida take control of this Council. Either we agree to fire them both, or you can expect me to fire Ida the moment she shows her overlong nose in the Hall of Witches.

Letter from Wicked Witch Agatha East to Good Witch
Tara South

HECTOR ROSE AND CARRIED IDA'S LEFTOVER CHEESE sandwich to the kitchen. She seemed so focused, so determined, no hint of distraction. Meanwhile he was a turmoil inside. It must be nice to be so unaffected by one's own magic that one could simply walk off to take an early evening nap, completely unconcerned by one's completely carnal preoccupations. When he saw the fear in her face, all he could think about was taking her in his arms and telling her he'd make it all right, and please, love him. Gods. Tinbit had been right about the balls. Getting rid of his heart hadn't helped at all.

Ida had once written that wickedness could never compete

against the power of a good heart, and while he'd appreciated both the insult and the challenge, there might be some truth in it. A good heart, a chivalrous sense of honor, a kind deed—those things went a long way in preventing a man from being overwhelmed by his baser feelings. His heart was gone, and it had never been good. Chivalry had gone the way of the unicorns long ago. But the kind deed he could manage.

He squared up to the dragon's stove, stacked two boxes of everlasting onions together, climbed up, tied an overlarge apron over his robe, and set the skillet on the burner.

He carried two slightly burned sandwiches along with a small bowl of rock-loganberry preserves on a tray to Alistair's room. The absence of them both at dinner suggested that Alistair, perhaps in an attempt to convince his father of Amber's worthiness, had decided to do everything according to dragon tradition. Once mated, a dragon must feed his mate to show he can provide, not only for her, but for the dragon eggs she will surely be expecting after their nonstop mating. The gifts generally took the form of fresh meat, a different animal each day for a full two weeks. The princess was probably sick of barbecue by now.

He knocked gently on the door.

"Yes?" she answered.

"It's Hector. May I come in?"

"Alistair isn't here."

"I would like to come in anyway, if you don't mind."

The door opened.

The princess had changed clothes. She wore another one of Alistair's long wool robes, a blood-red one, too long for her. The way the folds clung to her shoulders and hips, she wasn't wearing anything underneath. So she was adhering to dragon tradition too.

He thrust the tray with the sandwiches in her direction. "Grilled cheese and coffee. I'm not the cook my gnome is, or there would be hot onion soup."

Amber stuffed the sandwich in her mouth and started eating as fast as she could. "How'd you know?" She spewed crumbs as he poured a cup of coffee and set it on the table between them.

"I've spent many years being entertained by dragons. Please?" He gestured for her to sit.

"If you're here to talk me out of my marriage, I won't listen." She glared at him.

"I wouldn't dream of asking you to do something so hazardous to your health."

"Alistair would never hurt me."

"Or *his* health," Hector said. "Believe me, I have no intention of breaking up your mating unless it is a completely mutual rupture, and for that, I need Alistair. I take it he's out hunting."

"Yes." Amber glanced at the brazier in the center of the room that she'd fitted with a makeshift grill. Definitely tired of barbecue. She grabbed the second sandwich and started in on it ravenously. He wished Alistair could see this. His bride wasn't a dragon, and he couldn't expect her to behave like a dragon indefinitely.

"My dear, how long has it been since you had a proper bath, a fresh set of clothes, or eaten a green vegetable? This isn't sustainable."

Her eyes turned dragon-fierce. "I'm not leaving him," she said with her mouth full. "You can tell that to Ida too. She sent you to scare some sense into me, didn't she? Tell me all those horror stories about how Alistair will get angry and burn me up by accident, or how I'll say something wrong to his mother and she'll eat me in a single bite."

"Morga wouldn't eat you in a single bite. It would take two at least—she'd want to savor it. And as far as I know, Alistair has only burned one person in a fit of temper."

Amber snorted a laugh. "Who?"

"Me." Hector smiled and leaned back comfortably in his chair. "To be honest, I deserved it. He would not be so careless with the person he loves."

Amber's eyes widened. "You believe he loves me?"

"Of course, he does."

"Ida doesn't believe that."

"On the contrary; she's convinced you're both as in love as any prince and princess could ever be, as am I. It's magically induced. I know you don't believe any magic is capable of that—but believe me, it is." He sighed. "You underestimate the power of this kind of love magic on a susceptible heart." He certainly had.

"You are only saying this to get me to believe I wouldn't love him if the magic wasn't there. That's not true. Don't you understand? Maybe we did start to care for each other because of magic, but it's different now." She stood and walked around the room. "I don't know how to explain it. You're old. You're wicked. You've never loved anyone."

"Why don't you try me?"

She squared up to him, folding her arms in her robe, a curious expression of determination on her face that reminded him of Ida. "When Alistair carried me off, I thought he'd simply set me down in the field. We'd say goodbye. I'd walk home. He'd fly home. But when he told me he was sorry he'd ever let himself get involved in such a horrible barbaric ritual, and he hoped I could go back to my smithy and have a wonderful career because he could see I loved to work with my hands, it was like I'd found the second half of my soul. The way he looked at me, the way he held my hands in his claws, I knew he felt the same way. I asked him to take me to the mountains. I suggested it might keep both of us from being in trouble for a few days, but even then, we both knew. And the morning after, when I turned over in his arms and saw his eyes shining in the dark and the happiness in them, I realized I could see him every morning, in any form, every day until the morning I don't wake up, and I'd die happy. What is that, if it's not love?"

He winced as a sudden vision of Ida petting the fern in his library flashed across his memory. "It's magic. All magic."

"Who are you to say true love *isn't* magic?"

"But it isn't true love, and if you knew even a fraction of the risk you are taking—"

"I know what we're risking. Alistair told me if we mated, I would risk not only my life, but also his. I told him I didn't care about me, but him—I would do anything for him. If he wanted me to go, I would. Then he held me, and he said he could think of no one he would rather risk his life for, risk his life *with*. I felt the same way." She dropped the half-finished sandwich on the plate and walked to the brazier to arrange the coals. "Whatever he asks me to do, whatever we have to do to be together, I'm with him through all of it."

"Respectfully," he said, "I don't think you've thought this through."

"I've thought as long as I need to," she said. "And any other thinking that has to be done, we'll do together too."

He reddened. "Flamelords need an heir. They will expect an egg at the end of this mating. Did he tell you that?"

"Yes, as a matter of fact. We're going to adopt. The king egg is a function of temperature, and he will incubate it."

"But your human family—"

"My family will learn to love him as I do."

"They won't love him! They don't know dragons are anything other than man-eating monsters!"

"Something you've encouraged, no doubt." She huffed.

"Yes—because it protects them."

She rounded on him. "Dragons can take care of themselves, you know! Maybe Happily-Ever-After started out to protect people who couldn't protect themselves, but people evolve. They grow. They change. They learn. And that's killing you, isn't it, Your Wickedness? They don't need you anymore!"

"Princess, you don't understand—"

"Leave," she said, standing tall. "Alistair will be back soon, and I'll tell him you were here. If he wants to see you, he'll find you. But I'm not going to put him through the pain Ida caused him earlier today."

"She didn't intend—"

"He wept after what she said to him. He begged me to tell him to let me go. He asked me to tell him to take me home and he'd stay with me. He said he didn't want to return to the mountains if he couldn't be with me."

An intense chill ran down Hector's spine. "Amber, he can't do that! The people would—"

"Kill him? Yes, I know! This is the man you want me to leave so you and Ida can have your precious little Happily-Ever-After intact, so you don't have to take responsibility for the lives you've ruined, so you can go back to your castles and look down on us poor mortals from your thousand years of sovereign wisdom until you get to wreck the next generation of lives! Well, you aren't ruining my life, and you aren't ruining his."

"You're ruining your own!"

"If we are, we're doing it together," she said. "That's what matters. Now go."

He went.

Shaken.

44

Ida

Contrary to popular opinion, people in love, even magical love, don't always agree on everything. They stand together despite their differences.

MAGIC AND MISCHIEF–A THOUSAND
YEARS OF HAPPILY EVER AFTER: A MEMOIR

IDA NORTH

"I'M SORRY FOR LEAVING LIKE THAT," IDA SAID, FACING Hari's angry, raised shoulders. "Hector and I thought it would be best if we confronted the dragon and the princess ourselves and not put you and Tinbit in danger—"

"Danger? Danger?" Hari pulled down the bedspread and plumped Ida's pillow. "We nearly got eaten by a manticore! Tinbit and I barely got away. I've no idea if the pony escaped."

The bad luck kept coming like a landslide. Her crystal, her clothes, her books, not to mention all the roots and herbs Hector had insisted on bringing—just in case—were somewhere walking around the mountains or giving a manticore wicked indigestion.

"I really am sorry. I'm glad you saved the salamander."

"More like they saved *us*," Hari said. "But if they flame both your britches for running off and leaving them, I'm going to be there handing them matches." He stripped his dirty shirt and wiped a dark smear of smoke from his cheek. "I need a bath. Don't suppose they have anything here that would fit a gnome?" He glanced at the long red robe Ida wore.

"I don't think so," she said, hitching Morga's belt tighter around her waist.

"No matter." He sighed. "I'll wash my things out and dry them by the fire. Yours too. And then we both need sleep."

"Later, perhaps," Ida said. "I'd better go see if Hector needs help. He was counting on the pony so he could prepare wound balms for Adair."

"Tinbit was carrying as much on his back as the horse. He'll manage. I don't think there's much he can't do, except when he doesn't want to." He gave the pillow a particularly aggressive punch.

"Are you hungry? We ate grilled cheese. I'll make you one—"

He sighed. "You'd burn it. I'll eat later. Right now I want to bathe and rest my feet. It's a long way up a mountain when you've been running half a day trying to get away from a manticore with kits."

Feeling worse than before, she nodded. "Okay. I'll leave you to it. I'll go apologize to Cear."

Hari said nothing. Something must have happened between him and Tinbit beyond running for their lives.

Ida found Cear in what she'd termed the dragon's living room. She supposed Hector might call it a hospitality chamber, but had the furniture not been all stone with carefully arranged human comforts in various places, she could imagine the whole dragon family settling down to watch the latest sitcom on the crystal at night.

As in her room, a fire burned over the gas vent, soaring to the ceiling in a solid sheet of yellow, red, and blue, undulating softly. Sinuous and graceful, vaguely serpentine, Cear curled inside the flames, expanding, swimming back down, and as they turned, their eyes glowed a bright crimson, gazing at Ida.

"Are you well?" Ida asked, reaching for the sweetgrass bale. A few flakes were missing. Hector had seen to their comfort before going to attend Adair with Tinbit.

"I have not been so comfortable since leaving my home," they said, assuming more of a human face, but thin and angular, shining like a multifaceted jewel. "This is how we exist in our natural habitat. I hope I do not distress you with my form."

"Not at all," Ida said. "I wanted to be sure you were comfortable and to apologize for leaving you alone at the hostel."

"But I was not left alone. Your gnome is quite resourceful, and Hector's gnome equally brave. They attended to me as well as you or Hector might have done."

"We meant no disrespect. Hector thought we needed to speak with the dragon and the princess first, to ascertain how badly they were affected by the Happily-Ever-After. We were worried about its effects."

"On your gnomes?"

Ida fed a flake of sweetgrass into the flames a handful at a time. "Yes."

Cear curled down around the sweetgrass, nibbling it daintily. "Are you not concerned for yourself or for Hector?"

"I'm concerned for every creature who has been affected," Ida said, not without a twinge of wry amusement at referring to herself as a creature.

"But you hold Hector's heart," Cear said in a sibilant hiss. "He is the one you fear for. You care for him."

"Please don't tell him about the heart. I don't regret saving it, and I do plan to return it when all this is over, but I'd rather him not know that I have it for the time being."

"I will say nothing. But Ida, don't you wish to consult your own heart in this matter?"

"I don't have anything to ask it, Cear."

Her head ached. Somewhere far away, her heart probably ached too.

Fresh air might help with the first. Nothing would help with the second. She left Cear and headed for the cave entrance.

Outside the cave, dusk settled over the mountains like a gray blanket. The sun wouldn't be down yet, not at this hour. The mountains merely blocked it from filtering through any place but the mountain passes. These lit up like red and gold torches, spreading their flames through the valleys wherever the evergreen forests didn't swallow the light whole. Stars pricked the blue night above her as she walked a little way down the path.

She didn't go far, despite the urge to wrap Morga's overlarge robe around herself and walk home, dodging dragons, manticores, and bandits. Some good witch she'd turned out to be. She couldn't get Hector to listen to her. Couldn't get the princess to listen to her. Couldn't even get Hari to listen.

A soft cough made her slip into the shadows of a large rock, thinking of a dragon blowing fire if they sneezed, but it was only Hector, coming back up the path. He wore a worn, black dragon robe, probably something of Adair's, and leaned heavily on his staff like he wished it would bear up the whole world, not just him.

"Come to make sure I don't wander off?" she asked, stepping out from behind the rock.

He straightened. "I came out to look for the pony. I left Tinbit patching up Adair. He gets short with me if I try to help with bandaging."

"He brought enough herbs?"

"Apparently so. He was worried Hari might need him to mix a tonic or treat a blister, so he decided to carry it all on his own. He says I owe him. I checked on Cear, by the way; Morga put them in the fireplace."

"I saw," she said. "They looked happy."

Hector climbed the last few feet and stood next to her beside the rock, gazing back at the valley. "No sign of the pony yet."

"Wouldn't it run back home?"

"It would if I didn't have a compulsion on it," Hector said with a soft grunt.

"It will be hard for it to climb out of a manticore."

He chuckled. "If it got eaten, I pity the manticore," he said. "Goblins breed their ponies to be almost indigestible. Dragons used to hunt them, you know."

"It's hard for me to imagine them hunting," Ida said. "Now that I've met them, I can't see them being so barbaric."

"Humans are even more barbaric."

"You still feel the same way, don't you? You still want to fix Happily-Ever-After."

He hesitated. "To be completely honest, I've been trying not to think about it for the last hour and a half. I talked to the princess, you see."

She folded her other hand over his. "She's quite a formidable woman."

"Not unlike the witch who chose her." Hector smiled. "Whether she thinks she did or not."

She squared up to him. "I've been thinking. When we do get this sorted out, I'm going to resign from the Council. I'm going to tell them why I can't continue in my post. But I'm not going to tell them that I let the magic choose. Maybe—maybe it made the right decision after all. I'm not fit for my position. Maybe I never was."

"What are you talking about?" He put both hands on her shoulders. "You're not going to resign. I'm the head of the Council—it's my responsibility!"

"Hector, do you think Agatha could do half the job you do? All she does with any degree of proficiency is enchanted sleep and hauntings. She certainly wouldn't enforce the rules about not killing dragons. Remember when she fought you on whether or not dragons who died of natural causes could be harvested for their magical properties?"

"I remember—but when I'm gone, you'll be head of the Council, and you do care about it—"

"I don't want to be head of the Council, Hector!"

Hector took her hands. "Ida. Listen to me. If you really believe there is something intrinsically wrong with Happily-Ever-After, shouldn't you be the one to investigate that? And if it turns out that I'm right, you'll be the best one to fix it. You can convince the others. I have faith in you—"

"But they won't listen to me! I was responsible for the love magic after all." He wasn't saying this, doing this. She couldn't stand it if he left. She couldn't. "You're better at that than I am. If we talk to them together, maybe—"

"We can't both take the fall for this, and you know it," Hector said. "Forget about Agatha. What about Tara? Do you honestly think she would pick princesses and princes with any attention to their worthiness? She'd turn the whole thing into a cake competition."

Ida choked back a sobbing laugh. "But they need you. The prince. The princess. The dragons. What's going to happen to them if you leave? What about the giants, the goblins, and your silly old ghoul? And your plants? What would you do with all your plants at the castle?"

Hector turned away from her. "Perhaps you might adopt my plants. I personally wouldn't trust Agatha with a weed."

"And adopt Tinbit too?"

He sighed. "He won't leave me."

She clasped and unclasped her hands nervously. Hari had said not to, and she wanted to respect that, but Hector couldn't resign. He couldn't. She couldn't sit in the Council room and stare at an empty seat where he used to be, knowing she had caused it. "Hector—would you—if—I think Hari—" She took a breath. "It's just, he cares a great deal for Tinbit, and if he wanted to stay, to come live with you, would you be open to that? I'd so much like for him to have a happily-ever-after of his own."

"You know I would. But I don't think he'll ask, or you wouldn't have done it for him." Hector laughed mirthlessly. He leaned heavily against the rock, staring down into the gathering darkness. "You know, the more I think about it, the more I think you might be right. The problem with Happily-Ever-After is *us*. No matter what we try to do, it all seems to end up wrong, doesn't it?"

"It certainly feels that way," Ida said.

They stood quietly for a while, hand in hand, staring down the mountain path. A light breeze kicked up, but it felt more like a breath of winter despite the warmth of the late sun, gilding the snowy peaks of higher mountains with fire. Ida leaned into Hector's comforting warmth, grateful for the thickness of his robe in addition to hers. To her surprise, he pulled her closer to himself, and briefly, he touched his nose to the top of her head.

"They'll be all right," he said. "Whatever happens."

"I want to believe you," she said. "But I'm just so worried."

"Quite frankly, I'm more worried about the dragon and the princess. I'm no expert on humans in love, but I know dragons, and there's no mistaking it. This has gone way beyond Happily-Ever-After. They're in love, Ida. Worse, it *is* real."

45

Hector

The foremost skill a Wicked Witch should hone over a lifetime is their intuition. It's important to learn when to stay if a dragon invites you to dinner and when to run for your life.

A THOUSAND YEARS OF WICKEDNESS: A MEMOIR

HECTOR WEST

He hadn't expected her to take it well. She should be angry with him. She should be dismissive, to remind him that he knew nothing about true love—even if it was dragons. He was a wicked witch—heartless and utterly incapable of understanding it.

Instead, she slumped against the rock, glowing pink in one of the last shards of sunlight to bathe the grim face of the mountain. "I know."

"They can't stay together. It's completely impossible, for so many reasons."

Her eyebrows drew together, her cheeks sagged, her mouth pouted. "Like Hari and Tinbit, some obstacles they can't surmount."

"Hari and Tinbit see the difficulties and concede them. Amber and Alistair don't."

"I don't even know if they *can* concede them," Ida said. "They think they can overcome it all by the power of love. I'm sorry, Hector—I'm sorry for everything. If I'd not sent you the laughing charm, this wouldn't have happened."

What was he supposed to do now? If she'd drawn her wand and blasted him, it would have been easier. As before, he wanted to take her in his arms and comfort her, tell her everything would be all right, he would fix it all for all the good that lie would do. Still, he offered her his embrace, and she leaned into it, head resting against his empty chest, and for once he wasn't burdened by worrying if he was doing the right thing.

"Ida, Alistair would've burned me if I *hadn't* laughed at him, and I think I deserved it. Blame me for this mess—I sent you the candor curse."

She shook her head, eyes shut tight. "Amber would've come to see justice was done, and I'd have done the exact same thing I did. I know that now." She sighed. "There's an inevitability about this that would be serendipitous if it wasn't so…well, there's no serendipity in mangled magic, and that's the way everyone will see it. You're right. One of us has to go. It needs to be me."

"No." He swallowed hard. "I won't allow it."

"Hector—"

"No!" He couldn't stand the idea that she wouldn't be opposite him at the table, thwarting his every move, always ready with a scathing remark about his ineptitude, even when he knew she didn't doubt his ability. She never had. He fumbled for the words to tell her what an honor it had been, fighting her for almost a thousand years, but they seemed empty, hollow, and purposeless.

Instead, he pulled her tightly against him. He tilted her chin up with one hand, his other hand resting tenderly against her shoulder, and kissed her.

Frankly, *something* should've happened. Bats should've descended and swarmed them. Perhaps an attack of spiders. Or Sebastian could've leaped out from behind a rock and said, Gotcha! But nothing happened except that Ida melted into him, and he broke away, terrified, trembling, afraid of what he'd started. But something very different was happening in the rest of his body, an eagerness he'd forgotten except in very occasional dreams. "Ida, I—I want—just once—"

"I know," she whispered. "I do too."

"We shouldn't."

"I don't care!"

"But I care about you! If the Council finds out—"

"Fuck the Council!" She pushed against him hard, hands shaking. "If this is the end of Happily-Ever-After, if it's all I have left, can't I have you? Just once."

Oh, he wanted that too, and his fear mixed deliciously with desire. There were a million reasons why he shouldn't make love to Ida now, a million reasons why he shouldn't make love period, but if he didn't act now, he'd be sorry forever. "Come," he said. "Come with me."

"Anywhere," she said.

Hector pushed open the door of the stable.

Ida glanced around with interest. "This is…different."

He glanced down the empty corridor where various open doors showed the lack of inhabitants. The goblin pony would have the first stall when it arrived, filled to a plush depth with meadow straw and sweetgrass. The vanilla fragrance filled the place. He led the way to the end of the breezeway where a larger room had been carved into the rock and pushed the door open. "When I used to ride Napoleon here, back when he was alive, I sometimes stayed here. Dragons love to give parties for visiting dignitaries. They can be…intense. One needs a break some-times. These are supposed to be the groom's quarters."

They were roomy, if more spartan than the rooms dragons kept for important guests. But the bed looked inviting, and it still smelled of lavender and sweetgrass when he pulled the sheet back. Immediately upon entry, a tiny candle in the room lit up.

"A candle in a stable?" Ida asked, watching the light fill the space.

"It's everlasting flame. I conjured it to be safe. Fire is sacred to the dragons. Whenever there's a fire in a house or a heart, it becomes magic—"

He didn't get any further. Ida pulled him down and kissed him. The candle flickered brightly, burned hot and hard, blazing against the wall. How could he have ever missed how beautiful she was, her eyes so bright, her curiously changeable hair curling over her shoulders. He reached, trembling, and undid the clips holding it all back.

She undressed him slowly, sliding her hands beneath his robe. It dropped down to his ankles. "Well, I see you like to keep things well-aired."

He flushed, feeling the heat all through his arms, chest, and groin. "I took a bath. I didn't feel like putting on my dirty things afterward."

"Me either." She eased his hands underneath the shoulders

of her robe. He slipped the fabric down to her waist. The warm light cast shadows over all the lovely places he wanted to be. But there was one thing he had to do, had to say.

"Ida. I've never had sex before. I mean, I have studied the procedure—"

She cupped his cheek with one hand and planted a kiss on his lips, long, lingering. Her warm skin pressed against his, and he sighed and wrapped his arms around her, pulling her against him.

"It's been a long time for me too," she said.

"How long?"

"A very, very long time." She laughed. "And it's been a long time since I studied the procedure too."

He choked on a laugh. "We're supposed to be in charge of Happily-Ever-After, and neither of us knows how to make love." He kissed the top of her head, pressing his nose into her sweet-smelling hair. Roses. Red roses. He drew in the scent, and all fear left him.

"I don't know about that," Ida whispered. "Let's find out how much we *do* know."

He pulled her down into the bed with him.

46

Ida

The very best part about a breakup is the makeup.

MAGIC AND MISCHIEF–A THOUSAND
YEARS OF HAPPILY-EVER-AFTER: A MEMOIR

IDA NORTH

IT HAD BEEN MORE THAN EIGHT CENTURIES SINCE IDA had been in bed with anyone. She'd not forgotten the man's face, or the way he thought he was the Gods' gift to women. She'd not forgiven the way he handled himself, expecting his body would be enough to pleasure any manner of woman, any shape, any configuration—one cock to fill them all. She remembered him very well.

Hector was nothing like him.

He fumbled his way through sex, clearly trying so hard, until she pushed him over on his back and took over. He seemed delighted by the change of position, and the warm glow filled his eyes, already alight with candle flame.

"Thank you," he said. "I was wondering when you'd punch me."

She laughed and bent over him, forehead to his lips. "You

were trying. Believe me, trying goes a long way to making any woman happy."

"I don't want to make any woman happy. I want to make *you* happy."

"You great flatterer. Are you sure you haven't done this before?" His heart pounded in her chest as much for her as him. She flexed her hips, feeling the slight ache from that riding accident long ago. She'd be sore from a different kind of ride tonight, but Hector's trembling hands rested on the small of her back, and Gods help her, he was so involved, so intensely passionate, even in his clumsy attempts to do everything by the book. "Hector, touch me here." She guided his hands to her breasts. "Like what you did in the inn, where you—"

A happy gasp escaped her as he gently massaged. With a sly smile, he wet his fingers in his mouth, and touched her nipples. "Like this?"

"Gods." She leaned back, sitting on him, feeling him harden underneath her as she moved against him. She raised up, moved forward, and slid down on him. He gasped, his hands stopped moving for a moment, and his eyes closed.

She bent forward, sliding down on her elbows, hair trailing over his shoulders, rocking against him gently. "Is this good?"

His voice was a bare whisper. "Ida, I don't know how long I can hold back. I—I feel close. Very close."

She settled down against him, slowing down. Warmth burned in all the right places, softly simmering, like the candle flickering on the table near the bed. She tangled one hand in his hair. "I'm close too." He might feel his heart inside her chest, but she couldn't pull away from him. She imagined making love to him in his castle, with the black roses dropping a shower of petals on top of them both. She could smell the fragrance.

"Oh, Gods." His voice broke. He gasped. Pushed upward, panting. He shifted, and oh—oh, *that* had never been touched like he touched it, and she gasped, pressing down as he pushed up, pulling her down against himself, rocking her hips down as if he'd take as much as she'd give him, give as much as he could.

"Hector." She collapsed on top of him.

He jerked and quivered, but refused to let up, like he'd stay inside her as long as he could. She'd never made love to a fellow witch before. Their magic passed between them like fluid, but if this was Hector's wicked magic, it felt delightful—a deep, wonderful, softening warmth that melted into her the way she melted into him.

"Ida." He breathed a kiss on her cheek.

She didn't want to move either. She wanted to stay with him, nestled in his arms, glad for his warmth, glad for his body, glad for the soft light in his green eyes when he stroked her hair. "Are you happy?" she asked.

"So happy, but…but, Ida, I thought once would be enough. It's not. I want you again. Over and over again, every night, every morning."

She laughed softly. "Oh, Hector. You know we can't." She rolled off him, curled up next to his side, and snuggled into his arm when he embraced her.

"Well…not now." He curled his fingers in her hair. His voice took on a quietly contemplative tone. "Maybe…maybe when we're both retired, you can visit me. No one is going to care about one grumpy old witch in the woods entertaining another grumpy old witch, are they?"

"Who said I had to come visit you? You should visit me sometimes. We'll sit out on my front porch in our rockers and eat gingerbread and talk about how the kingdom has all gone to rot and ruin. I'll ask you in for dinner, and you'll just happen to lose track of time, and then it will be dark, and you'll stay over…"

"And by some strange coincidence, you'll only have the one bed, and neither of us will have any nightclothes. We'll snuggle close for warmth, won't we?" Hector chuckled.

"I don't think I've ever heard a nicer laugh, Hector West."

"I don't think I've ever seen a prettier smile, Ida North."

She kissed him.

"We'll just have to wait," he said softly. He wrapped his arms around her. "Until then."

"Until then," she murmured. His mustache and his beard scratched, but it wasn't unpleasant, although she worried what she'd look like tomorrow morning. Hari would almost certainly notice, even if he didn't ask her what kind of walk would put her back at the dragon cave after dark. But she didn't stop, and she didn't say they needed to get up and get dressed, although the urgency of it was pressing.

He was right. Once was never going to be enough.

How long had she wanted this? Maybe since the first day she'd met him, standing at that punch bowl, so nervous, completely overwhelmed by the enormous honor of being the youngest ever Cardinal Witch but trying so hard to look the part. And he *did*. The memory sent her burrowing against him again, hungry for his body, his touch. She'd thought him unbelievably arrogant that day, but over the centuries, he'd proved he was worthy of that honor. There was no one who cared more about the world on the Council. Whatever happened, she would *not* let him take the blame for Happily-Ever-After. All along—he'd been this man, the man who would go to any length to save what he loved, including her.

A door creaked.

Tinbit and Hari stood in the doorway. Hari's face wore an expression of shock, but Tinbit looked like he'd swallowed molten lead.

Hector sat up. "This…this isn't what it looks like." He yanked half the blanket over himself.

Tinbit snorted. "I think it's exactly what it looks like. You hypocrite."

"What are you doing here?" Ida asked Hari, frantically reaching for the sheets and pulling them up around her neck.

Hari blushed crimson, staring at the floor. "I came out to find you and saw the pony trotting up the hill. I went to grab it, then Tinbit came out and asked if I'd seen Hector, and—"

Ida rose and grabbed her robe. "The pony is safe?"

"I guess you'd be interested in that. I suppose you might like some clothes?" Tinbit sneered.

"Hari will help me, Tinbit. You take care of Hector's needs, not mine."

"I'd say you've already taken care of Hector's *needs*."

"That's uncalled for," Hector said, standing.

"Yeah, remember who I'm talking to," Tinbit scoffed.

"Yeah," Hari said quietly. "Remember who you're talking to. That's *my* Witch."

Tinbit rounded on him. "She's been trying to keep you away from me. You know that!"

"Ida has nothing to do with it! *I've* been trying to keep me away from you, and it's been the hardest thing of my life to do! Now, I'm thinking it might have been worth the effort."

Tinbit went white under his brown. "Hari, you don't mean that."

Hari squared up to Tinbit. "Back at the castle, you asked me to leave her for you! Up until now, I wanted to. But now I see how you really are. If I'm not exactly who you want or need when you expect it, you'll do to me what you do to Hector and Ida. Mock me. Hold me to standards I can't possibly meet. They can't help being in love! It's the damned Happily-Ever-After spell."

Tinbit visibly shrank with every word, cringing under them. "Hari, that's not true. I'm only angry because they tried to keep us apart—because they didn't want us to love each other."

"I'm going to feed the pony," Hari said. "And when this is over, I'm going home with Ida. Find some other gnome to dress up and play doll with. I'm not your toy."

He turned on his heel and stomped out.

"Hari—" Tinbit's wild plea came out as a gasp. He bolted out the door.

Ida glanced at Hector, shakily pulling on his robe.

"I need to get to him before he does something foolish," Hector said. "Keep Hari with you. Tell him not to go after Tinbit."

"What's going on?"

"A crisis of necomancy." Without explaining further, he left the room.

47

Hector

Necomancy remains the staple magic of the wicked witch for a number of reasons. First, the position means one generally has a surplus of dead bodies. Secondly, dragons don't cremate for free anymore. Thirdly, there are times in an immortal man's life when saying goodbye is too painful.

A THOUSAND YEARS OF WICKEDNESS: A MEMOIR

HECTOR WEST

AS SKILLED AS HE WAS, HECTOR KNEW HIS LIMITS, less determined by the spell than the person involved. He had known Tinbit since he was a gnomelet. Whenever someone rejected him, he catastrophized. Nobody loved him. Nobody cared for him. Nobody wanted him. Hector did everything in his power to manage the bouts of depression following every failed love affair, but he'd never been able to do anything about the anger beneath it all. Some wounds were too deep, even for a great witch to fix.

"Tinbit!" he called out into the darkness. "Tinbit, where are you?"

Silence.

Tinbit had a strong sense of devotion, but Hector had never tested it like this. He shouldn't have done it. He should've held back with Ida, should've conquered his desire. If Tinbit left him, there'd *be* nothing left.

"Tinbit?"

A sudden crash of a rock over a ledge startled him. He followed the sound.

The gnome sat on the edge of a precipice, legs hanging over the side. As Hector approached, Tinbit picked up a rock and hurled it. "Leave me alone."

"You know I won't do that. I never could."

Tinbit turned to look at Hector. In the moonlight, his brown skin took on a transparent sheen.

Hector flinched. "Can I sit with you?"

Tinbit jerked his head at the stone by his side.

Hector took a seat. "I didn't want this to happen. I wanted you to be happy."

Tinbit hurled another rock. "Some people aren't supposed to be happy."

"But there have been times you seemed content."

"Until him, I was. Honestly, Hector, I should throw myself off this cliff and be done with it."

"Tinbit, please—"

"You can't fix everything, Hector. You did the best you could, but the problem is me. I was a fool to think Hari could ever love me." He buried his face in his hands. "I wish I'd never sent that letter. I wish I'd never talked to him. I wish I'd never touched him and known what it was to be touched by hands that wanted me. Loved me. Held me. Oh, Gods, Hector—why did you have to raise me?" He wailed.

A million images of that horrible day returned to Hector with painful clarity. The skeletal housekeeper coming into his room instead of Tinbit, telling him a ghost wanted to see him. Then the icy chill in Tinbit's terrified eyes as he stood, a shade in the dark, gazing at his body, lying stiff and cold in his own bed, and the belladonna and aconite weeping a dark, miserable stain where in his death throes he'd knocked the cup over on the floor. He hadn't done it on purpose—it had been an accident, too much poison for too much pain…

It had been pure selfishness on his part, seeing Tinbit's dead body, knowing his poisons had done it. But guilt was a poor motivation for bringing a man back from the dead.

He touched Tinbit's shoulder. "Because I loved you. You deserved so much more life than you had."

"And you deserved a living person as a companion."

"So did you," Hector said. "You still do."

"Well, neither of us are getting that, are we?" Tinbit hurled another rock into the abyss.

No, he supposed not. He folded his hands in his lap. "If I told Hari about you, would that make it easier?"

Tinbit shook his head. "I don't want him to know. Let him hate me."

"He doesn't hate you. He's just angry."

"I deserve it. I shouldn't have said that to Ida. I shouldn't have said that to you. Hari was right. You couldn't help it. It's the spell."

"Yes." But he was no longer sure. "Come back with me. I'll fix your face, and we'll sort this out by daylight."

Tinbit took Hector's hand, and impulsively, Hector pulled the gnome against him and hugged him. "I'm sorry," he said brokenly. "I'm sorry, I'm sorry."

Tinbit wept. The moonlight shivered through him, showing the loving detail with which Hector had knit the bones together by magic, clothed the frame with flesh, and the heart, still and silent, in the cage of bones making up the most precious and difficult construct he'd ever made.

Tinbit took some fixing once Hector carried him back to the stable room. Strong emotions were never good for the dead, and tears were worse than acid. He patched the tissue with care, pressing it back and melding it to the bones.

"I'm sorry, Hector," Tinbit muttered. "I shouldn't have cried—it just came out. I love him, and now he hates me."

"He doesn't hate you," Hector said again. "If you'll talk to him—"

"I'm not speaking to him, except, of course, politely. If he asks me the time of day, I'm going to politely tell him to go fuck himself." Tinbit touched his face, and it seemed to meet with his approval, because he stood, left the bed, and went to find a mirror.

Hector, exhausted now, hands bloody and coated in dark magic, lay down on the bed. Somewhere, out on the mountain, ten strong trees who should have lived for many, many years yet, had shriveled up and died. Nausea twisted his stomach, his back ached, his shoulder hurt, and the warm, loving moment he'd spent with Ida felt like the faint scent of her wafting up from the sheets—fleeting and ephemeral.

He'd been so close to doing exactly what she wanted—standing up with her and telling the rest of the Council that Happily-Ever-After was ruined, unfixable, and he would not be part of it anymore. A million wonderful prospects would open up to him then. He saw his little gingerbread house in the woods—a gift from his mentor so long ago—bright with life and happiness. He saw himself in the kitchen, pulling out a tray of fresh gingerbread, calling out to Ida that it wouldn't be warm forever, her hands wrapping around his waist, dirty from potting out the little skunk cabbages in their bog garden, turning to kiss her, and then forgetting the gingerbread entirely to pick her up and carry her to their bedroom. All of these years, and he finally knew what he wanted. And now that he knew, he couldn't have it.

Ida had asked him what would happen to the dragons, the goblins, the giants—everyone who depended on him. Amber might be right. The dragons might have outgrown the need for his protection, but what about the others? What about the one who meant the most? Who would patch Tinbit up the next time he fell for the wrong man and fell apart as a result?

His jaw firmed. There were no happily-ever-afters for the wicked. He'd sampled what love could be; he'd seen what it would cost him. He couldn't justify it.

He lay still, reflecting on the image of Ida hovering above him, hair drifting over his face, soft, vulnerable, and yet utterly in control. He'd thought of dragons, how the female ruled the lair, laid the eggs, and won the male by her fighting prowess and strength of mind and heart, and he realized for once, he wasn't simply observing this mating game like he'd done most of his life, he was participating. For once, he was the one *in* love.

Tinbit was right. It would've been better if it had never happened.

48

Ida

When I reflect back on my childhood, it's like gazing at an ancient fresco in a dwarf city. My past, like that fresco, is hazy, cracked, and faded with the way memories fragment over time. But one stands out in perfect clarity.

I remember my stepmother, a sunny day, the rank smell of geraniums floating through the summer air. She held my hand tenderly, teaching me the rudiments of palmistry.

"See, Ida? That's your lifeline. You'll have a long, long life. See how long it is before the smaller line? That's where love will cross your path. You must be patient. Love is a slow-growing plant, and you'll wait a long time for it to flower."

Immortality, it turns out, is a very long time.

*MAGIC AND MISCHIEF–A THOUSAND
YEARS OF HAPPILY-EVER-AFTER: A MEMOIR*

IDA NORTH

HARI'S EYES WERE RED WITH WEEPING. HE RUBBED them constantly, claiming it was hay fever.

Ida didn't question him. She'd used the time to reclaim her robe and put her hair up in something resembling order. She had a million rat's nests where Hector had pawed through it. The thought of him made her blush and burn inside at the same time. She shouldn't have given in to her desires, that much was plain.

"You shouldn't have yelled at Tinbit," Ida said. "He was only angry with Hector."

"No, he was angry with *you*," Hari said. "All the way up here we were talking about it—he asked me to come live with him and Hector. He tried to tell me you were no kind of good witch, that you shouldn't have a hold over me. I told him he was full of shit, and he got snotty with me. Then we ran into the manticore. I didn't have time to finish telling him off. I guess this was his way of getting the last word."

"He's right, though. I don't want to hold you back."

"You aren't," Hari said. "But the way he's been acting, you'd swear he wanted to keep me and put me in a cage somewhere to take care of me. He's got control issues. I don't think I want to deal with them." But his eyes welled up with tears again as he said it. "Let's go in, Ida. I need to wash my face and get rid of this awful nettle rash."

The one great disadvantage to dragon guest rooms was the lack of a private bathing area. Hari washed in the large central pool while Ida busied herself unpacking her bags, trying to ignore his sniffles.

Most of her things were safe. Her crystal, at least, wasn't broken. She examined it carefully for any hairline cracks, wrapped it back in its velvet cloth and set it aside. Her silk nightgown was rumpled. She picked it up, brought it to her nose. It still smelled like the inn, like Hector. *Hector.* She couldn't regret him, and she wouldn't forget this night, not if she lived another thousand years. She laid it on the bed. The smell of him would be gone soon, but she'd not be free of her feelings, not in whatever was left of her lifeline.

Hari let out a choked sob.

She closed her eyes. "Please, Hari. I know you love him. You were never meant to be this sad. Stay with him forever."

Hari spun around. "And have him see me, find out what I really look like?"

She opened her eyes although she didn't want to.

The twisted wreck of his face glared at her from behind the illusions. He'd been so young when it happened. Always toddling around, lisping her name. And he liked to be with her, the first gnomelet who'd ever taken a shine to her. She couldn't have been happier.

One second of inattention to a boiling cauldron of magic was all it took. She'd been conferring with his mother about the meal plan for the week, and they'd gotten into a happy little gossiping conversation about the doings in the village between the butcher, the baker, and the candlestick maker—a love triangle if ever she saw one—and then she heard him scream, the gagging, terrible scream of a baby in pain beyond endurance.

Months of healing followed, wrapping his blistered, charred skin with herbs and rags. The healing salts hurt him so much he cried even under heavy sedation. But he survived. As soon as he was well enough, Ida set about reducing his scars. Fixing up bad transformations was something she was good at—it came with being a good witch. Frog-faced prince? No problem. A head like a horse? Fixed. But no matter how hard she tried with Hari, she couldn't undo the damage. He'd been scalded by *her* magic. She gave him the most beautiful face and body by illusion, but like most illusions, it meant she must maintain it for him.

"Tinbit would be so angry, so disgusted—" Hari tossed the bath towel across the floor.

"You don't know that!"

"You know what the first thing he said to me was? 'My Gods, you're so beautiful.' He won't want me this way. Please tell me we're almost done here. I want to go home."

She sighed. "We will be going home soon. I'm going to put an end to this mess, whatever it takes."

Hari glanced furtively at her. "What about you and Hector?"

"It was a mistake," she said. One of many, starting with ever writing a letter to him. One that would be hard to live down and harder to forget.

In her memories, she could see him, beginning to end— the young man who had impressed her enough to make her hate him, the acerbic witch who at five hundred showed her his wicked sense of humor, and finally the man who had shown himself to be every inch worth protecting, worth loving. A man she couldn't have.

There was only one way to end this situation. She'd separate the dragon and the princess herself. And then she'd go back to the Council, take whatever punishment was coming, and resolve to do better. Conscience be damned. Happily-Ever-After would have to go on, regardless of how she felt. She could never leave Hari on his own, disfigured and alone. She'd sacrificed herself before for the higher cause, to ensure the happiness of others. She could do it again.

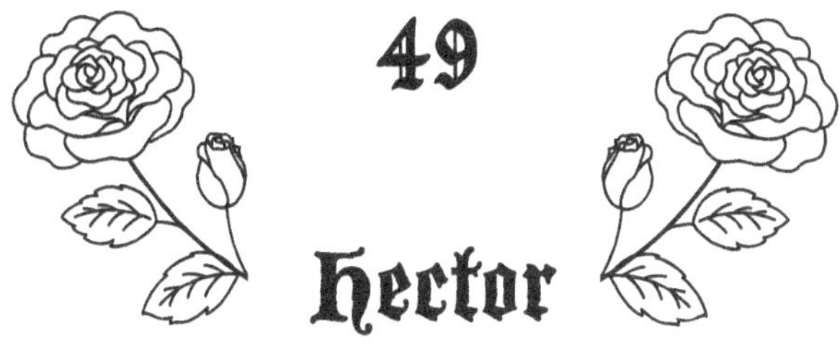

49

Hector

Among the most popular skills in a wicked witch's arsenal is the transfiguration of a human being into a monster. It provides the masses with an emotional boost thinking love has the power to take the monster out of the man. I find it ironic that the true meaning is lost in the transformation— the "monster" was, and always will be, worthy of love.

A THOUSAND YEARS OF WICKEDNESS: A MEMOIR

HECTOR WEST

HECTOR LAY AWAKE FOR A LONG TIME, LISTENING TO Tinbit snore. He'd done enough transformations over the years to be sure his spell would work. Would it give Ida enough leverage to keep her job when this was over? That was less certain. As much as he needed to keep his, he didn't want to be responsible for costing hers. He'd let her take credit for having known all along that Prince Archibald's true love was the boy next door, not the girl. It would make a good story. Aside from Amber's family, no one would be interested in what happened to the wrong princess, would they? They'd never cared what happened to nasty stepsisters or wicked aunts once there was a happily-ever-after. And it was essential that Amber stay with the dragons.

Short of killing Alistair, he couldn't remove the princess. Dragons mated for life. No magic Hector could conjure would combat the instinct, not even his strongest forgetfulness charm. Alistair might not know he'd had a mate, but he would feel her missing inside him nonetheless. He would be restless at first, then anxious, then determined to seek what was lost. Even if by some miracle, Alistair took another, there would be no eggs. The dragons would depose their heirless king and fight over the rule. Their carefully built society would fall apart then, and Hector would be the architect of their ruin. He wasn't going to let that happen if he could help it.

He worked the transformation out by midnight. Once Tinbit was snoring, Hector left the bedroom, staff in hand, and headed toward the dragon's lair, feeling that for once in the last two weeks, he'd finally done something right. This would preserve his bad name, save the dragons from themselves, Ida would keep her job, he'd keep his, and together, they'd do something about Happily-Ever-After so nothing like this would ever happen again.

The dragon's hospitality room was dark but for a thin stream of fire coiling from the gas vent to the ceiling. Cear dozed in the inky peace. Hector eased in, not wishing to disturb the salamander, and took a chair where he could rest until daylight. Strong necomancy took it out of him. Dismally he wondered how many plants in his garden he'd killed to make it happen. He'd have a desolation to replant when he got home.

Morning came late for Hector. He'd underestimated how tired he was, and when he woke to the sound of plates rattling in the kitchen, it was well past dawn.

Cear, consuming a small pile of sweetgrass in a leisurely fashion, gave him a side glance as he yawned and stretched. Somehow, he'd managed to sleep despite the discomfort. He ought to get up, go out to the stable, change his rumpled clothes and comb the tangles from his hair.

Tinbit's voice grated harshly in his ear. "No, I don't know where Hector went. I stayed awake as long as I could, but he slipped out as soon as I nodded off. What of it?"

Hari spoke softly. "Ida went out last night. I asked her where she was going. She said she needed fresh air. Do you think… they…well, you know, again?"

"No," Tinbit said. "Hector wouldn't. Your witch might; she's the mistress of love magic after all."

"Gods, Tinbit! Whatever you may think of her, Ida did nothing wrong. I demand an apology."

"I'm not in the mood to hand them out this morning—tend those eggs before they burn!"

"Mind the toast then; it's the last of the bread!"

Hector rose, sore and grumpy. He twisted his head from side to side. Sleeping in a stone chair wasn't good for the neck or the back.

Ida emerged from the hallway, looking cross, and sleepily tugging her robe around herself. She almost ran into him.

"What is it?" he asked.

"I thought I heard something," she said.

"Tinbit and Hari are in the kitchen making breakfast."

"No. It came from Alistair and Amber's room."

"A—"

He didn't finish his question, because a roar came from the hallway, the kind of roar that preceded fire. A huge, golden-brown dragon loomed in the doorway, chestnut eyes flaming. It bore down on him, jaws agape. "What have you done with my husband? Tell me now, or I'm going to eat you!"

It was the princess.

50

Ida

There are those who would say that vivomancy has fewer limitations and less potency than necomancy. This is a fallacy. Magic that relies on accelerating the natural processes of conception, growth, and birth is the most dangerous magic in the world and should not be treated as inferior or less powerful than magic that starts with a corpse and adds animation.

For this reason, transformation is not an art many good witches now indulge in, despite its seductive charm. It just takes too much magic to turn a man into a convincing monster if he isn't one already.

MAGIC AND MISCHIEF—A THOUSAND
YEARS OF HAPPILY-EVER-AFTER: A MEMOIR

IDA NORTH

IF NOT FOR THE BROWN EYES AND THE WAY THE dragon pinned Hector bodily to the ground under a huge, onyx-taloned paw, Ida wouldn't have known Amber. She was truly glorious—a huge female dragon with deep chocolate scales and bright dots of orange and green on her soft belly. Her teeth, sharp and amber-colored, dripped venom as she loomed over Hector.

"Where is he?"

"I haven't touched him." Hector gasped as Amber pushed down, crushing him.

"Amber, stop!" Ida said, quaking inside. "Hector hasn't done anything to Alistair."

"Alistair is gone! He probably turned him to stone or into a monster!"

Ida stared at Amber. The girl didn't know. She seemed utterly unconcerned about being a dragon. Every move she made looked exactly like what a dragon would do. It was a complete and perfect transformation. Under normal circumstances, Ida might have applauded Hector's skills. Not today.

She glared at him. "Hector—"

He squirmed under the dragon's paw. "If you'll let me up, Amber, I'll try to explain—"

"The only explanation I want is the one that tells me where Alistair is!" Her voice rose to a hysterical pitch.

"What's going on out here?" Morga appeared in her human form, pulling a gilt robe on as she came from the Flamelord's room. "Oh, Gods!" In an instant, she shed her robe and assumed her dragon form. She swooped in, shoving Amber off Hector. She bared her teeth. "Let him up right now!"

"But he took Alistair!" Amber backed up.

From the kitchen, Hari's frightened face appeared, and Tinbit, spatula raised like a sword, started forward.

"Hari! Tinbit! Don't move," Ida yelled. "Hector isn't responsible for Alistair's absence. I am."

"What?" the dragons hissed, and both of them flattened their ears and snarled.

"What?" Hector rose, straightening his robe.

"I changed Alistair into a man," Ida said. "He's in an enchanted sleep in a cave where only his true love can go. When Amber kisses him, he'll be transformed into a handsome prince and they can live happily ever after."

Morga stomped on Hector's feet in her haste to bite Ida. "You turned my son into a man?"

"Don't be absurd," Ida squeaked, nose inches away from bared teeth. "Once Amber presents him to the kingdom as the prince she saved from his dragonhood, they can get married in a double wedding with the prince and the captain of the guard, the Happily-Ever-After will be fulfilled, and then she can go back to the mountains. He'll revert to his natural state after that—I don't do long-term transformations!"

Morga stared at Hector, then at Amber. "Is Amber a temporary transformation as well?"

"Transformation? What are you talking about?" Amber thumped both her front paws on the floor.

"My dear, you are a dragon," Morga said. "Or at least that's how you woke up this morning."

The great, brown eyes opened wide in surprise. "What?"

Ida raised her eyebrows. "It might be more appropriate to ask why. Hector?"

"I should think it's obvious," he snapped back. "I cursed her into a dragon so she can marry Alistair properly! Then the dragons will accept her. We'll tell the Council that it was all part of your love magic to show that the prince's true love was the captain of the guard. There are precedents—the woman unworthy of the title princess *should* become a monster. No one needs to know it wasn't a punishment but a gift! There will be no need for the prince to save face and no need for the princess to ever go home. We can go back, our jobs are saved, the prince gets his man, the Flamelord has a mate, and you and I will have fixed Happily-Ever-After together."

"Fixed it *together*? I'm never speaking to you again, Hector West! What were you thinking? I had a perfectly good plan—"

"Well, you didn't enlighten me!"

Great tears like blood rubies filled Amber's eyes. "I…I can never go home?"

Ida rounded on Hector in a fury. "You and your necomancy. Did you even consider if Amber wanted this?"

"But I *do* want to be a dragon," Amber sobbed. "It's just…I want Alistair."

"You—you do?" Ida gasped. "You actually want to be a dragon?"

"If it makes things better for Alistair and me, why wouldn't I? I love him." She turned her fierce firelight on her mother-in-law. "Will you accept me now or do we need to fight?"

Morga took a step back. "Let's not rush things. First, I want to know how to fix my son."

Ida glared at Hector. "Alistair is in an enchanted sleep in a cave. A kiss will wake him, a kiss from a princess. I'm afraid I didn't account for the princess being turned into a dragon!"

"But if I kiss him, what will happen?" Amber asked. "Will he be a dragon or a man?"

Ida rolled her eyes. "A man. That's what kisses are supposed to do. They change monsters into men."

"Alistair was never a monster," Amber said. "It's you and the other witches who make people into monsters or men." She turned and stalked back to her room.

"Hector?" Morga's anxious voice echoed. "What if—"

"Don't worry. I will do what I can," Hector promised, patting her claw. "Ida, can we talk in your room about this?"

She was only too glad to flee.

Hector slammed the door behind them angrily. "Why?" he yelled. "Why did you do it? I had this fixed and you went and complicated it!"

"Fixed? You turned an innocent girl into a dragon—"

"You heard her! She's happy she's a dragon."

"Balderdash. Of course, she's happy now. But at some point she'll want to tell her family, to visit them, and how do you think she's supposed to do that? I had it fixed. She saves Alistair, he turns into a man, they go home together and she can tell them she's safe and happy. Then they can return to the mountains where they can both live Happily-Ever-After, no questions asked. But that's all pie in the sky now—why on earth did you turn her into a dragon? Now how will she break the news to her family? 'Sorry, father, I ran afoul of a wicked witch who turned me into a dragon, but I couldn't be happier? Oh, please don't mount a mob to come and rescue me, I'm perfectly fine!'"

His face tightened. "Well, I don't fault your logic, but you could've consulted with me!"

"As could you!"

Hector sat on the edge of the bed with a loud sigh. "Well, it's done. Now we need to undo it."

"There's nothing to undo! When Amber kisses Alistair, he'll turn into a handsome prince. There's no getting around that. I suppose I'll just have to be content with her turning into her human form for the trip, although Gods only know what her family will think of her if she's now twelve feet tall like Morga." She snorted.

"You *assumed* she could take human form?" Hector looked skyward, as if searching for his patience. "Do you know how long it takes a young dragon to learn how to shapeshift? Years! Years to learn, years to practice! I don't even want to think about how hard it would be for her to try to compress herself as an adult. Of course, she'll learn in time, but…"

"Years?" An icy chill of doom infiltrated her bones.

"Yes, years. What did you expect?" Hector flopped backward on the bed, clutching his head between his hands. "So now the future Flamelord is in enchanted hibernation in a cave somewhere, the current Flamelord is injured, the dragons are probably meeting in secret, and it's only a matter of time before the whole Witches Council calls for us to report on how we botched everything. This is just *ducked*."

Her heart pounded fearfully. Ducked indeed. "Well, excuse me for trying to save your ass! I was going to give you credit for transforming a fine young man into a dragon and letting Amber be the princess who saved him."

"I was going to let you take credit for saving the prince of the kingdom from a marriage to someone who wasn't his true love!" He huffed.

"Doesn't matter now." Ida flopped down beside him.

Hector was quiet for some time. He nudged her shoulder. "You actually wanted me to look like the big, bad witch?"

"Well, of course. It's good versus evil. If evil has to lose, it should look damned fine doing it."

"Thank you."

"And you wanted me to look like the wise old woman who knows love in all its forms?"

"Well, it's true," Hector said.

Ida smirked. "The old part is."

"Wise woman! Not old—good Gods." Hector snorted. "Why do you always do that to me?"

She cuddled into him. "Maybe I need you to make me laugh to keep me from being so scared."

He put an arm around her. "You realize that if this works out—and Gods only know if it will—we can't be together? We'll still be Cardinal Witches, and no one can know what happened between us."

She rested her cheek against his shoulder. "Hector, if this works out, we'll both come to accept it. The time when we could've been something passed a long time ago. But Hari and Tinbit, and Amber and Alistair, they have their whole lives to love and be loved. They deserve a chance. That's all I want right now."

"You're right, of course," Hector said. "Show me where you put the prince and I'll see what I can do to make that a reality."

She shook her head, feeling sick. "I can't show you. I can't even tell you. The moment the magic took him I couldn't find him again if I tried. Only one person can find Alistair: the princess."

51

Hector

So many spells are subject to the magic of truelove's kiss, it's a marvel lip balm companies haven't turned it into a slogan.

A THOUSAND YEARS OF WICKEDNESS: A MEMOIR

HECTOR WEST

THERE WERE MANY THINGS HECTOR DIDN'T KNOW about good magic. He'd concede his ignorance gladly most of the time. But then again, most of the time he wasn't riding between the backplate scales of a large, grumpy mother dragon, on his way to transform a beautiful prince back into a charming reptile, assuming Amber could find him. Wisely, Ida hadn't said anything about that to Alistair's parents. If she had, Hector might have been reporting back to the capital city alone, blaming himself for the dragons turning her into dinner.

Ida flew opposite him, perched precariously on the Flamelord's back. Although wounded, Adair wouldn't be left out of trying to save his son from becoming a hideous human for the rest of his life. Hector had reservations about having Ida ride him, but the princess was having enough trouble flying without putting a person on her back. She flapped in Morga's draft, her large brown eyes dilated with fright.

Morga glanced over her shoulder at her daughter-in-law. "Do you need to rest again?"

"I'm fine," Amber said, then dropped a foot because talking and flying at the same time was a feat her brain hadn't mastered yet. She flapped harder than ever.

"Set down on the next crag," Adair roared, also glancing back with worry written on his scaly face.

Hector smiled grimly. Something about watching the girl struggle with her new wings and her coordination must be reminding the dragons of their early days parenting Alistair. Or maybe it was simply what Hector told them: if this worked out, they'd get an actual dragon for a daughter-in-law, not a human in dragon skin. He'd felt it prudent to ignore the frightening possibility that Amber already wasn't human enough to give a true-love's kiss. Ida had been deeply concerned on that point. Had he said that, Ida would've been headed back to the capital alone to report their failure, and he wouldn't have blamed the dragons one bit for turning *him* into dinner.

He and Ida had consulted for most of the morning, leaving the lovely breakfast the gnomes had cooked largely uneaten.

"Handsome prince," he said, feeling hopeful. "Well, Alistair is a prince, and he's considered quite handsome. So if she kisses him, he could resume his dragon form after all."

Ida shook her head. "You are looking for a loophole, Hector, and I don't leave those. If a kiss makes a man into a prince, you'd better believe you'll get what I ordered. I ordered a handsome *man*, the way Alistair appears in his human form but truly human. And he'll stay that way for at least six weeks. I wanted to give Amber time to say her farewells, and then there's the media. They'll want interviews."

"Wait a minute," Tinbit spluttered. "*All* magic has loopholes. They're built-in for curse breaking."

"Wicked magic has them, although, I admit, I've been breaking Hector's magic long enough to know he doesn't leave many." Ida glanced thoughtfully at him.

He squirmed uncomfortably.

Hari, sitting close to Tinbit and holding his hand, asked, "Well, what about that?"

"What about what?" Tinbit asked.

"The loophole in Hector's spell? What is it?"

Tinbit grunted. "Probably the usual. A kiss from a handsome prince can break the curse. I don't suppose Prince Archie would be up for kissing a dragon's scaly bonce, though."

"That's *not* the loophole I left. I didn't want the princess ever becoming human again, not when she is mated to the future Flamelord."

"Well, what is it?" Ida asked.

He told her.

She hadn't talked to him since.

He'd wanted the impossible, and a dragon surrendering a firstborn child was about as impossible as it got, especially as it looked like Amber might be doomed to spend the rest of her life with a mate who couldn't even wake up, let alone be a Flamelord.

Adair banked sharply. Hector saw Ida clutch hard at the Flamelord's neckplates as he descended to a ledge with barely enough room for all three dragons to rest in reasonable comfort. Morga landed next, and Amber crashed between them. The two dragons kept her from spilling over the edge.

"I'm sorry," she panted, stepping all over Adair's feet and leaving bloody claw prints.

"Quite all right," Adair said with a soft grunt of pain. "Next time you turn a human into a dragon, Hector, give them muscles to obey their instincts."

"My shoulders feel like they're separating. I don't know if I can keep flying." Amber started crying.

"There, there." Morga bit Amber affectionately on the neck. "It's not much farther." She'd been saying it at every resting ledge to keep Amber going.

Amber leaned into the bite and even let Morga shake the nape of her neck a few times. Mothers-in-law were easily the biggest force in a young mated female's life, and Morga's affection and Amber's willingness to accept it were what Hector had hoped for. She was part of the family now. Of course, it also meant that if Alistair was stuck in an enchanted sleep for the rest of his life, they would undoubtably all eat Hector together.

"Do you have a feel for where he is yet?" Ida asked Amber.

She nodded wearily. "Yes. It's like a line from me to him. I would follow it until I fell from the sky. I can't tell if it's three miles or thirty, only that it's closer than before." She flopped down on the ledge. "I'm so tired."

Morga stretched her left wing over Amber. "I know, dear. Adair, let her draft behind you. I'll be on the side in case she falters."

Adair launched himself off the rock with Ida clinging on for dear life.

"Now, watch me," Morga said. "Let the thermals lift you. It will help. Even fit dragons get tired flying long distances. I'll show you."

Hector braced himself, but the fall into space sent his gut churning. Before he vomited with the dizziness, Morga rose, swirling in circles as the warm wind from the valleys carried her upward.

Amber launched herself. She flapped helplessly for a moment while Morga observed. Just when Hector thought she'd need to go after the girl and was preparing his stomach for the drop, Amber quit flapping and spread her wings. Slowly, inevitably, the current carried her upward.

"I must admit," Morga said, "she makes a good dragon. Once I teach her how to prepare a proper nest cave and give her lessons on fighting and hunting for her young, she'll fit right in. She has the fire for it." She swept after Amber as the girl set off more confidently into the mountains.

They reached the cave around sunset.

Amber veered suddenly south with a cry like a strangled scream and plunged toward a snowcapped peak lit with the last rays of the setting sun. A cunning place, it was accessible only from a narrow ledge. Amber landed. Adair tried and was forced to flap backward when he couldn't find room to stand. Morga landed and immediately condensed herself as Hector slid off her rapidly shifting mass. The cave entrance was far too small for a dragon to enter, but Amber clawed plaintively at the doorway. "Alistair!"

"He can't hear you. He's in an enchanted sleep," Ida said as Adair made another attempt and managed to shift down to his human self. She slid from his shoulders and landed on her knees. "Ouch!"

Hector helped her up. "How in blazes did you get him in there?"

She pushed his hand away. "He flew here, transformed, and walked in of course. You must remember I intended for a human-sized princess to rescue him. Oh, my back." She stretched with a grimace.

Hector eyed the slit in the rock with deep misgivings. "How far back in the cave is he?"

Ida brushed herself down. "I don't know, Hector. He walked in. At some point he lay down and became a dragon in an enchanted sleep. We must find him, animate him, and walk him to the door so she can kiss him." She sounded confident, but he could see the way she bit the corner of her lip when she didn't think he was looking.

He'd simply have to put a good face on things. With a calm smile, he patted Amber on the nose. "Don't worry, we'll get him out in a few minutes." If they didn't, hiding in the back of a cave with a dragon in an enchanted sleep might not be a bad idea.

He slipped through the crack. Ida followed him.

Inside it was dark beyond all reckoning. Amber's nostrils jammed the doorway immediately after they entered, blocking out the thin light of the setting sun. Hector lit his staff, and a few frightened bats took off and sailed around the cave in a panic when they found a dragon outside their door. But there was no dragon inside.

Ida's face withered in the light. "He should be here. It's nice and roomy, the logical place for him to lie down."

"No. He's a young dragon in dragon country," Hector said.

"He wouldn't lie in state where anything could come and eat him. He'd look for a good place to hide. Let's go farther in."

Two side caves parted ways at the back of the gallery, one with a low ceiling. Ida immediately rejected it. "I don't do well with tight places. I'll take the other if you can explore this one. If you find him, call me."

Hector stooped into the tunnel, ducking to get past the low overhang. He didn't state the obvious—if Alistair had reverted to his dragon shape in the tight tunnel, they couldn't walk him out. But how much more transfiguring could an enchanted, sleeping dragon stand? How much more could *he* take? He'd used so much necomancy on the transformation of Amber. Most of his greenhouse was probably dead because of it, possibly every plant he owned. It might take a forest, and if he did that, Agatha would certainly take him to task for it. He didn't know what else of his own that he could sacrifice to transform Alistair, even if only for the moments it would take to get him to the door. His hope sank into his boots when he came out through the narrow space and saw the dragon.

Alistair lay wedged comfortably under a ledge, cocooned in rock.

"Ida?" he called, trying not to panic. "He's in here." He found a flat rock and sat down gingerly. As far as he was concerned, dragons were never meant to be ridden.

Ida joined him quickly—she evidently hadn't gone far down the other tunnel. "It was a dead end," she explained. "I was already on my way back." Then she saw Alistair. "Oh my. How did he do that?"

"Shapeshifting," Hector said. "Parts of him are compressed, others inflated. It's so no one can drag him out."

"Oh." She sat on the rock next to him.

"Can you do anything to reverse your spell?" he asked. "Anything at all?"

Ida bit her lip. "No. Only a kiss from the princess will break the enchantment and make him a prince."

"I can't transform him," Hector said. "I used a lot of magic on Amber, and there's only so much death I can use before there's an inquiry."

"Well, I'm about at max myself," she said. "I created a lot of life last night to bring Alistair here and make the enchantment to turn him into a man."

"Life?"

Ida touched Alistair's face. "Your magic makes you pay in death. I pay in life. When I make magic, trees fruit, grains swell, and animals give birth. Why do you think we do Happily-Ever-After in the spring? I can get away with it and not risk upsetting the balance. If I use too much vivomancy, too many twins are conceived and sometimes the animals can't give birth. We've already seen the crops are out of season. And I've upset the balance more with what I've done here. I probably shouldn't have done it, but I thought it would fix everything."

"Regardless, one of us has to either get him out of here or get the princess in here. Short of flying in a team of goblins to open up this tunnel and the entrance, I don't see a way to do the second."

"How feasible would that be?"

"First, I'd need to convince the goblins it's in their best interest to help the dragons. Then they'd have to vote on it. Then I'd need to go to the dragons and present the demands the goblins want in exchange for their help and—"

Ida held up her hand. "Stop. I know how dangerous that would be."

Hector gnawed his knuckle. "What about waking him? If we could do that—"

"He would still be trapped here, wouldn't he?"

"I don't think so. He's still a dragon. He might well be able to shapeshift and make his way out."

Ida considered. "Break half the spell. I've never even considered such a thing. But I couldn't wake him, not entirely. The best I might be able to do would be no better than sleepwalking."

"If you can do it, even for a few minutes, I think I can transform Alistair enough to help him hold his shape, at least long enough to get him out the door." But at what cost? He shivered.

Ida closed her eyes. "If I use the eagles or ravens here for magic, perhaps I could do it. But I feel terrible. It's not nesting time here yet, is it? The chicks might starve."

He winced. "We don't have a lot of choice."

"No, I don't suppose we do. But what will you do? You have to kill someone long enough to get Alistair to the princess. Who?" She blanched. "Not a dragon…"

"No. I don't need a dragon's death for this. I know what I'm going to do." He couldn't bring himself to meet her eyes. *Please, let her think it's the pony.*

Tinbit wouldn't be harmed. At least not irreparably.

52

Ida

The one drawback to immortality no one ever tells you about? Remembering every mistake you've ever made makes for a lot of sleepless nights.

MISCHIEF AND MAYHEM—A THOUSAND
YEARS OF HAPPILY-EVER-AFTER: A MEMOIR

IDA NORTH

IDA HAD BEEN A WITCH FOR CENTURIES, BUT STILL, each swish of her wand reminded her of every hour she'd spent learning the basics of magic and all the endless mistakes too. Standing over Alistair wedged in the rock and snoring like an asthmatic ogre, she remembered so many mistakes, she almost feared to begin.

The time she accidentally gave an elf a mermaid's tail and couldn't take it off.

The time she charmed a dryad's hair red, and it turned her leaves red for the entire year.

The time a whole village of people barked for a day.

She glanced at Hector, standing with his staff poised to cast the reanimation spell once she wakened Alistair. "Ready?"

He nodded grimly.

She held her wand at waist level, pointed it at Alistair's snout, letting the magic flow through her, and thought about eggs.

Somewhere, in some great nest, a great eagle laid an egg. She felt the formation of it, the way the life crept into it, the meeting of two parts to make one whole. Sadness overwhelmed her. It might not survive hatching, even if the weather went back to normal. There had been ice in that air. But as Hector said, there wasn't anything else they could do. A warm, springlike sense of early blooming flowers, green leaves, and cool rain filled her middle, moved into her arm, and ran down her hand, breaking forth from the tip of her wand with the smell of basil and orange blossoms.

Alistair blinked his eyes once or twice, gave a tremendous stretch, and shuddered. He yawned.

"Hurry, Hector. I don't know how long I can keep him awake."

Hector raised his staff and pointed it at the sleeping dragon. A shock of cold, frozen meat aroma startled Ida. She wrinkled her nose. But the effect on Hector was more marked. Every part of him seized up, his face clenched into a grimace of pain, and then relaxed, but not in the way of relief. More like the way a body relaxes when life leaves it. A stench filled the cave—rotting death and roses. Alistair's hands and feet changed shape, then his nose, until he became a handsome man, wedged in a cozy crack in the rock.

"Are you all right?" she asked.

"Yes," he said, but he was shaking and a film of sweat coated his forehead. "It was a lot after last night, that's all."

Alistair flexed his long arms. His fingers curled like claws.

"I don't know how long I can keep him moving without reversion." With a wave of his staff, the inert form of Alistair became active, wriggling and flailing its way out of the crevice with a peculiar snakelike twisting and writhing.

Ida shuddered as the dragon-man fell on the floor with a thump and eagerly wriggled forward toward her. "Ugh. Can you make him move…more like a human?"

"No," Hector said. "He went in there in dragon shape. His mind still thinks he's a dragon. Let's go."

Ida led, and Hector followed. Alistair squirmed between them with interminable slowness, inch by inch, out of the back of the cave and into the corridor. Each second, more of him took on a dragonish quality beyond the rippling movement. He grew claws again. His nose elongated into a snout. His mouth, too, took on a sharper shape, and his head grew larger.

"Hurry," Hector said as the wiggling became frantic. "Go tell Amber to get ready!"

Ida backed through the crack, bumping into Amber's warm nose, and Alistair followed, but with a sudden sickening sound like a swelled frog popping, Alistair's head turned into a massive dragon's skull. Hector's cry of despair was the last thing Ida heard before he was cut off completely.

Alistair's human eyes vanished, and his hair too, but he still sported human flesh, all of it turning purple. The door was too small and he was choking.

"Hurry!" Ida stepped back as Amber shot through, trying desperately to get her mouth into some configuration for a kiss, but dragons, it seemed, didn't have lips.

"Alistair!" Amber screamed, biting his nose, his eyebrows—

Ida sucked in a great gulp of air. Someone needed to be calm;

she couldn't panic. "Amber—listen to me. You must transform. You've got to grow some lips, girl—come on, you can do it!"

"I can't—I can't!"

"Yes, you can! Transform! You're a dragon—you can do anything!"

"Alistair!" Amber bit him again, then hunched, squealed, and a strange, fleshy shape took the place of her dragon snout.

Alistair gasped, his tongue protruding from between his teeth.

"Alistair!" Amber screamed, trying desperately to compress herself. She thrashed her wings, and the leathery skin clubbed Ida in the back, pushing her aside. She tumbled backward off the ledge.

For the first quarter second, she didn't believe she was falling. This was a dream—a terrible dream, but she'd wake up and be back in the dragon's lair, or in the creepy hostel with Sebastian's head floating above her like a doomsday alarm clock. Better yet, she'd wake up in the hotel room in Kingsmanor, nothing had gone wrong, and everything would be fine—

The sky fell away as she dropped down. She screamed. She'd hit rocks in a moment.

The world went red.

"Hang on!" Hector yelled.

Adair swirled past in a flurry of scales and wings.

"Hector!"

The wings flashed into view again.

"Grab on!" Hector yelled.

She reached out, missed him.

The wings vanished.

She twisted in the air again, the rocks shimmered below,

another blur of crimson, and then a pair of knifelike talons cut into her shoulder. She screamed again.

The rocks stopped, and she rose upward.

"Hector!" She sobbed. Blood warmed her skin as it flowed down her throbbing arm and back, and then she was back on the ledge.

Hector knelt beside her. "Stay calm." He pushed both his hands over her wound. "I'll stop the bleeding."

"It hurts!"

"It will only take a minute."

She gritted her teeth and risked a glance. Her robe was saturated with blood, and meat and tendons sprouted obscenely from the ruined fabric. "Oh, Gods." She tried not to faint. Hector drew a knife from his belt and cut away the lower part of his robe to make a bandage.

"How—how is…"

"Alistair is fine, for a handsome prince, that is. He's with Amber. Don't move. There's not much room on this ledge with them on it."

"But Adair and Morga are flying. Ouch!"

Hector tied a knot in the robe and then stood. "So they are."

"Where's…Amber?"

A large, scaly face loomed over her. "Sit tight, Your Goodness. We'll get you out of here."

She groaned. Call her optimistic, but she'd really hoped one kiss would magically fix *everything*.

"You better fly me back," Alistair, a decidedly handsome prince said, stroking Amber's face. "I can help you. Dad and Mom will take Hector and Ida."

"Are you sure, sweetheart? I don't want to drop you."

"You'll be fine. The key is to always breathe the same way—in, out, in, out—like that. It's good practice for when the eggs come."

Ida stared. "Eggs?"

Alistair looked curiously at her. "You didn't think we were celibate, did you?"

"No, but—"

Hector looked as stunned as she felt. "I thought you said you'd use eagles."

"I did! I found the biggest eagle so that maybe it would be able to feed its—oh."

Amber startled. "Eggs?"

Hector smiled. "If you want me to be godfather, Alistair, I believe it would count against my curse. Should Amber want to take you home to meet her parents, you could both go, no more transformation needed. Of course, she'll need to wait until the eggs come in a few weeks."

Alistair grinned back, showing all of his pearly white and decidedly handsome human teeth. "Well, if it's a boy, I'll choose you. If it's a girl, Amber picks."

Amber blinked. "I'll pick Ida. Will that do?"

Ida laughed. "I'm not sure. I'm not a wicked witch."

"It counts," Hector said, putting his arm around her. "Loopholes, you know."

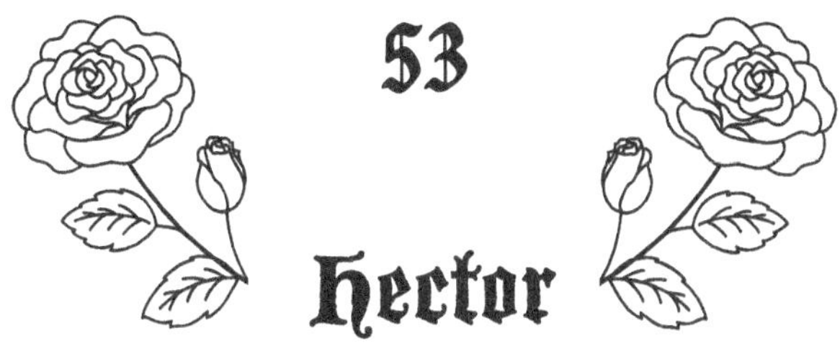

53

Hector

While I've always thought necomancy a beautiful thing, I concede there's nothing pretty about death.

A THOUSAND YEARS OF WICKEDNESS: A MEMOIR

HECTOR WEST

HECTOR WANTED TO RIDE BACK WITH IDA ON ADAIR, but Ida insisted she could manage. The Flamelord flew ahead of them all, carrying her on his back. Alistair rode astride his mate. Periodically, he leaned forward to stroke her neck with the kind of ease that made Hector cringe. If the prince fell, Amber would try to catch him, and he wasn't exactly confident in her midair rescue abilities, especially after seeing the damage Adair's talons had done to Ida's shoulder.

Morga flew slowly, staying close to both her son and her daughter-in-law, burbling happily about the coming eggs. Hector wouldn't put it past her to completely redecorate Alistair's room and order a new lair built for the expectant mother, the kind of comforting den any dragon would want when brooding and rais-ing her hatchlings. He could practically see the ideas churning in Morga's head. But he wished she'd fly faster. Adair was already out of sight, and he wanted to get back as quickly as possible.

By the time Morga and Amber landed, Adair was already in the lair, back in human form.

Hector marched in. He didn't need to ask where Tinbit was. He could follow the crying.

Ida, face pale and angry, sat on the couch in the hospitality room, holding a sobbing Hari. On the other end of the couch, watched by the salamander, lay the inert form of Tinbit.

"How could you?" Ida gasped, glaring at Hector. "How could you?"

"This isn't what it looks like." Hector knelt next to Tinbit and touched the icy flesh, winced at the terrified, staring eyes, the grimace of pain—there was nothing pretty about killing someone, even someone who had died long ago. He gathered the gnome in his arms. "Tinbit died over five hundred years ago."

Hari blanched. "He…he's a…"

"A construct, yes. I brought him back. I'm sorry. I should've told you both."

"But—but what happened?" Hari stared helplessly at Tinbit sagging in Hector's arms.

"I had to take his life for the magic I needed. I'll put him in my room for now. Once I get him home, I'll make the magic I need to make him live again. He'll be fine."

"But what about me? What about us? Will he even remember me?"

"Of course, he will," Hector said, surprised. "I…I just wasn't expecting—"

"You didn't think I could love a dead man?" Hari asked, face flushed and furious.

"Something like that," Hector said.

"Who are you to tell me who I can or can't love? Put him back down. I'm not letting him out of my sight again. I'll take care of him." He folded his small hand over Tinbit's. "I'm going to take care of him forever."

"You're sure?" Ida touched Hari's shoulder.

"Not you too! Of course, I'm sure. I'd love him until the day I died, and I'm still alive. When Hector brings him back, I'm not breaking that promise. I'll stay with him if he'll let me."

Ida hugged Hari. "I'm so happy for you, sweetheart!"

Hari burst into tears.

Baffled, Hector gently set Tinbit on the couch again. Cear gazed at him with something approaching pity in their blue eyes. He wished they wouldn't look at him that way. But when he glanced at Ida, there was no pity in her face as she rocked the sobbing Hari. Only understanding.

Hector would've preferred a few more days in the mountains in which to contemplate his future. He didn't look forward to going home, where he'd have about a hundred messages waiting on the crystal ball, all requiring his immediate attention. But he had a dead gnome to raise, and Ida needed far more healing than they could get from Tinbit's salves.

Adair flew off to get a giant early the next morning. And although Hector insisted he didn't need to, he took Hector on his back while the giant carried Ida, Hari, Cear, and Tinbit's corpse in his basket.

"Once they learn you enchanted the princess so she could stay with my son, what will happen?" Adair asked, flapping quietly. "What will they do to you?"

"I don't know," Hector lied. Take his assets certainly, considering what he was planning to do. He still owned his mentor's old gingerbread house deep in the woods, and anyway the retirement homes in the city would never suit him. They certainly wouldn't allow him to bring his skeletons, whatever plants still lived, his hellhound, and his immense library. And what about Tinbit? He would argue, but in the end, he would probably go with Hari. Ida would certainly take care of them both. Hector would have to make this raising permanent so he didn't have to maintain it anymore, and what would that cost him? He no longer had a heart to sacrifice.

"You'd always be welcome to stay with us," Adair said.

"It's a great honor, but I can't," he said. He'd worked most of his life to make sure the dragons were safe. There was no guarantee he'd be able to do that now. "Besides, you'll have enough to do without entertaining guests," he said, with a forced laugh.

"You're not a guest, Hector—you're family," Adair said. "In two or three weeks, Amber will be laying her eggs. I owe you. Not only did you give Alistair his mate, you gave the dragons their next Flamelord. I'm already planning a feast in his honor once he's back to his dragon self. I'm going to eat an entire rock buffalo. I have to grow fat and comfortable to be a good granddragon. I'd like you to be there for that."

"I'll try." He could promise nothing. The outcome was so far from certain. But at least the journey home should be completely uneventful. And it was, until they reached Sebastian's hostel.

"What happened?" Hector asked, climbing from Adair's back as he landed at the base of the hill. There was no hostel. All that remained were a few stone walls. A column of dense black smoke rose from the ruin.

"Why are we stopping?" Ida sounded tired.

"The inn." Hector gaped. "Where's the inn?"

Sebastian's head popped out of the middle of the air, livid. "Those stupid knights burned it, that's what happened to my inn! Where's that awful witch? I want to give her a piece of my mind!" He pulled his gray brain out of his skull and shook it in Hector's face.

Ida stood in the basket, face pale, shoulder stained with blood through the bandage. "I'm here, you dreadful old ghoul."

"You! You…you horrible hag! You malicious monster! How dare you!" Sebastian pointed his middle finger at Ida. "She sold me good magic! She's responsible for this mess!"

Hector raised an eyebrow. "What would you want with good magic, Sebastian?"

"To sell it, what else?" Sebastian threw his hand up in the air and caught it. "But they wrecked my inn and it's all her fault! What are you going to do about it—eww." He'd caught sight of Tinbit. "You aren't leaving that with me? I don't even have a freezer to put a fresh corpse in, let alone an aged cheese like that."

Hector raised his hand. "Tell me what happened."

"I asked for pleasure spells—something to sell to randy knights out on quests. I didn't expect to have customers so early, but there were four of them, all out questing for the Holey Pail— the chumps—so I offered them a good time. No sooner did those fellows buy them than they wrecked my inn! They freed my ghosts, unleashed the demons—one of them got eaten and the demon died, poor thing—and then the remaining three ran off with my best banshees to 'escort them home.' I hope they get their livers ripped out."

"*True* pleasure comes from doing a good deed," Ida said. "You might try it sometime."

"No thanks, it might kill me." Sebastian snorted. "Again."

"What, precisely, do you want me to do about it?" Hector asked.

"Turn her into a frog. An ugly one. This is the second time someone has burned down my house."

Hector shook his head. "I'm not going to turn Ida into a frog. For one thing, she's a good witch, and it's her business to provide good magic. For the second thing, black market magic is illegal and I think you got what you deserved."

"I've got a living to get."

"As you so eloquently said, you're already dead."

"But…but it's my home," Sebastian whined, shedding maggots. "Where will I go? What will I do?"

Hector sighed. The ghoul wasn't the only one contemplating that decision. "Come along to the castle. I'll see what I can do."

"And ride with that?" Sebastian said, wrinkling his nose at Tinbit. "Really, Hector."

"You'd prefer to ride me?" Adair bared his fangs.

Sebastian dropped his jaw and picked it up from the ground quickly. "On the other hand, what's a dead body? I love dead bodies. They're so sweet and cute when they're rotting." Sebastian flung his head into the basket before he crawled in and parked his lower half in the back, folding his legs before setting his head in his lap.

Hector climbed in after him.

Immediately, Sebastian handed him his head. "Now, let's talk about what I'd like in my next establishment. I want three stories, not two, and I want a haunted ballroom, upscale, with some of those sparkly vampires, no more wretched bats. You can import sparkly vampires, right?"

When the topmost towers of his castle glittered in the afternoon sunlight, Hector was all too glad to see it.

"Let me down here," he told the giant. "I'll walk the final mile."

"Wait!" Sebastian howled. "Don't you want to hear my plans for the quicksand spa?"

"No." He got out. "Take them to the courtyard," he told the giant. "I'll be along as soon as I can."

There was something he needed to do first. Someone he needed to kill.

54

Ida

Magic would seem to present a witch with a number of paths to take in life. With magic, a witch can cure a plague, transform a man into a monster, cause a person to fall in love, or stop a war by turning everyone into ravens. The prospect of such power seems unlimited.

In actuality, it's much less complicated.

The only question a witch must ask themself: Will I be good or will I be wicked?

*MAGIC AND MISCHIEF—A THOUSAND
YEARS OF HAPPILY-EVER-AFTER: A MEMOIR*

IDA NORTH

HECTOR'S SKELETON ROSES LOOKED SICK. THE VINES hung on the walls of the courtyard, dark green and bloated, weeping strange juices. The paving stones were strewn with sticky, graying leaves and faded black petals.

Hari climbed out of the basket and landed gently next to her. "What happened here?"

"Hector," Ida said. She gazed wearily at the immortal rose, undead and rotting, a fitting symbol of the fate that awaited both of them when they went back to the capital to explain. The rest of the plants in the courtyard were wilted and she could distinctly smell decaying fish. She thought about the funny little sensitive fern, drying out on the table in the library, its poor little fronds curled around itself in the agony of death. And Hector would need to kill to resurrect Tinbit too. She felt sick.

She touched the bloody bandage on her shoulder. The wounds no longer oozed. Adair himself had licked the cuts clean. His venom provided the antidote to the toxin in his claws. He'd told Ida not to worry; one of Hector's skeletons had been a superb physician in his day. He'd donated his body for necomancy, intending to one day build an army of the living dead to take over the world, but when he discovered he wasn't so keen on that after becoming a construct, having a new appreciation of what it meant to die, Hector had employed him as his personal doctor. *Typical.*

Ida glanced at Sebastian. The ghoul angrily directed his body out of the basket and then screamed when it walked off without his head. Even that worthless ghoul was a recipient of Hector's compassion.

"Hari, help me get Tinbit out of the basket. I don't think he would want Sebastian carrying him, and I'm not sure I can carry him with my shoulder."

Hari patted her hand. "Don't you even think about trying it. I'll carry him. You go inside and rest. I'll take him to his house. I think that's where he'd most like to be until Hector revives him."

She squeezed his hand. "And when he does, you'll stay with him."

"Well, if he'll have me." Hari laughed, but it sounded harsh and scared. "It's up to him. I know his secret now. It's only fair he knows mine."

"When he sees you, he will love you," Ida said. "I've no doubt."

He flung himself around her legs and hugged her. "I wish you could stay too—here with me and Hector. You love him, I know you do, and I want you to be happy too."

"I *will* be happy," she assured him. "And so will you. You'll have Tinbit, you'll have Hector, and everyone here will adore you. Even that old ghoul—once Hector tames him."

"Don't count on it, Witch." Sebastian strolled by, bouncing his head. "Now, can someone show me where a guy can get a cold bone and a hot bath?" He strolled in the door, scowling.

Ida turned and followed Sebastian through the doorway.

Ida found her way to her old room with no trouble. The hellhound wasn't there. She didn't want to think about what might have happened. She'd refused to even glance in the library. She'd burst into tears if she saw the fern. Instead, she stoked up a small fire in her own personal grate and set the firepot down beside it.

"Your Goodness?" Cear climbed out of the pot.

"Yes?"

"Are you—are you well?"

"More or less, apart from my shoulder." She sat on the bed. "But I'm tired and more than a little sad."

"The dragon and the princess are happy. Tinbit and Hari will be happy. The prince and his lover are happy. Does that not make *you* happy?"

"Of course it does. But some Happily-Ever-Afters take a little longer to feel than others," she said, lying down on the bed. This was going to be one of those kind of endings. There was so much left to do, so much she had to arrange. Hector would take care of Hari for her, of course, and that was the most important thing. But once she confronted the Council, she'd be fired. There was no escaping that now. The dragon and the princess would not be coming back with them, and the only explanation she had left was the truth.

At least Hari and Tinbit would have a home, but she was going to miss her castle. She would take cuttings from the gardens, though, send some to Hector to replace what he'd lost, and plant the rest at her new house. But where would that be? Somewhere far away from Hector. Living close to him would be a recipe for disaster. Maybe she'd go back home. A sudden, horrible thought came to her of walking back into that tiny village grown to a large town, seeking out the oldest cemeteries, looking hopefully for headstones of her family that had long since crumbled into dust, and she wanted to cry.

Cear's voice was curiously gentle. "You wanted things to be different for you and Hector."

She sucked in a great gulp of air. "I wish many things were different. I wish Hari had never fallen into a potion as a child, I wish I'd never written those hateful letters to Hector, and I wish he'd not needed to kill his whole garden for me. I wish I'd been more willing to call him a friend a long time ago. We might have had a whole eternity to know each other better. There's no opportunity now."

Cear regarded her with those deep, fire-blue eyes. "Opportunity still remains. If you are willing to take it." They stepped into the flame and became one with it.

Someone knocked on her door.

"Come in," she said, rising and crying out as the wound twinged.

Hector came in, with him a tall skeleton who was missing one arm. He ground his teeth at Hector, and he nodded. "Yes, you can start. I want to talk to Ida."

The skeleton carefully unwrapped Ida's shoulder and examined the wounds with his bony fingers.

Hector sat on the end of the bed. He was holding one of the wilted flowers from the Skeleton Rose, twisting the stalk absently between his fingers . "I've restored Tinbit, but I need your help."

"What's wrong?"

"He's the same grouchy, irritable gnome he's always been— but he won't talk to me and he says he doesn't want to see Hari. I want you to talk to him."

"Me?"

The skeleton pressed his fingers into the wounds, and she yelped.

Hector sighed. "Tinbit had always been somewhat prone to despair. Also, he's not too happy with me right now, which is completely understandable. There's nothing pleasant about dying twice. I think you're in a better position to make a proposal to him."

"What kind of proposal?"

"I want you to take him home with Hari. I want him to be happy. You see, I won't be able to give him life again should anything happen to him."

"Far be it from me to question your skills, but why?"

Hector touched the rose and a single petal fell to the floor. "It took a lot out of me," he said in quiet tones.

Ida shuddered. "You didn't. You didn't kill the dog? The fern? Oh, Gods, Hector—not Napoleon?"

"No, no, they're fine—well, Spot and Napoleon are. I haven't checked the fern yet—"

"Hector? Who did you kill?"

He stared up at the ceiling. "Myself," he said.

"What?" Ida gasped.

"I sacrificed my immortality. Whatever time I've got left is all I have." He smiled. "I'll take the blame and resign from the Council. Then whatever comes next will be your decision."

"Hector—" She stared down at the white bones knitting her flesh together with thin, black thread. Whatever medication the skeleton had put on his needlelike fingers, it numbed the wound. She couldn't feel anything but the pressure of skin touching skin, pulling together, but her eyes stung and she blinked back tears. "Hector—"

"For once in your life, don't argue with me," he said, touching her knee gently. "It's best this way, and you know it. It took me a little longer to understand, but you were right. No one should have this kind of power, no matter how much they want to do good with it."

"Hector, I don't want to—"

"One of us had to take full responsibility. You and I both know this is what needs to happen. If the world is ready to let go of Happily-Ever-After, you are the most qualified to guide them—not me."

"But you thought it wasn't. Hector, what if—" She half rose from the bed, but the skeleton made a horrid grating sound in protest. She settled back down while it dressed the newly repaired wound with a salve that smelled almost like the rotting roses outside. "What if you're right? What if they aren't ready? What if this world falls apart the minute we let go of the strings?"

"It might," he said, rising. "But that doesn't matter. You were right. We never had any authority to do what we did." He sighed. "Maybe that's why it was doomed to fall apart from the beginning. And you're the best one to tell them that, too."

"They won't believe me! I'm the one who insisted the magic choose. They'll say I'm the one who didn't do my job! Don't you understand? Coming from you—the one witch who was there at the beginning—they'll listen when you tell them it's time to give up controlling people's lives and loves."

"And what does a wicked witch who kills everything he touches know about life or love? Nothing," he said. "Logically, you're the best choice to remain on the council. Now, that's settled. Will you come with me to see Tinbit?"

She touched her shoulder briefly, but the skeleton swatted her hand and started to fix a bandage. "I'll go with you." This wasn't settled, at all.

Hari waited in a chair outside the library, a scared little smile on his face. She turned to Hector.

"I thought Tinbit would be in your workshop."

"This *is* my workshop," he said somewhat apologetically. "Once I created my staff, I didn't need a full necomancy suite anymore, and my books migrated here, and so…"

Ida pushed the door open gently.

The fern sat on the stand, curled up into a brown, miserable ball in its pot. She stared at it sadly, trying not to remember how it had reached for her. She wanted to ask Hector if it was dead entirely, or if somehow, with enough care and fertilizer, it might come back from the roots. Then she saw Tinbit. He sat by the fire, naked except for a towel over his shoulders. It was warm in the room. She could smell him.

She glanced at Hector.

"The scent of decomposition will wear off," he said. "The first few days are the worst."

"Hari's not with you, is he?" Tinbit said in a rusty, disused voice. "If he is, I'm not speaking to either of you."

"Hari's not with us," Ida said.

Tinbit turned.

Ida tried not to gag.

His face looked melted. The skin hung limp and sallow over his cheekbones. His eyebrows overshadowed most of his eyes, and they weren't filled with life but shrunken and dried up. His face slumped as he glared at her. Dismally, he tried to push it back up. "Yes, I know I look bad," he said. "Why do you think I didn't want to see him?"

Ida glanced at Hector again.

"It…should be better in a few days," he said. "The longer between death and resurrection, the longer it takes the skin to go back to normal and—"

"You should've left me dead," Tinbit growled.

"I couldn't do that," Hector said. "I owed you an explanation—"

"You could've explained it to my corpse!" He rubbed his slack face angrily. It oozed raw and red about the mouth and chin, like a scab. "He won't want this. And I don't want him to see it."

Ida set her hand on Tinbit's rotten one. "But he wants to see you. He has something he needs to say to you."

"I don't want to hear it. I don't care anymore. Tell him death ruined my brain. Tell him I can't remember him. Tell him not to care."

"But he *does* care," Ida said. "He's waiting outside."

"I don't want to see him!"

"Tinbit, he won't go, not without talking to you first."

"Please, Tinbit," Hector said. "I think you should see him. If you don't want him to stay after that, I know he'll go, but talk to him, please. I want you to."

"Why should I do anything for you when you've done this to me? Leave, Hector. I only wanted to talk to Ida."

"Very well." Hector nodded to Ida before he left Tinbit and stepped out the door.

Tinbit stood and dropped the towel around his waist. She didn't look down—the rest was surely as bad as his face. "You have to tell him for me. I want him to understand why I can't be with him. This has to end here. And then I want you to take away his memories of me with a potion. Hector says he won't do it."

"What makes you think I will?"

"Because you love him. You don't want him hurt either."

She closed her eyes. "Tinbit—"

"Look at me!" Tinbit yelled. "Look at this! You don't want this for him anymore than I do! I'm a rotting corpse—stinking, fallen apart, incapable of being the man he loved. The man he thought he loved."

"Tinbit, he doesn't care about that—"

"*I* care! I don't want to talk to him!"

Ida folded her arms over her chest. "I'll make a deal with you, Tinbit. I'll do what you ask—but only if you listen to him first and only if he wants the same. But he won't. He loves you."

"He can't love this!" The corner of Tinbit's mouth cracked

and bled, a black stream running over his too-scarlet lip. He reached up and touched it gingerly. "How could anyone love this?"

She turned to the door, open a crack the way Hector had left it. "Hari, will you come in now?"

Tinbit jerked around in the chair. "No, wait—don't—"

Hari entered, holding his hat in his hands, but he stopped halfway across the room when Tinbit glared at him.

"Well?" he said. "Didn't they warn you?"

"Hector did. He said you weren't yourself," Hari said, sitting beside Tinbit and folding his hands in his lap. "But you're alive, and that's what matters. How are you feeling?"

"I'm *not* alive!" Tinbit yelled. "This is me—a dead man who has nothing to give you. I never should have written you that letter. I never should have loved you. I'm sorry."

Hari glanced at Ida. "Okay, Tinbit. Maybe you shouldn't have. And maybe I shouldn't have done that, either, because if you knew what I really looked like, you'd have run." He stiffened as Ida gently lifted the charm.

Hari's handsome face slid away. The scars of his burning showed clearly—white, livid blazes and slashes across the pink-and-brown skin. His eyelids had no lashes, his brows grew no hair, and his head was covered with bald patches where his hair would no longer grow. His hands were equally horrible—fused skin between his fingers, missing nails. He took Tinbit's hand. "This is me," he said, "a man who lied to you with a spell, who thought he could hold you because you loved beautiful things. I was scared to death when you said 'I love you' because I wasn't the man you fell in love with. That's why I didn't want to leave Ida. If I did, she couldn't maintain the illusion, and when the spell was lifted, you'd see. You'd know I wasn't beautiful."

Tinbit reached out and touched Hari's face. "I didn't love you because you were beautiful. I love you because you said you loved me."

Hari cupped his hand around Tinbit's slack jaw. "You said it first."

"Pretty sure it was you."

"No, I'd never say that on the first date. I'd save it for the second one."

Tinbit laughed. It sounded as rough as his voice and almost as angry, but instead of pulling away, he raised Hari's mishappen hands to his cracked lips and kissed them. "I do love you," he said. "I love you so much. I can't ask you to stay."

"Not a chance," Hari said. "I kissed you raw trying to wake you from the dead, and now you're back, I can't let you go again."

"Kissed me?"

"Probably about a hundred times. It works in all the stories."

Tinbit chuckled. "When will you ever stop believing in happily-ever-after?"

"Never," Hari said, leaning forward. He brushed the hair out of Tinbit's face. "After all, I work for a good witch." He glanced at Ida again as if asking for her permission.

Ida smiled encouragingly, although Hector's heart felt tight and pained in her chest. She'd miss him. Oh, she'd miss him so much.

Hari's mouth firmed. He dropped down on one knee in front of Tinbit. "Marry me."

"Wha—"

"You heard me," Hari said. "Marry me. And I want Ida, and

Hector, and the dragons, and everyone to come to our wedding, because you are the most amazing man in the world, and I'm so lucky you love me."

"Hari, I'm dead."

"Well, we can hold the funeral and a wedding at the same time. Twice the food and twice the tears."

Tinbit laughed so hard he cried. He hugged Hari, pressing his nose against Hari's cheek. "Yes," he said. "Yes, to eternity."

55

Hector

My dearest detested Ida,

The black rose is dead. I killed it forever when I destroyed my own immortality. Happily-Ever-Ater is now effectively destroyed, and you won't need to lift a finger.

One day, I hope you'll understand why I didn't tell you. First of all, I had to ensure you didn't sabotage my plan, as I knew you would. You're far too devious—it's one of your most endearing character traits, by the way. Secondly, you are the best person to watch over Tinbit. I know you're worried about maintaining him once I'm gone, but by sacrificing my immortality for him, I've made the necomancy permanent. He'll live out his normal lifespan, just as I will live out mine. And I'm sure both Hari and Tinbit will prefer your castle to a rundown gingerbread house, although I hope all of you will come visit me.

Thirdly, you are right about Happily-Ever-After. Always remember that, no matter how tough things get. They might, but I hope my resignation and suggestions to the Council for the future will alleviate that somewhat.

But just in case I don't see you again after today, I want to tell you how much I've enjoyed your companionship, not just over the last week, but over the last thousand years.

There was a time when I thought that I alone sacrificed every-thing for Happily-Ever-After, which I did gladly given the world we lived in. But I was wrong. You were always there with me. This is my way of returning the favor. I will never forget your kindness, your compassion, or the way you loved a man who has always, although he never would have admit-ted it until now, loved you.

Yours wickedly ever after,
HECTOR

TINBIT SAID THEY SHOULD ALL GO BACK TO THE CAP-ital together. Hector said no. He put his foot down so sharply that Tinbit, sitting at the skullery table supervising Hari as he flipped eggs and turned bacon, shut his mouth and didn't say any more about it. But Hari wasn't so easy to shut down.

"We ought to be there," he said, serving Ida first. "Let us come—we can tell them what we saw. No one should judge either of you until they hear from eyewitnesses."

"We have an eyewitness. Cear will tell them everything they need to know." Hector rubbed the small of his back painfully. He'd wrenched it on one of Adair's sharp turns rescuing Ida, and it was plaguing him this morning, largely because he'd been up most of the night trying to put his thoughts into words and fail-ing utterly. The library fireplace was full of bits of charred paper.

"But Cear can't tell them all that we could," Hari said. "We'd tell them how hard you both worked to fix Happily-Ever-After—"

"Which wouldn't help anything," Ida interrupted. "Hector and I will handle this together. You stay here with Tinbit. He needs you to take care of him, and Hector is right. Nothing you can say will help." She winced, twisting slightly as if her shoulder still bothered her. Hector noted this with concern. He'd wanted to take the coach, but she'd refused. They would have two days' hard ride to the city on his constructs, and it wouldn't be a comfortable one, even with extra padding.

Hari didn't look pleased, but appealing to his love for his husband-to-be worked. He dropped his protests, gazing with doe-like adoration at Tinbit's frowning face.

"Are the horses ready?" Hector asked the skeleton who passed through.

The grating reply assured him they were.

"Are *you* ready?" He turned to Ida.

"As I'll ever be." She drained her teacup and rose.

His uneasiness increased. Ida couldn't do much to sabotage him on the way to the city. But all matter of things might go wrong when they got there. She was too compliant, too subdued. Moreover, she'd said he was *right*. That alone would keep him up tonight if his back didn't.

He was right. It did keep him up. Nothing went wrong on the trip, however, other than Napoleon deciding he was a young colt and shying at every fluttering leaf, jumping deer, or manticore scat they encountered. He unseated Hector once, and only a quick grab around the horse's bony neck column saved him from a ridiculous spill. Ida's horse, Scary Mary, behaved herself. Periodically, she gazed at Napoleon out of large, crimson eye sockets like she couldn't believe he was being so silly.

They camped in the woods that night, far enough away from the road to avoid bandits, or so Hector thought until four highwaymen came into their camp determined to rob and steal. But one of them was the innkeeper's son. He recognized Hector before Hector could turn all four men into stone as a reminder that not all travelers were helpless. The affair ended with the robbers sharing their supper and begging a bag of everlasting salt, which Ida gave them with good grace. After that, they both settled down to sleep with the two skeleton horses piled in comfortable heaps under the leaves, but Hector couldn't get comfortable, although he did his best not to toss and turn. As far as he could tell, Ida didn't move all night. But she didn't snore, and that let him know she was as wakeful as he.

They rose as soon as the morning sunlight began to seep into the gray beneath the trees, and were on their way again, with nothing to prevent them from reaching the capital that afternoon.

Ida sighed and slowed down when the turrets of the castle came into view. After a few more steps, she pulled up completely and stared down at the shining buildings, clasping Cear's firepot in her arms.

"What is it?" Hector asked, turning around in the saddle. "Is your wound hurting? I knew I should have changed your bandage last night."

"No, it's not that," she said, rubbing her shoulder ruefully. "Well, it does hurt, but that's not it. I was only thinking how different everything looks now."

"How so?"

"Ever since I was a girl, I've thought that castle was beautiful, even back when it wasn't much more than a stone fortress and a moat. It always sparkled, like something out of a fairy tale. I used to dream about living there. But today it doesn't look so lovely. It needs something, I think."

"I believe the king intended to request some magical renovations later this year, to celebrate the prince's marriage. A new treasury building, singing windows in the queen's quarters, upgrade the nursery with some screens to keep malicious fairies out—that sort of thing. I suppose those will be on hold until they sort out how they want to handle succession."

"I suppose you'll say I need to visit the king and queen this evening to talk about that."

"It would be a good idea. It might go a long way toward getting them ready to accept change."

She folded the reins into one hand and brushed her hair back with the other. "Somehow, I don't think it will. But I don't suppose it can be avoided." She lifted the reins and her mare broke into a gallop.

Napoleon bucked, and Hector had to get him under control as he raced to catch up.

When they cantered into the courtyard of the Hall of Witches, a tall sylph with white hair and blue skin was waiting to take their horses. An equally impressive salamander took the firepot from Ida's arms without a word.

"Take good care of them," Ida said. "They've had a long journey."

The salamander said nothing and walked away. Ida's gaze followed them with a curious intensity. She was planning something—he knew that look. Well, he'd have to get ahead of her, that was all.

"Are you ready?"

She sighed. "Whether I am or not, there's no point in delaying this, is there?"

"I don't suppose so." He reached for her hand. "Ida, whatever happens, I—"

She raised her eyebrows.

He let go of her hand, a soft smile curving his lips. He hadn't needed to write that letter after all. He didn't need to say anything when she could read the look on his face so well.

They walked into the Hall together.

Tara and Agatha were waiting for them, each with their elemental attendant. The fire crackled on the hearth as Cear emerged, dusting ashes from themself, and took their place beside Hector. Agatha stared at him impassively, but Hector saw the look in her eyes. Pure, unadulterated hatred. They'd always been professional rivals, but this was something different. Momentarily, he wished he'd brought his staff. But both he and Ida had agreed that if they were to get the other witches to listen, it would be better if they didn't go in armed.

Ida walked toward her usual chair, turning to say something in a quiet tone to the sylph, who nodded and melted into the air.

"Are you going to sit down, Hector?" Agatha asked in a dangerously pleasant voice. "Or remain standing on your dignity?"

"Standing, I think," he said. "I've been sitting most of the day."

Ida eased around him, pulled out her usual chair, and sat. Tara stared at her with a sweet smile, but there was professional malice in her gaze. "Well? Is that it, then? No princess. No dragon. No prince. And no wedding."

Ida spoke with acid in her voice. "Tara, don't pretend you don't know the prince has already married. I saw the news in the first mud puddle I happened upon."

"And yet, Happily-Ever-After doesn't seem to be working, given the flooding along the river or the unseasonable blizzard that wiped out two-thirds of the grain in the north, not that it was a huge loss, as it had ripened before it was ready and was already ruined."

Agatha pressed her fingertips together, leaning forward in a ridiculous parody of the way Hector often sat when he was hearing people out before deciding against their proposal. No wonder Ida had thought him such an insufferable egotist.

"No, it isn't. And it's my fault," he said quietly. "I'm prepared to take full responsibility."

Ida glared at him. "You ought to be. It's been your fault the whole time."

Oh, thank the Gods. She *was* going along with his plan. He'd been concerned, but at least the fiasco with Alistair and Amber had taught her that when they'd decided on a course of action, unity was the best policy.

"I'll tell you what's wrong with Happily-Ever-After," Ida went on. "Long ago, four witches thought they knew what was best for the world. And so they brewed a potion that forced a prince to marry a commoner—a sacrifice that would ensure the peace they paid for with their hearts would last. They even made it look good—a pumpkin coach, oversized white mice to draw it, glass slippers that pinched they were so tight. Everyone was happy. The long war was over. No one would ever be hungry.

The clouds of magic polluting the sky were gone, the rivers became clean, and no one ever needed to worry about their future, because they would all live happily-ever-after."

Wait a minute. No, no, no, no, Ida. He was supposed to explain this. Not her. "If I may interject here—"

"But was it Happily-Ever-After?" Ida rose, folding her arms behind her back, one much more slowly than the other. The dragon wound was clearly bothering her. "When was it better to take away anyone's choice for peace? I'm not just talking about the right to fall in love with and marry whom you choose. We denied the world the chance to fix itself. We fixed it for them. We erased all the horrible things they'd caused, and worse, we told them that all they had to do was perform a little ritual to keep it that way—to stage a fight with a dragon instead of fighting the monsters inside themselves. That's when we failed Happily-Ever-After. That's when we failed the world. Ironic that we cut out our hearts when maybe if we'd kept them, we'd never have done this horrible thing to the people we were trying to save."

"Ida, I—"

But she wasn't even looking at him.

"This year, the courage of one woman, the valor of a dragon, and the subterfuge of a captain of the guard who couldn't bear to lose the man he'd given his heart to almost destroyed the foundation of this world we worked so hard to create. But for their love—real love—Hector and I might not even be here today. We didn't make Happily-Ever-After for them. They made it for themselves out of the wreck of that spell. And yes, there are going to be consequences that we'll have to live with and fix. We owe it. It should be our penance for ever thinking we were wise enough to fix the world's mistakes with a spell."

Agatha's sharp mouth curled upward at the corners.

Tara, though, looked down at the table. "Do you hear your-self, Ida? You're saying you *want* Happily-Ever-After to end? After all it's done for the world? For us? It's kept the kingdom happy for a thousand years. If we let it expire, what happens to us?"

"What do you mean, *what happens to us?*" Hector asked. "Didn't you hear what she said? We have work to do. There will be famines to fix, levies to build on the river, and it rather sounds like someone needs to go summon a warm front."

"You too?" Agatha glared at him.

"I—" He looked at Ida. "Yes. Yes, I do think it's time for it to end. We've been in charge long enough. It's time we stepped aside and let the world handle itself with our help, but not our control."

"Next you'll be saying you set this up on purpose to fail this year," Agatha said.

"As a matter of fact—"

"He didn't," Ida said. "I did."

"What?" Tara gasped.

"I destroyed Happily-Ever-After. It happened at the very beginning when I didn't choose the princess this year. I asked the magic to do it, without oversight, without thinking about the consequences of what I did, and worse, I didn't tell anyone what I'd done. I didn't trust anyone but myself." She gazed at him, and a warmth filled Hector, and a peace that he didn't think was possible. "But I'm glad it happened this way. If it hadn't, I'd have never known just how wicked I really was. Or how good other people could be."

He reached across the table and set his hand over hers. "You were supposed to let me take the blame," he said. "We agreed."

"Yes, well—I knew you'd come to see it my way in the end," she said. "Besides, you know I could never let you win."

Ida turned to the others. "It's time to abolish Happily-Ever-After forever."

56

Ida

My dearest, most horrible Hector,

I couldn't let you do it. I couldn't let you stand alone. Maybe someday you'll forgive me for my complete distrust in your ability to make a proper Happily-Ever-After, but after all, you are the Wicked Witch of the West. I know my duty, and it's thwarting you at every turn. Besides, I couldn't stand being head of the Council without you there. As soon as it's over, I'll go home and tear the red rose up by the roots. Nobody will be able to fix this awful spell once I'm done with it. I simply can't take the risk that if I allow that plant to flourish, some other fools will come along and repeat our mistake. I know they'll come after me for it, but don't worry. I can take care of myself.

I wish I had the words to tell you how much your friendship means to me. It's the hardest thing in the world, stepping down when all I want is to spend every day working with you, but I think we both know that if anyone is qualified to lead us into a new era without Happily-Ever-After, it's you and not me.

I'll always have the greatest respect for how much you sacrificed for Happily-Ever-After. Perhaps one day, you'll understand why I had to do the same.

Yours forever,

Ida

Hector stood so stiffly, as if his back hurt. It probably did. Her back wasn't feeling wonderful after lying on the hard ground in the forest all night either. She hadn't been able to sleep, and from the way Hector shifted around in his blankets, she didn't think he'd slept either. Probably worried about what she would do.

He hadn't wanted it to end this way. She could see it in the way his jaw clenched, as if he anticipated the pain she was about to endure as his own. She didn't suppose it hurt any less if one sacrificed one's own immortality.

"I agree with Ida," he said, "although despite what she says, she didn't destroy Happily-Ever-After. There's no provision that says she shouldn't have chosen the princess the way she did. But had she not let the magic choose, we'd have never known that the magic was flawed from the beginning. And it was. I know that now." He drew himself up. "That's why I'm resigning. I'm leaving the Council in her capable hands. The world will need a witch of her ability to navigate the consequences, and I can think of no one better for the job."

"You go too far, Hector," Agatha said, clenching her hand around the handle of her wand. "You're talking about abolishing the one thing that has kept us in charge for the last thousand years. You're really ready to turn the world over to…who, exactly, Hector? The prince and his husband? The common people? You're asking us to return to anarchy!"

"Who said anything about anarchy? I think we need to remain advisors to the crown and the people, to guide, not to control. I see that as our role in this world—as it should have been from the beginning."

"And you think they'll listen?" Agatha laughed. "You really

aren't with the times, are you, Hector?"

"Maybe they won't at first," Ida said. "But who are we to say they won't listen eventually?"

"The ones in charge," Agatha snapped back. "That's who. I'm not about to give that up because you two have gone senile." She raised her wand.

Hector started. "Agatha, what are you doing?"

"Firing you to start with!"

A freezing, burning sensation filled Ida from her limbs to her chest where Hector's heart pounded. Her wand was back on Scary Mary, in the saddlebag, and Hector's staff was back with Napoleon—he'd wanted to retain it after his resignation, and he'd been concerned that Agatha might demand he break it. He'd said he was rather attached to it, having received it as a gift from a dryad queen for his five hundredth birthday.

"You don't have the authority to fire him," Ida said. "I'm the only one who does. I have seniority here, not you!" Losing *her* immortality was one thing, but Hector had already lost his. If Agatha tried to fire him…

"I think you'll find I do," Agatha said. "Don't be so surprised. You were just saying that you thought both the crown and the people would continue to listen to the witches in charge, and they did. The queen herself gave us her blessing and her royal permission to get rid of both of you before she ran off to mourn the marriage of her son. So, which one of you wants to go first? Age or beauty?"

"Hold on a minute, I said I was resigning—" Hector said, but Agatha's wand was trained on his chest; in a second he'd be dead.

"No, Agatha, stop!" Ida threw herself in front of him.

She thought she was ready for it, but nothing—nothing

had ever hurt like this. The blast hit her like a thunderbolt. The immortality was ripped away from her like skin ripped away from her body, and it wasn't loose or worn, but tight and clinging to the bones. She cried out, grabbing at her chest, and fell to the floor. This is what Hector had endured to resurrect Tinbit. She couldn't imagine pointing her own wand at herself to do it as he had. The room blurred, went dark.

Then someone was holding her, stroking her forehead, someone warm, strong, and smelling of black roses.

"Ida? Ida?" Hector's face came into focus at the same time the room did.

"What—what happened? Agatha!" She tried to sit up.

"Slowly." Hector helped her, supporting her in his arms.

"Agatha—where is she—" She glanced around wildly, trying to rise. She would not let Agatha hurt Hector; she couldn't lose him.

"I told you slowly! Agatha is incapacitated for the moment," Hector said. He folded his hand around hers, and she looked wonderingly down at the handle of a wand.

"Where—where did you get that?"

"It's the wand I owed you," he said. "I ordered it when we got to my castle, and it came in while we were with the dragons. I was planning to give it to you today after this meeting as a token of my respect when you ascended to the head of the Council."

Ida gazed in horror at the decidedly stony visage of Agatha, still posed dramatically in the middle of casting a spell, or it might have been dramatic if her mouth hadn't been open.

"Limestone?" she ventured.

"Granite," he said. "It will take her a year to chip her way out, but I rather think she deserves it. Do you think you can walk?"

"I—I think so. What about Tara?"

Hector glanced at the Good Witch of the South, snoring softly, her cheek resting on her pastry. "Well—I'm sure she's got a true love. Somewhere."

Cear emerged from the hearth, dusting ashes from their hands. "All is arranged, Your Wickedness," they said. "You won't be pursued for several hours. Your horses are waiting."

"Thank you, Cear," Hector said, pulling Ida to her feet. She collapsed against him, leaning hard into his shoulder as he half-guided, half-carried her out of the Hall.

Hector put her up on Napoleon before mounting up behind her. "Come on, Mary," he called, and the mare cantered after them as they rode out of the courtyard with a whinny that made every hair on the back of Ida's arms stand up, it was such a horrible grating sound.

She leaned back into Hector's chest as he spurred Napoleon's bony flanks and the undead horse put on a fresh burst of speed. They were leaving a trail of bone dust on the cobbled streets that anyone could follow, but once they left town, they'd be much harder to follow.

"We need—my home—"

"I know," he said.

She bumped along in front of him, feeling the severed ends of her life curling up like a plant dying in the hot sun. Everything had gone so wrong. She should have known that nothing she or Hector might say would convince the other Cardinal Witches to give up any power. She'd been a fool not to see it.

"I'm sorry," she said eventually.

"What for?"

"I should have…told you. If you'd known I planned to get myself fired, you could have done it. It probably would have hurt less."

"I couldn't," he said. "I don't think I could ever cast a spell against you again if my life depended on it."

The gates to Castle Peerless stood open.

Hector guided Napoleon into the courtyard, slowing him to a trot. Ida, still dazed and sore, glanced around at her former castle. While the walls shone, white and sun-kissed as usual, the castle itself had an air of neglect about it, like it had stood vacant for years, not a week and a half. The daily papers had been delivered. They sat in a neat stack in the doorman's hut.

Hector dismounted first and then held his arms up to catch her as she slid down after him.

"How long do we have?" she asked, refusing to look at the glorious tangle of red roses blooming divinely on every wall.

"Cear will hold off inquiry for at least a day as I requested," Hector said. "Maybe even longer, depending on how long Annabeth and Rupert decide to pout in their resort getaway." He caught Scary Mary and tied her up next to Napoleon. "Nevertheless, I don't think we can dillydally."

No, they couldn't, although she thought Cear might give them far more than a day from what the elemental had said. *Opportunity still remains if you are willing to take it.* "I—I just have a few things I need to do first," she said. "I won't be long."

No one was in the castle at all—no housekeepers, no maids, no manservants. Even the kitchen was utterly deserted, although it was spotless as always. Hari's mother, unwilling to take a vacation with anything undone, had scoured them before leaving. Ida went through the drawers in the linen closet, picking out the thinnest ones. She would use those to bag up cuttings of her favorite plants. She could still give them life in new ground, although now that her immortality was gone, she expected her vivomancy to diminish over the rest of her life. But at least this way, she'd always have a memory of who she'd once been—Ida, Good Witch of the North, now Ida Moonshadow. Most everything else would have to stay behind. She certainly couldn't take all her books, or her hat collection, or more than six or seven pairs of shoes. But there was one thing she absolutely had to have.

She was pulling it out from under the bed when she heard the downstairs door open. "Ida?" Hector called from the entryway. "Where in the name of magic have you got to?"

"Third floor, turn left at the landing, second door on your right."

She set the box with her heart on the bed and turned to the closet to get her travel bag. She could shrink a few things down to fit—the magic mirror, her favorite dresses, the ever-growing manuscript of her memoirs, and Hari's hats. He wouldn't be happy if she forgot his hats.

"What are these?" Hector glanced at the stack of pink, yellow, and purple tea towels on her dresser.

"For cuttings from the garden. I wanted to replace some of the things you lost, not that they are wicked plants, but perhaps you can breed from them. Maybe turn the snapdragons into proper snapping dragons?"

"Possibly. Can I help?"

"I'm almost done." She glanced around. "You know, in a way, it's for the best."

"How do you mean?" Hector sat down on the edge of the bed, pulling the box toward him and glancing at the embossed markings curiously.

"Well, imagine if I'd worked another hundred years and then retired. It would have taken the rest of my life to figure out how to downsize. This way, I can only pack essentials."

He grunted an assent. "I suppose."

"Hector, I know it's not what you wanted—"

"No, it's not." He rose and paced the length of the room and back. "Ida, what will you do now?"

She picked up her heart box. "Honestly, I haven't decided. I had thought about going home—my home when I was a child. Thought I might explore the area, find a spot I can enchant with protection, build a house, live happily ever after. Of course, there's Hari and Tinbit's wedding to attend first, and I'll need to pick up my books from your castle, and I really should find Hari's mother and tell her Hari has found his happiness. And after that, I'll try to find my own happy ending." She opened the box.

Hector stopped pacing. "Your heart," he said, gazing down at the ruby-red organ gently palpitating in the box. "You—you never got rid of it."

"That's right," she said. "And I'll need it inside of me now, which means you'll need this back." She reached inside herself and took his heart out of her chest. "It's not a bad heart, Hector, although sometimes I think it's a rather foolish one."

He took it and held it for a long moment before glancing at her face. "Sebastian."

"Really, Hector, you were going to let a ghoul eat it?"

He half smiled. "It seemed the best option at the time."

"Did it?" She folded her arms over her empty chest. "Tell me something, Hector Prim. You could have killed anything to resurrect Tinbit, couldn't you? A forest, the swamp, those obnoxious mire imps, but you chose yourself. Did you think you could force me into staying on the Council by sacrificing your immortality?"

He turned away. "Not…not entirely—"

"Gods, Hector." Ida sighed. "You did."

"I said not entirely! I *did* want you in charge of the Council, I won't deny that. You understood earlier than I did that Happily-Ever-After should end; you had a clear vision of what you wanted—"

"What I wanted? Hector, when did you ask me what I wanted? You think I wanted to go back, to sit in your chair and pass judgment on you, and stay there, staring at a new face where yours used to be, thinking about your life draining away one day at a time while I stayed where you put me—immortal and all alone?"

"That's not what *I* wanted." His face flushed a dusky pink in the rose-colored light flowing through the window glass.

"Then what did you want?"

"I…I couldn't stand it," he said after a long pause. "When I thought about you leaving, being fired, I couldn't even imagine standing by when you'd done nothing to deserve it. I was there when Happily-Ever-After happened. I took the black rose and grew it. It was my duty to answer for what I'd done."

"Your duty." Damn the man. Damn him and his foolish heart that couldn't let go of his duty and responsibility.

"What's wrong with that?"

"Oh, nothing." She contemplated throwing her heart at his head. Instead, she crammed it back in the box before she could act on the impulse, grabbed her valise, and stalked out the door.

57

Hector

You heard it here first, folks! King Rupert and Queen Annabeth Divorced! Queen claims King cheated on her with Lady Gray, first lady-in-waiting and highest in the confidence of the queen. King denies all—says Queen is carrying on with the Head Gardener Exclusive from Lady Gray on page four!

I Was Seduced By A Two-Headed Strawman With A Giant Eggplant—one woman's sizzling erotic encounter with a scarecrow continues to top the bestseller's list...

—*THE SORCERER'S STAR*

Crown Prince Archibald Quentin Rupert II and his consort Caedan Cay visited the flooded province of Westfale today where unseasonably heavy rainfall resulted in a dam break on the River Fale. Over a hundred people are confirmed dead and many others remain missing. The prince is expected to go before the Parliament of Commons and ask them to match the offer from the royal treasury to assist in recovery efforts.

In other news, the annual quest for the Holey Pail remains in jeopardy after three knights errant and their scouting master were reported missing. Knights Lanceboil,

Piercenavel, Galehead, and master Arthur Pin-Dragon were last seen in the company of three banshees headed for Lake Wildmere. Anyone with information on the missing men should contact the Wildmere Sherriff's Office.

—THE KINGDOM WALL JOURNAL

Last chance to sign up for Witches' Weeds Annual Garden Contest—Don't Miss Your Chance! All new this year: Best Bog Competition!

Sale on Jack-in-the-Beanstalk's Magic Root Powder!

Shop Cinderella's Emporium for all Your Giant Pumpkin Needs!

—WITCHES' WEEDS

"GODS." WHAT HAD HE SAID THIS TIME? ALL HE WAS trying to tell her was that he would never have forced the issue had he not been so sure that she was right about Happily-Ever-After. Couldn't she see how much he cared? How could he have fired her and spent the rest of his life alone without her to keep him company? Because he couldn't lose her now. He'd known it from the moment he watched the immortality leave her eyes. It had been all he could do to restrain his anger and not shatter Agatha as soon as he turned her into stone. He clutched his heart protectively. No wonder he'd felt her pain so intensely. Part of it had been his own. *Ida, why? Why does it always have to be this way between us? Why is it so hard to just say what I want to say?*

He stomped down the stairs. It wasn't hard to see where she'd gone. The crystal doors that led into the garden stood ajar.

"Ida!" he called, pushing both doors open. "I didn't mean it like that! Of course, it wasn't all about duty—I simply thought you were better equipped to deal with the aftermath than I was. I don't understand love magic—or even love for that matter. I never have!"

"You got that part right." Ida knelt at the base of a lily, digging it up with a hand spade. With an angry jerk, she lifted it and divided it with her fingers. She set a slip in one of the tea towels, then settled the remaining plant in the ground before waving her hand over it. Golden sparks drifted downward like fertilizer. "If it wasn't all about duty, then what else was it about?" She moved on to the next flower bed. He followed, picking up the stack of tea towels she'd left behind.

"If you couldn't bear to sit in the room and stare at the chair where I used to sit, what makes you think I could?"

She stopped digging but didn't look up. Her rose-gold hair fell partly over her face, covering it.

Now. Now or I'll never do it.

He squatted down next to her, touching the leaves of the plant in front of them both. "I know…I know I'm an old fool, and I know you and I…well, I doubt we'll ever agree fully on anything, even when to have dinner, but these last few days—" He set his hand on her shoulder. "Ida? Will you look at me please?"

She turned toward him, face pink in the light flowing through the roses.

"Ida, I've lived more with you in a week than I have in a thousand years. When I thought about living another day without you, I knew I'd never want it. I'd be dead inside, truly heartless. I…I didn't know if…"

"…I felt the same way?" She looked full in his face then, melting lavender eyes warm and wanting.

"I couldn't tell you I loved you before. How could I when I knew what I'd done would make Happily-Ever-After impossible to restore? I killed the rose, Ida. When I destroyed my own immortality, I destroyed that magic. If they had demanded you restore it, I'd be nowhere to be found. It was the least I could do for you, to make things right. But now you've sacrificed your immortality for me, I dare to hope. Ida, if you could find it in your heart to stay by my side, to be my constant companion, there's nothing I want more."

"Oh, Hector." She buried her face in his chest while he held her.

He pressed his nose into her hair, breathing in the warm scent of her. "Come with me. We can protect each other. I don't want you to go anywhere else. I want you with me until the day you die, and when that happens, I won't be far behind. I don't want to be alive if it means I don't have you."

"Oh, you, you stupid, stupid—you amazingly foolish man. How do you do this to me? I think I know what you want, and then you go and"—she thumped his chest with a gentle fist— "you ruin everything, you blow my plans up in a word, you turn over everything I do." She gazed up at him, purple eyes filled with tears, but she was smiling. "And I don't even care."

"Say you love me. Do you? Please say you do. Please say you'll come back with me. I have a little gingerbread house in the foothills of the Dread Mountains. It's old and the foundation might be a bit cracked in places, and the style is hopelessly out-of-date, but I think I still have the batter recipe. We can fix it up together."

"How did you know I love gingerbread houses?" She laughed, tears running down her cheeks.

"Is that a yes or no?"

She shoved him sideways. "That's a yes. For now. Until you make me mad and I leave in a fury."

He raised her hand to his lips and kissed it. "Well, since *that's* unavoidable, perhaps I can make you laugh enough to stay."

She cupped her hand around his cheek. "And I hope I make you annoyed enough that you'll never get tired of me."

"I think you can count on that," he said.

"So, I do annoy you." She huffed, eyes sparkling.

He pulled her close. "So much that I don't think I'd ever have a happy day if you weren't there to do it."

"You infuriating man," she said as he helped her up. "You could have told me all of this instead of just sacrificing yourself and telling me you wanted to resign. I'd have understood."

"At first, I was afraid I was being selfish. That I'd let my desires rule my decisions. Or worse, that I didn't care if they did. And I had hoped that possibly…"

"…the Council might listen to us if we both explained."

"Yes." He brushed a strand of hair from her forehead. "I think your optimism rubbed off on me."

"And your pessimism on me." She gazed sadly at the red rose, glowing brightly in the afternoon sunshine. "They didn't."

"No, but I hold out hope that the world is ready to rule itself regardless of what the Council thinks," he said, breathing in the scent of those ancient flowers—wild, intoxicating—so like the flowers of his Skeleton Rose that he could almost believe they'd never been different species at all, more like variations on a theme. "Amber said that the dragons had outgrown their need for me. Perhaps the people will prove just as capable of handling their own affairs without us."

"In time, maybe. But right now—no. I can see a manhunt happening as soon as the king and queen find out there will never be a Happily-Ever-After again."

"Probably." He curled his fingers around his staff. It felt so final, the end of Happily-Ever-After. Odd. He'd always thought he'd pass on the seeds from the black rose to an apprentice, much as they'd been given to him. He'd thought about it often, but every time he considered it, something held him back. Perhaps there was a destiny to it after all. He'd seen it come into being. Now he'd be here at the end of it.

But not alone.

He reached for her hand, and she took it.

Together they walked toward the garden wall where the root of the enormous rose grew, thick as a tree trunk and guarded by thorns as long as Hector's hand. She bent over and picked a small bloom, twirling it between her fingers. "This is where it was planted, Hector, so long ago. My mentor brought me out, gave this seed to me and said, 'I've been needing to hand this over to you for some time. It's going to be your responsibility in the future. You might as well be in charge of it now.'"

He smiled. "I received almost the same speech." He reached into the pocket of his robe and pulled out the crumpled, wilted bloom he'd taken from the Skeleton Rose. He kissed it gently. "I had rather hoped that we could have made this a bigger event. I'm not one for spectacle, as you well know, but I think the *Sorcerer's Star* would have liked front row seats." He set the tip of his staff on the ground beside the rose and let the power flow through him. A sudden stinking smell of death, decay, and rancid meat filled the air to mingle horribly with the roses.

Ida watched the plant wilt with a firm, resolute look on her face. "I don't suppose there's any point in explaining to anyone else, but I think I'll send a note to the prince and his husband to explain things. Maybe they'll listen."

"I was thinking of doing the same for Alistair and Amber. I plan to suggest he send an envoy to Archie and Caedan, just to feel out the possibility of formal diplomatic relations."

"And if that doesn't work out?"

"Then they'll know where to find me when the fighting starts." He glanced up at the rose bush, now curling and blackening in the sunset. He reached out and plucked a fading blossom and handed it to Ida. "A keepsake. Hold onto it like holding onto hope."

She pressed her forehead against his shoulder. "Like holding onto you." She tucked the red rose in her hair. "My horrible, horrible Hector."

"My dear detested Ida." He kissed her.

A gust of wind picked up the drying petals and showered them with crimson.

The End

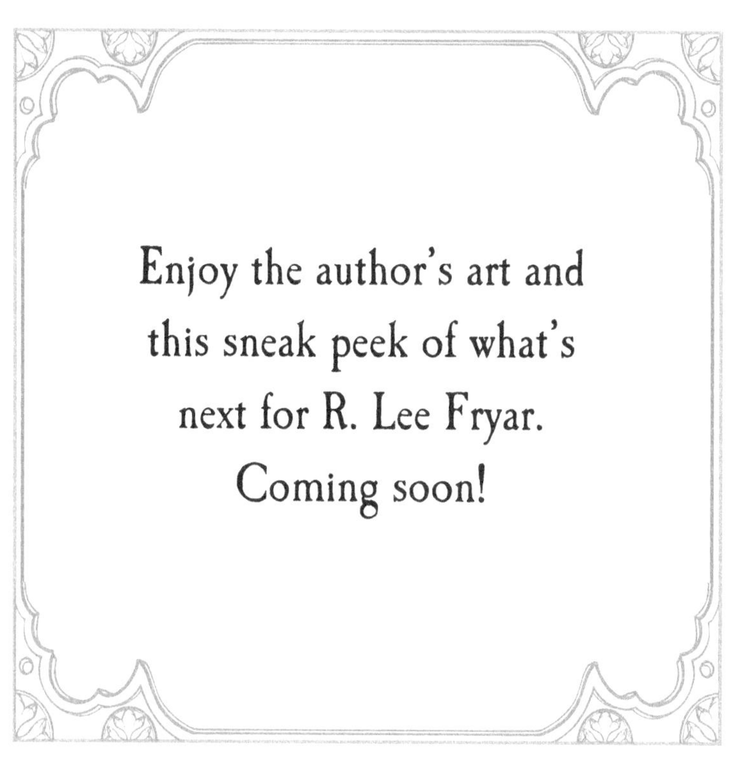

Enjoy the author's art and
this sneak peek of what's
next for R. Lee Fryar.
Coming soon!

FUGITIV
Missing witche
after having last be
former Cardinal Witche
year's Happily-Ever-Afte
on their whereabouts to th
armed and desperate.
In related news, Cardina
condition. Healers are considering
her out, but are having trouble c
wouldn't be any great loss."
h Tara South in good conditi
kiss from a pastry chef.
DRAGONS ON
Prince Archibald an
Peace envoy
Flame lord
concern
but
Dear Lda,
Have gone to the forest with Jumblet to gather honey mushrooms for supper. There's fresh gingerbread cooling for this afternoon if you could mix the icing.
Love,
Hector

JACK'S BEST MAGIC BEANS
Rapunzel's Rampion
ONCE REPORTER
Voted This Kingdom's Most Trustworthy Ne... Readers Like
TCHES STILL AT LARGE!
st and Ida North remain at large a month
king the Capital on a skeleton horse. The
ed for questioning in connection with this
Citizens should report any information
uthorities. The witches are considered
ath a East remains in a petrified
n Hector
ng is in the buckets out back. Hari
in the vegetable garden planting
d the sensitive fern.
tell you otherwise.
Love,
Ida
KING AND QUEEN DIVORCE FINAL!
King Rupert is said
merry Lady Jane Gray
secret passion for years!
SORDID DETAILS ON PAGE
HOLEY PAIL QUEST KNIGHTS MISSING
The search continues for
Knight-Errant master Arthur
incompetence and misappropri
defected! It is rumored that
uncomfortable for years with
"arranging accidents" to eliminate
potential political threat to
RHF 5/2025

1

The amount of money a magical life is assigned is based on the relative importance of the target and the amount of danger involved in apprehending them. It's paid out by the Council of Witches upon delivery of the rogue witch or, in my case, their wand or staff. Quite frankly, taking a witch who doesn't want to come quietly—and none of them do once they see me—is a colossal pain in the ass.

EDRICK HARPER

WHEN THIS JOB IS OVER, IT'S REALLY OVER. I'M RETIRING.

Edrick had said that to himself so many times over the last ten years, it had all but ceased to have any meaning. Like the late spring rain pelting down, that thought was a constant drizzle, making his drought of a life a little less endlessly dry, but making him miserable at the same time. He shifted in the saddle as he approached the castle, gaze drifting from the front, to one side, then the other, then to the back, and front again. Twenty plus years of being a witchfinder had taught him to always watch his back. And there were way too many witches here. Playing fast and loose with his safety could get him turned into a toad or worse—and toads were bad enough. Given his special talents, he could undo the enchantment without much fuss, but getting turned into an amphibian, even for a few seconds, always gave him hives afterwards.

The rain fell steadily as he rode through the castle gate under the watchful eye of Queen Annabeth's guards. He ignored the cobblestone road that led to the Council Hall of Cardinal Witches. He'd heard that once the two buildings housed separate governing bodies, but he'd never known the world to be any different than now—the queen's castle towering like a throne, and the Witches' Hall on bended knee before it. Ostensibly they served the queen like he did, but unlike the queen, they didn't like him. He killed them, after all.

"If the queen pays you today, can I have some new shoes? These damned things are killing my feet." Moiry stumbled over a cobblestone, hooves clattering.

"Quiet, Moiry. This isn't the place to be complaining."

"Where is the place for complaining, then? My feet are rotting off."

"The blacksmith said you have a mild case of hoof fungus. Your feet aren't rotting off. In fact, they're in better shape than mine. I'm not sure I have soles left on the bottom of my boots."

"No comparison. You aren't walking on them and carrying my ass like I'm carrying yours."

"If I promise to get you shoes, will you shut up? It's one thing to tell the yokels a witch enchanted you before I killed them; it's quite another for the guards to tell it to the Witches' Council, who could tell them that's not possible given how I actually operate." He cut his eyes at a guard who gave him a sideways glance, the kind generally reserved for people ranting in the streets. Moiry took a perverse pleasure in shutting up just in time for him to look like an idiot. But it was true—it absolutely wasn't the way he was supposed to work, and he didn't like conjecture. That was every bit as bad as toads.

Moiry snorted. "If it pisses you off that much, then take the enchantment off me. We both know you could do it as easily as breathing. But if you're making deals, I promise I won't utter so much as a dirty limerick if you make sure I get a full meal with my new shoes—and I don't want moldy hay, even if it's been raining. And I want them to take this saddle off and let me catch my breath. I'm twenty-five; I don't deserve to be standing around all tacked up in the stable while you sip red wine and eat petit fours with the queen."

"It's hardly like that," he said. "I don't intend to stay long. I only want to pick up my pay for that last job and see if she has any more assignments for me."

"Oh, Gods," Moiry groaned. "You said this was the last one."

He clenched his teeth. "It was, but that was before that giant broke me, and then you had colic and I had to get your stomach pumped—"

"That was your fault. That grain was atrocious—"

"But of course, you ate it—"

"What else was there to eat? And the whole giant thing was your fault too—he didn't throw you clear across a field into the barn. That was all you and your magical gas attack—"

"Shut it, alright?" Edrick spat back. "We can argue about this until we both go hoarse and not agree."

"That's supposed to be funny? One more bad pun out of you and I'll beg whoever you're supposed to kill to kill me before they do you in." She snorted, tripped over another cobblestone, and went on muttering to herself about workaholic witchfinders who couldn't solve their own magical snafus, let alone anyone else's.

Edrick didn't try for the last word. For one thing, the Council Hall was close. For the second, Moiry was right. Bespelling her to talk had been more of a magical gas attack than intention. He didn't know why magic sometimes exploded out of him without warning. Like with that giant. One minute he was standing in the field, feathers fanned, eyes on fire, siphoning the very life out of the giant. The next minute, he was regaining consciousness in the middle of a barn that he'd blown out a half-mile away, his arm was broken, and Moiry was looking down at him with a decidedly worried look on her horsey face. Months of bedrest and healing spells later—none of which were effective, and he wasn't about to tell the healers why—he was whole again. Well, as whole as a man like him ever could be. But he was also bankrupt and out of the precious artifacts which had sustained him during the long convalescence. It had taken him a lifetime to collect that many. He needed another assignment that paid well, and soon. As Moiry said, she wasn't getting any younger, and whether he wanted to admit it or not, he didn't want another horse. He was getting sentimental, that was the problem. But it would be nice to spend those last few years with a companion, even if it was a horse who stepped on his toes every time she got the chance just to hear him yell. She was the closest thing he had to a friend.

"I'll make sure you get new shoes," he said. "And we'll take it easy until I've got my full strength back. No giants. No dragons.

Nothing stronger than a couple of hedge witches with a vanishing cat. Okay?"

Moiry harrumphed. She wasn't what he'd call an intelligent animal, but she was smart enough to know when he was bullshitting her. He'd never once taken it easy—on himself, or anyone else.

He left her at the stable doors and went to see the queen.

Edrick had been to this room in the castle before—many times, in fact. The first time, he'd been entirely overwhelmed by the opulence. He'd never seen red velvet upholstery on places where a person was supposed to put their feet or known that there were curtains that rivalled ladies' dresses for embroidery, or that a fire could actually contain enough wood to warm a room. He'd stood there in all his nineteen-year-old naivety, back to the fire, rubbing the chill out of his fingers, his hawkish shadow falling long on the floor in front of him, darker than every mysteriously inviting nook between the bed, the couches, the breakfast table, and the open wardrobes. He'd wondered why, of all places, the queen would choose her bedchamber in which to meet with him. He'd been so green it still embarrassed him.

That was long ago. This time, Edrick sat down on the nearest couch without bothering to brush the thick layer of mud drying sluggishly on the back of his knee-high boots. His duster hung in tattered ribbons almost down to his toes, and he was sweating beneath it in the heat of the chamber, but he didn't remove it. He wasn't in the mood for the queen's games today. He'd never figured out why she played them with him, of all people. If there was one thing Edrick couldn't stand—besides witches—it was games he couldn't hope to understand.

He turned his hands over and studied his gaunt arms, the way the thin greenish blood vessels twisted under the skin of his wrists. They pulsed like worms, a sure sign that he would be needing fresh magic soon. He could only live on magical artifacts for so long. Moiry had it right—he'd never retire at this rate. He'd always need magic, and there was no artifact left in the world that could keep him going for more than a few months. Fresh blood was what he most needed. He wished Annabeth would hurry up and get it over with. The sooner he left, the sooner he could feed his hunger, the sooner his pulse would stop throbbing like a hammer's fall, the sooner his hands would stop shaking. But Annabeth had never been known for her promptness, at least not with him. She was probably still deciding what to wear. Edrick estimated that he'd seen her in a hundred outfits by now, and none of them had ever been repeated. Meanwhile, he'd had this same tattered coat for the last twenty years, patching it by hand whenever he'd torn it, cleaning it in the rain, drying it in the sun. It was as steeped in death as he was, and almost as threadbare as he felt most days.

A soft click behind him let him know that the queen had entered through the hidden door.

"My lady," he said, rising, one hand straying to the pommel of his nearest knife. Habit. But with Annabeth, he often felt it necessary. He lived by her mercy, and she wasn't exactly known for that any more than she was for showing up on time.

"Edrik, my darling!" She rushed toward him in a rustle of satin and lace and threw her arms around him. "It's been an age. Kiss me, sweetheart."

"Six months, exactly." He took her hand in his and brushed the back of it with his lips. If he didn't, she'd probably go right for his face like she had the last time.

Annabeth laughed. "You charmer—" She grabbed his feathery hair and pulled him down for a kiss.

He gave up. It didn't matter how many times he tried to be professional—even brusque at times—she seemed to think she'd melt that ice around his heart with her passion. What was it about being a taciturn, bitter, middle-aged asshole that made certain women swoon? And never the ones he might actually have warmed to, given enough time. It was always the ones who either wanted to make love to a man they considered dangerous or the ones who wanted to take him home, clean him up, and reform him. The first group was obnoxious, the second group deluded. Generally, he could make himself exasperatingly distant with both, but Queen Annabeth was different. She couldn't take a hint.

"I heard about the giant," Annabeth said, letting him go as quickly as she'd grabbed him and turning away. "I was worried."

"I'm gratified, my lady." Not that worried. His letter had gone unanswered, although he'd humiliated himself enough to ask politely for his payment. She'd ignored that part too.

"Of course, I needn't have been concerned," she said with a light laugh. "Of course, you were victorious. You're always victorious, my dear, dark, deadly knight," she purred.

And now with the alliteration. He stifled a sigh. "May I ask why you've summoned me?"

She stuck out her lower lip. "Oh, Ed. Six months since we've seen each other and that's all you can talk about? Business?"

He flinched. He hated when people called him Ed. "You did

ask me here, Majesty. I assumed it was for something more than a polite visit."

She smiled and fluttered her eyelashes. "Naturally. But unlike you, I like to mix business with pleasure, and you, my dear, are certainly a pleasure." She touched his nose with a long, painted nail. "Don't worry, sweetheart. That nasty Witches' Council can wait. I know you're supposed to be meeting with them today as well."

"News travels fast."

"I have my ways."

Ways he'd like to know about. Granted, he'd been a witch-finder for years now. It made sense that the queen would keep a close watch on him, just to make sure he knew exactly where his loyalty had to lie. But it irked him, too—not that she would doubt his reliability, but rather that she questioned his sanity. He knew better than to turn to the Council for his welfare. He'd killed too many witches for them to want him in good health, and every one of them knew that Edrick was the last thing they'd see before their magic vanished into the ravenous maw that was his endless hunger if they stepped out of line. The queen was no more trustworthy, but she needed him. He was her best defense.

"I take it you wanted to talk to me about the same matter as they do?"

"Not exactly." She left his side and went to a table where there was a decanter and two glasses. "Rose Brandy," she said, pouring him a glass. "I know you don't drink much, but I had this brought especially. It's made with enchanted roses so it should be good for you."

He accepted the cup, although he didn't drink until she did. It was good practice—more than half of all poisonings could be avoided by making sure the other person drank what they served him. Less than half were smart enough to poison the glass instead of the decanter, and those he avoided by always carrying a mixture of clay and charcoal pellets in an inside pocket of his duster just in case.

Not that he actually expected to be poisoned at this juncture. She wanted something from him, and evidently it was a matter of some importance and delicacy, or she wouldn't have gone to all the trouble of serving something as difficult to acquire as Rose Brandy. Finding roses that still contained some of the original Happily-Ever-After magic in their blooms was a tricky business. And it was, indeed, "good" for him, although he doubted the medicinal value for other people. He sipped the liquid, hating his gratitude, but loving the way it made his bones ache less and eased some of the demands his body expected from him.

"I'd heard that you were looking to retire after this mission," she said.

"I'm sure you can understand that there are very few lines of work for a man of my…particular skills. And those skills come with particular needs."

"But you're so young. You're still in your thirties, yes?"

"Thirty-five, but my work has taken a toll on me." That, at least, could not be questioned. His was a high-risk profession—as far as he knew, no one had ever been tasked with killing giants since Jack the Giant Killer, and Edrik certainly didn't intend to end his career in the same way as that famed serial killer. Working for royalty didn't end well for anyone if they didn't get out before it was too late. "I'm sure you can appreciate that there aren't a great many people who have my talent, and fewer that suffer for it as I do."

She giggled. "You don't have to be so coy with me, darling. You might as well come out and say it—you don't think there are enough magical creatures left in this part of the world to satisfy your needs. I suppose you blame me for that."

"Not at all, my lady. Rather, I thank you for giving me the opportunity to work." He'd have been labeled a murderer otherwise. "But as you say, there *aren't* many magical creatures left. Those I haven't killed have fled to the Dread Mountains. I don't see you needing my services much longer, and I already have a residence in mind."

"Yes, but you'll need servants, people to protect you, things of that kind. A man like you must have some powerful enemies in the more…dangerous…parts of the world." She toyed with her glass. "And I know that the Witches' Council pays better for live capture than dead, so you've probably not made enough to let you retire to a life of ease. You do deserve that, my precious bird." She set her glass down and stroked his cheek with the back of her hand. "What do you say to retiring on my dime? Your own castle in the Eastern Mountains where the weather is so nice, with all the retinue you need to keep the world away if you desire. And for your magical needs, the strongest artifacts in the world from my private collection to feed on. How does that sound?"

Too good to be true. He smiled. "That's a tempting offer. But I assume you want something for such a generous proposal."

"Of course," she said, inspecting her fingernails. "Tell me, Ed, how much do you know about Happily-Ever-After?"

He winced again, but he could let that go. Rather, he had to. He took a sip of the rose wine. "I know the roses that make this drink grew in that time. That's about it." Of course, he knew about Happily-Ever-After. That was when the world ended for people like him. His jaw tightened.

Once upon a time, the world had been a better place—a kindly place where magical creatures and humans mingled. Undoubtably, that's why he'd been conceived. But that all had changed in a heartbeat. Shortly before he came squalling into the world, his mother had abandoned him as an egg and fled. When Edrick crept dripping from that egg, a blind, featherless chick, he'd crawled instinctively toward the drunk man lying on the floor for warmth and safety, curling up in the crook of his arm, because there was nothing else he could do. He still had no idea why his father kept him instead of tossing him in the river. It could only have been cowardice. The man certainly had never had a heart.

But Edrick lived, and he wasn't mistreated—his father knew all too well what Edrick's gift was after the first time he pounced on a dying man like a starving raven on a helpless mouse. Had his father been a better man, he probably would have run a knife through Edrick while he slept, or at least dumped him out in the swamp just east of the town to die. Instead, he kept Edrick, mostly because dead men and women didn't care if he rifled through their pockets for money to buy drink. So when his father went from tavern to tavern, plying his trade as a bard, Edrick went too, calling himself Harper and playing the instrument during the evenings while draining people of their life for their purses in dark alleys at night, and hating every minute of it. He'd relished burning that harp the day his father died.

"Do you know the names of the witches responsible for ruining it?"

Everyone did. "Hector West and Ida North, I believe. They've been missing for decades."

"Missing and wanted. The Council plans to send you to find them and kill them."

That was a death sentence. "The last time anyone saw them, they were riding toward the Forbidden Forest. No one who goes in there ever comes out."

"They say that your…special skills…will give you protection. They plan to send you as soon as you can get ready. I don't need to tell you that they don't expect you to succeed."

"I gathered that." He ground his teeth. Maybe Annabeth would let him kill some of them as traitors. Those mediocre witches weren't much of a meal, but at least he'd enjoy it.

"I, on the other hand, do expect you to succeed. And when you do, I will give you the wand of Ida North and the staff of Hector West as your reward."

He was momentarily stunned. A thousand years of magic were in those objects—he might never have to kill so much as a fairy to feed himself ever again. "That's generous of you."

"It's you," she said, shrugging. "You're going to have to go either way, Edrick. And I think you'll go willingly if you know there's a reward at the end of it."

He would have to go. Choices for people like him had always been limited. But there would be a catch to this offer. There always was. "What do you want?"

"I want you to bring them to me alive," she said. "They're no use to me dead. You see, they know where my son is hiding. And once I have him, there will be no one to oppose me as the rightful ruler of this land." She leaned in toward him, teeth glinting in the firelight. "Secure my future, witchfinder, and I'll make your dreams come true."

Acknowledgments

It really does take a village when it comes to writing a book. *Wickedly Ever After* wouldn't be what it is without the help of my lovely critique partner, S. Kaeth, who was a sounding board for everything Hector and Ida through many revisions.

I also want to give special thanks to my awesome agent, Lucienne Diver, who oversaw the most major changes to the manuscript and in doing so, brought forth the heart of the book, unearthing it from beneath the poisoned apple tree.

Additional gratitude goes to my editor Mary Altman and my team at Sourcebooks, including Gretchen Stelter and Nia Saxon, for helping me comb all the tangles out of the manuscript at multiple levels, and to the artist—Jessica Cruickshank—and production staff—Stephanie Gafron, Tara Jaggers, Diane Cunningham, India Hunter, Lynnette Gonzales, Dayna M. Reidenouer—for spending so much time making this book as lovely as it is.

More thanks must go to my local writing group, River Valley

Writers, for sitting through many an hour listening to this story in the local library and offering suggestions and support, and the librarians who heard, and have made it their lives' mission to put books like *Wickedly Ever After* on their shelves.

And lastly, thanks to my better half and my two kids, who have learned to wait patiently while I pull my headphones off before asking questions.

About the Author

R. Lee Fryar writes fantasy and speculative stories from her lair in the Ozark Mountains. In her other life, she's a mild-mannered veterinarian. She also gardens badly, paints rather better, and is "favorite person" to two spoiled cats and one tiny, but fierce, mouse.

Website: rebeccafryar.com

www.ingramcontent.com/pod-product-compliance
Lightning Source LLC
Chambersburg PA
CBHW061039310726
48969CB00004B/1018